THE MANY DEATHS OF COMRADE BÌNH

TALES FROM THE VIETNAM WAR

THE MANY DEATHS OF COMRADE BÌNH

TALES FROM THE VIETNAM WAR

KENNETH LEVIN

BLINDMAN'S PRESS, OAKLAND

ISBN: 0615905552
ISBN-13: 9780615905556
Library of Congress Control Number: 2013919277

CreateSpace Independent Publishing Platform
North Charleston, South Carolina

Dedicating this Book

The dedication in the first manuscript of this book was to Max Cleland, the former US Senator from Georgia. As typical of him, he wrote me that "it would be more appropriate to dedicate your book 'To all those who suffered in the Vietnam War.'" He may be right, but this is my book. So I dedicate this book with great admiration and respect, and more than a little envy of his writing skills, to the Honorable Max Cleland who served my country in war and peace with a patriot's heart, and to all those who suffered from the Vietnam War.

Kenneth Levin

Human life is incidental to both victory and defeat...

TED MORGAN, *VALLEY OF DEATH*

CONTENTS

PREFACE

While writing my first book, *Crazy Razor*, I realized I had a whole lot more to say, but the practicalities of publishing forced me to stop. In butcher's terms, *Crazy Razor* was the roasts, chops, hams, and ribs of the pig. But I still had a whole of pig left over, so I decided to make sausage. This book is a case of sausages, each story a link.

The impetus to make all this sausage started with a story, a true story, told to me by the daughter of a North Vietnamese Army veteran via an exchange of emails that must number in the hundreds. Although it appears toward the end of this book, that was the first link. Tales and memories and imagination fill the other casings.

For want of a better term, this is a collection of war stories. As in *Crazy Razor*, the stories are really antiwar stories. War is a terrible thing. It not only affects those who are in battle, it affects their families, their friends, their enemies. And it allows human beings to act inhuman. Shakespeare's "what a piece of work is man" becomes deeply more complex when man is affected by war.

Despite that they are about the Vietnam War, some of these sausages are savory, some sweet, some spicy, and some terribly bitter.

In mid-September 2013, I was sitting on a bench at the elevated rapid transit station platform in Lafayette, California, waiting for my train back to Oakland. Across the tracks, highway, and parking lot, I could see a hill covered in white crosses and a few stars of David. Each marker represents an American service member's death in Iraq. The hillside is so crowded with these markers that it looks to be painted white. I don't know the size of that white field—probably half a dozen acres so. There are four thousand crosses there now. The number of crosses added hasn't kept pace with the actual deaths, but the running tally on a sign at the memorial site stood at more than 6,700 in March 2013.

Fifteen such hillsides would be needed for the Vietnam War.

THE MANY DEATHS OF
COMRADE BINH

C omrade Binh died seven times. At least seven times. According to the Army of Vietnam, Navy of Vietnam, the United States Army, the United States Navy, and the United States Air Force. And the CIA. Seven dead Comrade Binhs. One bullet, one corpse. But seven dead Comrade Binhs.

* * *

The People's Army—better known as the North Vietnamese Army, or NVA—decided that they needed a post-1968 Tet assessment of the struggle for unification in the Mekong Delta. They and their comrades in the National Liberation Front—better known as the VC—had lost too many men and too much in equipment, supplies, and ammunition to call the Tet Offensive a tactical success.

There was no grand uprising, the Southern forces did not run away from the battle, and the US forces refused to back down from the fight. But the Tet Offensive may not have been a strategic loss for Hanoi: much to their surprise, the North Vietnamese and their southern communist counterparts seemed to have scored a victory inside the United States. American public opinion was changing. Support for the war was waning.

Hanoi girded itself for a war of attrition. They would wear the enemy down both in battle and from within the American citizenry. To do that, Hanoi needed to replenish the NVA and VC troops, equipment, and supplies. And they needed an assessment, an accurate assessment, from the South. NVA officers were dispatched south to Cambodia via ship, or by way of the Ho Chi Minh trail through Laos and Cambodia and into South Vietnam.

Comrade Binh, a twenty-eight-year-old NVA captain, was sent into the Mekong Delta. Dressed as a peasant with identification papers saying he was a shell-shocked, disabled ARVN veteran, Comrade Binh roamed the waterways of the delta, often using the homes of the local VC cell leaders as a temporary base. He sent out coded reports via couriers and radio at least once a week.

Comrade Binh was a snob. Educated in Paris and Moscow, the son of a party elite, he disdained the southern communists as ignorant, uncultured, and congenitally stupid. As a result, Comrade Binh was not always a welcomed guest in the cell leaders' homes. He was also inconsiderate and demanding. An arrogant asshole.

The village of Chu Co May was the home of the cell leader for the entire eastern half of the Mekong Delta. And the cell leader was getting good and tired of his guest, Comrade Binh. He was tired of the constant criticisms, the dismissive responses to all suggestions and recommendations, the sneer that seemed to be a permanent feature of Binh's face, the sense of entitlement for the largest helpings of food and drink, and the demanding orders as if his hosts were his servants. But what bothered the cell leader most was this northerner's frequent routine of getting drunk and then flirting with his wife.

It was apparent that Comrade Binh liked his accommodations at Chu Co May and was quite happy to use it as his permanent headquarters. Occasionally he would venture out of the village for a day or two, but he always returned for a refreshing and relaxing stay of a week or more.

Finally, the cell leader had had enough. He went to his superiors and complained, but was told that for the importance of solidarity between Hanoi and the South, and for the sake of unification, he had to bear with Comrade Binh who was doing an important job.

Straightforward suggestions by the cell leader to Comrade Binh to move on and assess areas other than his wife's body were ignored. Why should Comrade Binh ever leave? He had free food, free liquor, and charming company.

Worse, the cell leader's wife seemed to be responding to Binh's charm. It was time to do something about Comrade Binh.

* * *

The US Army ranger captain walked into the US Navy advisors' hooch—slang for their makeshift living quarters, essentially a plywood and corrugated steel shack—in Vung Tau. He was the liaison between the local CIA office, the local US forces, and the Provincial Reconnaissance Unit, or PRUs. Having earned the ranger badge, he was qualified for special and unconventional warfare, and put in charge of the Phoenix Program. Phoenix was the new name for an old CIA program that targeted the VC, using sneaky tactics to weaken its popular support. The PRUs he worked with were a dozen or so Cambodian mercenaries, all of them apolitical, their allegiance given to whomever paid the most. These mercs were the Phoenix Program's soldiers. They were rough, tough, and well paid.

The four American navy advisors worked with the South's junk force. The junks' original mission was coastal patrol, trying to stop the waterborne influx of supplies and men to the VC. However, since Tet, patrolling to stop smuggling or infiltration from the sea had produced few results. The mission had morphed into river patrol, ambushes, and psychological operations to "win the hearts and minds of the people."

Over cold cans of grape soda, the ranger shared some intelligence he had just received. An NVA officer was operating just to the north—some bigwig from Hanoi who was doing a strategic assessment, probably in preparation for a big offensive once the rainy season replaced the hot and dry summer weather. The snotty weather it would bring would neutralize the deadly efficient US air support.

In three days the NVA officer would be traveling by himself in a sampan from the village of Chu Co May through the delta. Putting his index finger on the map on the table, the ranger pointed to the place where he wanted to ambush the man, the juncture point of the two rivers. If the intelligence proved correct, the man should be in the killing zone sometime between 1900 and midnight.

* * *

The coin of the US military realm in Vietnam was the body count. The McNamara Department of Defense kept statistics on every measurable parameter. Somebody there could provide data on the number of bullets used, the gallons of JP-5 jet fuel consumed, the cases of C-rations eaten, the tons of bombs dropped, and the number of gonorrhea cases treated.

For Americans, the Vietnam War was a conflict that lacked a measure of success. There were no front lines, at least none that meant anything. Little territory remained captured for long. Ammunition used, villages pacified, and troops in-country all meant nothing in the long run. The only thing that mattered was the body count—the number of enemy dead, whether they were in fact enemies or not. Every night, the folks back home could hear Walter Cronkite recite the grim statistics of the body counts on the news. He never once told the listening audience how many rolls of toilet paper the US military used in Vietnam, although that statistic was available.

The higher the body count, the closer the light at the end of the tunnel. The greater the ratio of enemy dead to US dead, the more likely Hanoi would say it had had enough. Or so the US forces thought. As a result, everyone scrambled for kills. For career military officers, KIAs could mean the difference between getting promoted or not. For draftees, KIAs became the only tangible justification for being in the godforsaken jungle.

4

Commanders of units and advisors to the Vietnamese were anxious to be included during missions so they could tally up some body counts. The operation to ambush Comrade Binh was no exception. By the time the planning was finished, three units were involved: the PRUs and the US Army ranger; the junk force and one of its US Navy advisors, who would provide transportation on rubber boats from the main waterway to the ambush site; and a US Navy Swift boat that would tow the rubber boats on the main waterway, act as a command center, and then provide gunfire support during the operation.

By the time the operation was over, the number of units would double.

* * *

As the sun set, the cell leader handed Comrade Binh a cloth-wrapped package of food, enough to last him two days. They briefly discussed the river and canal route from the village to Comrade Binh's first stop. Although he knew Comrade Binh would refuse, the cell leader again offered to go with him. Comrade Binh did not need any handholding from a stupid, uneducated southerner, even one with a sexy wife. The cell leader steadied the sampan as Comrade Binh boarded, then pushed the boat clear of the riverbank. He waved goodbye and said he'd see Comrade Binh in a few days. The NVA officer grabbed the large stern oar and sculled the sampan into the river current. The cell leader knew that if the Americans did their job, that was the last he'd see of Comrade Binh.

* * *

The big Swift boat ran at full throttle up the river, towing the two rubber rafts filled with PRU passengers, the army ranger, and the junk force oarsmen. A hundred meters before the inlet that would be the ambush site, the Swift boat flashed a light at the rubber boats, got two flashes in return, and released the towline. The

5

Swift boat continued upriver another kilometer at high speed, then dropped its speed to a bare steerageway and turned around, drifting with the current back to the drop-off spot.

The navy advisor stood next to the Swift boat's officer in charge and nervously hovered around the silent radio. Most planned ambushes never materialized. Despite all the intelligence and preparation, they usually ended as nights wasted doing nothing more than sitting in the mud trying to stay awake until the sun came up and it was time to extract and go back to the base. But the advisor had a feeling that this one would be different. The Phoenix Program's intelligence sources had so far proven far more productive than the South Vietnamese or American navies' sources.

The sailors paddled the rubber boats to a spot around the bend from the ambush site and beached. Silently, the PRUs and the ranger climbed onto the muddy canal bank and walked around the bend. They moved into the bordering mangroves and waited for Comrade Binh. The sailors stayed with the rubber boats.

Midnight came and went. The radio on the Swift boat remained silent except for a double spurt of static on the hour, the signal that the ranger had keyed his handset twice. Checking in. A half hour after the 0200 check-in, the lead PRU tapped the ranger on his forearm and pointed upstream. A low shadow was moving on the water. The American readied a pop flare, a hand-held illumination flare much like a single-shot Roman candle. The PRU tapped the ranger's arm again and nodded. The American could see a figure standing in the stern of the sampan, sculling.

The ranger slammed his palm into the base of the pop flare. The resulting *whoosh* was the "open fire" signal for the ambushing mercenaries, who started shooting their Swedish-K machine guns as the little rocket climbed into the sky. One of the bullets hit Comrade Binh in the back of his skull and blew out his forehead and left eye. His corpse collapsed into the sampan. No other bullets hit him. The Cambodians kept on firing until the little flare popped open and, hanging from a handkerchief sized parachute, illuminated the killing zone. The PRU leader ordered his men to cease firing.

With its lifeless cargo, the sampan drifted to the bank, snagged on a mangrove root, and stopped in front of the PRUs. In perfect English, the Cambodian PRU leader said, "He's dead. But they usually send out two or three when they move on the water. Did you see anyone go over the side?"

"No. But it was all shadows," said the ranger. "Your guys see anyone else?"

The PRU asked his men, and they weren't sure what they had seen. They had been shooting at shadows until the flare illuminated the killing zone.

"Roller. Fiddler, over," said the ranger into his radio handset.

The voice of the advisor on the Swift boat answered. "Fiddler, this is Roller. Heard the noise and saw the flare. Over."

"Roger that, Roller. Got one enemy KIA here. Looks like he's carrying papers, which we're harvesting. Can you pop some bigger illumination for us? There may be some more in the river or the other bank, over."

"Roger, will illume ASAP, over."

"Request you call in a team of grunts to search for any bad guys that got away. And an observer for aerial recon. Over."

"Roger, search team and air recon, Fiddler. Anything else? Over."

The Swift boat's 81 mm illumination round opened overhead, bathing the scene in brilliant white light. The PRU leader searched through Comrade Binh's pockets and carrying bag. Besides food and a pistol, he found several files of papers.

"Yeah, Roller. Looks like we got the right guy. Let's get him and his goodies out of here. Request we get a house call to pick up the body and the info. No rush, the guy's dead. I'll go along. Over."

"Got it, Fiddler. Medevac low priority to pick up KIA and you. That right? Over."

"Roger, Roller. You got it. Fiddler, out."

During the next six hours, a platoon of Army of the Republic of Vietnam soldiers was delivered by US Army helicopters. The ARVN searched both banks and the nearby rice paddies but found nothing. A US Air Force forward air controller flew over the ambush site and saw only the sampan, the Swift boat, the ARVN, the PRUs, the rubber boats, and the Vietnamese sailors. A medical evacuation helicopter picked up Comrade Binh's body and the ranger and took both to the PRU base. The rubber boats brought the PRUs back to the Swift boat, and the Swift boat returned to its base.

* * *

The ambush was a success, at least in some people's minds. The information carried back by the ranger and analyzed by the CIA and military intelligence people provided a peek into Hanoi and VC relationships, the status of the pacification—or lack of pacification—in the eastern Mekong Delta, and the rearmament of the VC. In the long run, however, it did absolutely nothing to defeat the VC and NVA. Still, it did provide a KIA. One KIA.

After each operation or firefight in Vietnam, the units involved sent after-action reports to their superiors, who then sent the information all the way up the line to the Pentagon. After-action reports followed a simple format that included who, what, where, and when. The most important part, the parameter most valued, was the subparagraph that included the numbers of killed, wounded, and captured.

The ranger sent in his report, which listed one KIA, the late Comrade Binh, and no friendly casualties. The advisor to the junk force sent in a report that also listed the one KIA, Comrade Binh. Others sent in reports, each dutifully listing one KIA, Comrade Binh: the Swift boat officer in charge, the helicopter detachment that delivered the ARVN search team, the US Army advisor to the search team, the Medevac helicopter pilot who picked up the dead Comrade Binh and the ranger, and the USAF forward air controller who had flown above the ambush scene looking for Comrade Binh's nonexistent companions. In all, Comrade Binh's body was counted seven times by the Americans. And probably two or three times by the South Vietnamese.

All the reports went up various chains of command: special forces, US Army, US Navy, USAF, advisory commands, Vietnamese military commands. The further from the source of the after-action reports, the less personal the reports became. Analysts too busy to check would not have the time to notice that the forward air controller and the Swift boat officer in charge had been reporting on the same operation. Or that the advisor to the ARVN was counting the same body as the advisor to the South Vietnamese Navy.

The end of all the chains of command was the president's desk. Not only did the buck stop there, so did the body counting. And the enemy body count number that LBJ read in October 1968 included Comrade Binh. Multiplied by seven. And the number of dead that Walter Cronkite told his TV audience included seven Comrade Binhs.

In the end, it didn't matter much if Comrade Binh lived or died, much less if he died seven times. In seven years, the country would be unified under the communists. Comrade Binh's death may have helped a few people, though. The ranger, the US Navy advisor to the Vietnamese Navy, the Swift boat officer in charge, the US Army advisor to the ARVN, a few helicopter pilots, and a forward air controller were all promoted. One KIA for each did not mean much, but it certainly did not hurt their careers.

But one person definitely did benefit from Comrade Binh's death. That was the person who made sure that the PRU's intelligence organization knew Comrade Binh's travel schedule. The VC cell leader in the village of Chu Co May received five thousand piasters for that information. And he no longer had to feed or house Comrade Binh. He no longer had to suffer through the insults and arrogance. And although his wife was upset when she heard that Comrade Binh had died, she got over it.

9

BUDDHA'S BIRTHDAY

Gunner's Mate Third Class François "Frenchy" Ducasse sat on the edge of the patrol boat's machine gun tub. In the dark. In the rain. Not thinking about much of anything except that he was craving a cigarette. It was 0315 in the morning, April 18, 1969. Buddha's birthday.

For the past three days, Frenchy's boat and another had been on the Saigon River escorting a group of Vietnamese assault craft loaded with South Vietnamese and American soldiers. At noon on the seventeenth, a radio message from headquarters related that a twenty-four-hour truce and cease-fire in recognition of Buddha's birthday would begin at midnight. The boats were ordered to stop operations at 1800, find a secure part of the riverbank, and tie up the boats until the truce ended.

The two patrol boats were tied to the same tree at the upstream end of a clearing. Downstream sat the five river assault craft. The Vietnamese and American army troops manned a security perimeter. Those not on guard duty or watch relaxed. Most napped, cleaned their weapons, read tattered *Playboy* magazines or old letters, or ate C-rations and chatted quietly. A few of the Vietnamese sailors fished. The patrol boat crews set up a security watch. Even though it was quiet and nothing was expected to happen, the sailors would rotate standing watch throughout the truce. The machine guns were loaded and cocked.

Frenchy's watch started at midnight, as did the truce. In his four years in the navy, he had stood over a thousand watches. Some had been on the bridge of a destroyer as lookout, helmsman, and messenger. Other watches were on the quarterdeck of the same ship in port in Newport, Rhode Island. A few were on the pier in Guantánamo and Naples where he had guarded the garbage.

When Frenchy heard that the navy was looking for Gunner's Mates to go to Vietnam, he volunteered. After a couple of months spent training in San Diego, he reported to the patrol boat squadron, and was assigned to his boat as the gunner. This suited Frenchy fine.

The 31-foot fiberglass boat was nothing like the destroyer he had left. But it did remind him a lot of the lobster boats he had worked on in Maine before enlisting. He liked the fast boat, he liked his crewmates, and he liked the informality and the lack of chickenshit. Maybe he'd stay in the navy. Maybe not. He'd decide at the end of his twelve months in-country.

Three hours into Frenchy's watch on Buddha's birthday, the wind picked up and the normally still and humid air turned chilly. Lightning and thunder came rolling out of the east toward the clearing. Frenchy put on his poncho just as the rain started.

"Frenchy, you fucking moron. What are you doing sitting there in the rain? Get under the canopy," called the boat captain, a chief petty officer.

"Nah, I'm fine, Chief. I got my poncho, and there's only about half an hour left. Can't see shit from back where you are," answered Frenchy, without turning around.

"Suit yourself. Nothing to see out there anyway except dark and trees and rain. Want a cup of coffee?" offered the boat captain.

A bright flash of lightning and instantaneous thunderclap meant the storm was right over them.

"No thanks, Chief. Coffee won't let me sleep after I'm relieved. I'll take a beer, though."

"Yeah, you and me both. Call room service and order me a six-pack."

The two men chuckled. The rain came down in sheets. Frenchy went back to staring at the riverbank. The lightning flashes were ruining his night vision.

He felt something thump on the fiberglass deck and then bump against the gun tub. A metallic click followed, as did a brilliant white lightning flash that illuminated the boat and clearing. Instinctively, Frenchy reached for the olive drab grenade that was rolling between his boots and threw it as hard as he could over the bow at the riverbank.

"Grenade!" he shouted. "Get down! Grenade!"

The grenade detonated, peppering the boat with shrapnel and mud. The grenade blast and another lightning bolt froze the image of three men in black pajamas pointing their guns at him. Frenchy jumped into the gunner's seat behind the twin machine guns and opened fire. Green tracers arced over his head. Frenchy sprayed the riverbank in front of the boat. He kept on firing until he felt a hand on his shoulder.

"Cease fire, Frenchy! Goddamnit, cease fire! You're going to burn out the barrels. You got them. Stop it!" ordered the boat captain.

White flares illuminated the clearing. Soldiers and sailors came running toward the two patrol boats. Frenchy sat back in the gunner's seat, hands shaking. The acrid firecracker smell of cordite hung in the air. He struggled to stand and get out of the tub, but his legs wouldn't hold his weight. Something salty ran over his lips.

The thunderstorm had stopped. An army medic pushed back Frenchy's poncho and pressed a bandage against his face below his left eye. He shined his flashlight in Frenchy's eyes.

"Hold that, press it hard," ordered the medic as he put Frenchy's hand on the compress. "Where are you? What's your name?"

"Where am I? Where the fuck do you think I am? I'm on the fucking Saigon River in Vietnam."

"What's your name?" asked the medic.

"My name? I'm Richard Nixon. What the fuck do you need to know my name for?"

The medic smiled and looked over at the boat captain. "Chief, I think he's fine. Looks like some shrapnel got him in the face, but I don't think there's any metal in there."

Two of Frenchy's crewmates helped him out of the gunner's seat and guided him aft. He sat down under the shelter of the canopy. His heart was beating in his ears. Someone put a cigarette in his mouth and someone else lit it. Frenchy took a deep drag and started coughing, settled down and puffed on the cigarette.

The officer in charge of the two boats and another navy officer attached to the assault craft walked up to one of the army officers standing on the riverbank. Pieces of what had been three Vietnamese in black pajamas, three AK-47s, and a satchel of grenades were scattered on the mud and splattered on the trees. The tree that the two patrol boats were tied to looked as if it had been inexpertly pruned. An ARVN first lieutenant and US staff sergeant walked up to the three officers.

The sergeant held a blood-soaked map case. He showed it to the trio. "There are three more KIAs about ten meters behind these three, loaded with B-40 rockets and grenades. Found these documents and intel on one of them. Whoever was shooting that .50, well—I'd like to meet that guy."

Later that morning three men sat on the riverbank in the shade of one of the assault craft. They were talking about what Frenchy had done five hours earlier.

The patrol boat's skipper said, "It seems to me the only question left is, what medal do we put him in for? What do you think, Chief?"

"Sir, if that was me sitting out there last night in the rain, I would have shit in my pants and been blown up along with the boats and crews. How the hell he remained calm enough to throw that grenade back, sound the alarm and get those guns firing is beyond me. That's beyond heroic."

"I agree with you, Chief," said the third man, the advisor to the assault craft group. "He saved a lot of lives. I think he deserves nothing less than a Bronze Star. Probably a Silver Star or Navy Cross. Maybe a Congressional?"

"Yeah, Marines get the Congressional for jumping on a grenade. He did more than that. Let me write something up and see how far I can get it," said the boat officer.

Several months later, as Frenchy neared the end of his in-country tour, he was ordered to report in his whites to the vice admiral who commanded all the US Naval Forces in Vietnam. Puzzled, Frenchy rode to Saigon in a jeep alongside his boat captain, with the officer in charge of the boats in the back seat. They wore their jungle fatigues, protecting their white uniforms from the road dust and soot.

To Frenchy's surprise, the admiral came out to the jeep to greet them, told them to change into whites in his office, and said lunch would be waiting for them.

At 1300, before ranks of sailors and officers lined up in front of the flagpole at the admiral's headquarters, Gunner's Mate Third Class François Ducasse was called front and center. A South Vietnamese Navy commodore awarded him the Cross of Gallantry. Then the admiral's aide read a document that promoted Frenchy to Gunner's Mate Second Class. The admiral shook his hand, and Frenchy was about to return to the ranks when the aide read another citation, this one awarding him a Purple Heart. The admiral pinned the handsome medal on Frenchy's white uniform blouse and again shook his hand.

The admiral smiled at Frenchy and said, "Better stay here, Ducasse. One more."

The aide read another citation, awarding the newly promoted Frenchy the Navy Cross. After the admiral pinned on the bronze medal with the dark blue and brilliant white ribbon attached, he stood beside Frenchy, grabbed his hand again and the two men smiled at the photographer.

Frenchy left Vietnam and worked a year as a recruiter in Portland, Maine. He returned to civilian life and used his GI Bill to study mechanical engineering. He got tired of people asking about the scar on his cheek, so he grew a beard. A year after graduating college, however, his girlfriend said she'd only accept his proposal of marriage if he shaved off that scratchy beard.

Forty years later, his four-year-old granddaughter opened an old shoebox she had found in a closet and discovered the medals. Her grandfather pinned them on her. Every visit thereafter, she asked to wear the Buddha Birthday jewelry.

BIG FAT UGLY FISH

The apex of the Iron Triangle is about twenty-five kilometers northwest of the urban sprawl of Saigon. It's formed by the junction of two rivers that mix their waters in a sluggish journey to the South China Sea.

The Viet Cong—Charlie—controlled the Iron Triangle. Despite frequent attempts by the US and South Vietnamese forces to obliterate Charlie and the North Vietnamese Army forces in the area, Charlie stayed in control. Pacification, winning the hearts and minds of the people, defoliation, bombing, infantry sweeps, psychological operations, and amphibious assaults usually failed to wrest control away from Charlie. Any successes were short-lived, measured in days, sometimes just hours, before the VC were back in charge.

Due to the nutrients in the two rivers, the mixing by the currents, and the blended temperature of the waters, fish proliferated at the point of the Iron Triangle. Big, fat, ugly fish thrived in the unique environment, growing bigger, uglier and fatter. These were not sleek and pretty freshwater fish such as rainbow trout or steelhead salmon; these were river fish from waters that were anything but fresh. Silt, dioxin, hardy smaller fish, insects, drowned rodents, rotting vegetation, farm animal and human waste, an occasional body, napalm, high-explosive residue, and pinches of diesel fuel and motor oil flowed through the gills and stomachs of the Big Fat Ugly Fish of the Iron Triangle.

Most Vietnamese seemed to be marvelous cooks. Those that lived in the area prized these fish. For one thing, a single fish could feed several families. For another, the fish were versatile. The fatty meat could be roasted, stir-fried, braised, broiled, or grilled, and the head, skin, skeleton, and fins used for soup. The village dogs relished the innards. But these fish rarely made it to the local tables.

It was hard to catch one of these river fish. For whatever reason, they seemed very fickle when it came to baited hooks on the end of a fishing line. Sometimes they'd bite, but often they did not. They seemed very content to eat whatever happened to swim past or to nibble at the organic buffet spread on the river bottom. The swirling currents made netting impractical. Even dropping a grenade into the water from a patrol boat rarely worked. The few that made it to the cooking pots were usually those clubbed by kids wading in the shallows.

* * *

Over a year and a half had passed since the Tet of 1968, and there was no light at the end of the tunnel as far as Lieutenant Commander Abe Todd was concerned. Todd was the US Navy officer assigned to the South Vietnamese Navy's River Assault Group 8, or RAG 8. Todd's job was to advise his counterpart, Lieutenant Commander To, on how to fight the war—the same war that To had been fighting for nearly a third of his thirty-two years. Compared to To, Todd was a newcomer to Vietnam and war.

Todd's ultimate boss, President Nixon, had demanded that the Vietnamization of the war be accelerated. Nixon had no desire to follow LBJ's example, and wanted out of the quagmire with as little mud as possible on his shined shoes. And, of course, he wanted victory over the VC and NVA. Todd had been in-country nearly a year. He was weary and wanted to go home, or at least to return to the familiar comfort of the "real navy" of oceangoing modern ships: "Haze gray and under way." Although he rarely acknowledged it, deep down inside he knew that victory wasn't attainable. But he did his job as best he could. It was his duty.

The officers, sailors, and lone advisor of RAG 8 had been away from their home base for two weeks. They were on the upper reaches of the Saigon River carrying a company of South Vietnamese rangers and their US Army advisor, and they were getting the snot knocked out of them. Rangers and sailors had been killed and wounded. Two of the RAG boats had been so badly shot up that they had to be towed behind the armored command boat. The survivors were jittery, grumpy, sleep-deprived, and dirty. But they kept on doing their jobs.

Up until that day, river operations had followed a predictable pattern. In the past, there had been little resistance, if any, to the RAG 8 moving upriver. The insertion of troops was usually quiet and rarely opposed, as was extraction. And there was always one ambush on the way downriver back to the home base in Phu Cuong. The tactic employed by the RAG when ambushed was dictated by the boats' slow speed and heavy armor. They turned into the ambush, opening up with every weapon the boats could bring to bear, and nosed the boats onto the riverbank to land the soldiers. Most times, the soldiers simply mopped up and counted the dead VC. For the rare stubborn holdouts, Todd would call in attack helicopters or artillery.

On that day, however, their firefight was against a particularly obstinate group of VC that would not stop firing, Todd even called in an air strike, dropping HEs—high explosives—onto the enemy's location. That stopped the VC. Afterward, when the sailors searched the bombed riverbank and mangrove stumps, all they found were some unidentifiable chunks of bones and muscle tissue. No weapons. No radios. No backpacks. Just chunks of people—maybe enough parts to account for at least two whole people. Whether the two had been VC or peasant farmers was impossible to tell. But since they were dead, the after-action report listed two enemy KIAs.

Todd's boss in Saigon got a call from some army general about that particular firefight. The general said that bombs and jet fuel were expensive, and asked why those kids on the river didn't just shoot their way out of it. Spending all that money on two lousy KIAs, he said, seemed inefficient and Secretary McNamara demanded efficiency. Todd's boss passed the general's criticism to Todd but added that some desk-bound general wasn't the one getting shot at on the river and told Todd to do whatever he thought was needed to save friendly lives.

The last two weeks of river operations had not followed the same predictable pattern. VC activity had been more intense and aggressive. The RAG had had to fight its way upriver as the VC shot rockets and fired AK-47s at them. When they landed their troops north of the Michelin Rubber Plantation and positioned the boats as a blocking force, snipers pinged away at the sailors; sappers threw a satchel charge into one of the boats; and mines detonated in pillars of water whenever they moved the boats. When the rangers extracted four days later, they carried out half a dozen wounded and four full body bags. Several other wounded had been evacuated by helicopter. They had run into battalion-size opposition. Charlie was there in force.

More bullets, mortar rounds, water purification tablets, bandages, and cases of C-rations were airlifted to the RAG, and the assault group stayed upriver for another week of insertion, extraction, and getting shot at. There were only two bright spots: the enemy KIA count was increasing, and the rangers uncovered a cache of rice. The latter was especially welcome at the time since the Vietnamese sailors and soldiers had almost run out of rice.

On the twelfth day upriver, the RAG and its passengers were ordered to cease operations and return to their base forty kilometers downriver. Todd and To knew that they would have to fight their way home. The rangers had lost nearly a third of their soldiers. The RAG had lost fewer men, but had two boats out of commission. The VC were aggressive, well armed, and in force. Charlie ruled.

Within an hour after they started downriver, the boats were attacked by large-caliber weapons, rockets, and machine guns. As usual, the assault group turned into the fire, but could not suppress it. Finally, after an hour of fighting and calling in artillery, the incoming fire stopped, though the lull was probably due to Charlie running low on ammunition, not because he was dead. The boats moved on.

After five more kilometers, the boats were hit again, this time by just a lone rocket and AK-47 fire. The incoming fire stopped when the boats turned toward the bank and opened fire. Hoping that this was a sign that they were moving out of Charlie's concentration of strength, the boats landed the soldiers.

The rangers left the boats and walked right into a booby-trapped clearing and a murderous crossfire. They called in helicopter gunships and artillery fire, and slowly the firefight ended.

As they loaded their wounded, Todd and To took a quick inventory. They were low on everything but rice and water purification tablets. There was enough fuel to get back to base, and, at the current rate, enough ammunition for two, maybe three more firefights. For food, all they had was a couple of cases of C-rations and a lot of rice; lack of variation might be a problem with that diet, but loose bowels would not. With fewer than thirty kilometers to go to their home base, their supplies would not be replenished. And the sailors' families had missed a payday.

To smiled grimly to Todd. "*Thieu Ta* Todd, do you know what I would like right now?"

"A cold beer?"

"That would be good, but no."

"A truce?"

"No. That would also be nice, but that will never happen."

"So, what would you like right now, *Thieu Ta* To?"

The Vietnamese officer's smile widened. "I would like some fresh food. Fish. Maybe duck. But fish would be nice. With sauce and rice."

The American chuckled. "That does sound good. Two weeks of C-rats are two weeks too much."

The boats got under way, hoping to make it past the juncture of the two rivers without another ambush; once south of that point, they'd be out of the Iron Triangle and in South Vietnam government controlled territory.

Around dawn, they neared the apex of the Iron Triangle. Tossing an empty C-ration can over the side of the command boat, the American army advisor to the rangers told Todd and To that he would not send any troops ashore if they got into another firefight. The three agreed that if they got shot at one more time, they were calling in an air strike to bomb the shit out of the place. They were frustrated. If the United States of America ended up spending thousands of dollars on jet fuel and bombs to scare a single VC and blow up a bunch of trees...well, that was just tough shit. Fuck the general in Saigon.

Fifteen minutes later, a B-40 rocket crossed the bow of the lead boat, and then green tracers sprayed the column of boats from the mangroves on the left bank where the two rivers joined. As in all the other attacks, the boats opened up with every weapon available; unlike in all the other attacks, however, the boats did not turn into the fire, land on the riverbank, or put the rangers ashore. Instead, the column of boats continued their slow creep downriver, fighting its way out of the killing zone.

With a finger in his left ear to mute the cacophony of gunfire and the handset of his radio pressed to his right ear, Todd called for help. Within in seconds he was talking to the tactical operations center at the big US Army base in Cu Chi.

"Receiving heavy incoming from coordinates 755206 north bank of Saigon Thi Tinh river junction. Moving boats half a klick south. Request air strike. Napalm and HE. Over." Klick was the war's slang for kilometer.

Thirty seconds later a small gray spotter aircraft zoomed low over the boats. Todd's radio crackled to life. It was the forward air controller or FAC.

"Two birds on the way. Marking target with smoke. Observe and correct my darts, over."

The FAC fired a rocket at the point of land that still spewed green tracers, which were now arcing up at the plane. Todd observed the smoke from the rocket through binoculars. To did the same, then nodded vigorously and held up his right thumb.

Todd keyed his handset. "Observed smoke. On target. Bomb from the shoreline north. No friendlies in the area. Over."

The little plane zoomed over the boats, fired another rocket that landed a hundred meters north of the first, did a wingover, and dived close to the river surface and sped south.

A silver Super Saber fighter-bomber streaked in a steep dive from the south, pulled up, and lofted two dark shapes into the air. As the deafening sound of the plane reached the boats, the dark shapes arced through the sky and descended between the two columns of the smoke markers.

The tip of the Iron Triangle silently exploded in a black and gray eruption of dirt and shattered trees. A few seconds later, a wall of thunderous sound reached the boats, rippling the flat water of the river. Another Super Saber came out of the east and flew directly over the target, dropping two silver bombs of napalm. Horrible black and orange cauliflower blossoms whooshed upward, sucking up air. The sailors and soldiers on the boats cheered as the smell of gasoline and the heat of the flames wafted over them.

The little FAC plane circled overhead, assessing the damage. A string of green tracers reached up to it. The plane dived, unleashed another smoke rocket, and again sped south at low altitude. The Super Sabers dropped more HE and napalm. The FAC flew low again, observing the damage. Todd's radio came alive.

"Looks pretty quiet down there. I can see some crispy critters. Birds are low on fuel. I'm sending one home. The other has two HE left. I don't want to have him take that home. Okay to drop on target? Over."

Todd smiled and keyed his handset. "Great job. Can you drop the HE at the water edge? Right on the riverbank? Over."

"Riverbank. Roger that. Good target practice. Watch for some real precision work. Over."

"Will do. When you're done, we'll land the troopers and count bodies and collect weapons. If any. Will include you in after-action report. Over."

The final two bombs hit near the riverbank. One fell into the shallow water, the other a few meters away into deeper water. Great fountains of river water and mud plumed into the air. With a rocking of its wings, the FAC made a final low-level pass over the boats and flew back to base.

Blackened and bare, the target area smoldered as the boats approached. In the river water were floating tree limbs and leaves and clumps of earth. And *fish*. Lots and lots of fish. As Todd had hoped, the surface was covered with fish stunned and killed by the underwater explosions of the last two bombs. These were not just fish; these were Big Fat Ugly Fish.

While the rangers counted bodies and body parts and collected pieces of weapons, the sailors loaded fish into one of the small patrol boats and ferried tons of Big Fat Ugly Fish to the larger boats. For the next two hours, the sailors stacked fish on the boat decks, covered them with canvas, and wet the canvas with river water.

RAG 8 tied up at its base in the middle of the afternoon. Wounded that had not already been evacuated by helicopter were loaded into waiting ambulances or carried into the sick bay. Body bags were loaded into the covered bed of a lone truck. The rangers, each carrying fish wrapped in a poncho, boarded three troop transport trucks. The convoy of wounded, dead, and fish-bearing soldiers left the base just as two empty civilian pickups pulled in.

Sailors loaded fish into the two trucks until at least a thousand kilograms of fresh fish filled the beds. The senior enlisted sailor climbed into the cab of one of the trucks, and the vehicles left the compound and headed into the town of Phu Cuong. An hour later he returned, having negotiated the sale of the fish to the Phu Cuong fishmongers. He gave To the money so it could be distributed among his sailors.

As the sailors finished securing the boats, those not on watch left to be with family and friends. Each sailor carried a couple of the Big Fat Ugly Fish.

That night after showers, shaves, and naps, Todd sat at To's dinner table. The Vietnamese officer's wife scurried around the small dining room and kitchen, directing her children and mother-in-law as she prepared her husband and his American friend's welcome-home meal. She set before them a bowl of steaming rice and a platter of redolent vegetables surrounding a large filet of braised fish covered with a garlic sauce.

That night Todd wrote his wife about the finest meal of his life. Big Fat Ugly Fish, which he had helped catch.

A Bright and Shining Light

USS Willett was on its way home. The big guided-missile frigate was steaming east out of the Gulf of Tonkin, on its way
back to San Diego. The ship and its crew were returning from
ten exhausting months of operations: protecting the aircraft carrier, coordinating other ships, collecting intelligence, providing
gunfire support, and looking for aircraft, submarines, and surface
vessels. The ship had been relieved on station by another frigate,
fresh from Newport, Rhode Island. She had beautiful, sensuous
lines—seductive features that hid her ability to destroy other men
and their ships and airplanes.

The captain reviewed his night orders, made a few additions,
walked out on the bridge wing, and scanned the horizon in the
warm, heavy air and the wind generated by his ship's forward
movement. The night was that inky black that only sailors know.
Overhead...a canopy of stars. Gentle sea swells bubbled into a
phosphorescent froth of bow wake.

The only sounds were the wind whistling around the signal flag
halyards and the ping, ping, ping of the sonar as it sought out submarines, whales, and schools of fish. The men on watch were silent,

doing their job, guiding twelve thousand tons of steel filled with 362 men through the blackness to San Diego, half a world away.

The captain nodded to the lookout on the wing of the bridge, told the officer of the deck that he was going down to sleep, and thumped down the steel ladder to his at-sea cabin. He had not slept in thirty-six hours, and his sleep before that had been nothing more than a short nap. The war had made sure that for him, rest was a rare commodity. He was out as soon as his head hit the pillow.

Fifteen minutes before midnight, the frigate's newest OOD walked onto the bridge to relieve the watch. This young officer was one of the few in a new program: a junior aviator aboard a surface ship. The new Chief of Naval Operations, tired having what he called "three navies," wanted to integrate the surface, aviation, and submarine communities. Cross-pollinating with hard-charging young officers was his solution.

The young aviator had been aboard six months and just qualified as an OOD. With the strong endorsements of the executive officer and senior watch officer, and despite the fact that qualification as OOD usually took a year or more, the captain signed the aviator's qualification without hesitation. There was no doubt in his mind that the young man was ready to take on the responsibility of guiding the ship safely through the seas and, if need be, leading her and her men into combat. Freshly promoted to lieutenant, the officer was proud of his rapid qualification, although he still had some butterflies about his ability to do the job right. The aviator found the man he was to relieve standing by the radar repeater.

The two officers started their formal exchange of information:

"Course 274; speed 18 knots; plant cross connected with both port boilers on the line; all radars on line; sonar sweep search, no sonar contacts, three surface contacts, of which Bravo is the oiler moving east; helm and lee helm not yet relieved; skipper's in the rack."

"When's our next course change?"

"Not until the morning watch. Captain wants us to keep an eye out for Bear overflights; he got a message from CINCPAC. Track with the air search only. Something's up on the diplomatic front, I guess." A Bear was the Soviet's long-range bomber and reconnaissance aircraft, an ungainly and dangerous vulture of an airplane. CINCPAC was the Pearl Harbor–based commander of the Pacific, a four-star admiral.

They discussed the midnight rations that were on the wardroom table—peanut butter and bread—and the lack of mail since they had not received an underway replenishment for a week. The aviator walked around the dark bridge and wings, recognizing faces in the glow of the radars and instruments, looked over the quartermaster's shoulder as he plotted the last navigation fix that confirmed they were on course and schedule, walked back to the on-duty OOD, stood at attention, saluted and said:

"I relieve you, sir."

"I stand relieved. You have the watch and conn." The off-going officer then turned to the bridge front and shouted, "Mr. Thornton has the watch and the conn!" His friend and shipmate had the watch and would be in control for the next four hours. A chorus of "Aye aye, sir!" came out of the shadows.

The young officer then turned to the bridge front and loudly proclaimed the formal declaration, "I have the watch and conn! Continue course and speed as before. Inform me of any changes in contacts."

The helmsman reported, "Aye aye, sir. Steering 274 true, 272 magnetic." The lee helmsman followed, "Aye aye, sir. All ahead full. Making 18 knots at 82 rpm. Two boilers on the line, one on standby, one off line."

The OOD quietly replied "Very well." He then went to the log and made his entry, the official acknowledgement that he was responsible for whatever happened to this US Navy vessel until he was formally relieved. The senior enlisted watch stander, the boatswain mate of the watch, was at his elbow, handing him a mug of hot coffee.

As he sipped the bitter brew, the OOD looked at the BMOW. A good sailor, salty as an anchovy. Ten years ago a judge in Texas had offered him the choice of going to jail for some drunken highjinks or shaping himself up by joining the armed services. A Texas jail's loss turned into a national defense asset. Sailors like Petty Officer Second Class Watson formed the backbone of the US Navy. Rough, smart, untiring, dedicated. On the promotion list for first class petty officer.

"How you doing, Boats? When do you get to sew on the new stripe?"

"Doing fuckin-A outstanding, sir. I think I get the promotion papers as soon as we're in San Diego. And I'm up for orders. Put in for a river squadron in-country. First class gets me my own boat."

The lookout on the starboard wing called out, "Sir, contact starboard bow. On the horizon."

The OOD walked out to the wing. He recognized the young sailor who was the lookout: Seaman Ewashko. Newly reported aboard, trying hard to please. Reliable.

"Where is it, Ewashko?"

"Fine on the bow, sir. Right on the horizon. Pretty bright now; I can see it without the binoculars."

The OOD looked and saw a very bright light on the horizon. He walked back into the bridge and checked the surface- and air-search radar repeaters, but they showed no such contact. He picked up the phone to talk to the watch officer in the Combat Information Center in the bowels of the ship to see if they had anything. Again, nothing.

A single white light at sea is anathema to a warship. It has to be investigated. It could be a vessel over the horizon with just its masthead light showing; it could be a vessel's stern light; it could be a reflection off a submarine's snorkel; it could be a low flier; it could be a fishing vessel's worklight; it could be a missile. Or it could be a Soviet Bear heading right for the *USS Willett*.

The OOD moved back to the starboard wing as Ewashko started to say something. The light had grown even brighter and seemed to have almost an elongated vertical shape on the horizon.

"Ewashko, that thing is brighter than before. It must be really moving."

Ewashko put down his binoculars and said, "Mr. Thornton, I think it's the..."

But the OOD was already moving back into the bridge, taking another look at the radar repeaters and then walked back onto the wing.

"Shit, it's even brighter and I don't have it on the screen."

"Uh, sir, I think..."

"Be right back, Ewashko. Keep an eye on that. I had better call the skipper." The OOD walked back into the wheelhouse before the lookout could finish his sentence.

None of the officers had had much sleep lately. The OOD felt as though his eyes were filled with sand, his teeth had grown fur, and his mouth was tarred with coffee-flavored asphalt. The captain had had the least sleep of all of them, but he had left no doubt in any of his night orders: if there was a concern, the OOD was to notify him immediately—sleep or no sleep. The OOD grabbed the bridge phone and pushed the captain's sea cabin button. A sleep-clogged frog of a voice answered, "Captain."

"Captain, this is Mr. Thornton, the OOD. We've got a single white light on the horizon that's moving at us pretty fast, but I can't get it on the surface search or air search. CIC has nothing and sonar's all clear."

"How do you know it's moving fast?"

"Sir, it's gotten bigger and brighter in just the last minute. Still nothing on the radars."

"Okay, be right up."

"BMOW, Captain's coming up!"

The BMOW was standing next to Ewashko on the wing. The OOD ran out and looked at the light. It was even brighter and more elongated then before. Sort of the horn of a crescent.

The BMOW touched the OOD's sleeve and said, "Sir, that's the..."

The OOD turned as he heard the captain's footsteps on the ladder and said, "Be right back, Boats, skipper's coming up." He walked back into the bridge as the watch standers chorused, "Captain's on the bridge."

31

The captain looked around, trying to accustom his eyes to the night. He focused on the OOD. "Show me it, Jerry."

"Yes, sir, Captain. You can see it through the bridge windows, fine on the starboard bow."

The BMOW coughed loudly behind the OOD, then cleared his throat. He moved up behind the OOD and whispered, "Uh, sir, can you come over here to the wing for a second?"

Irritated, the OOD barked back, "Boats, I'm with the captain, I'll be right with you."

The captain scanned the horizon to the right of his ship and then moved out onto the wing, staring into the darkness. "Where is it?"

Jeez, the old man must be blind, thought the young OOD. *That thing's big enough and bright enough to read by.* "Captain, that's it, about 005 relative, fine on the starboard bow, that bright skinny thing."

"Where? I don't see anything."

Fuck, he is blind. "Right there, Captain." He pointed, his finger dead on the target.

"I don't see anything. Put the pelorus on it."

The OOD bent to the pelorus's small telescope sitting atop the compass repeater and put its crosshairs smack on the middle of the bright silver crescent-horn of light. He stepped back. The captain looked.

"I still don't see it. Maybe I knocked the crosshairs off of it. Take a look."

The OOD looked but the crosshairs were still smack in the center of the brilliant light. *Hell, the old man was not only blind he was also nuts if he couldn't see that.* "Nope, the crosshair's are still on it, Captain."

The captain bent to it again. In the glow of the compass repeater, the OOD could see just how tired his skipper was. His normally handsome face was lined and covered with a day's growth of stubbly beard. The captain squinted.

"No, I still don't see it. Is it to the right or left of the moon?"

"Moon, Captain?"

"Yeah, to the right or left of the moon? You've got the crosshairs on the moon."

Aw shit. Called the skipper out of his rack to come up to the bridge to watch the moon rise. He looked behind him at Ewashko and Boats, who both nodded and smirked and shrugged their shoulders. The helmsmen softly chuckled.

The captain turned to his newest OOD and said, "I'm going back to sleep. Call me if you need me."

The next afternoon Lieutenant Thornton sheepishly went up to his captain and tried to mumble out an apology. From his throne of a bridge chair, the commanding officer listened gravely, then climbed down and walked his youngest OOD to the starboard wing.

He put his arm around the young man's shoulders. "Listen, Jerry. I would rather come up a thousand times to look at the moon than to once miss something that I really needed to know. Besides, you're going to get enough razzing about this for the rest of your tour on this ship. Seems like a pretty good lesson, huh?"

"Yes, sir, it does."

"If you want to apologize to anyone, better do it to your lookout and BMOW. Those guys are always worth listening to and should never be ignored."

"Aye aye, Captain."

The skipper then patted his young officer on the back and told him to get something to eat. And to hit the rack and get some much-needed sleep.

H&I

T he slow armored boats of the river assault group plied the
Saigon River from the little town of Phu Cuong upriver all the
way to the Cambodian border. They carried US and Vietnamese
troops, landing them at one spot on the river and picking them
up from another. The river the boats operated on was the border
between several big US Army and ARVN divisions. It was also an
artery through Viet Cong and North Vietnamese Army operating
areas, known in GI slang as "Indian country."

After the thwarted Tet Offensive of 1968, the pace of attacks
and ambushes of US and South Vietnamese forces had dropped
dramatically. Rumors that "the enemy shot his wad" and news clips
repeating that some general could see "the light at the end of the
tunnel" encouraged Saigon operational planners to go on the
hunt to finish off the elusive enemy.

For a few months, the big boats encountered little opposition
as they lumbered up and down the river with their cargoes of
troops and, occasionally, defoliants: a rocket or two fired from the
riverbank, a half-hearted spray of precious AK-47 bullets, a rare
mortar shell. But not much else. Most of the troops found little to

shoot at and kill during their forays from the river and back. For war, it was a very quiet time. Sometimes the army commander of the embarked troops even asked the boats to pull into an inviting beach area so his men could go swimming in the fetid waters of the Saigon River, while the Vietnamese sailors remained on their boats watching and commenting on how hairy the Americans were.

Gradually, the tempo picked up. By the end of 1969, the boats could count on at least one firefight as they came back downriver. The encountered more rockets, mortar shells, bullets, and even water mines. The troops ashore ran into ambushes and booby traps. Contact with the enemy occurred more and more frequently as the soldiers humped their way inland, then back to the riverbanks. People on both sides died.

The generals wanted the enemy escalation stopped. The ragamuffin VC and NVA were obscuring the light at the end of the tunnel. Free-fire zones were set up from curfew to dawn. The official definition of a free-fire zone was a single sentence from a field manual: "A specific designated area into which any weapon system may fire without additional coordination with the establishing headquarters."

Translated from the purple prose of the military bureaucracy to common English, the definition meant that if there was a target in the zone and you had a weapon, you were free to fire it. What this meant to the grunts in the field and the sailors on the riverboats was that if a person was in the free-fire zone, that person was by definition the enemy and needed to be killed.

Hand-in-hand with the free-fire zones came *harassment and interdiction,* or H&I. This was usually artillery or mortar fire on an area suspected of being used by the VC to hide, set up rockets, ambush, infiltrate, escape, and transport equipment and supplies. It didn't matter if Charlie was there or not, shells could be lobbed in. Supposedly, H&I fire missions were intended to kill the VC or at least keep him uncomfortable and off balance.

Five-year-old Nhung lived with her parents and her little brother in a strategic hamlet northeast of a big US Army division base across the Saigon River. Strategic hamlets were a miserable failure of the South Vietnamese government. Peasants were relocated from their homes and family plots of land to these shoddily built collections of huts to separate them from the VC. The strategic hamlets were fenced with barbed wire and sharpened bamboo sticks. The Nazis would have considered them poor imitations of their concentration camps.

The hamlet dwellers were separated from their fields, fishing grounds, and ancestral land holdings. They had to get up early in the morning to walk to their crops, sampans, and fishing nets then hurry back at dusk before the curfew. If they weren't against the Saigon regime before having been relocated, many of them certainly were after. Probably the biggest accomplishment of the strategic hamlet program was the creation of a large population of VC and VC sympathizers.

Nhung's father and mother made charcoal in three large domed charcoal ovens a two-kilometer walk from their hamlet. As did many of their neighbors, they took considerable pride in providing charcoal, food, and clothing to the nearby VC base camp and the tunnel network located off a path to the Saigon River. Sometimes they carried messages to People's Army couriers who visited the hamlet in the middle of the night. The Americans and South Vietnamese had targeted that path as an infiltration and escape route used by the local VC battalion. From sunset to dawn, the path was in a free-fire zone.

Two men were visiting her parents, talking in low voices in the night. Awake on her sleeping mat, Nhung could see the outline of the men and their guns. Although she couldn't see their faces, she knew who they were. They were Daddy's friends who lived with the other men at the end of the path that went to the river. She stretched and stood up, scratching her tummy as she padded over to the adults. Mommy smiled at Nhung and gave her a hug, then told her to be quiet so as to not wake up her little brother. Nhung went out to urinate near the scrub bushes behind the hut.

When she came back, the men had left. Mommy noticed that they had forgotten to take with them the warm steamed tapioca root, peanuts, salt, and a bunch of nutritious morning glory vines.

Mommy gave the warm bundle to Nhung and told her to hurry after the men and give it to them, then to come right back.

It was very quiet in the Tactical Operations Center ten kilometers across the river from Nhung's family hut. The American first lieutenant running the TOC was bored and fighting to stay awake. He had already disassembled, cleaned, and reassembled his .45 pistol, which had not been fired since he cleaned it the day before. He had finished the *Stars and Stripes* crossword puzzle two hours ago. Except for some routine patrols checking in, the radios were silent. He wanted something to do. Anything to burn up some time. He looked at the map on the board hanging behind him, studied the grease-pencil borders of a free-fire zone, and put his finger on the path that ran from the little hamlet through the free-fire zone to the river.

To exercise his brain, he plotted the coordinates of the path at hundred-meter intervals, starting with the hamlet and moving down the path to the riverbank. Then he picked up the radio handset, called the howitzer crew—they were as bored as he was—and ordered H&I fire, starting with the first coordinate and ending where the path joined the river. Twenty shells in all.

Nhung was about two hundred meters from her home when the first 105 mm round exploded directly over her. The air pressure crushed her to death instantly. Nanoseconds later, the explosion incinerated her, vaporizing the little girl into superheated molecules of carbon dioxide and water. Nhung ceased to exist ten seconds before the second shell exploded a hundred meters farther down the path.

The bored first lieutenant had ordered twenty rounds of H&I fire. He was unaware that he tore up a dirt path, destroyed seven trees, and erased a little five-year-old girl from the face of the earth. Forever ignorant of the consequences of his action, he sat down at his desk, radioed the artillery crew that the firing mission was over, and thumbed through a well-worn *Playboy*. In another hour, he'd leave the TOC, grab some breakfast, and then catch some sleep.

Two years later, the generals decided that H&I was too expensive and possibly counterproductive, and eliminated H&I—for "budgetary reasons."

Forty years after Nhung disappeared, an amusement park opened on the site that included the path and the strategic hamlet. Tunnels, farmland, huts, and hard laterite soil were bulldozed and covered with asphalt, cement, amusement rides, and manicured gardens. Families arrived at the park by bus or automobile. And tourists from Ho Chi Minh city took motorboat rides on the Saigon River that let them off at the riverbank. An ice cream parlor sits where that first shell exploded.

LA BAMBA

The version of La Bamba *in this story is not the rock-and-roll hit version released by Ritchie Valens in 1958, though it is based on the same Mexican folk song from Veracruz. This is the version that Harry Belafonte sang and danced to at Carnegie Hall in 1960—the one that starts with a slow and lyrical waltz of love before turning into an energetic, whirling and foot-stomping folk dance. —KL*

From the first time I heard it, the prelude to *La Bamba* has always choked me with emotion. I feel like crying, but I'm not sad. This time, I lifted my granddaughter when the music started. She wrapped her right arm around my shoulder, snuggled her cheek next to my stubble, and put her little left hand in mine. We waltzed around the den, stepping and gliding gracefully between the rocker, exercise mat, toy cups and saucers, and the two stuffed animals strewn on the floor. We waltzed into the dining room, through the kitchen, and back down the hall into the den. She was smiling, happy. I felt as good as I've ever felt. The two of us were unconditionally happy with life.

Dancing to the lyrical part of *La Bamba* with her, I was graceful and kept perfect time. We spun around the den as I softly sang the beautiful lyrics to her. I sang that I'd always love her and told her about the crabs that walk in reverse. She held onto me. She loves dancing with Grandpa, even though my left foot is withered and spastic leg movements make me clumsy. She doesn't care that Grandpa can't see and feels his way around the cluttered floor with his bare feet. And Grandpa loves it because I can just be myself. No people helpfully, constructively criticizing, trying to aid me, no one watching out for my stumble or anticipating the mess I might make. And my granddaughter doesn't care when I just stare off to nowhere, saying nothing.

When the lyrical and romantic waltz ended, *La Bamba* abruptly changed to wild festival dance music. I put her down and we jumped and twirled to the lively beat. She smiled and laughed, chubby arms and hands held above her blond hair, spinning, running short little distances, jumping. Her little feet tapping, knees pumping. We only stopped when the music ended and the Carnegie Hall audience burst into cheers and applause. As did the two of us. Clapping our hands, laughing.

She had never heard that song before. Looking at me, she said in her two-and-a-half-year-old voice, "Grandpa, that song is hard." Then she buried her face on my knee and wrapped her arms around my legs. I picked her up and hugged her and we sat on the rocking chair. Saying nothing, just snuggling.

I was at war the first time I heard that recording. With sound legs and good balance. Able to see everything I looked at. The music, especially the first part, seemed to be a dream to me. A dream away from the war. Beautiful. Now I was cuddling the dearest thing to my heart. I was again in a dream away from the war. Far away from the war.

SUPER BOWL III

On January 11, 1969, the National Football League was king. Monsters in football jerseys and helmets. Rough, tough. No one could beat the NFL. The American Football League, on the other hand, was a collection of dinky teams playing sloppy football. A good college team could probably beat any AFL team. Two years before, the AFL had had the audacity to challenge the NFL. The best of the teams of the two leagues would play to determine the world's greatest football team. That was 1967 and Super Bowl I. The AFL team got creamed in Super Bowl I. As did the AFL team in Super Bowl II in 1968.

Super Bowl III was scheduled for January 12, 1969. The team representing the NFL was the Baltimore Colts, a collection of the finest football players in the world. They had thirteen wins and only one loss in the mean and tough NFL. The Colts were so tough that the defensive linemen got more press than the rest of the team. The NFL Baltimore Colts were like one of the US military's elite units. No one could beat them.

The Colts would be playing against the best team in the weak AFL, the New York Jets. The Jets were 11–3 in a league that was going to lose its third straight Super Bowl. No doubt about it.

Everyone knew that the Colts were going to kill the Jets knew it, as did sportswriters, bartenders, barbers, even housewives. They all knew that the Colts were going to roll all over the Jets. The Jets would be like a bunch of little guerrilla fighters getting smashed by a crack US infantry division followed by an artillery barrage followed by an air strike. Obliterated. Pick up the remains with a blotter.

The quarterback for the Jets, Joe Namath, was just a few years out of college. Most quarterbacks in professional football had to sit on the bench and play backup for several years before they took over the starting job. Some never got the chance to start. But not Joe Namath. He started as a rookie and he was good. Namath was smart, and although he couldn't run well, he could do almost everything else better than any quarterback in professional football. Still, he was playing in the AFL, the pussies' league.

Namath announced that the Jets would beat the Colts.

The press, the public, and especially the Colts thought Namath was nuts. How could any team in the AFL beat the Colts? And how could anyone be dumb enough to say his team would win against the Colts? The Jets were the VC and Namath was a very brash Ho Chi Minh. The light in the end of the tunnel for the Colts was only a football field length away.

The NFL was so confident that the Colts would win that they agreed to go to Vietnam and show the game films to the troops in the field. This would be a wonderful morale booster, great public relations for the NFL, and a chance for the Colts to boast about how they beat the shit out of the Jets.

On January 12, 1969, the Jets beat the Colts 16–7. Namath was Super Bowl III's MVP. And American football has never been the same.

Two weeks later, Lieutenant Junior Grade Sam Chabot and Chief Petty Officer Chuck Whipple carried their gear from the South Vietnamese Navy's coastal force junk to their hooch. They had been on patrol for a week and were tired, hungry, and—despite, or maybe because of, having jumped into the delta water to cool off and bathe—dirty and smelly. The two were advisors to the

44

South Vietnamese Navy. Chabot was a Chicago Bears fan; Whipple liked the Cleveland Browns. Like most NFL loyalists, they were shocked when they heard that the Jets had won.

They dumped their gear on their racks and Whipple took two cold sodas out of the refrigerator. Chabot drafted his after-action reports and called them into the Tactical Operations Center on top of the hill in Vung Tau. Sitting across from his chief, Sam put down the landline phone and opened his soda can. The landline phone rang and Whipple picked it up.

"Advisory Group 33, Chief Whipple speaking." He listened for a pause. "Yes, sir, we just got in. Mr. Chabot sent in the reports about five minutes ago." Another longer pause. "Yes, sir, he's right here. Hold on, please."

Whipple handed the handset to Chabot. "It's the boss, sir. Looks like we've got an invite." Whipple stood up and started stripping off his dirty uniform.

"Mr. Chabot speaking, sir."

"Sam, I told Chief Whipple already. You guys stow your gear and clean up. Then come over to Geralds Compound. The NFL is going to show us the Super Bowl films. Meet and greet. Should be interesting."

Half an hour later, the two advisors drove their jeep into the gravel parking area of Geralds Compound. This was the housing for most of the US Navy personnel assigned to the Tactical Operations Center, communications center, intelligence office, and administration headquarters for this part of the Mekong Delta. The compound was a low, single-story brick building that had been converted into two dozen rooms, showers, and toilets, as well as a lounge area for watching movies and US Armed Forces Radio and Television, Vietnam (AFRT, Vietnam). It was named for a navy lieutenant who had died after falling off the back of a motorcycle while trying to evade MPs who were raiding a skivvy house.

Outside the compound stood group of sailors and officers and three giants in jungle fatigues. A smaller, more normal-size person with styled hair was also there, but everyone was talking to the giants. As Chabot and Whipple approached, the guy with the nice hair came up to them, introduced himself as somebody with the NFL and thanked them for coming. He turned to the first giant, a tall, slender, yet heavily muscled black man Chabot recognized as Irv Cross, all six feet two inches and 200 pounds of him. His name was embroidered over his left fatigue blouse pocket, "NFL" over his right. Cross was a defensive back for the Philadelphia Eagles.

"Mr. Cross, you did your student teaching at my high school," said Chabot.

"Really? You went to Evanston? Bear fan?"

"You bet, but these've been lean years."

Cross laughed, his face a wide smile. "I think we might all be saying that. Thanks for letting us come over and meet with you guys. This means a lot to us."

"Means a lot to us, too, Mr. Cross," said Whipple. "How's it feel having to go around and show the film of the Jets winning?"

"Call me Irv, please. Feels lousy, to say the least. But not as bad as those two feel." Cross pointed at the two blocks of humanity standing by the table with soft drinks. He walked Chabot and Whipple over and introduced them.

The first was Dick Szymanski, the center linebacker for the Colts. He was taller than Cross and a good eighty pounds heavier. Shaking hands with him was like grabbing a cement catcher's mitt. The other goliath was a true legend of the Colts, their ferocious defensive tackle, Billy Ray Smith. He was taller than Szymanski and looked a little lighter. But he was still a very big human being. After some chatting, it was movie time.

Cross gave an introduction. He made no bones about it. The NFL had been so confident of a win that they had committed to take the films around Vietnam to show the troops. Billy Ray Smith just shook his head and stared down at his size-thirteen feet. Szymanski wore a sick smile.

Billy Ray Smith stood up, thanked Cross, and in his country-boy twang, asked the guy with the nice hair to start the projector. The game film was what the national television audience had watched January 12, 1969—minus the pregame kibitzing, commercials, and half time. Smith talked over the sportscasters and often asked for the frame to be frozen or to back up the scene so he could point out things that only a professional football player would recognize. He was erudite and kept the two dozen sailors and officers riveted in their seats. At the end, he took questions.

One of the sailors asked "What happened, Billy? What went wrong?"

He rubbed a big hand over his mouth and answered, "What happened is that they beat us. We played as good as we ever did. With a healthy team. Namath just beat us. Fair and square. Nothing went wrong; they were just better than us."

"You surprised at that?" asked another sailor.

The big man laughed and said, "Surprised is the right word. If I knew that was going to happen, do you think I'd be standing here tooting the Jets' horn?"

The questions got around to NFL and AFL competition.

After a little discussion, Billy Ray Smith looked around at the sugarcane and rice paddy in front of the compound. He said, "Y'know, fellows, I've been thinking. On the plane. And now here. Since that game, it's a new era in professional football. Maybe January twelfth was our Tet."

RIVER DANCE

The boats of Assault Group Zebra motored up the Saigon River about ten kilometers from the Cambodian border. The air was a warm, wet, mildewed sponge. It smelled of the sickly sweet rotting vegetation stink of the river, mixed with the boats' diesel exhaust and the sailors' sweat. A full moon was rising.

At this part of the river, the assault group always found itself in a firefight. The group's commanding officer, a twenty-something American, knew that they would be hit again and had his Vietnamese radioman standing next to him with the air strike and artillery radio frequencies already dialed in. The Viet Cong and North Vietnamese Army regulars owned this real estate— "Charlie Country."

The anticipation of a battle was as bad on the nerves as the battle itself. All they could do was wait; they had no control over when or what would happen. The lack of control was, for most of the group, the worst.

The lead boat had just reached a bend in the river when green tracers erupted from the riverbank with the barking rattle of gunfire a second or two later. The bullets raked the boats. One group of men, the mixed crew of American and Vietnamese sailors, had been ambushed by a large and well-equipped group of other men entrenched in the riverbanks and paddy dikes. Men shouted orders and the boats turned toward these other men, the ones on the riverbank, and opened fire. Men started to die. Men who had been mothers' little boys. Men who were husbands. Men who were little girls' daddies. Men who were gentle and men who were animals.

The air filled with the acrid firecracker smell of cordite and the unique sweat-smell of fear. As if in slow motion, the young American officer watched three red balls of fire, the exhaust trails of B-40 rockets, converge on his command boat. The first hit forward. The second passed a few feet above him, its exhaust blowing his unstrapped helmet off his head. The third hit and exploded on a stanchion just outboard of him and his radioman. The beautiful explosion blossom expanded until it engulfed them.

The American was deafened by a screaming silence of wind. Hot stinging smoke went up his nose and filled his mouth. His eyes stung. The force picked him up, peppering him with hot, stinging steel shrapnel. With detached crystal clarity, he watched the boat rapidly move away as the explosion carried him through the air and dumped him on the far riverbank below a rice paddy dike. The American landed on his back on top of all that was left of his radioman—a severed left arm—and the radio.

Numb.

No pain.

Then the warm, wet black wool that covered him started to lift. His brain was befuddled, but images were clear, outlined in stark moonlight. No noise but that screaming wind in his ears. Hot blunt pain seared his back. His left side from his shoulder down: paralyzed. The American lay there, on top of the radio and a dead man's arm, watching red and green tracers crisscross like brilliant hornets above his face. The chicken-feather smell of burning flesh reached his brain.

The boats fought their way downriver and out of the firefight. The only sound was that high pitched hurricane ringing in his ears. His thoughts remained muddled, but the pain ebbed. It didn't hurt so much. Cotton muffled the hurricane. He felt cold, detached.

Moonlight painted the riverbank blue. A skinny and shriveled Vietnamese in a uniform walked in a crouch out of the brush with a pistol in his right hand. The young American's hearing was clearing. The pain was coming back. As his brain cleared, the shock lifted. He hurt worse. Anxiety and panic briefly surfaced when he realized he couldn't feel his left side. The radio beneath him crackled static.

The Vietnamese cautiously walked over and nudged the big man with his rubber-tire sandaled foot. The American looked directly at his face. Thin, prominent cheekbones narrowing down into a triangle of a jaw and chin. Full and brooding lips. Wide, flat nose with flared nostrils. Beneath his pith helmet, wide eyes, filled with adrenalin and the fear of battle. A red star on the pith helmet, four pockets on his faded dirty uniform shirt—the sign of an NVA officer. A small man.

The Vietnamese must have thought the American had died with his eyes open. He bent over to take the radio, a prized piece of equipment and intelligence. The radio was wedged between the American's back, the severed arm and the riverbank. The slight Vietnamese couldn't move it. He straddled the corpse and tried to roll it off the radio.

With his right foot, the American kicked him as hard as he could in the groin. Grimacing with pain, the Vietnamese officer instinctively fired his pistol wildly, emptying its clip. One bullet went through the American's numb left wrist. Another ricocheted and entered his open mouth, breaking two teeth before coming to rest with the shattered teeth on his tongue. A third cut his left earlobe. The fourth entered the left side of his chest, and he started to lose precious blood. He choked, gagged, and then spit out blood, shattered teeth, and the smashed bullet.

In an animal rage, the American reached with his left hand and tried to grab the Vietnamese, who was still straddling him. But his left hand was a bloody useless club. He reached up with his right hand, knocking off the pith helmet, and grabbed the little

Vietnamese's thick black hair and pulled him down. The NVA officer pummeled and scratched at the big American.

They were fighting for their lives. The Vietnamese was flat on top of the American, their eyes inches apart, their hot breaths intermingling. He tried to choke the American. The American still had the Vietnamese's hair in his right hand; he jerked the small man's head back so his neck arched, pulled him closer, and bit his throat. Rolling over, they did a passionate dance of death as the American crushed the little man's windpipe with his teeth. When the Vietnamese's breath turned to a gurgle the American relaxed his bite and the small man started to flail and kick. The American's teeth went deeper into the arched neck, severing the little man's jugular vein.

He could taste the little Vietnamese officer's salty, metallic blood. The Vietnamese bled into his mouth. He held the dying man's hair with his one good hand, his throat with his teeth sunk deep into the flesh, until the body went into spasms and died. Rolling off the little dead man in an adrenaline-induced high, the American was full of life. He lay there in the blue moonlight.

Through the buzz in his ears, the American could hear voices in the paddies, probably the NVA officer's men looking for him. He didn't know how long he had been unconscious. Freezing cold, chilled despite the steamy heat and the fever of battle, he stuffed two fingers into the hole in his chest, hoping to stem the bleeding long enough to be found alive—either by them or his own people.

Sleep—sweet seductive beautiful sleep—was beguiling him to escape the pain. But he knew if he closed his eyes he'd never open them again. For the rest of that night he fought the second fight of his life. He tried to recognize the stars above. Tried to name the states and their capitals. Watched a nocturnal bird in a tree limb above him—innocent nature amid this man-made carnage. He lay there in shock, in pain, fingers stopping the bleeding, the severed arm and radio beneath him. To his side lay a dead man with his throat opened as if mauled by a jungle cat.

A burning thirst made his throat feel like sandpaper. He couldn't swallow. For reasons unknown, the phrase from Hamlet kept going through his mind. He had read it in college just a few years before, but remembered it more from an inscription on a statue in a big city park: *"What a piece of work is man! How noble in reason, how infinite in faculty! In form and moving how express and admirable! In action how like an angel, in apprehension how like a god!"*

What a crock of shit, he thought. As he lay there with the dead man's blood dried on his face and lips, it seemed hysterically funny to his blood-deprived brain. He silently giggled in the dawn.

With sunrise came the noise of boat engines and then a voice with a thick New England accent. "Jesus motherfucker. What the fuck happened here? Is he alive?"

Someone pushed a compress against the hole in his chest. He could feel a needle prick in his right arm. The cold lip of a canteen was pressed against his lips and a trickle of delicious water entered his mouth. Strong arms picked him up.

WITNESS TO HEROISM

One late night in 1969, Gary Harding was sitting in the squadron office on the Swift boat base in Cat Lo. He was a lieutenant and the skipper of PCF 84. But this night, he was also the squadron's watch officer, responsible for monitoring the radios and the security of the base.

A single-lane road bordered the land side of the base. Across the road sat a ramshackle line of huts, two hundred meters from the squadron office. Most of the rickety structures were bars and whorehouses—if a couple of cots in plywood cubicles behind the bars could be called houses. A minefield with barbed wire and concertina wire fences filled the area between the road and the base, protecting the Quonset huts, piers, and boats. Sailors in helmets and flak vests stood guard at an iron gate that opened into a narrow roadway that led into the base. More sailors carrying radios and M16s patrolled the perimeter from sunset to dawn.

While Harding sat in the squadron office trying to keep awake by reading Truman Capote's *In Cold Blood*, Charlie Teague was enjoying a postcoital beer and cigar in one of the bars. It was his eleventh beer of the evening and his first cigar. Teague was also a lieutenant, but he was a supply officer, referred to by most in the navy as a *pork chop* due to the shape of the supply corps insignia. He didn't serve aboard any of the squadron boats. Instead, he ordered, dispersed, and tracked supplies and money. Beans, bullets, fuel, and toilet paper.

Teague was drunk as a skunk. Not unusual for him. He half slid, half fell off the flimsy barstool and stumbled through the curtained back door, where he pissed on a motorbike and down his pants leg. Back in the bar, he bought another beer, drained the bottle, waved at the whore behind the bar, and walked out to the sticky night. He stood alongside the road for a few moments, swaying and looking at the cigar smoke in the moonlight. Teague crossed the road and stood at the barbed wire fence. The gate and the roadway through the minefield were about a hundred meters up the road. He'd have to walk to the gate, wait for the sentry to let him in, walk down the path to the base, and then walk all the way through the base to his quarters.

But he could see his quarters just on the other side of the fenced minefield. It was right over there. Shit, he could fling a beer bottle at it from this distance.

Teague determinedly stumbled back to the bar. Ignoring the hookers' protests, he picked up a bamboo and plywood table and carried it across the road. After clumsily putting the table over the fence and on the concertina wire, Teague belly flopped onto the table top, flattening the fence and the razor wire. As the fence collapsed, bells and tin cans attached to the wire clanged.

A sentry yelled out, "Halt! Who goes there? Stop or I'll shoot!" An illumination flare popped and lit up the minefield. The flare dangled beneath its little parachute.

Oblivious to the sentries and the flare, Teague slid down the length of the tabletop and landed on his face, hands, and knees inside the minefield. He stood up, picked his cigar out of the dirt, popped it into his mouth, and started to walk across the minefield.

In the office, Harding heard the mine go off. The minefield was bathed in light and he could see one of the sentries standing by the fence talking into his radio handset. Across the road was a small gaggle of girls from one of the bars, looking to see what happened. He put down his book, grabbed his helmet and flak vest, jumped into his jeep, and drove down the roadway through the gate and out onto the road. By the time he got there, another sentry and one of the hospital corpsmen were on the scene.

It took them twenty minutes to extricate Teague from the wire and load him into the back of the jeep. He was conscious but barely so, due more to booze than wounds. His right foot hung by just some skin.

* * *

Teague lost his leg. He was sent back to the big hospital in Oakland, where he recovered and was fitted with an artificial foot and lower leg. After several months of physical therapy, he was honorably discharged and awarded disability payments by the Veterans Administration. The navy hired Teague as a civilian supply manager at the Naval Supply Center in Oakland.

Working with Teague was a young Vietnamese supply officer, Ensign Pham Tran Hoi. Because of his excellent language skills, the Vietnamese Navy had sent him as a liaison officer to the supply center, where was told he could expect to stay until the war ended.

South Vietnam fell in 1975, stranding Hoi in Oakland. There was no home to return to. Resigned to not seeing his family again, Hoi sought resident status and eventually became a US citizen. He worked as a logistics specialist for engineering firms in San Francisco.

Harding left the navy after Vietnam. Using the GI bill, he picked up an MBA and went to work for an engineering firm in San Francisco. In 1982, he hired a Vietnamese logistician who had recently become a US citizen: Pham Tran Hoi.

By 1994, Harding had lost most of his hair, put on a few pounds, and grown a beard. He bore little resemblance to the lieutenant and Swift boat skipper of twenty-five years ago. He was also the west coast vice president of the engineering firm. Hoi was the firm's logistics and supply manager. The two men became friends as well as coworkers. Occasionally they talked about Vietnam and the war. But not much.

One day Hoi took a phone call while Harding happened to be nearby.

"Sure thing, Charlie, let me look at my schedule and I'll call you back," said Hoi, then hung up the phone. He looked at Harding. "That was a guy I worked with at NSC Oakland. Charlie Teague. Wants to do lunch. Retiring from civil service, and I think he's starting to network, looking for a job. Wants to meet me for lunch."

"Charlie Teague? We had a fellow by that name in Cat Lo. Supply corps type."

"Yes, that's him. Lost a leg over there. Navy retired him, then hired him as a civilian." Hoi chuckled. "Big party animal. Drank his way through two marriages when I was working with him. But he knew his stuff."

"That fits as I remember him. I was the duty officer when he got hurt."

"No shit, Gary? I guess it was quite a firefight he was in. Said he got a chest full of medals and wanted to stay in but the navy said they didn't want a peg leg hobbling around in uniform."

"He said that?" Harding smiled and shook his head. "When are you going to meet him?"

"Let me see...I'm free Thursday for lunch. Want to go with us? Might be interesting."

"Sure, count me in. Do we need anyone with his experience, Hoi?"

"Not really, Gary. We could use a junior logistician in the Los Angeles office, but I think Teague would want too much money and probably wouldn't want an entry-level job. We could use a project manager here for that navy civil engineering contract we picked up. He might be good for that."

Harding thought for a minute. "Let's ask Orlando to join us. That contract will be in his department. Set up lunch for the three of us and Charlie Teague. You pick the place."

On Thursday, Harding, Hoi, and Orlando Silva walked into the crowded restaurant. A gray-haired, florid-faced man in a blue suit drained his drink, said something to the bartender, then limped over to Hoi and shook his hand.

"Hoi, goddamnit, you little shit! You look great!" He slapped Hoi on the back, then turned to Harding and Silva. He thrust out a beefy palm and introduced himself with boozy breath. "Charlie Teague, glad to meet you."

As soon as they sat at the quiet corner table, Teague waved a waiter over and ordered a Manhattan. He turned to the other three. "Whaddya guys drinking?" Teague did not seem to notice or care that they ordered iced tea.

While they waited for their meals, Silva said he had heard that Teague was retiring from the civil service after a long stint at the naval supply center. He asked him what he did there.

Gesticulating, loud and animated, Teague talked about managing a major integrated logistics program for new construction ships. He said he was doing a great job, but that the supply center was on the chopping block and if he wanted to stay in the job he would have to move to San Diego. He didn't want to leave the San Francisco Bay area, so he had his feelers out and was starting his networking.

Silva asked him about his education. Then about his work before the naval supply center.

Teague slapped Hoi on the arm. "I was fighting this guy's evil buddies in Vietnam. Navy. Full lieutenant. Mekong Delta. Saw a lot of action. Got pretty banged up..."

Harding cut him off in midsentence. "I know, Charlie. I was there."

"Yeah? You were in-country? When were you there?"

"I was there when you got hurt. Squadron command duty officer at Cat Lo. You were our pork chop. I drove you in my jeep to the hospital at Vung Tau."

Teague quit talking. He seemed to deflate. "Oh, yeah. Sure. I think I remember your name now. Uh, yeah, sure, didn't recognize you." His voice was quiet, the bombast gone. He ate his meal quietly, asking polite questions about the civil engineering contract and how the firm was doing in general.

They shook hands outside the restaurant. Harding, Hoi, and Silva turned to walk back down the hill to the office.

"Uh...Mr. Harding, can I speak to you for a second?" asked Teague. Harding turned and walked back to Teague, leaving Hoi and Silva to go ahead.

"What is it, Charlie?"

Teague sighed and looked at the pavement, then into Harding's eyes. "I...uh— I...uh...just want to thank you for not...uh...going into the details of that night. It's nothing I'm proud of. I cover it up with a lot of bullshit. Sorry."

"Charlie, good luck with your job search. I don't see a fit for you with us." Without shaking hands, Harding turned and walked down the hill.

CHRISTMAS DINNER

T he acceleration of the Vietnamization of America's war in Vietnam started when President Lyndon B. Johnson realized that his war could not be won. Before that, Walter Cronkite had broadcast *his* doubts of victory—whatever in the hell victory meant in that war—to the American public. Johnson knew it was time to get out of the quagmire. Vietnamization was the American disengagement from Vietnam. A better but more awkward term may have been the de-Americanization of the war, as equipment and supplies were turned over and areas of operations returned to the South Vietnamese.

Some American navy units, such as river squadrons, were replaced man by man with Vietnamese naval officers and sailors over the course of a year or more. For a few weeks, an American and a Vietnamese sailor would work side by side as the latter became familiar with the equipment and his new job. Eventually, all the Americans in each unit were reassigned, usually out of Vietnam.

All accept two. The US commanding officer was given the title of senior naval advisor and the senior US enlisted sailor was given the title of senior enlisted advisor. These two stayed on. Their counterparts were the new Vietnamese commanding officer and his senior enlisted sailor. Supposedly, the two Americans would advise the Vietnamese in the operation of their new equipment and how to fight a river war in Southeast Asia.

The senior naval advisor, Lieutenant Bob Fields, came from the Midwest. He had trained for deep ocean operations on a destroyer. The senior enlisted advisor, Chief Petty Officer Santorino "Sandy" Rizzo, was a Bostonian. His last job had been as chief of the boat of a San Diego submarine. The officer had been in the US Navy for under four years, the chief about eighteen. Up until ten months earlier, neither had ever seen men die in combat.

And now the two were to advise the Vietnamese on how to fight a war that those people had been fighting since the end of World War II. The last peace any of the Vietnamese sailors could remember had been a brief respite when the Japanese and Vichy French left in 1945. Most of the Vietnamese had no idea of what peace *meant*: they had been born into war and surrounded by it ever since.

The American advisors were also there to bring the power and might of the American gunfire and air support to the battlefield—assets that the Vietnamese were not allowed to control. The most lethal weapon the advisors possessed was their radio, which they used to request and control the incoming shells and bombs, and their most valuable asset, their radioman. For Fields and Rizzo, that asset was Nguyen Van Duong, Radioman Second Class.

In all navies, there's a hierarchy of skills, talents, and intelligence in the enlisted ranks. The South Vietnamese Navy was no exception. Their boatswain mates and gunner's mates were the foundation of the Vietnamese Navy, responsible for the seamanship and weapons. But they were not always the smartest enlisteds. The sailors responsible for operating and maintaining the boats and their engines—the enginemen and machinist mates—were the next level up. At the pinnacle were the sailors whose specialties were electronics and communications: the radiomen.

Duong fit that category. Fields and Rizzo's favorite, Duong was smart and spoke far better English than the advisors spoke Vietnamese. Gifted with a sense of humor, Duong was the river squadron's satirist and an unflattering mimic of the senior enlisted and officers of the squadron, as well as the advisors. Duong smiled easily, and his smile was infectious. He was also brazen. Radioman Duong didn't care if he occasionally made a fool of himself; his quick wit would always save him.

Within a few days after the start of the turnover of the river squadron to the Vietnamese, all 112 pounds of Petty Officer Duong replaced the 220-pound hulk of Radioman First Class Johnson, who had been sent home to enjoy a reunion with his family in Norfolk, Virginia, before he had to report to a cruiser. Once they had him, Fields and Rizzo never let Duong and his radio get too far away.

While the politicians and diplomats debated seating arrangements and chair heights in Paris, the river squadron patrolled the upper reaches of the Saigon River from the bridge at Phu Cuong up to the Cambodian border. They set ambushes and were ambushed. They carried Vietnamese and US Army troops and inserted them into booby-trapped riverbanks and rice paddies. And they were shot at from the Michelin Rubber Plantation, but were forbidden to shoot back because somebody in Washington, DC, did not want to pay the French for the damage to the rubber trees.

The American brass in Saigon was worried about Vietnamization and the execution of the war. Over cocktails and steaks at the rooftop restaurants in Saigon, with the miniskirted bar girls at hand, the senior officers groused how a unit lost its aggressiveness when the Vietnamese took over. Those damn people just didn't seem to want to fight and die like Americans.

The farther away from the miniskirts and headquarter officers and the closer to the operating units you got, the less criticism of the Vietnamese you heard. The river squadron's advisors well understood what the Vietnamese sailors were doing. They were trying to stay alive, trying not to die before the elusive peace came. No one on the river ever talked of victory. They only hoped for peace.

As the Paris talks ground on, the politicians would seize on an event and propose a unilateral cease-fire, a truce for a day or two. The event was usually a holiday such as Buddha's birthday or American Thanksgiving. Tet, the Vietnamese New Year, was nevermore a candidate for a truce or cease-fire after the disaster of 1968, when the Viet Cong infiltrated the population centers.

A major problem that the Saigon warriors failed to understand about these truces or periods of cease-fire was that although the US and South Vietnamese forces were notified by radio to stand down, the Viet Cong and even North Vietnamese Army units in the South were often out of communication with anyone but themselves. Forced to rely on runners and word of mouth, field commanders operated on their own initiatives for the most part—they rarely received orders in a timely manner from Hanoi. So, although the US and South Vietnamese forces would stop fighting and stand down, their enemy didn't always get the word. It's hard to stop a war, even temporarily, when only one side puts down its arms.

Starting at 2200 Christmas Eve, a cease-fire was declared until 0600 the day after Christmas. For those thirty-two hours, the US and South Vietnamese forces had orders not to shoot unless shot at first. Several days before the cease-fire, the sailors and their boats carried a company of US troopers from the riverbanks near their base at Cu Chi and inserted them many miles upriver. The boats were positioned along the river, acting as a blocking force to stop any movement across the river as the American company swept through several villages and surrounding paddies.

With the news of the truce, the troopers' commanding officer radioed the American advisor on the boats to come and pick them up at a coded grid coordinate. On the big command boat, Fields discussed the extraction with his counterpart, the Vietnamese commanding officer. They knew if Charlie did not honor the cease-fire, or more likely did not even know of it, they would have to fight their way in to the pickup spot, hope they could get the troopers aboard, and fight their way back down river. But they had to get the troops out.

Whether the Viet Cong knew about the cease-fire, whether they were just feeling charitable, or whether they were all dead, the boats picked up the American army company without a shot being fired. They lumbered back downriver waiting to be ambushed, but by 2200 Christmas Eve, all had remained quiet. The boats nosed into a flat spot on the riverbank, the troops put out a perimeter of watch posts, and the men settled into damp and mildewed ponchos to sleep in the muggy air.

The men and boats would stay in that spot on the river until the end of the cease-fire. Then they would be given orders to either bring the troops back to Cu Chi or reinsert them somewhere else on the river.

Christmas morning, the troops' CO went up to Fields and told him that since it was Christmas and it looked like the cease-fire was being honored, the brass back at Cu Chi was sending a Christmas dinner with all the trimmings. He asked if he should include the Vietnamese sailors in the numbers he was passing back to Cu Chi for Christmas rations. Smiling at the idea of a treat for the Vietnamese sailors, Fields told the army CO to add another sixty sailors to the list.

At around noon on Christmas day, the army CO's radio crackled. A helicopter was on its way with Christmas dinner. The pilot, his voice warbling with the helicopter's vibrations, requested a secure landing zone and smoke to make sure he was not flying into an ambush. The *wopwopwopwop* of the big green two-engine helicopter could be heard before the sailors and soldiers could see it flying down the river. After they had popped a smoke canister and gone through the authentication procedures, the boats and men were whipped by a rotor-produced cyclone. The aircraft settled onto its ridiculously small wheels and the stern ramp opened. Out marched several soldiers in full combat gear, along with cooks in aprons carrying collapsible tables and large, olive drab, insulated containers. The helicopter lifted off, causing a second windstorm.

Under the direction of a sergeant wearing a white chef's toque and apron over his olive drab tee shirt and camouflage pants, a food line was set up. Behind the tables stood three more toque-topped soldiers with ladles and tongs at the ready. In the middle of the table sat a three-foot tall plastic pine tree decorated with tinsel and a silver star. Christmas dinner was served.

Fields, Rizzo, the company commander, and the South Vietnamese Navy's commanding officer decided that the soldiers should eat first while the sailors took over the perimeter guard. When the army men finished, Fields would lead the Vietnamese through the food line. The soldiers, glad for a change from C-rations and water laced with Halazone tablets, loaded up their paper plates. No mess kits for this meal. Fruit cocktail for starters. Southern fried chicken. Mashed potatoes. Gravy. Rice. Green beans. Cookies. The ubiquitous bug juice. The sailors watched the soldiers load up their plates and chowed down.

Finally, the hungry Fields and Rizzo led the sailors to the feast served up by the waiting chefs. The two stood back and waved the sailors to the food tables. In typical paternal American military tradition, which the Vietnamese were copying, the officers did not eat before their senior enlisted, who did not eat before the enlisted men. Take care of your sailors, officers were taught, and they'll take care of you.

The young Vietnamese sailors walked up to the food and just stared. No one wanted to be the first in line. Hungry and a little frustrated that the Vietnamese sailors were not taking plates and food, Fields called Duong over and told him to start before the food grew cold and the helicopter came back. Never one to walk away from a challenge, Duong rakishly cocked his sailor hat over his left eyebrow and did a John Wayne walk up to the fruit salad. Immediately the rest of the sailors followed. Now the problem was that they were not sure about the food.

Explaining to his fellow sailors like a South Vietnamese Navy version of Julia Child, Duong ladled some fruit salad into a paper cup. Fruit salad they all knew and considered it an expensive and, frankly, frivolous treat. Duong moved to the middle table and stared at the fried chicken. His eyes lit up as he recognized what it was. Due to the wetness of the Saigon River plain, duck was the common poultry in this part of Vietnam. Chicken was a luxury for the well-to-do. Although he had never tried fried chicken before, Duong bravely held out his plate as the chef tonged him a large breast and wing. The server next to the chef plopped a shovel size scoop of mashed potatoes onto Duong's plate, while the next server dropped a ladle of rice onto the one clear spot left.

Rice, of course, Duong knew. But mashed potatoes were another story. A quizzical look at Fields brought an explanation. Potatoes, okay. But mashed potatoes? Well, the Americans did some funny things with food. A pile of beans went into the center of the food. And there the procession stopped.

A small swimming pool of gravy waited in front of Duong. The line of Vietnamese sailors telescoped around him. They discussed the viscous, hot, brown, savory liquid before them. Again, a look passed to the advisor.

"It's gravy, *Trung Si* Duong," said the American.

"Gravy, *Dai Oui?*" questioned Duong.

"Yeah, gravy, Trung Si. Same-same sauce. Uh... *nuoc cham.*"

"Sauce?" A murmur rose from the Vietnamese sailors. Sauce to them meant *nuoc mam*, the clear amber odoriferous fermented fish sauce, not this brown thick stuff.

"Here, Trung Si, like this." Rizzo grabbed the ladle and poured some of the gravy onto his own mound of mashed potatoes.

Duong looked at Rizzo and the brown lava trickling down the mountain of mashed potatoes on this plate.

No, that couldn't be right.

"Good, Trung Si. Good. *Tsu mot*. Number one," Fields assured Duong as he put a plastic fork full of gravy covered potatoes into his own mouth.

Duong watched. He slowly shook his head. Then the light went on. He smiled at the advisors and his fellow sailors. Duong looked around, saw what he was looking for by the bug juice canister. Striding purposely to the container, Duong picked up a large paper cup, ran back to the gravy bowl and dumped a big ladle of gravy into the cup.

Holding the cup above his head, Duong proudly turned to the Vietnamese sailors and said, in English for the benefit of the culinary challenged Americans, "Soup!"

Then he chug-a-lugged the paper cup of gravy.

* * *

During the remaining months of the squadron's Vietnamization and the American advisors' tour of duty in Vietnam, the Americans always wanted Duong near at hand to operate the radios. They just liked having him near. He was quick, expert, funny, exasperating, irreverent, and made them shake their heads and smile.

Fields and Rizzo had one operation left before they would say goodbye to the squadron and Duong, pack up their gear, go to Saigon for a debriefing and a steak or two, then board the freedom bird back to Travis Air Force Base outside of San Francisco. The operation had started off quietly with an unopposed motoring upriver to insert some Vietnamese soldiers. The soldiers swept through an area and were picked up by the boats three hours later. Hot, sweaty, tired, but all intact and not a bullet fired.

With just five kilometers to go before they reached the squadron's base, a rocket fired from the riverbank hit Duong, killing him and throwing his corpse into the river. His radio was destroyed. Fields and Rizzo were standing a meter away from Duong and the explosion. Both were burned by the blast, deafened, concussed, and peppered with shrapnel. A medevac helicopter took them to Saigon and a week later they were transferred to Oaknoll Naval Hospital in Oakland. A month later they were released from the hospital and reassigned.

The navy sent Fields to graduate school at MIT and Rizzo to instructor duty at the Submarine School in New London, Connecticut. The two made it a point to see each other with their wives for dinner at least once a month. And each dinner started with a quiet toast to Radioman Duong.

BLOOD THIRST

The front-page article in the Sunday *Los Angeles Times* on April 11, 2011, was titled "Anatomy of an Afghan War Tragedy." It described the sequence of events that started with a radio call from an aircraft that reported two vehicles blinking their lights at each other, and ended with the death and wounding of nearly two dozen civilian men, women, and children.

A US Army captain was responsible for telling two attack helicopters to shoot their missiles at the innocents. His rules of engagement were clear enough: weapons and imminent threat to his troops warranted opening fire. He made his decision from bits and pieces of intelligence that came from a Predator drone several miles above the civilians and from intercepted cell phone communications. Drone operators in Nevada, video screeners in Florida, and communication intelligence linguists outside Washington, DC were passing real time information that made up these bits and pieces.

The Nevada-based Air Force drone pilot and camera operator were in direct communications with the army captain on the ground in Afghanistan. They were distilling the flood of information through a filter of interpretation. And they were reading into their interpretations more of what they wanted to see than what they actually could see, encouraging the army officer in his decision to attack the target.

Despite no positive identification of weapons, some questions about whether there were children in the target, and the target being a dozen miles away from the captain and his team, the threat was judged as imminent and the helicopters attacked. Two hours later, Afghan and US forces administered first aid and medevaced the survivors to hospitals. The dead and wounded were all noncombatant civilians.

After months of investigations, the United States of America apologized and gave each survivor about $3,000, and the families of the dead about $5,000. A two-star general said, "Technology can occasionally give a false sense of security that you can see everything, that you can hear everything, that you can know everything." What no one mentioned was that blood thirst can make you see, hear, and know what you want to see, hear, and know.

* * *

Forty-two years to the day before the *LA Times* article was published, US Navy Lieutenant Junior Grade David West had been sitting on the muddy riverbank of a small tributary of the Saigon River. It stunk from the rotting vegetation and human and animal waste fertilizer in the paddy on the other side of the dike behind him. West had been fighting to stay awake ever since he and the eight Cambodian mercenaries had moved into their ambush position at midnight, five hours earlier.

Next to West sat Sen, the leader of the mercs. Short, scarred, and well educated, Sen was in the fight for the money. He and his men were well paid, far more than any junior officer in the US Navy.

West was there because he had been ordered to Vietnam. Until a year before, all his military experience had been at sea on the Atlantic aboard a destroyer. He had been picked to go to counterinsurgency and Vietnamese language schools, then assigned to the

South Vietnamese Navy as an advisor. From haze gray and under way to Sneaky Pete missions in the stinking mud in less than a year.

According to the personnel detailers in DC, the assignment was a plum. If he was going to make a career of the navy, the job would put him well ahead of his peers. Sitting wet-assed in the mud while insects sucked his blood in the middle of the sticky night, West wasn't sure he wanted a naval officer's career. He could leave the navy and use his GI Bill for law school. And an uncle wanted him to learn the stockbroker business and take over his brokerage. The girl he had left behind wrote letters about how she was looking forward to him coming home and not having to go to war and sea.

He did like the navy, though. It was interesting and challenging, and he didn't have to worry about profits and losses. The officer's uniform seemed to garner respect—although from what he could read in the *Stars and Stripes* and the occasional *Time* and *Newsweek*, that might be changing. But at least he didn't have to worry about what tie went with what shirt and what socks went with what shoes. And the navy satisfied his patriotic streak.

West was keeping his options open and trying to do the best he could as an advisor to the Vietnamese. Doing well in Vietnam meant two things: not getting killed or maimed, and killing a lot of the bad guys. West was hoping this mission would go well.

For the previous two months there had been reports of a VC tax collection team in the area. Depending who was reporting, the two men were either savage thieves or Robin Hoods. The South Vietnamese Army—the ARVN, short for the Army of the Republic of Vietnam—had been hunting the duo but had had no success. Most of the ARVN operations were too late—surrounding a village only to find that the VC had left the night before. Or the ARVN ran into booby traps and ambushes. Good intelligence was lacking.

West and his South Vietnamese Navy counterparts had read the reports on the tax collectors, but had never been involved in an operation to capture or kill them.

The navy advisor's counterpart's intelligence, for the most part, was better than the ARVN's. Fed by an elusive informer West had never met, their operations were more successful. If the informer said that a cache of weapons or medical supplies could be found at a certain spot, at least half the time the supplies were there. If the informer's intelligence predicted a river movement between two VC base camps, an ambush set up on the riverbank just might end up in a firefight and dead VC. By unwritten rule, if a Vietnamese died because of an American or South Vietnamese bullet, that dead Vietnamese was a dead Viet Cong and added to the body count.

One evening, West met with the local CIA office chief and a US Army ranger captain. They had received information that identified the two tax collectors as important National Liberation Front leaders. The elimination of these two was a high priority. Worried about information leaks from the ARVN to the VC, the CIA wanted to mount an operation to kill the taxmen using their Cambodian mercenaries, but they had to locate these tax collectors first. Could the informant who was supplying West's South Vietnamese counterparts help them get these two?

Two weeks later, they had the informant's report. The two VC would be moving from a little fishing and farming village down the tributary to the Saigon River at dawn. At midnight, a South Vietnamese Navy fast patrol boat had dropped West and the eight mercenaries at the mouth of the tributary. They paddled two black rubber boats up the muddy, fetid waters to a blind bend. After pushing their rubber boats onto the bank, the nine men waded around the bend to their ambush site.

The plan was simple. If the taxmen came down the tributary, West would pop an illumination flare and open fire with his M16. The mercenaries would then open fire with their weapons, which included two grenade launchers. If they needed help, West would call for the patrol boat to fire its mortar. Or he'd call in the helicopter light-fire team he had asked the ranger to have standing by. Once the firing stopped, he and the mercs would count bodies, pick up the VCs' weapons, collect documents, make a radio report, and paddle the rubber boats back to the river to be picked up by the patrol boat. Simple. Two KIAs, a couple of pistols, and a shitload of documents would be the plunder.

But most ambushes never happen. The would-be ambushers sit in place for hours, even days, then give up and go back to base with no scalps hanging from their belts. While West was hoping the VC would show up on schedule, he knew the odds were against it. Still, it would be nice to kill these guys.

Fighting to keep alert, West tried calculating the number of seconds in a year in his head. He felt a soft nudge on his arm and turned to see Sen pointing at his wristwatch. It was 0500. Every hour on the hour, West checked in with the patrol boat idling five kilometers away on the Saigon River. He put his radio handset to his ear and clicked the key once. Within a few seconds, he heard the double click from the boat. Message received.

The sky was lightening to the east. It would be dawn in about 45 minutes. He'd wait until 0700. If nothing happened by then, West would call it quits and lead the mercs back to the rubber boats and out to the river for a tow back to base and some hot food and sleep. Until then, he'd sit in the mud and stink, listening to the chirps of frogs and bugs and try to stay awake.

Then he heard, or thought he heard, a faint *putt-putt.*

West sat erect, trying to pick out the sound. *Putt-putt.* It was there. Soft but steady, coming from up the tributary, coming from the village where the VC were supposedly staying. He looked over at Sen, who was also erect and alert. The two men exchanged stares and nods.

The sound gradually grew louder. It was the sound of the ubiquitous little two-stroke engines the fishermen used to propel their sampans. West put his radio handset to his ear and pressed the key three times, paused, then pressed three more times. A double click from the patrol boat acknowledged his cryptic signal that the targets were approaching the ambush site.

As he reached for the illumination flare, West felt Sen grab his forearm and hold it tightly. The Cambodian shook his head and leaned close.

"This is no good. No good. Do not open fire," the mercenary whispered. "Not right. No good."

Incredulously, West pulled his arm away and in a hoarse whisper said, "Sen, what the fuck to you mean 'no good'? These guys were supposed to leave the village before dawn and make it to the river. This is exactly what the intel said. I'm popping this fucking flare and opening fire. You tell your men to stand by and get ready to kill these assholes."

"No, no shoot. Not right." Sen grabbed his arm again, and held it tight, keeping West from reaching for his flare.

"Are you fucking nuts, Sen?" West considered hitting him, knocking him out. Maybe even shooting him as soon as the ambush started. The sampan was moving toward them exactly as the intelligence report said it would. Adrenalin had sharpened West's senses. He could hear the *putt-putt* and his own heart beating like syncopating kettledrums.

Sen held onto West's arm and said, "VC would not use a motor. Too much noise. This is no good. Don't shoot."

"I'm going to shoot your yellow ass if you don't let go, Sen."

"No shoot. Pop flare, then I will shoot over sampan to make it stop. We see first. If VC, we shoot."

West didn't have to see first. He didn't need to verify anything. His orders were to get these guys. The intelligence was right on target. Besides, it was still during curfew, which would make the area a free-fire zone. If any swinging dick was moving, that swinging dick was a VC.

Sen stared at him, an iron grip on his forearm. The clear sound of the sampan motor meant it was about a hundred meters upstream from them.

For reasons that West did not know—even forty-two years later—he nodded at Sen and said, "Okay, Sen, you tell your men not to fire. I'll pop the flare, you fire the warning shots. If they fire back, we open up with everything." Sen let go of West's arm and turned to the other mercenaries and briefly whispered orders.

The shadow of the bow of the sampan rounded the bend. A few seconds later, West could clearly see the low dark hull of the boat and two small figures huddled in the stern. He pulled the cap off the illumination flare, put it on the firing end, and hit it with his palm. As the flare shot skyward, Sen fired his Swedish-K machine gun in front of the sampan, red tracers disappearing into the trees on the opposite bank.

In the white light of the flare, West could see two children, eyes wide with fright, staring at him from the sampan. The boat swerved out of control and beached its bow right in front of him, its engine racing loudly. The bigger child was a trembling girl of about thirteen years old, the other a crying little boy of six or seven. Fishing nets, an aluminum thermos bottle, a ball of rice wrapped in cloth, and a beer bottle full of fuel with a rag for a stopper were all the boat contained.

West felt empty and weak-kneed. He sat heavily back in the mud, forearms resting on his knees, and his head on his chest as the sun came up. His heart was pounding and he felt like crying. But he didn't.

The mercenaries and West waded back to their rubber boats, pulling the sampan and the two kids. Escorting the sampan, they paddled downriver to the waiting patrol boat. After an interrogation and a stern lecture about violating curfew from the patrol boat captain, the children were given food, soap, and candy and sent on their way to tend the family fishing nets.

Back at the base, West radioed in an after-action report of no enemy contact and tried to sleep. He couldn't and finally got off his cot and wrote his girlfriend a letter. He told her that he was applying for law school.

West had no Predator drone to take pictures to be analyzed, he only had his eyes and a flare. He had no linguists to intercept communications, just his ears to listen for a sampan motor. West had an intelligence report that he blindly believed. He had been blinded by blood thirst. But unlike the US Army captain in Afghanistan, West had had Sen.

Genuwine VC Flag, Guaranteed

Gunner's Mate Second Class Abraham Wilson had been in Vietnam nearly a year. He liked it. In fact, he liked it so much that he asked to be extended another year in-country. Happy to not have to find another GM2 to take his place, the Bureau of Personnel quickly granted his request.

Wilson, better known as "Ape" owing to his resemblance to a cute, stuffed, toy gorilla, along with a corruption of "Abe" by his shipmates, found much to be happy about in-country. He liked where he was. He lived in a roomy hooch on the South Vietnamese junk base in Vung Tau with the three other American naval advisors. Vung Tau was a resort city and the in-country R&R center for US, Australian, and Korean troops. The other enlisted man was a good guy. The two officers were a mixed bag. The boss, a lieutenant, was a chickenshit snob who couldn't wait to leave Vietnam and get back to his ass kissing and climb up the rank ladder. The other officer, a young JG, was okay but dumber than shit. Each of the four had their own specific duties as advisors and, fortunately for Ape, the other three never interfered with his. Ape was the advisor for weapons and boat handling.

Small arms were something of a novelty to a gunner's mate. Most of the guns that Ape had worked on during his tours aboard a destroyer, cruiser and, just before he came in-country, a battleship, threw projectiles that ranged from five inches to sixteen inches in diameter and weighed up to a ton. Here Ape worked with what he considered tiny weapons: M16 rifles, M79 grenade launchers, M60 machine guns, and the .30- and .50-caliber guns that were mounted on the junks. He could hold a pile of their bullets in his meaty palms. Ape loved working with these guns and with the Vietnamese sailors. He was good at it.

He was also good at taking care of the hooch. More accurately, at taking care of Ba Yung, their hooch housekeeper, cook, seamstress, and laundress. Ba Yung was formidable in appearance and action. In her midthirties, Ba Yung wasn't bad looking. She was not the typically delicate and petite Vietnamese female but husky, although in a feminine sort of way. Her normal expression was a brow-furrowed frown, but her face was occasionally lit by a smile that showed off a gold-capped front tooth. About the time Ape came to Vung Tau, Ba Yung dumped her alcoholic and jobless husband. With the pay the advisors gave her and the informal agreement that anything not in use, including the garbage, was hers, Ba Yung was comfortably well off. A month after Ape's arrival, she didn't need any husband to keep her happy. She had Ape. And she smiled a lot more.

In addition to his talents as an advisor, weapons expert, and Casanova, Ape was a master cumshaw artist. Cumshaw was the informal barter of goods and services in the navy. While the Naval Supply Centers in Saigon and Nha Be could provide everything from bullets to slide rules, requisitions had to be filled out and whatever you wanted had to be justified—and paid for. The fact that you really wanted cold beer or a jeep was not enough. You had to show that you really needed the beer or the jeep, and that there was money to pay for it. And often the length of time to get what you really needed—like bullets or engine parts—was so long that you just couldn't wait. So you traded.

For example, Ape had a surplus of fiberglass repair material. The only fiberglass boat they had was the skimmer, but the supply center had sent him enough resin and cloth to build a fiberglass aircraft carrier. One day he went over to the medevac helicopter squadron at the hospital landing pad and traded some cloth and resin for two bottles of scotch and a field surgical kit. The kit was traded to the senior army medic at the hospital for a bottle of Remy Martel cognac. The two bottles of scotch and the bottle of cognac were traded for two cases of frozen steaks, a five-gallon box of chocolate milk, and a case of grape soda. One case of steaks, the chocolate milk and the soda went into the hooch's refrigerator. The other case of steaks went up the hill to the Australian Explosive Ordnance Demolition team's cave for two cases of Australian beer and a bush hat. And so on and on it went.

Determining the value of a cumshaw article was complicated. War trophies, such as Chinese Communist pistols or a VC flag, were the most valuable. The farther away the customer was from combat, the more valuable the item became. For example, a Chicom automatic pistol with an ammunition clip would be worth a new pair of boots, a couple of days of guard duty, and a choice selection of various pharmaceuticals and herbs at a forward fire base. In Saigon or Vung Tau, it was worth a jeep. Aboard an LST or destroyer off the coast, it was worth more than anything a crew-member could possibly give.

After one firefight between two of the junks and a squad of VCs protecting a riverbank food cache, Ape went ashore and walked around. There was blood and what looked like pieces of raw chicken meat splattered on the foliage, but no bodies. AK-47 casings littered the riverbank mud. Several big burlap bags of rice, five cans of cooking oil, and a box of French pharmaceuticals were the spoils. As Ape watched the Vietnamese sailors load the rice bags onto one of the junks, he noticed a red and blue rag in the thick vegetation at the water's edge. He had found a VC flag.

The flag was shredded and barely more than a rag. It was about a meter by a half-meter and made from rough cotton cloth. The bottom half was blue, the top red, and a holed yellow star was in the center. Ape tried to brush off the mud and finally dipped the flag in the delta river water and wrung it out. Dark brown stains covered a third of the battered flag, probably blood. It must have been used as a bandage. It was a genuine VC flag. Captured in battle. Well...really after a battle.

Back at the hooch, Ape washed out the flag and spread it on the sand bags to dry in the sun. The cloth was not much more substantial than a worn tee shirt. The blue and red were faded and the yellow star was mottled with the dark brown bloodstains. All four edges were frayed. The cumshaw value of this war trophy was considerable. Or so Ape thought.

US Navy LSTs beached to unload cargo at the terminal right next door to the junk base. These ships shuttled boringly back and forth between the Philippines and Vietnam. Although the terminal was in Vietnam and therefore in a combat zone, the crew rarely saw any combat. Occasional forays ashore were usually trips to a restaurant, bar, or USO show. The LST sailors were a prime market for Ape. Not only were they hungry for war trophies, they had access to great barter items: frozen meats, tools, fiberglass and resin, first aid kits, cigarettes, pancake mix, white and chocolate milk, C-rations, uniforms, ice cream, and boots. And the barter items were in such great quantity that no one would care or notice if a few went missing.

Ape knew most of the leading petty officers on the LSTs. He walked up the bow ramp of the *Caddo Parish* as forklifts and trucks unloaded cartons, crated equipment, and corrugated steel boxes loaded with supplies. The VC flag was stuffed in his jungle fatigue blouse. If things went well, the flag would be traded for one of the new 50 HP Johnson outboards sitting in the cavernous well deck of the ship. His buddy, a first class boatswain mate, stood at the end of the well deck, supervising the off-load.

"Hey, Boats, I've got something for you," said Ape.

"Ape, you've always got something for me. What do you want this time?" asked the LST sailor.

Smiling, Ape took the flag out of his blouse, shook it open, and proudly held it by its top corners, stretching the tattered, faded, stained, and holed cloth to its full width.

"What the fuck's that? Your Kotex?" growled Boats.

"That, you dumb fucker, is a genuine VC flag, captured in battle by yours truly."

"Yeah? Looks like a rag to me, Ape. What are you going to do with it?"

"I'm going to give it to you if you got some decent cumshaw in return," said Ape as he refolded the flag.

"For a rag? You're shitting me, Ape. Hell, I'll give you a cup of coffee but you can keep that rag. I'll give you a cigar for it. What the fuck am I going to do with that? Shine my shoes?" Boats laughed and shook his head.

"You don't want it, that's your dumb decision, you dumb fuck," said Ape as he stuffed the flag back into his blouse. "Believe me, this is worth a lot. Where's my cup of coffee?"

An hour later, Ape walked back to the junk base, the flag still in his blouse. He had managed to get a pity gift of five pounds of coffee, so the trip wasn't a complete waste.

There were several good marketing opportunities in Saigon, especially his contacts who ran the military exchange that sold everything from nail clippers to TV sets. He'd trade the flag for a case or two of cigarettes, a better currency than gold among the Vietnamese. Early the next morning Ape bummed a ride on an army helicopter from Vung Tau to Tan Son Nhut, then rode into Saigon in one of the frequent US forces' shuttles.

Late that same evening Ape jumped off the cargo ramp of a Royal Australian Air Force Caribou transport as it made an un-scheduled stop for him at the air base in Vung Tau. He waved to the crew chief and walked over to the flight line shack to call the hooch and see if someone could pick him up. Despite having vis-ited the military exchange, the Naval Supply Center, Army and Air Force Depot, Commander Naval Forces Vietnam headquarters, the marines at the US embassy, and even the USO, Ape still had the VC flag. Everyone he had shown it to saw absolutely no value in a dirty rag.

Puzzled, but not discouraged, Ape put his marketing genius to work on the problem. He was certain that a VC flag had consider-able value. It should be a coveted item by those removed from the battlefield. He had no doubt about that. Yet everyone, including the most trophy-desperate, had dismissed his captured flag as a rag. A dirty, tattered rag. Why was that?

It came to him as he leaned back in his chair and looked around the hooch. Ba Yung was bustling around the kitchen, wearing an *ao dai*, the most feminine and graceful piece of attire in the entire world. An *ao dai* is the traditional Vietnamese woman's dress—a silk dress that flowed from a tight-fitting bodice to shoe top, slit up each side to the hip and worn over silk trousers.

Ba Yung knew Ape was looking at her and stood in silhouette. She inhaled deeply while sucking in her stomach, showing off her ample—at least by Vietnam standards—breasts. Ape thoroughly appreciated the display, but also noticed the tailoring of the silk *ao dai*. He also noticed the American flag standing in the corner of the hooch.

The flag was clean, its red, white, and blue brilliant in the sunshine that came through the louvered windows of the hooch. The cloth was slick, smooth, tightly woven. That flag was anything but a rag. If he ever retired from the navy to a domicile with a den, he'd have a flag like that displayed on the den's wall.

That was it! No one wanted a dirty rag hanging on their paneled den wall. They wanted something handsome, something that they could boast about. They wanted VC flags that were clean and brilliantly colored—VC flags not made from coarse cotton but from silk.

Ba Yung made her own *ao dais*. That meant she had a sewing machine. It also meant she was skilled as a seamstress. Ape felt excited as the prospect of a new market developed in his mind. He was also excited by Ba Yung's tantalizing sweeping through the room, bending over to display her ample derriere, arching her back to look at some phantom dust on the ceiling fan, and accentuating her bosom, all accompanied by her heavy-lidded, sidelong glances. It was time for a nooner.

While enjoying a postcoital cigar, Ape cuddled a naked Ba Yung and posed his idea to her. He'd buy red, blue, and yellow silk and thread, and she'd manufacture VC flags. To make them genuine, they'd be splattered or dipped here and there in chicken or duck blood, which was in abundance when she butchered fowl for a meal. Bulletholes would be provided by a burning cigar. Not too much blood, not too many holes. Just the right amount.

She protested that it was against the law to possess, much less manufacture, VC flags. Ape thought about that for a few smoke rings. It wouldn't be a problem, he announced. Although he had no legal basis for saying so, he said that the hooch was really property of the USA, so the laws of Vietnam didn't apply within the hooch. Like diplomatic immunity. So, they'd just move her sewing machine to the hooch and set up shop. Quite pleased with himself, Ape treated Ba Yung to another orgasm and took a nap.

To the amazement and amusement of the other three Americans, flag production started the very next day. Ape took the first flag off the production line and walked over to the terminal where the *Caddo Parrish* had just returned. Half an hour later, he was back at the hooch empty handed. Ape took the jeep and returned a few minutes later with two cases of frozen steaks, ten pounds of coffee, a tool chest, four cases of soda, and $15 in greenbacks—not Military Payment Certificates.

Gunner's Mate Second Class Abraham Wilson was promoted to Gunner's Mate First Class six months later. Five months after that, Ba Yung gave birth to Abraham Junior. Ape and Ba Yung were married twice shortly after that, first by a Buddhist monk and then by a navy chaplain.

A year after producing the first VC flag, Ape, Ba Yung, and Abe Junior moved to San Diego. After ten years in San Diego and two more children, Ape retired as a senior chief petty officer. They open Ba Yung's, a Vietnamese restaurant, in Chula Vista.

During the twelve months of VC flag production in the hooch in Vung Tau, 114 flags were produced. A little over half were traded for various edible luxuries or hard-to-find replacement parts for diesel engines and outboard motors. Many were bartered for cigarettes or cognac, which was then sold to Vietnamese civilians at very reasonable prices. The proceeds from those sales paid for several visits by Ba Yung to Hong Kong to exchange money and invest in gold and the Hong Kong stock market.

One of the flags was given to an admiral's staff that had it framed and presented to the admiral when he left Vietnam. The admiral's wife hung the flag above the fireplace mantle in his den in their house just outside Washington DC.

Two flags are on display in Ape's den in Chula Vista. One is an immaculate and handsome stars and stripes. The other is a framed, tattered, faded, and stained rag of what was once red, blue, and yellow cloth.

Ape is very proud of both.

CARROTS

T he soldier's green uniform and red hair were in sharp contrast to the yellow laterite soil dike that separated the river
from the fallow dry rice paddy. He lay on his back on top of the
dike, knees bent, his right forearm shielding his eyes from the
brilliant hot sun. Two men on their knees hovered over him, an
American army medic and a Vietnamese navy corpsman.

Two officers stood on the deck of a riverboat, ten meters from
the redhead. "He looks okay to me," said the American navy officer to the man's company commander. "It doesn't look like he'll
need the dust-off."

"I don't know. Doc says he needs it. So do those other guys."
The army captain waved his hand at half a dozen American and
Vietnamese soldiers and sailors sitting or lying on the cracked
mud of the rice paddy floor. All were bandaged. Two army medics
walked among them, administering words of comfort and checking vital signs and IVs.

"I guess, but look at him. Color's good, I don't see any wounds.
Be a shame to lose your radioman. Seemed like a good guy." The
navy officer took a gulp of water from his canteen.

Half an hour before, the riverboats and their cargo of soldiers had been strafed with machine gun fire and a rocket. The rocket missed, as did most of the AK-47 bullets. Those that did hit the boats bounced harmlessly off the thick steel hulls. As they always did when fired upon, the boats opened up with all their guns, turned into the incoming fire, and prepared to land the troops. But after the initial spray of bullets and the single rocket, there was no incoming fire.

The bow ramps dropped open and the soldiers fanned out and walked into the heart of a minefield. Two died instantly. Seven, including the redhead lying on the dike, had been wounded and needed evacuation. A dust-off was called in to take away the wounded and as many of the dead as space would allow.

The two officers stood still, watching the medic, the corpsman, and the redheaded man. "What's that kid's name again?"

The company CO cleared his throat and spat into the river. "Hudson. Sergeant Hudson. We all called him 'Carrots.' Best fucking soldier I ever worked with."

"Yeah, I got that idea. Still looks okay to me. Why we medevac-ing him? Shock? Concussed?" The *wopwopwop* of the helicopter was getting closer. One of the platoon leaders, a second lieutenant butter bar, stood in the middle of the rice paddy, the wind at his back, an orange smoke grenade pluming at his feet.

The rotor blades caused a small dust storm as the helicopter flared in to land. His red hair tousling in the wind, Carrots tried violently to sit up. Both the medic and the corpsman tried to push his shoulders back. His arm knocked the Vietnamese off the dike, his flailing legs kicked the American medic, who was able to hold onto the struggling soldier's chest and waist. The other two medics ran over to help as the Vietnamese corpsman clambered back on top of the dike and grabbed the twisting man's arms. The helicopter landed, its rotors now slowly turning. The redheaded man lay quietly.

Two of the dust-off crewman, one carrying a collapsible stretcher, ran to the paddy dike. Both the American medic and the Vietnamese corpsman waved and pointed them away to the six other wounded.

They followed them, leaving their patient alone on the top of the dike. Not moving, peaceful, quiet. Pale.

The six bandaged wounded were loaded into the helicopter. Then the soldiers piled the two dead, one on top of the other, on the chopper's cabin floor. The medic and the corpsman ran back to Carrots, picked him up by his arms and legs, dragged him to the helicopter and put his body on top of the dead men.

The navy officer shielded his face from the dust as the helicopter with its cargo of wounded and dead took off, circled the boats and flew southwest to the big base at Cu Chi. He looked at the army company's CO. Tears washed rivulets through the dirt on the soldier's face.

"Chuck," said the navy man to his friend. "We'd better get your men aboard and move these boats downriver." He wanted to hug Chuck. To hold him tight to his chest. But that would be inappropriate. Men like him and Chuck didn't do that.

"Yeah, Burt. Let's get these boats moving."

GARBAGE DUMP HEROES

War's a funny thing. About 2.5 million Americans served in Vietnam or in other Southeast Asian countries or seas during the eleven years of the war that ended in 1975. Twenty-five years later, about a quarter of those veterans had died. Yet during the 2000 census, nearly 9.5 million Americans claimed to have served in Vietnam. Claiming to have served in a lousy war when you didn't must be a generational phenomenon that defies reason.

Most of the soldiers, marines, and sailors in Vietnam were in their twenties. Mostly men, they were the sons of the veterans of World War II, the "good" war. They were fed a diet of Saturday matinee war movies starring handsome and heroic icons like John Wayne and Cary Grant. Every little boy in the 1950s had a set of olive drab plastic toy soldiers and had built model World War II airplanes and ships. For many of these kids, the highlight of a summer barbeque came when the beer loosened up their fathers and uncles and the vets would tell war stories. Growing up and going to war was seen as honorable, patriotic, and something that made your parents proud and turned on the girls. Coming home be-medaled was guaranteed to get you laid, or at least get you a free beer at the hometown tavern.

The number of people who actually saw combat in Vietnam remains a mystery. Since the whole country was a combat zone and everyone collected combat pay, one could say that all 2.5 million were in combat. But being in a combat zone does not actually mean that a person was in combat and shooting and getting shot at. Some sages have said only 8 percent were in combat. Others say 15 percent, 25 percent, and 90 percent. Since nearly 15 percent of the 2.5 million who served wound up dead, missing, or wounded, the number must be closer to half or more.

Some servicemen did not see combat. They were supporting the troopers, aircraft, and boats. For every person in the field hunting or being hunted by Charlie, there were probably seven or eight supporting him—administrators, mechanics, communications and electronics technicians, intelligence analysts, dentists, shrinks, stew burners, bomb loaders, and all the other supporting characters to keep soldiers and marines in the fields, aircraft in the sky, and boats on the rivers.

In the World War II classic *Up Front*, Bill Mauldin described some of the supporting warriors as "garritroopers"; these, he said, were those too close to the front to have to wear ties or salute, and too close to the rear to get shot at. In his cartoons, Mauldin portrays these garritroopers as tough-looking characters wearing officers' sunglasses and paratrooper boots, sitting at a sidewalk cafés in starched uniforms while infantrymen slog past on their way back to the front.

US Army First Lieutenant Jeffrey Budwine neither looked nor acted like one of Mauldin's garritroopers. He looked like his nickname, "Buddha." While not fat, Lieutenant Budwine was round with a protruding belly accentuated by his short stubby legs and arms and easy smile. Buddha—short for Buddha Belly—was a nickname he had picked up in high school that had followed him to college and then to the army. Much to his irritation, some of his fellow officers even rubbed his stomach for luck.

Jeffrey Budwine's aptitude for mathematics landed him a full Army ROTC scholarship to the University of Michigan, where he excelled in mathematics and engineering. He liked his ROTC uniform and always made it a point to stop at the student union snack bar on his way back from his military science classes. Carrying an order of fries and a Coke, he would scan the room and invariably head to a table next to a gaggle of coeds. One girl in particular was always nice to him. Meredith May. At the beginning of his senior year, he gathered the courage to ask her out, and after half a dozen dates he even got to make out with her. She was the first and only girl he had ever kissed on the lips.

ROTC did not go as well for Buddha as did his other studies. While he knew all the information, he lacked charisma, leadership skills, military bearing, an aptitude for decision making, and, even though he regularly worked out, physical fitness. The ROTC professor had real worries about recommending him for a commission as a second lieutenant. After many meetings with the ROTC instructors and several phone conferences with the army's personnel command, it was decided that ROTC Cadet Budwine's dual degrees in mathematics and electrical engineering could be put to good use in the army's new world of data processing and computers.

In June of 1966, Second Lieutenant Budwine graduated and left Ann Arbor and Meredith May for his first duty station, the Pentagon. For the next two years, Buddha haunted the bowels of the building, wearing civilian clothes and working with civilians programming mainframe computers, developing algorithms, and wearing out several pocket protectors and clip-on neckties.

Back in Michigan, Meredith was teaching in a Benton Harbor grammar school. Lieutenant Budwine wrote her frequent letters, always on stationary with the eagle of a US Army officer's insignia embossed at the top of the sheet. He visited his parents in nearby Holland, Michigan, every few months, and always drove over to Benton Harbor for a date with Meredith. In his uniform. Always in his uniform.

During one visit, as Buddha climbed out of his mother's Volkswagen and put on his officer's hat, Meredith got out of a Jaguar XKE roadster with a tall, flat-stomached, white-haired man. This was Meredith's father, and within a few minutes Buddha was in the cramped space of the Jaguar's passenger seat on the way to a country club for lunch.

Meredith's father smiled a lot, white teeth matching his hair. After a quick scotch, he asked Buddha where was he stationed and what was his job?

"I'm in the Pentagon, Mr. May," he answered. Then he added, "I can't talk about what I'm doing." That was not true. There was nothing classified about writing algorithms to keep track of C-rations and truck tires. And, more importantly, there was nothing glamorous about it either.

Daddy gave him a skeptical look, and then nodded. Buddha was saved from further explanation by the waiter who took their orders.

Later, pushing her empty plate away, Meredith turned to her father. "Daddy, tell Jeff about what you did in the war. Wasn't the air force part of the army then?"

The white hair shook and Daddy demurred. But after some cajoling Buddha found out that Meredith's dad had flown Thunderbolts over France and Germany, won the Distinguished Flying Cross, was wounded twice, and spent the last four months of the war as a POW.

"They going to send you to Vietnam, Jeff?" asked Daddy.

"Well, Mr. May, I've asked to go," lied Buddha. "It's a question of whether they...uh...can better use me there or in DC. You know."

"I didn't know you had volunteered for Vietnam," said Meredith with some irritation in her voice.

"Uh...yeah, Meredith. I did. I probably shouldn't have even mentioned it given...uh...the sensitive kind of work I'm doing." Daddy fixed him with another icy blue skeptical eye.

The rest of the visit was miserable for Buddha. Daddy seemed glued to his daughter. Whenever he looked at Buddha, his pearly white teeth smiled but his eyes did not. After a few more hours of avoiding eye contact, Jeff made up an excuse that he had to get back to his parents' house for some family event, and drove his mother's VW back to Holland. Despite the cold autumn wind off Lake Michigan, Jeff had deep dark sweat circles under his arms.

Three months later, Buddha was in Benton Harbor, walking out of the movie theater with Meredith. They had just seen *The Green Beret*, a movie where John Wayne plays a full colonel who walks point on a patrol and a skeptical David Jansen drops his civilian journalist typewriter and picks up a gun and kills a dozen VC. Buddha was nervous. The next morning his dad was driving him to O'Hare Airport and putting him on a plane to San Francisco. From there he'd take a bus to Travis Air Force Base and a chartered plane to Saigon.

Going to Vietnam wasn't making him nervous. What was making his heart pound and his armpits drip was how he would execute his plan to seduce Meredith. To get his slice of the pie. To make it past first base and go all the way home.

He had practiced his lines and his moves. Going to see *The Green Berets* was no coincidence. He had seen it before he left Washington and figured he'd act the part of Jim Hutton, the courageous and loveable screwup who dies horrifically in a barbaric booby trap. Meredith would feel so bad about the dangers her boyfriend and soon-to-be lover were facing, and the fact that she might never see him again, that of course she'd have to put out for him. He had a condom in his wallet, another in his hip pocket, and a third in his shoe.

Hiding the erection bulge in his pants with his sport coat, Buddha walked Meredith up to her apartment building's front door. She turned and looked at him, then grabbed his hands.

"Jeff, you promise me that you'll be careful, okay? And write me. And send me pictures, okay?" She squeezed his hands.

Before he could say or do anything, she continued, "You've got to get up early tomorrow to get to O'Hare. Be safe. Have a good trip." She leaned over, kissed him on the cheek, turned and went inside, shutting the door behind her.

Ninety-six hours later, First Lieutenant Budwine was being shown around the air-conditioned computer shack in the center of the large airfield in Vung Tau, south of Saigon. His boss, a Department of Defense civil servant, introduced him to the four young enlisted men who would be his staff. This was not what Buddha thought going to war would be like.

Despite the fact that he had been issued jungle fatigues, leather and nylon combat boots, a flak vest, helmet, M16, .45-caliber pistol, ammunition clips, poncho, camouflage blanket, and first aid kit, Lieutenant Budwine had been told in no uncertain terms that the Secretary of Defense had put data collection and analysis at the highest of priorities, and he was too valuable to send to a combat unit. His boss was delighted with Buddha's education and experience and jumped at the offer to utilize his expertise.

Buddha had mixed emotions. His working and living conditions on the airfield were better than those he had left behind in the Pentagon and DC. The work he would be doing was challenging and stimulating, right up his alley. The four young men over whom he was in charge seemed smart, much smarter than the draftees and career soldiers he had run into before. Vung Tau was the in-country R&R center for the US servicemen, and offered fine beaches, lots of good places to eat, many bars, and seemed to be the most secure spot in Vietnam. If Charlie was near, he was probably on R&R, too.

But all that was part of the problem. Buddha had gone to Vietnam to fight a war, win some glory, and return to his parents and Meredith a modest hero. He wanted to send home letters written from a foxhole with maybe a blood stain and a photo of him smiling with his helmet pushed back and his rifle casually hung over his arm holding a VC flag. Maybe a glimpse of a bandaged forearm from a Purple Heart winning wound.

And while he really hadn't thought much about a career in the military, the airfield posting would be a dead-end job for a lifer. When his year was up, he'd have to transfer to some combat arm like infantry or armor to get on a career path. And the grunts and tank drivers might not want him. Most likely he'd be heading home to a civilian life.

Letters home to Meredith and family were short and numerous. He purposely did not write about what he was doing because it would be all about flow diagrams, computer programming, analysis, and synthesizing data looking for trends. Buddha thought that would be boring to anyone other than someone like him. And more importantly, would Tyrone Power or William Holden star in a movie about crunching numbers and algorithms? *The Fighting Statisticians* would never draw a crowd. A photo of him sitting at a desk in an air-conditioned office with slide rule in one hand and drafting pencil in the other would drive no woman to wild sexual fantasies.

With the help of a few vague comments that he couldn't really write about what he was doing, Buddha's letters had a touch of mystery about them. The unwritten would spark the imagination. Or so he hoped.

One evening as he was closing up the office he noticed a photograph on one of the enlisted men's desk. Looking closer, he recognized all four of them, in full battle dress, with arms around each other standing before a blazing fire emitting thick dark smoke. Had these four been in an infantry platoon before they came to work in the computer shack? Hadn't they been under the same restriction that he was under? Weren't they too valuable to send to a combat unit?

The next morning, Buddha asked about the photo. The four men looked at each other and laughed.

Sergeant Hernandez, the senior in rank, said, "Lieutenant B, that's one of our hero photos to send home. For the ladies."

"Were you guys in an infantry company before this?" asked Buddha.

"No fuckin' way, sir. We came here just like you did. Selected for our ability to count in hexadecimal and think in Venn diagrams."

"But how'd you get into combat?" asked Buddha, picking up the photo and looking at it closely.

Hernandez pointed at the photograph. "Sir, that's no combat. See that sand hill behind us there? That's here, on the east side of the base. It's the garbage dump for the hospital and the air base. Every Tuesday they burn all the garbage. Douse it with diesel oil and gasoline, throw a thermite grenade into it, and *whoosh*. A couple of Tuesdays ago we skipped lunch, put on our John Waynes, and did a photo shoot. One of the medics took it. There must have been twenty guys, even a couple of nurses out there, sir. All in helmets and flak vests, toting empty M16s or first aid kits. I heard one rumor that they even took a stiff out of the hospital morgue once so they'd have a body to attend to."

"No shit," was all Lieutenant Budwine could say.

Later in the afternoon, he went up to Hernandez. "Sergeant, how about the next time you guys take pictures, let me know. I want to go along."

"Sure thing, Lieutenant B. These photos are guaranteed to get the panties wet." He winked and smiled then added, "And I've got a buddy in bomb disposal. Every so often they go over to one of the islands on the other side of the shipping channel, unload a lot of out-of-date ammunition and blow it up. Spectacular. Even better than burning garbage."

Like everyone else serving in-country, Buddha was entitled to a week's R&R in places like Honolulu, Hong Kong, Tokyo, Bangkok, Kuala Lumpur, Singapore, and Sydney. He fantasized about meeting Meredith in some place far away from Michigan for a week of passion. Starting about halfway through his tour, he started hinting to her that he had a week's R&R, it would be nice to see her, and he thought about her all the time. Her letters seemed to ignore all that and instead related her classroom experiences, the Michigan weather, being so busy, and always ending with a caution for him to be careful.

It was time for Buddha to make his move. He had put off his R&R until he had only a few months left in-country, figuring it would make the remaining months go faster. Now he'd put his plan into gear.

On his desk were two pictures. One showed him standing before a mushroom of dust and flame, helmet pushed back, aviator sunglasses shading his eyes as he stared into the camera. He had one hand on the butt of his holstered pistol, the other on his hip. A bandage wrapped around his forearm. His open flak vest showed a smoke grenade hanging from his web belt.

The other photograph showed him on one knee holding the stock of his M16, flak vest zipped up, fatigue pants bloused atop his combat boots, arms bare and smiling. Behind him stood his four young enlisted men, all similarly garbed, arms on each other's shoulder. Black charcoal dust dirtied their faces. Behind a small sand dune, dark heavy smoke swirled up into the sky.

The letter by the two pictures read as follows:

Dear Meredith:

I've finally got some pictures to send you. The fellows behind me are my men. We've lost a few, but these guys have made it all the way with me. It will be good to get back to base for some hot chow, good water, and a shower.

I'm planning to take my R&R in Honolulu the 28th of next month. I think of you all the time and really miss seeing you. Can you join me in Honolulu on the 28th? Please write back as soon as possible so I can finalize my plans.

I hope you're enjoying your teaching and the weather's getting warmer. Say hello to your father for me.

Again, missing you very much, with love,

Jeff

A week later to the day Buddha read Meredith's letter.

Dear Jeff:

I've so much to tell you, I don't know where to begin.

First, thanks for the pictures of you and your four buddies. It's good to see you looking happy. And safe. I'm frankly jealous of the obvious camaraderie you all have. I wonder if that's a male or military thing because it's rare with us females. I'm glad you're okay because I've worried about your safety since you left. The war has become very unpopular here. I'm sure you can agree with that.

Now here's my exciting news and I hope you're happy for me. I'm engaged!!! That's right, engaged to become Mrs. Booth Coleman on June 6. I think you won't be home yet but if you are, I hope you can attend the wedding. You're certainly going to get an invitation. I met Booth at Daddy's country club and found out he's working right here in Benton Harbor. He's an engineer with Whirlpool. How's that for convenience?

Okay, I've got to run. Thanks again for the pictures. Say hello to your friends and please be careful.
Meredith

Jeff never responded to Meredith's letter. He moped around for a week, depressed and pissed off at Meredith's infidelity. Hernandez asked what was wrong and the response was, "Nothing, Sarge."

"With all due respect, sir, it sure doesn't look like nothing. Anything we can do for you?"

Buddha looked at Hernandez, then at the other three men doing their job, and he thought his behavior was fucking silly. How could he have ever thought of building a relationship with anyone when he was trying to be something he was not? Fuck it—from now on he was being himself. No more shoots at the garbage dump. Hell, he wasn't Audie Murphy, he was Buddha. Be Buddha. His mood immediately lightened. He walked over to his four soldiers and asked them if they had any recommendations on where he should go for his week's R&R?

Hong Kong was where Buddha went. And he had a very good time, sightseeing, eating, shopping. A tailor at the Royal Navy's China Fleet Club fitted him for two suits and a sport coat and slacks that made him look less round, less tubby. He bought gifts for his family and a polished bronze statue of a sitting, laughing Buddha.

An envelope from Meredith's family containing a wedding invitation was on his desk when he returned from R&R. He sent his regrets along with the bronze Buddha and a note wishing the newlyweds well. Then he took the garbage dump hero pictures off his desk and dumped them into the trashcan. From there the photographs made it to the garbage dump where they were burned the next Tuesday. He was enjoying being himself.

Jeff left Vietnam and used his GI bill to get his doctorate in systems analysis at MIT. He took a job in Seattle and then met a woman who was as skinny-straight as he was round. She liked him. A lot. A year later she married Buddha, not some decorated war hero who looked like Peter Lawford. A son and daughter followed.

Other than to say he didn't do much, Buddha never talked about his tour in Vietnam. In 2000, he noted on a census form that he was a veteran who had served in Vietnam.

COLLEGE KID

P ham Nghia's father was a landowner. He owned prime rice-growing properties around the town of My Duc, northwest of Hanoi. A little river ran alongside his rice paddies, serving as the waterborne thoroughfare from My Duc to the Perfume Temple.

In 1954, the French left the country and Vietnam was partitioned into North and South. Although a landowner, Nghia's father was sympathetic to the communist Viet Minh. Despite the urgings of his prosperous friends and business acquaintances, he did not move to the South. Rather, he gave all but his ancestral landholdings to the Viet Minh for redistribution.

After a year or two, the government officials around My Duc changed. As the first officials moved up the bureaucratic ladder and were promoted to positions in Hanoi, Haiphong, and Vinh, they were replaced with graduates from the civil service academy. These new men were well schooled in communist political doctrine, but ignorant about My Duc and the local population.

In late 1956, Nghia's father was accused, tried, and punished for having been a landowner and depriving the people. After a year of reeducation and imprisonment, he returned to My Duc. One zealous local official was not happy that this landowner and criminal had spent so little time in prison and had been granted a full pardon. He also resented being told by his superiors to leave Nghia's father alone.

"He is a good man," said the senior official in Hanoi. The local official did leave him alone, but kept a mistrustful eye on him.

Nghia was the eldest of three children, all boys. When he was twelve, he started to row a cargo boat on the little river. He delivered foodstuff to the landing by the Perfume Pagoda and brought back empty crates. In school, Nghia impressed his teachers with his quick and nimble mind, especially in math. With a few months of high school left, the school principal encouraged Nghia to apply for entrance to the Hanoi Polytechnic University to study engineering.

Going to the university would also mean a deferment from conscription into the People's Army. While Nghia felt strongly about serving his country in its struggle for reunification, the school principal and the senior teachers told him that his country needed a good engineer more than they needed another soldier. He applied.

Months passed and Nghia received no response from the university. No acceptance, no rejection. He was conscripted into the People's Army and went to basic training, saying goodbye to his family. A month after the Tet Offensive of 1968, Nghia and twenty-seven other men, all with river experience, were formed into a platoon and sent down the Ho Chi Minh trail to the Saigon River.

When the American war ended and the country was reunified in 1975, of the twenty-eight men, only Nghia was still alive.

After spending another two years helping to locate and identify remains in the area around Cu Chi in the South, Sergeant Nghia returned to My Duc and his family. One of his brothers had died in Qui Nhon. The youngest brother, assigned to an antiaircraft defense unit in Hanoi, had made it through the war unscathed. Nghia's father and mother were in quiet retirement, while the youngest brother ran the family rice-growing business.

For a month Nghia helped his brother, but soon realized that while his brother welcomed him, there really wasn't much for him to do. My Duc offered little in way of other employment and challenge. With the encouragement of his father, Nghia decided to go to the university and become an electrical engineer.

He took a bus to Hanoi and then a *xyclo* to the Hanoi Polytechnic University. After wandering around the large administration building, he found the admissions office. When a young woman looked up from her desk as he entered the office. Nghia told her that he was interested in applying for the electrical engineering program, but that he had been out of school for nearly nine years. What would he have to do to matriculate? She handed him a sheet of paper that spelled out the requirements for admission.

"This hasn't changed in nine years, has it?" asked Nghia. "It's the same as when I applied before."

"Oh, you've applied before? Were you accepted then?"

"I don't think so. I never received an acceptance or a rejection. I just assumed I did not meet the admission standards."

She looked at him for a few moments, studying his face. "What's your name? Let me see if I can find out what happened."

While he sat on a bench in the hallway, watching students and faculty walk by, she searched the admission records. He saw her coming down the corridor, a thin folder in her hand, smiling.

"You are Pham Nghia from My Duc, right?"

"Yes, that's me."

"You don't have to apply again. You were accepted in March of 1968. We sent you a letter of acceptance via the government office in My Duc. I don't know why you did not receive notification."

"I...uh...I am accepted? I was accepted? I...I...can enroll here?" Nghia was stuttering in amazement.

"Yes," she laughed. "You can start this upcoming semester in September. I assume I can write in your file that you are accepting our offer of enrollment?"

Yes, yes...of course. Yes...thank you so much."

The next day, Nghia and his father went to the government office in My Duc. The official was the same man who had accused and prosecuted Nghia's father twenty years before. Unlike many of his peers, he was stuck in the same shitty little town sixty kilometers northwest of Hanoi. No advancement, no recognition. Stuck. He glared at Nghia's father and then looked at the young man standing next to him.

The young man asked, "Do you have a letter for me? I am Pham Nghia. The letter is from the Hanoi Polytechnic University. It was sent here on March 24, 1968. Do you have it?"

"1968? Why would I have a letter that is nine years old? I don't remember any such letter. Maybe it was sent to your father's home and he lost it."

"Maybe," said Nghia. "But I want you to check anyway. You are a servant of the people, aren't you? So please do your duty and check your correspondence files. I'm sure you keep a file as required by the people's government."

"Who are you to tell me my duties? I am not going to tear apart my files for a letter that does not exist. Go!"

Nghia reached across the counter and grabbed the man by his throat with one hand and then slapped him with the other. "I am not going anywhere. Why don't you call your supervisor and then he can tell you to do your job." Nghia slapped him again and did not let go of the man's throat.

The man's face was red and his eyes wide with fear. He seemed to be flopping about like a fish on a line. Nghia let go and the man crumpled to the floor.

"Where are your correspondence files, sir? I will save you the labor and I will go through them for you. 1968? I know you're the type of person who would never violate orders and discard official correspondence, right?" Nghia stood over the man who pointed at a filing cabinet.

The second drawer was marked "Correspondence 1965 to 1975." In the middle of the drawer, Nghia found a file with his father's name on it. Inside was an acceptance letter from the university to Nghia.

"So this is the letter that you never received and my father must have lost? How fortunate that you have now found it. I am sure your supervisor will be happy to hear how efficient you are, Comrade." Nghia bent over the man who cowered on the floor.

"Here, Comrade, let me help you up. You must have tripped on something, yes?"

Pham Nghia started his college education that September. At the age of thirty-one he graduated with a degree in electrical engineering. He was hired by a West German engineering firm that had just opened offices in Hanoi and Ho Chi Minh City. Nghia married his girlfriend from college—the young woman in the admissions office.

The man in the government office in My Duc never lost a letter again.

BOMBS AWAY

Sergeant Barry Lawson, Royal Australian Air Force, loved his job. Just flat-out loved it. Hell, he even loved Vietnam. Life was very good for Bazza, which was his nickname in the RAAF's 35 Squadron.

His squadron operated out of Vung Tau, the nicest spot in all of South Vietnam. The tucker was good, and the barracks the best he had experienced in the RAAF. His squadronmates were also the best. The officers were fine pilots and not a bunch of asses. He had just been promoted. And his girlfriend, Quoc, was gorgeous.

But most of all, he loved being the crew chief on the RAAF's Caribou, serial number A4-140. He had not missed one flight on his airplane during the nine months he had been in Vung Tau. If the plane flew, he was aboard it. To say Bazza was proprietary about the plane would be a gross understatement. The RAAF owned it, the pilots flew it, and the squadron leader dictated where and when it went, but A4-140 was his. If DNA tests had been available in 1968, a perfect match would have been made between the Caribou's hydraulic fluid and the sergeant's blood.

Born in 1964 in Canada, the plane was pure function and absolutely no beauty—although people like Bazza thought the Caribous graceful and gorgeous. Rugged, like all of De Havilland Aircraft of Canada's aircraft, the Caribou could take off and land on short, unimproved runways and fields. It flew fast and far enough to get you where you wanted to go in good time, and high enough to keep you safe from VC bullets. It was loud and it vibrated. The slightest turbulence or thermals turned the sky into a road filled with potholes, steep hills, and gullies. To spoil the aim of the enemy, the squadron's pilots took off steeply, weaving as soon as the wheels left the ground. Landings were little more than controlled crashes that amazingly did not damage the plane, cargo, crew, or passengers.

Though it was a compact airplane, the Caribou could carry four tons of supplies and people. It had a large ramp in the back to make loading and unloading easy, and allow a quick exit for paratroopers.

The Caribous of 35 Squadron soon became known as Wallaby Airlines. The typical run for one of these Caribous was...well, there were no typical runs. From Vung Tau, they flew north and south to drop supplies at American special forces camps and to members of the Australian Army Training Teams across the Central Highlands. In addition, Bazza and his plane frequently flew wide-ranging unscheduled flights, including transporting military and civilian passengers, sick and wounded, precious personal mail, and badly needed food, fuel, ammunition, plasma, and spare parts. A few times, they even delivered water buffalo, pigs, and ducks. And too often, the cabin was silent with dead soldiers in body bags.

Takeoff and landing were always hazardous. Most landing strips were outside the bases' defensive perimeters. Except for the concrete pads of Tan Son Nhut and Vung Tau, most were short and often eroded by the monsoon rains and flooding. The planes made tempting targets for the VC and North Vietnamese Army. Heavy monsoon thunderstorms didn't help matters much, either.

Bazza loved it all. He was never bored. A4-140 and its crew had become known as the best of the best. When General Westmoreland dispatched a gaggle of senior US Army officers to Vung Tau to see how the Aussies did it, the RAAF Wing Commander made sure the army brass hats talked to the crew of A4-140.

When some colonel in starched jungle fatigues asked Bazza to describe their missions, he replied, "Sir, we do it all. We do everything except drop bombs."

And even that was about to change.

* * *

A4-140 was sitting in the hot sun on the tarmac at Cu Chi. A platoon of soldiers and their gear had just disembarked. Bazza carefully watched the refueling, checked the landing gear and engine intakes, and inspected the control surfaces as he walked slowly around and under the plane three times. His hands and eyes examined the airplane like a doctor examining a favorite patient. Then he tidied up the cockpit and cabin, and supervised the loading of two crates of cargo. He looked at the schedule. Most of the heavy lifting for the day was finished.

"Hi, Sergeant. Any room on Wallaby Airlines to Vung Tau?"

Bazza looked up from his manifest and loading plan. Standing in the shade of A4-140's fuselage was Lieutenant Gordon, the lone American navy officer advisor to the South Vietnamese river squadron stationed a few kilometers down the road on the Saigon River. He had hopped rides on A4-140 several times before. The last time, he had expressed his appreciation by presenting the crew with a freshly made Viet Cong flag. It even had bloodstains from a chicken Gordon's hooch mama had slaughtered for dinner. She had sewn the flag together before she started her dinner preparations. The counterfeit flags were better than Military Payment Certificates when it came time to barter.

"G'day, Lieutenant. Sure, sir. I've only got three passengers and some light cargo going north and two passengers coming back. Plane's light. We've got the cargo aboard. As soon as the passengers show up and Skipper and his mate show up, we'll be on our way. About ten minutes, sir."

When Gordon gave him a thumbs-up and a smile, Bazza noticed Gordon's left arm was covered in an olive drab bandage and in a sling.

"Sir, what happened to your arm?" asked Bazza, pointing with his clipboard at the sling.

"Ambush, Sergeant. VC seem to have recovered from Tet. At least in this neighborhood."

"Bad one, sir?"

"Yeah, Sergeant. Wrecked one of the boats, killed two sailors. Wounded six of us."

"That's not good, sir. Where?"

Gordon took a map out of his fatigue pants pocket. He unfolded it and pointed at a point of land that jutted into the Saigon River. "Right here. Got us telescoped together when we slowed to round the point. Opened up with a mine, rockets, and a hell of a lot of bullets. They seem to be pretty well entrenched there."

"Tough, sir. Going for R&R?" Bazza was writing Gordon's name and unit on the manifest.

"I wish, Sergeant. Some meeting with your army guys and the Koreans."

Two well-built men walked up to the plane. Both wore tropical fatigues without rank, name, or service insignia. Floppy hats sat on their heads. They carried small duffels, and wore 9 mm pistols on their hips and Swedish machineguns slung over their shoulders.

"Hello, Mr. Gordon," said one. "You joining Bazza and us today? Going to visit us, sir?"

Before Gordon could answer, Bazza said, "Nope, mates. He's going on to Vung Tau. You guys all ready? I got your crates aboard." He looked at his manifest and checked off the names "Jones" and "Smith." He knew the two SEALs and their real names, which were not Jones and Smith.

A jeep drove up as the two SEALs and the navy officer walked up the ramp into the comparative cool air of the plane's interior. A Vietnamese woman in a white *ao dai* over black silk trousers got out of the passenger seat of the jeep, picked up a lather briefcase and a small overnight bag, thanked the driver, and walked up to Bazza.

110

"Good morning, ma'am. Are you Mrs. Toh? Destination Tan Son Nhut?"

She smiled behind her dark sunglasses. "Yes. That's me. Am I late?" Her accent was more French than Vietnamese.

"No, ma'am. Right on time. " He waved at the two pilots walking toward the plane as he helped her up the ramp.

Bazza sat her in a jump seat on the left side of the plane, figuring that his weight, combined with hers and Gordon's, would just about balance the weight of the two husky SEALs across the cabin. The two cargo crates were already lashed to the center of the deck. He checked his manifest one more time, put on his flight helmet, plugged his headset cord into the jack mounted by the crew chief's seat, and hooked a long woven nylon tether onto the harness built into his flight suit.

He walked around the cabin making sure his four passengers were securely strapped into their canvas jump seats. Then he tugged on the heavy straps holding the cargo crates. Satisfied, he rechecked his manifest and loading diagram. People: 370 kilograms. Cargo: 280 kilograms. After another quick look around the cabin, he nodded to himself in satisfaction. Clean, everything properly stowed. He hit the button that raised the ramp, sealing them inside the bowels of A4-140.

Bazza keyed his headset. "Skipper. Everything secure. Light load. 650 kilograms. Loaded centerline and amidships. Fuel topped off."

The copilot's voice answered as the propellers started to turn, the engines winding up and vibrating the aircraft. "Good, Bazza. Where's everyone going?"

"Our two friends and the cargo to Special Forces Camp Echo. The civilian lady to Tan Son Nhut. Lieutenant Gordon to Vung Tau."

The pilot's voice commented, "Gordo's aboard? Haven't seen him for a while. We owe him a few drinks for that flag he gave us. Who's the lady?"

"Dunno, sir. Attractive enough Sheila, for sure. Must be someone important; she's carrying a briefcase bigger than she is." He looked at the manifest again. "Her unit ID says MACV G2. Must be some intelligence analyst or something. "

"Okay, Bazza. Better buckle yourself up." The plane was rumbling toward the runway for its takeoff.

"Buckled up, Skipper. Lieutenant Gordo says his guys got shot up at that point of land on the south side of the river across from the Michelin plantation, sir. Might want to avoid that."

"Will do. We'll turn away from it until we get some altitude then pass to the southwest. Hold on, mates."

A4-140's engines made a synchronized roar, shaking the aircraft violently. The navy officer and the two SEALs just sat calmly, but the woman's knuckles turned white as she squeezed her shoulder straps.

As soon as the brakes were released, the shaking diminished, replaced by a bumpy rolling and bouncing as the plane accelerated down the runway. Then the cabin tilted upward and the harsh movements gave way to wallowing and pitching as the plane gained altitude. The screaming engines quieted to a hoarse drone. For the next hour, the plane imitated a gentle roller coaster, never straight and level.

The pilot's voice interrupted Bazza's concentration on the *Stars and Stripes'* crossword puzzle. "We're making our approach to Echo Camp. How're our passengers?"

"Corkers, Skipper. The guys look like they're napping. Mrs. Toh's not enjoying the ride, sir. She's looking a little pale and has a death grip on her seatbelts."

He could hear the pilot's chuckle. "Nervous flier, eh? Okay, we'll do a 180 and sneak ourselves in. Hold on."

The plane turned sharply to the left, came around, and then made a steep and rapid descent, flared out, and jolted hard as it touched down. With engines screaming and propellers in reverse pitch, the plane bounced and jarred down the dirt runway. As the plane slowed to a halt, Bazza lowered the tail ramp. Hot and humid air entered the cabin.

A jeep with a trailer pulled up to the ramp. An American waved at Bazza from the driver's seat, and four Vietnamese in unmarked jungle fatigues jumped off the trailer and walked up the ramp. With no greetings or preliminaries, they unstrapped the two cargo cases and, with the help of the two SEALs, carried them out of the plane and onto the trailer. With a wave and shouts of thanks, they drove off, the Americans in the seats and the Vietnamese sitting on the cargo.

"Clear, Skipper. Ready to go," reported Bazza as he raised the ramp, trapping hot air and engine exhaust in the cabin.

"Hold on," answered the copilot.

A4-140 immediately turned around, its engines revving to full power, and started a teeth-rattling ride down the short field. Engines screaming, the plane stood on its tail and took to the sky, weaving and bobbing like a boxer looking for an opening. After a minute, it leveled off, winged over, and headed north.

Mrs. Toh's complexion was now the color of blue-tinged ivory. She took off her sunglasses and wiped the sweat from her forehead with her sleeve. Bazza had seen this many times before. And, as in everything associated with his airplane, he was prepared. Stashed beneath the crew chief's seat was a package of airsickness bags. The plane settled into its roller coaster ride.

They flew another twenty-five minutes before making another controlled crash landing at another remote camp to pick up a Royal Australian Army special forces officer. Besides his duffel and weapon, he had a paper bag with grease stains on it.

"G'day, Sergeant. Looks like you're pretty empty today."

"Yes, sir, Captain. Just you and our two other passengers. Next stop is Tan Son Nhut to drop off the lady, then to Vung Tau and we're done. About an hour to Tan Son Nhut, then twenty minutes to Vung Tau."

"Good on ya, Sarge. Here's some tucker for you and the crew. Fried chicken. Still hot." He took a paper towel, drumstick, and thigh out of the bag, and strapped himself into a jump seat across the cabin from Mrs. Toh.

Bazza passed the bag around the cockpit crew. Then he offered some of the chicken to Gordon, who gratefully took a breast, wing, and a paper towel. Mrs. Toh turned from pale blue to not-so-pale green, smiled weakly, and shook her head as he offered her some chicken from the greasy bag.

"Skipper, it's pretty hot in the cabin. Everything's secured. I'd like to keep the ramp open from here to Tan Son Nhut to let it cool and air out."

The copilot answered through a mouthful of chicken. "Good idea, Bazza. This chicken's pretty good. You tried it, yet?"

"As soon's we're up, sir."

"Hold on, turning around and then we're off."

As Gordon and the Australian officer ate their chicken, A4-140 screamed and shook its way into the sky. The cabin immediately cooled and, except for an occasional whiff of chicken grease, aired out.

The ride south was a smooth one, the plane flying relatively straight and level. The view through the open tail ramp was majestic: blue sky, white puffy clouds, green jungle, brown mud. And the horizon, due to the gentle motion of A4-140, cycled every fifteen seconds or so from below and out of sight to above and out of sight.

Mrs. Toh slid her eyes from the man across from her eating his chicken with greasy fingers, to the man to her left eating his chicken with greasy fingers, to the man in the flight helmet to her right eating chicken with greasy fingers, and settled on looking out the ramp and watching the world go up and down, up and down, up and down. Sweat trickled down from her hairline. She started gulping air. Her complexion matched the jungle fatigues the men wore. She looked down at her lap and watched sweat drip off her face onto her *ao dai*.

Above the roar of the engines, she heard "Ma'am?" and saw a pair of flight boots by her feet. Looking up she saw the man in the flight helmet holding out a clear plastic liter-size bag to her. She tried to smile, then quickly pulled the bag out of his hands, opened it, and vomited up her breakfast and last night's dinner.

Bazza stayed in front of her with another bag and a wad of wet paper towels at the ready.

"Skipper, she's chundering. A real Technicolor yawn. I think this may be a two-bagger, sir."

114

"I guess she won't be eating any of this chicken, eh? We'll be landing in about thirty-five minutes. She going to last?"

"She'll be okay, sir. But I think she may never get on a plane again." Bazza took the full bag from her and handed her the empty one. Twisting the top shut, he held the full bag behind him and out of her sight and put the cool wet paper towels on the back of her neck as she bowed over the new plastic bag. She nodded her head in thanks but kept her mouth over the bag.

As the two other passengers munched chicken and sucked meat off the bones, she filled the second bag halfway, then leaned back. Bazza took the bag and shouted over the engine noise. "Mrs. Toh, you okay? Want me to call ahead and have a medic for you?"

Her color had returned to pale blue, almost white. She wiped her face with the wet paper towels. "Thank you, Sergeant. I'll be okay. As soon as I can get off your airplane."

Bazza put the two puke bags out of her sight by his seat. He took the empty chicken bag and collected the bones and paper towels from the passengers and the cockpit. He walked back to his seat and looked out the ramp opening. They were over the Saigon River. His altimeter read 2,200 meters. Then he looked at Lieutenant Gordon's bandaged arm and sling.

"Skipper. We're high enough to be out of Charlie's range. How about we fly over that spot where Lieutenant Gordon got hit and I drop Mrs. Toh's chunder and our chicken scraps on the VC?"

For about half a minute, his earphones were silent. Then the pilot's voice came on. "You mean, we turn this plane into a bomber?"

"Sort of, Skipper. Not sure I'd call these things bombs. Sort of more like editorial statements, sir."

After another long silence, the pilot's voice came back on.

"Okay, here's what we'll do up here. We'll figure out the wind and time to drop and then pick an aiming point. As soon as we get over it, you drop the bombs. We should be over the aiming point in about four minutes. I'll circle around if we need more time to make our calculations. Stand by."

Laughing to himself, Bazza thought just how much he loved this job. Best in the world as far as he was concerned. He looked over at Mrs. Toh, who was leaning back in her jump seat, her face now devoid of blue and green, her eyes shut, her sunglasses on her forehead. The other two passengers had their eyes shut, napping probably.

"Pilot to bombardier, approaching aiming point. Standby."

"Ready when you are, Skipper." Bazza walked to the open ramp, holding two barf bags and a greasy bag of chicken scraps in this right hand, his left hand steadying himself on the ramp doorframe.

"Ten seconds to drop. Five, four, three, two, one. Drop."

Bazza heaved the three bags out of the airplane, and watched as they fell toward the riverbank below.

"Bombs away, Skipper."

* * *

Three days after Bazza threw the barf bags and chicken bones out of A4-140, Captain Bob Neal, the advisor to the South Vietnamese Army's Fifth Infantry Division G2 intelligence officer, read a report just handed to him. The author, his most trusted intelligence analyst, Staff Sergeant Norman Feckler, stood casually across the desk from him, studying his boss's face. Neal shook his head in disbelief.

"Let me get this straight, Sergeant. You say these two VC defected to us because of some biological warfare attack on their ambush site three days ago? Just like that, they came waltzing in here and said they want to join our side?"

"Yep, sir. That just about sums it all up. The two decided that the war was hopeless and decided to *chieu hoi.*"

"What happened? Who in the hell used biological warfare?"

"Beats the shit out of me, Captain. Here's what we've been able to find out. Those two were scared shitless," said Feckler with a shrug and a smile.

"Tell me. I'm all ears."

"It seems those two were manning that ambush spot on the spit of land across from the Michelin, sleeping underneath some tree canopies. It must have been about 1400 or so. All of a sudden, both wake up because they hear something falling through the branches and then two *wops* and a thud. They were bracketed by whatever caused those sounds."

"*Wop*? What goes *wop*?"

"That's the same question we asked them. They just said it went *wop*. Made a bunch of noises with their mouths to demonstrate. *Wop*'s about as close as I could come in writing it."

Neal laughed as Feckler continued.

"They hunkered down in their holes for a couple of minutes, waiting. But it was quiet, nothing moving. So they go looking. It seems what went *wop* was some busted balloons or something that had been filled with what they said was foul-smelling liquid gunk. They guessed about a liter and a half of whatever was stinking up the place. In the other direction where they heard the thud they found a bunch of bones and wet paper."

Captain Neal's eyes were wide with wonder.

"Captain, we questioned both these guys separately and then together. Their stories are identical. And they're sticking to it."

"So they decided to defect"

"Yes, sir. They said they were sure it was a new form of biological or chemical warfare and they were probably exposed. If they decided to *chieu hoi*, we'd be able to give them a shot or something. And if we were deploying such weapons, they wanted to be on our side."

"Do we know what these things are?"

"I sure don't, sir. I checked with every unit I could, including the CIA house in Ba Ria. Nobody was around there at that time. I talked to the flyboys and they weren't dropping anything, not even propaganda leaflets, near there."

"Are those two showing any symptoms?"

"Looked fine to me, sir. But I had our surgeon and the ARVN doc look at them. They said they're both healthy. The ARVN's got them now, starting their *chieu hoi* indoctrination."

"Anyone looked at that ambush spot?"

"Yes, sir, ARVN sent a platoon in there and they nosed around. But it's been raining pretty heavy and whatever might have been there has probably been washed into the river. Found nothing other than some cooking gear and sleeping mats."

"Think these two VC are nuts?"

"Definitely, sir."

* * *

In late 2009, after forty-five years of continuous service, A4-140 was retired. It is now on display at the Australian War Memorial in Canberra. Retired RAAF Warrant Officer Barry "Bazza" Lawson and his wife Quoc were among the guests invited to the airplane's retirement ceremony.

The official flight logbooks of RAAF Caribou A4-140 tell of countless missions. Carrying supplies and people. Medical evacuations. Humanitarian relief flights. The plane flew millions of miles, and delivered thousands of people and tens of thousands of tons of supplies. But missing in the official log of A4-140 is the time it bombed the ambush site on the Saigon River.

And that's a shame.

THANKSGIVING DAY
PARADE BALLOON

I just didn't like him. There was something about him that irritated me. And with twenty-two days left before getting on the freedom bird and leaving the goddamned shit-hole country, I didn't need to be irritated. I just needed to get my ass out sane and in one piece.

He seemed to want to hang around me, though, like an ugly puppy or the jerky kid on the schoolyard playground.

The command boat was idling in midriver with the big monitor and one of the little patrol boats—all holdovers from the French days—tied up alongside. We were waiting for the American and South Vietnamese troops to board the troop carriers. Once they were loaded, all the boats would motor upriver into Charlie's territory and land the troops for a major search-and-destroy mission. The boats would shoot up the landing zone, unload the troops, and then sit there for three days as a blocking force.

Dirty and soaked with sweat, stinking of body odor and paddy shit, the soldiers would slog back. They'd file aboard, and then we'd motor downriver with all our guns manned. We always got shot at on the way back downriver. Finally, we'd unload the troops at their pickup point, wash down the boats, refuel, and then moor at the little river town that was our home base. Routine. Same old, same old.

Then I would have fewer than twenty days to go. A week to fart around the base and get things ready for my relief, then a few days to meet my relief in Saigon and show him the ropes down there, and then bring him back up here. Take him out on an operation and, hopefully, not get him or me killed. Kiss him and the assault group and the Vietnamese goodbye, and then I'd be down to Saigon to debrief the brass, fill out forms, burn my jungle fatigues, put on my khakis, and fly back to Madison, Wisconsin, via half a dozen stops. A few days with my parents, buy a Mustang, and then drive around visiting friends on the way to Annapolis for two years of shore duty as a midshipman company commander with no one shooting at me.

The year in-country had been good to me. Or rather, good for my career. Joint duty with the army, advisor to an allied nation's navy, high visibility with the brass—all good stuff. But the year took its toll. Getting shot at and hit, infections, goofy dreams, skin rashes, weird food, jumpiness, short temper, insomnia, and a loose stomach. I think the best part of going home may be my first solid shit.

The worst part of the year may have been the "Dear John" letter from Terri. She wrote that she was going to get married to some fucking dental student, adding that she will always love me like a brother. Who besides a brother wants to be loved like a brother? Bullshit. Fuck her. I hope she gets fat and her husband's breath smells like his asshole.

And then, just weeks before I'm out of here, some dork started hanging around me like a shadow. In my eleven months in-country, I knew all the Vietnamese sailors. Every once in a while we'd get a new sailor fresh from boot camp or maybe a navy technical school. I didn't know this guy. I noticed him when the patrol boat tied up and he came aboard our boat to pick up some radio batteries. After paying his respects to his commanding officer—my counterpart—he walked up to me and introduced himself with a salute and a proffered hand.

I shook his hand and told him to not salute me when we were on the river. That would mark me as a target for any sniper watching us. That was bullshit—any guy with a scope could easily pick me out since I was half a foot taller than the tallest of the Vietnamese, and obviously a round-eye.

For the most part, the Vietnamese officers and sailors were a good-looking group. Handsome features beneath mops of thick, black hair. Skinny and bony but square-shouldered and thin-hipped. Not this kid. When they were handing out looks, he must have been absent. His face was round, jack-o'-lantern round, with thick blubbery lips, a wide, flat nose, and beady porcine eyes behind black-rimmed glasses. Zits. His shoulders were narrow and sloped, his hips wide, and his ass round. Charley Chaplin feet and soft, moist marshmallow hands.

His English was excellent, spoken with a French accent. He wanted to talk, and although I had nothing much to do but sit on my ass and watch the troops load up, I didn't want to spend any time with him. He irritated me and seemed to invade my personal space. If I edged away, he followed. So, I listened, grunting a word or two in response. He sort of sprayed through his oversized teeth when he talked and his breath smelled of fish sauce and garlic.

He told me that after graduating from college with a degree in business and economics, he had gone off to boot camp and come out as a simple seaman, an enlisted sailor without a technical specialty. That was unusual, especially with his education. He must have been from an influential family that had lost its influence. People with his background did not become enlisted sailors.

The sailor must have read a quizzical expression on my face, as he explained that he had joined the navy because he liked boats. After the war, he wanted to go into maritime logistics—the shipping industry. He said that he hoped to be able to talk to me about America and economics.

I couldn't give a shit.

I told him to return to his boat; the troop boats were ready to get under way.

The big boats lined up in midstream, single file, led by the two minesweepers hugging each riverbank and the two patrol boats moving up and down either side of the column. Humming "We're Off to See the Wizard," I quickly forgot about the sailor and busied myself with maps, binoculars, and radios.

I tried to count how many times I had done that same thing during the last eleven months and stopped after two dozen, sure I had missed some operations and double counted others. They had all been pretty much the same. Motor upriver. Light up the beach with every gun we had. Land the troops. Sit and wait. Nap. Pee over the side. Shit off the fantail. Eat fish and rice and C-rats. Read. Nap a bit more. Then, load up the troops and go downriver.

Downriver trips were always tense. We knew for sure we'd get hit; we just didn't know where or when. The VC and NVA knew that there was only one way back home and that was the river. We couldn't take an off-ramp and bypass all the trouble. They'd pick a nice, juicy ambush spot, plant some mines, dig in, and wait for us to come by nice and slow.

We had another hour to motor upriver to the insertion point when I heard the deafening clang and *whomp*. Behind me, I saw the smoke cloud drift across the river, and one of the patrol boats veer drunkenly toward the monitor. It bounced off the big boat's bow, then wheeled down its side, scraping the splinter shields of the 20 mm cannons and Honeywell grenade launcher, before it slid clear. The patrol boat coxswain and one of the gunners, both drenched in blood, were trying to regain control of the boat. The boat's starboard side was blackened, its wheelhouse canopy torn and flapping, and the canopy stanchions bent and twisted and broken.

All of the other boats opened fire, raking the eastern riverbank. One of the troop boats beached and lowered its ramp, disembarking a platoon of soldiers who fanned out, shooting their M16s as they advanced on the riverbank. My counterpart asked me to call in a dust-off to medevac the wounded.

The soldiers found nothing. The helicopter picked up two of the patrol boat's crew, one with blast burns, the other peppered with shrapnel. Another sailor was missing, apparently having been blown over the side. After an hour-long search of the river and the banks, the boats continued up the river. No body was found.

The strike was unusual. I had been in-country nearly a year, and that was the first time we had ever been attacked going to our mission, going upriver.

We left the damaged patrol boat and its remaining uninjured crew tied up to a riverbank tree. On the way back downriver, we'd pick them up and tow the boat home.

The rest of the trip upriver to the insertion point was quiet, but when we landed the troops, all hell broke loose. Although we softened up the landing zone with our cannon, mortars, and heavy machineguns, Charlie opened up with a recoilless rifle, rockets, and small-arms fire. The incoming let up after we returned fire. I figured Charlie was withdrawing, but when the troops moved off the landing zone, they walked into a minefield and booby traps. The VC opened up again with a crossfire that scythed the sugar-cane and razor grass. Their firing only stopped after we called in artillery and attack helicopters.

As the medevac helicopters shuttled back and forth picking up wounded, the soldiers walked into the tree line. To search and destroy. For the next two days they did a lot of searching but found nothing to destroy. Dirty and exhausted, they walked out of the tree line and across the landing zone to the boats. Single file, they scuffed their muddy boots up the ramps onto the troop carriers, and collapsed on their packs, their helmets on their stomachs and their rifles alongside them on the deck. We backed off the river-bank and motored downstream, every boats' guns manned.

At every bend in the river, someone popped up and sprayed us with AK-47 fire, shot a B-40 rocket at us, or detonated an under-water mine that shot up a column of river water, mud, and dead fish. Other than giving the boats a wash-down and chipping some paint off the thick steel armor of the hulls, no damage was done to our boats, sailors, or soldiers. But it had been a lousy operation.

One of our boats put out of action, a sailor missing and probably feeding the crabs on the river bottom, two of our sailors wounded, and a lot of soldiers wounded and three dead. I had no idea how much damage we had inflicted on Charlie. I didn't really care. I had fewer than twenty days to go. *Just get me through this shit alive.*

We reached the damaged patrol boat and the monitor took it under tow. I could see one of the minesweepers and the other patrol boat moving out of line toward the western bank a few hundred meters farther downstream. They were pointing at something in the reeds alongside the bank.

Trying to see what they were pointing at, I grabbed my binoculars. My counterpart, the assault group's commanding officer, was standing next to me, doing the same.

"It's our dead sailor," he said through lips that held one of his acrid French cigarettes.

"Where?"

"Look at the minesweeper's stern. He's right there." What looked like a gray balloon was bobbing behind the sweeper.

As we motored closer, the balloon took shape. I thought it looked like a grim version of the Pillsbury Doughboy, or maybe the Michelin Man. The body was floating high in the water. The left foot was bare and looked more like a gray baby's pudgy foot except that it was gigantic. A foot long, maybe a foot wide. It looked like an overblown rugby ball. The other foot was shod, but the swollen ankle tightly filled out the denim trouser leg above it. The shoe was stretched tight. The torso was swollen and round, pulling the blue denim shirt out of the dungarees. All the clothes were soaked and dark, stretched to the point of ripping apart by the swollen corpse. His head was bare and swollen, face down in the river, his black hair slick. What wasn't covered by his shirt or trousers looked like a dull, gray plastic balloon.

I imagined him being towed down the street in the Macy's Thanksgiving Day Parade in New York City. A bunch of guys holding onto ropes to keep him from floating away.

One of the minesweeper crewmen tried to snag the dead man's belt loop with a boat hook. He caught the loop and started to tow the bloated corpse around the sweeper's stern. The body caught on the boat's propeller guard. With a violent tug, the sailor tried to free the dead weight. A rough edge of the propeller guard dug into the ballooned body and punctured the taut skin.

With a hiss audible over the engine noises, the parade balloon deflated, spewing out a slaughterhouse stink of death and rot. The sailor dropped the boat hook, bent over the side, and retched his stomach empty. Two other sailors also vomited while the others put their caps and flak vests over their mouths and noses. Even forty meters away from the deflating body, with the wind blowing at my back, I gagged.

After a half hour, the minesweeper sailors with wet rags tied over their noses and mouths finally muscled the dead man aboard and zipped it into a rubber body bag. Then they used bucket after bucket of river water to wash down their boat's side and deck.

We arrived at the base in the late afternoon. I put a tarp over the back seat of my jeep and two sailors dropped the full body bag onto it. Then they wrapped the tarp around it and taped it closed. With one of the Vietnamese corpsmen riding shotgun, I drove to the nearby Vietnamese Army compound and waited while two medics unloaded the body and carried it into their morgue. My corpsman escort handled the paperwork. Despite the sealed body bag and the tightly wrapped tarp, my jeep stunk.

I showered and scrubbed myself raw trying to get rid of the smell. In my mind was the image of one of those parade balloons. As a midshipman, I had once marched in that parade. I knew that the balloons didn't stink.

Ten days later, I was with my replacement waiting to take him out on his first operation. It would be like all the others of the past eleven and a half months—except for the one two weeks earlier. We would wait midchannel, load up the troops, then go upriver to the insertion point, then back downriver to the disembarkation point, then back to base. A firefight probably, shooting up the landing zone for sure. While we waited for the troops to load, it occurred to me that I hadn't seen that irritating sailor with the blubbery lips and glasses.

With not much else to do, I asked my counterpart what happened to that new sailor. I hadn't seen him. Was that kid assigned to the base staff now?

He looked at me through the cigarette smoke with squinted eyes for long seconds in silence.

"He's dead," he said. "He died when the patrol boat got hit on the last operation."

"That was him? Killed on his first operation?"

"Yes."

* * *

Twenty-four years later, I was an attorney living in a suburb of Milwaukee. It was Thanksgiving. Both my son and daughter were home from college. The television in the family room was on. My son and one of his high school buddies had made themselves comfortable on the couch for a day of watching football, starting with the Bears and the Lions. It was still early for the game. On the screen, the Pillsbury Doughboy's tummy was being playfully pushed by someone's finger and then the scene shifted back to the Thanksgiving Day Parade. A gust of wind hit one of the big balloons—a light blue pig cartoon character—and the rope handler guiding the cartoon character's feet lost his grip. The rope handlers connected to the pig's chest and shoulders and head held on. The character's feet slowly lifted up and then he lay there in space, floating face down. Bobbing.

My daughter had just walked into the den and look at me. "Hey, Daddy, you okay? You look sort of pale."

A wave of nausea swept over me and my scalp tingled. "Uh, sure, Sugar Pie. Yeah, I'm okay." I sat down on the overstuffed armchair and put my feet on the coffee table, then shut my eyes and leaned my head back. I could hear the horrible hissing of gas and could smell that never-to-be-forgotten stink. I tried to fill my lungs with air.

After a few minutes, I stood up and walked back to the master bathroom and locked the door. I sat on the toilet and leaned my head forward, my face in my hands. Tears streamed down my face and I felt so bad, so guilty. I saw the balloon in Times Square floating on the Saigon River and then the sailors with cloths around their faces like cowboy bandits hauling the dead sailor onto the minesweeper's deck. Hissing noise mixed with diesel engine rumble and the exhaust smell swirled with the acrid French cigarette smoke and the stink of rotting human innards and chestnuts cooking over charcoal on Columbus Circle in Manhattan. I could see it, I could hear it, I could smell it. I could taste sickly sweet and salt spit. I couldn't catch my breath, and I was chilled.

I had spurned that man's friendship and then he died. Lonely and alone and fucked over. Killed by a rocket's concussion and blown into the brown Saigon River water. He was probably about the age my kids were that Thanksgiving Day.

My tears stopped. All I saw was the bathroom tile. All I heard was the faint fan noise moving warm air out of the heating vent. All I smelled was the Dial soap and Pert shampoo. I rinsed my mouth out with cold water. A vague exhaustion that I could not explain overcame me. I could not think, my brain was empty and blank. My limbs felt heavy, leaden. Without bothering to wash my face or even dry the tears, I lay on the bedcover and fell into a deep, dreamless sleep.

I awoke with a start, disoriented. "Hey, Dad. Mom says to get you up. You missed the whole game. Grandma, Uncle Rick, and Auntie Ginny just arrived and we're gonna eat in about twenty minutes. Mom wants you to carve the turkey. Or you want me to do it for you?"

I walked over to my son and wrapped my arms around him and hugged him. He gave me a weird and quizzical look. "Uh...Dad? What's that for? You have a weird dream or sumpin'?"

"Nope, I'm just grateful for you, and Mom, and your bratty sister, and all that I have. You carve the bird, I'll assist. Happy Thanksgiving to us, buddy."

Eye Patch Leadership

The Tet Offensive had ended a month earlier. The Saigon River had become quiet, almost peaceful. Assault and patrol boats could travel the full length of their areas of operations and not get shot at. No rockets whizzed past out of the mangroves, rubber trees, or sugarcane. No rifle shots bounced off the hull. No mines douched out the entire column of boats. It was so quiet.

A month earlier, it had certainly not been quiet. Firefights every time they moved the boats. All troop landings fiercely opposed. Trucks trying to resupply the boats from Nha Be and Cu Chi ambushed or mined. The sailors' flak vests and helmets, rarely used before Tet, were now worn all the time. They stunk of sweat and dried blood and mildew. But the sailors wore them.

Two American advisors sat on the upper deck of the assault group's command boat. One was a US Navy lieutenant, the advisor to the assault group's Vietnamese commanding officer. The other was a US Marine Corps captain, advisor to the embarked South Vietnamese Ranger company's CO. Both had been in-country for ten months, arriving in April 1967.

The navy lieutenant had spent his entire time in-country advising the river assault group. The marine had spent his first three months assigned to a company of marines in I Corps near Danang. Then he was sent to advise the rangers, their previous advisor having been wounded and sent home. The two Americans had been on many operations together and were buddies.

The boats peacefully moved upriver to their home base. Despite the lull in fighting, all the guns were manned. The two advisors sat in the shade of the command boat's canopy, clad in flak vests, helmets on their heads, their radios beside them on the deck. The navy officer was reading a week-old *Newsweek*, the marine a two-day-old copy of *Stars and Stripes*.

"Dave, looks like *Newsweek*'s not been listening to that bullshit about how we scored a great victory during Tet. This is a pretty good article. A post mortem on the whole thing. Lots of blame to go around."

The marine looked up from his newspaper. "Yeah, I read that. We certainly got caught with our pants around our ankles reading *Playboy* on the thunder throne. I'm not sure how history's going to look at that one, Ed."

Ed thumbed through the magazine and stopped at a picture of Moshe Dayan, the Israeli defense minister. "Look at this guy. Throw an eye patch on Yul Brynner and he could play him in some movie. This is what you call charisma, and I understand the guy's a pussy magnet."

"For real. Before that six-day war in June, he was out with us in I Corps as an observer. He said he was observing 'modern warfare.' Shit, he should have observed his own troops for that." The marine looked around and then picked up his radio and made a routine communications check. "I met the guy. He went on a patrol with us."

"No, shit. What was that like? A bunch of bodyguards around?"

"Nope, he put on a flak vest and a helmet, grabbed an M16, and went for a walk with us in the boonies. We had the colonel accompanying him, but that was it. Asked a lot of what I thought were pretty pertinent questions. Y'know, 'Why you doing this and why'd you do that and how good is your intel?' Spent a lot of time looking at the gear we carried and how we were organized when on patrol. Seemed friendly enough. Smiled a lot."

"Get in a fight?"

"We skirmished outside a village, but that wasn't much. Got into a real firefight later on a trail. He and the colonel got airlifted out the next morning and then I think he went out with another company, then went over to the flyboys in Danang. I heard he was real interested in the Phantoms."

"Yeah, I guess those old French Mirage jets are getting tired and they must be looking to replace them." Ed got up and stretched. He looked around at the riverbanks. "Another half an hour to go and then we drop you and the boy scouts off."

Dave nodded. "I was thinking about Dayan. They took on Egypt, Syria, and Jordan, three pretty well-armed neighbors. And then six days later, they're done. They won.

"And while they're doing that, our brass is making noises about lights at the ends of tunnels, winning hearts and minds, and something about playing dominoes. Our secretary of defense is fighting the war with a slide rule and statistics, measuring everything but my dick."

Ed laughed. "Six-day war for Dayan in June. Then, what, eight months later over here and the guys we're supposedly beating the shit out of decide to go on a rampage all over the country? Think we got a leadership problem, Dave?"

The marine smiled, thought for a moment and took a drink from his canteen. "Look at Dayan and look at our secretary of defense. I think the only thing our guy has over Dayan is that our guy has a bigger selection of neckties. I've got an idea."

Three weeks later, the most senior administrative assistant in the Pentagon opened a package addressed to the secretary of defense and marked "personal." It took a while for her to recognize what it was.

When the secretary of defense returned from a meeting half an hour later, he found in his inbox an olive drab eye patch.

HOMO

"**A**dmiral, I'd like to close your door," said Captain Alan Michelson, his hand on the doorknob.

The three-star admiral looked at his chief of staff with a frown. "Al, every time you start a conversation with wanting to close my door, I know I'm going to hate what you'll tell me. Sure, shut the door and have a seat. You want some coffee?"

The chief of staff told the yeoman in the outer office to not disturb him and the admiral, shut the door, and took a seat in one of the armchairs by the gray metal desk.

"I'll pass on the coffee, Admiral. Stomach's acidity already in the red zone and I don't need to be any more jittery."

"That good, huh, Al? What mess are you bringing me now?"

"It's a delicate one, Admiral."

"Like how delicate, Al?"

"Like delicate enough that I don't think we want the embassy involved."

"I'm all ears."

Captain Michelson took a deep breath, let it out, and leaned forward, elbows on his knees, staring at the dark blue carpet. He looked up and locked eyes with his boss.

"Sir, the Vietnamese commander of their fleet command in I Corps told me that one of our advisors is engaging in homosexual activity. A lieutenant advising the skipper of one of their gunboats out of Danang."

"What kind of homosexual activity?" asked the admiral without expression.

"Rumors of mutual cocksucking with a Vietnamese sailor, a member of the gunboat's crew."

"What do you mean, 'rumors,' Al?"

"Just that, sir. Rumors. No evidence, no witnesses. At least that's what I was told. No investigations or requests for investigations by the Vietnamese. So far."

"Who said this to you?"

"Captain Vinh, commander of their deep water assets. The destroyer escort, patrol craft, gunboats, and those LSTs we just turned over."

"What your take on Vinh? Have I met him?"

"You met him, sir. A few times. Last time was at the ambassador's residence and before that at the fleet turnover conference. Fairly tall for a Vietnamese, gray hair."

"Yeah, Vinh. Seemed like a decent guy. Just got back from Newport and War College a year ago?"

"That's the guy, Admiral. He seemed genuinely embarrassed by it all and made a trip to Saigon just to meet with me and discuss the...allegations. He thinks the advisor is the best one he has in Danang. But in his opinion, we have to get him out of there."

Reading the look on his boss's face, the chief of staff answered the unasked question. "Vinh's a square shooter, Admiral. This isn't any of their bullshit politics and conniving, sir. He'd never have come to us if it wasn't a real problem in his mind."

"Who's the advisor?"

"Alexander. Phillip Alexander. Lieutenant. Nine months in-country, three to go. In the zone for lieutenant commander, and detailers have him slated for an XO job on a destroyer. His boss in Danang is Commander Steve Brooks. Steve's also Vinh's counterpart."

"Phil Alexander? He was the engineer on the best can in my flotilla. That ship had the best engineering department in its squadron and the flotilla. Best in the whole Atlantic fleet as far as I was concerned." The admiral ran his hand across this face, staring at his chief of staff. "Married?"

"No, sir."

"How's he done so far as an advisor, Al?"

"You signed off on his last fitness report, sir. Steve gave him a four-oh fitrep and recommended early promotion and early command. You endorsed both those recommendations very positively, sir."

"Indeed I did, Al. Indeed I did." The admiral leaned forward, elbows on his desk, fingers steepled at his lips. Then he sighed, pushed away from the desk, stood up and walked into the bathroom at the corner of his office.

Captain Michelson leaned back in his chair, stretched, and scratched his balding head. The sounds of flushing and running faucets came out of the bathroom, followed soon thereafter by his boss.

"Al, let's take a walk around the corridors and the compound. People get nervous when they see my door closed." Reaching into a little refrigerator behind his desk, the admiral took out two cans of Coke and gave one to Captain Michelson.

For twenty minutes, the two men walked through the headquarters building and around the compound perimeter, talking in low voices. This problem was unique. Sensitive. Compared to body counts, transferring American assets to the South Vietnamese Navy, and dealing with the army and the embassy, many would consider it insignificant. But neither of these two men did.

They walked back into the building and down the hall to the admiral's office.

"Okay. Here's what I want you to do. By 1700, give me a quick summary of the situation, taking our discussion into account, what decisions must be made, what the law requires, and your recommendation. No copies. The only ones going to read this will be you and me. Don't give it to the yeoman to type. If you can't type, write it by hand. Do not date it. Do not put any 'to' and 'from' and 'subject' on it. Don't sign it. Then meet with me at 1800."

The chief of staff looked at his watch. It was 1430. "Aye aye, sir."

Two hours later, Captain Michelson walked into the admiral's office and handed his boss a sealed envelope.

"Thanks. Come back in here at 1800. If I'm on the phone or talking to someone, just walk in."

At 1800, the admiral was talking to a civilian and an army two-star general when Captain Michelson knocked on the door jam and walked into the office. Addressing his two guests, the admiral stood up, thanked them for taking the time to brief him, and said he regretted not being able to join them for drinks at the American Club. As he led them out of the office, he introduced them to his chief of staff.

Smiling and shaking his head at the chief yeoman sitting at the desk in the outer office, the admiral said, "Fucking DC paper pushers trying to get some combat pay and souvenirs, Chief. Please get us coffee and two cups."

The admiral and Captain Michelson sat in silence waiting for the chief to bring the carafe of coffee and two paper cups. No cream, no sugar. After putting the tray on the admiral's desk, the chief walked out and shut the door behind him. Captain Michelson poured a cup of coffee for his boss and another for himself. He took a sip and made a grimace.

"Panther piss, Admiral. Hot, black, panther piss."

His boss opened his middle drawer and took out a folded sheet of paper. He read it through again.

"Al, your handwriting is worse than even mine. You should have been a doctor."

"I thought about going to med school, Admiral. But I figured I'd kill fewer people in the military than I would as a doctor."

The admiral chuckled. Waving the paper, he said, "Good job on this. Give me your verbal summary of what it says and let's talk."

For an hour the chief of staff talked, interrupted by questions and comments from his boss.

Until they formally learned of any homosexual activity, they were not required by navy regulations or the Uniform Code of Military Justice to do anything. But if formally notified or requested, or if they had a *reasonable* suspicion of such activity, an investigation was required. Depending on the findings, action ranging from doing nothing to filing charges would be dictated. Being told of rumors did not constitute formal notification. An investigation could always be initiated at the admiral's discretion.

The South Vietnamese Navy captain who had reported the rumors was considered a man of integrity. There appeared to be nothing for him to gain personally by reporting such rumors. His actions were a warning of possible problems. In the opinion of Captain Michelson, there was probably a factual basis for the rumors.

In those days, Vietnamese culture was similar to America's in commonly expressed view that homosexuality was an aberration and an immoral character flaw. Both navies considered homosexuality a reason for discharge. Homosexual acts were crimes in both navies.

Vietnam was turning into a public relations disaster in the United States. Public sentiment was increasingly against the American involvement in Southeast Asia and the press was ravenous for any hint of fiasco or scandal. The war correspondents were sensitive to rumors and quick to sniff out their source. Vicious rumors could destroy a unit's battle efficiency and morale faster than defeat in combat. Like a festering boil or tumor, a rumor could damage everything around it, and was hard to excise.

The intercom on the admiral's desk interrupted Michelson's summary. It was the chief yeoman. He had taken the liberty of ordering hamburgers, French fries, and Cokes from the snack bar.

"Bring them in, Chief," replied the admiral. "We'll take a break."

"Al, Bureau of Personnel is waiting for the flag board to meet before they cut you orders," said the admiral after swallowing a mouthful of burger and fries. "I'm not blowing smoke up your ass when I tell you I've been strongly recommending you for selection to rear admiral. You're the best officer I've ever had working for me. You'll make a good flag officer. The navy needs men like you as flags, especially now with this mess going on."

Captain Michelson took another bite of fries, smiled and shook his head. "Admiral, I'm not holding my breath. Making flag would be my dream come true, but the pyramid gets awfully skinny at the top. If I make it, great. If I don't, I'll be disappointed, but I understand the odds."

"Where do you want to go if you're selected?"

"I'd like a cruiser destroyer flotilla, sir. Or maybe use my graduate degree and lead a technical branch in the Bureau of Ordnance."

"And if you don't get picked? Retire?"

"That depends what BUPERS has in store for me. If it's a fun job or one that improves my chances at the next selection board, I won't put in my papers. But if not, I'll probably retire." The chief of staff took another bite of hamburger and through a mouthful said, "I think my wife would like that. Hell, I know she'd like that."

Dumping their paper plates, napkins, ketchup packets, and soda cans into the wastebasket, they returned to their discussion of the problem at hand.

Lieutenant Philip Alexander was one of the top performers of his rank in the in-country navy. The gunboat he was advising was doing well and had become the vessel that Captain Vinh relied on the most to handle the tough jobs. Alexander had 102 days left before he'd leave Vietnam for his next job as the executive officer of a destroyer. His replacement was in counterinsurgency school in San Diego and due to arrive in-country in eighty-eight days.

"Al, good summary. Let's talk about what you recommend I do."

"Sir, I laid out what I see as only three possible ways to go. First, we do nothing. We do not act on the rumors. Let Alexander stay in place and finish out his tour and send him on his way to his next job."

The admiral nodded but said nothing.

"I see problems with that, Admiral. To me it's like burying our heads in the sand. Captain Vinh is nervous about keeping Alexander aboard that gunboat. Rumors don't die. If something overt happens, we could be in for a real scandal. It could get messy if some correspondent starts asking why we didn't do something sooner. I think you, in particular, Admiral, could become a real target and it could hurt you later. It's no secret around here, sir, that you're in the running to be the next Chief of Naval Operations."

The admiral barked. "Al, until I get my orders, that's just a rumor. Just like the rumors about Alexander. Let me worry about my career. Your next recommendation?"

"Apologies, sir, I didn't mean to be presumptuous about your career."

As if swatting at a fly, the admiral waved his hand. "Fuck it. Go on."

"The second alternative is to bring him down here to headquarters as soon as we can. That takes the heat off Captain Vinh and separates Alexander from the rumor source. We keep him here until it's time for him to rotate out. There are a couple of good lieutenants with over half a year to go on the staff that we could send up to Danang to take Alexander's place."

"What would you have Alexander doing here, Al?"

The chief of staff smiled. "Well, sir, I could really use a deputy. It would be nice to go from a twenty-hour work day to a sixteen-hour one. You'd have a much better rested chief of staff, Admiral. And I could keep an eye on Alexander and an ear to the rumor mill."

The admiral chuckled and Captain Michelson continued.

"He could also become your aide, sir. Your current aide is one of the guys I would recommend take Alexander's place if we bring him down here."

The admiral nodded his head, but said nothing, waiting for his chief of staff to continue.

"The problem I see with this action is that I don't think the rumors will stop, no matter where Alexander is or how he behaves. It's just one step removed from burying our heads in the sand, although we would have done something. We would have taken him off that gunboat and brought him into our enclave. But how would we answer the correspondent or congressman who asks us if we knew we had a homosexual aboard and why we did nothing about that? That's another potential scandal or public relations disaster, sir."

With tight lips and a quick shake of his head, the admiral motioned for Captain Michelson to continue.

"The last action to consider, sir, is to bring Michelson down here and conduct an investigation of alleged homosexual conduct. By the book. If nothing comes out of the investigation, we've conducted our due diligence and we're done. Alexander can move on. If something is uncovered, then we follow the rules and do whatever the law requires of us. We do this quickly and efficiently. That will protect us from the question of why we didn't act."

"I'm going to pee, Al." The admiral got up and went to his bathroom. He left the door open as he urinated, flushed the toilet, and washed his hands. Sitting down heavily, he rubbed his hand across his face.

"Al, you laid out three scenarios for me. Do nothing. Bring Alexander down here to work until he rotates out. Or bring him down and conduct an investigation."

"Yes, sir."

"What do you recommend?"

"Admiral, I recommend we follow the book. We bring him down here and conduct an investigation. That exposes Naval Forces Vietnam to the least criticism."

The admiral stared at the captain for a long silent minute.

"I'm not going to hang Alexander out to dry, Al. An investigation will brand him for the rest of the time he's in the navy, no matter what the security, no matter what the outcome. He'll always be known as the guy who was accused of being queer. I don't want that. I don't give a shit about his sexual preferences. The man's an outstanding officer and the navy needs him. I need him. I'm not going to throw talent away."

Captain Michelson sat silent, watching his boss, who stood up, paced behind his desk then sat down again.

"Al, here's what I'm ordering you to do. ASAP, bring Alexander down here and make him my aide. Assign whichever of the lieutenants on the staff you think best suited to advise that gunboat skipper. Let me know who it is. I want to retain veto power. Have him stay here until Alexander arrives and can give him a briefing. Then ship him up there as fast as you can. Let Captain Vinh know he's getting a good replacement. Belay that last one, I'll call him and tell him."

"Investigation, sir?"

"No fucking way am I going to start a witch hunt based on rumors from who the fuck knows where."

"Aye aye, sir. Anything else?"

"Yes, Al. Two things. One, find someone who's underemployed and assign him to be your deputy. Two, I appreciate that your recommendation was made for what you consider to be the good of the navy and to protect me. I appreciate that. But this is my decision, and I think keeping a man like Alexander is what's best for the navy. I don't care if he doesn't like women or even humans. If there's any flak from this, that'll be my problem to handle. If it costs me my fourth star, it's still worth the price."

"Yes, sir."

"Let's you and I get out of here. This has been a long day."

That night Captain Michelson wrote his wife a letter. In it he wrote that he thought the admiral was the most courageous man he had ever met. He told his wife that he doubted his own ability to make the really hard decisions needed of a flag officer. Not decisions of tactics or strategy, but a decision of people and doing what is right.

Lieutenant Alexander spent his last ninety-nine days in-country as the flag aide to the Commander, Naval Forces Vietnam. His departing fitness report from the admiral recommended him for accelerated promotion and command at sea. After twenty-six years of active duty, then-Captain Alexander retired to Seattle to work as the head of design and engineering for a shipyard, living with his long-time companion on Mercer Island just outside Seattle.

Captain Michelson was not picked to become a rear admiral. His last fitness report from the admiral was a good one, an outstanding one, but not as good as the previous one. And it was not good enough for the selection board trying to pick the best of the best. After a tour as the Professor of Military Science at the UCLA Navy ROTC unit, Michelson retired from the navy, got his state teaching credential, and became a high school mathematics teacher in Monterey.

GECKO

Twelve hours. That's all he had left. Twelve more hours and then he'd strap himself into seat 36C of World Airways flight 612 and say, "Goodbye, Vietnam." Lieutenant Andy Vogel, US Navy, had been in-country one year and two days and he was ready to leave. In fact, he had been ready to leave after about seven days. But he had done his duty. And done a pretty good job of it. Now he was a short-timer—so short he could do pull-ups on the lowest rung of a bar stool.

Three days ago, he had turned over his command of the patrol boat squadron to his replacement. *A very good guy*, thought Andy. That night he had burned his faded jungle fatigues and made it a point to talk and shake hands with each of his officers and sailors. The next morning he had put on khakis and climbed aboard a Huey for a quick lift to Nha Be to debrief his boss. *Another really good guy*, thought Andy. Then he took a jeep ride to Saigon to fill out forms, pee into a bottle, give blood to some vampire corpsman, and bend over for the doc. He checked into the Le Qui Don, a little hotel not far from the Presidential Palace. The US Army had leased the Le Qui Don to use for a Bachelor Officers Quarters, but most of the assigned beds went to many of the navy officers

143

working in Saigon, or out-processing and waiting for the freedom bird home.

The old hotel was pretty threadbare and had an impressive collection of insects, lizards, mold, and mildew on all its walls. But the dripping shower heads could produce hot water and the noisy air conditioners spewed out cool and dry air with a hint of must. Compared to a year of life on the rivers, the Le Qui Don was pretty fine living.

After taking a late morning nap in his air-conditioned room, Andy shaved and showered, put on fresh khakis, and buffed his jungle boots. He hitched a ride with some MPs to the admiral's headquarters for a debrief and farewell handshakes with the admiral and the chief of staff. Andy was officially done. Nothing to do between now and getting on the plane except sleep, eat, and drink.

Or so he thought.

One of the admiral's staff, a lieutenant commander, asked Andy for a favor. It seemed that this staff puke was the senior resident of the Le Qui Don. As such, he was responsible for having a duty officer at the front desk from curfew, which lasted from the 2200 start of curfew until 0600 the next morning. The fellow scheduled for the duty that night was inconsiderate enough to have had a malarial relapse and was in no shape to stand the watch. Would Andy mind taking the duty? There really wasn't much to the duty officer job other than call the Saigon operations center once every hour on the hour, and answer the phone if the VC decided to pull another Tet uprising. To return the favor, the lieutenant commander would give Andy a ride to Tan Son Nhut the next morning and buy him an early lunch before he got on his flight home.

Andy said, sure, he'd do it. He had absolutely nothing else planned and it was obvious the Saigon warrior needed a warm body.

Andy strolled around Saigon for a bit, and visited the big PX in Cho Lon to kill some time. After an early dinner and a beer, he took another nap. At 2200 he went down to the Le Qui Don's small lobby. The staff officer was there, signing the night orders and giving Andy temporary custody of the duty officer's .45 pistol, full ammunition clip, holster, and cleaning kit.

Andy wished the lieutenant commander a good night, and sat behind the front desk. In a chair next to him sat the night manager, an older Vietnamese man. Outside the hotel door that opened onto the street corner sat a policeman in a concrete kiosk. The policeman wore a helmet and flak jacket. Andy called in on the phone to tell whoever was at the other end of the line that he had assumed the watch and had nothing else to report. All was in order.

He opened up Joyce's *Finnegan's Wake.* Since his last semester in college over five years ago, Andy had tried about thirty times to read it. He had never made it past page sixteen. Now that he had a whole night of nothing to do and a long airplane flight ahead of him, he was determined to make a dent in it. Maybe even understand what the hell it all meant.

As the old gentleman sitting next to him dozed off, Andy turned to the first page and tried to read. Through the open door he could hear the nasal twang of a Vietnamese song coming out of the policeman's portable radio. The only other noises were the night manager's deep breathing and the quiet chirping of whatever insects or lizards were in the lobby.

After thirty minutes of reading the same sentence over and over again, Andy shut the book. It was useless. He looked around the desk and opened the desk drawer. Inside was a pad of paper, a ballpoint pen, and a stash of well-read and worn *Playboy* magazines. Surprised at his complete lack of shame, Andy dropped Joyce in the wastepaper basket next to the desk and opened up the top *Playboy*, last year's January issue. Much to his delight, the centerfold was still intact and there was a short story by Jean Shepherd.

By 0400, Andy had read each *Playboy* cover to cover. He had walked outside and tried to chat with the policeman, who spoke worse English than Andy spoke Vietnamese. He had peed. He had decided not to write any letters home since he'd be there before they'd arrive. He was bored. His snoring deskmate was not much of a conversationalist.

High upon the wall across from the desk, two geckos lay in wait for some juicy insects. These two kept Andy's attention for about half a minute. Afraid he'd fall asleep if he didn't do something, Andy decided he'd clean the .45.

Cleaning that pistol must have been a common occurrence at the Le Qui Don. The gun was spotless. Even the bullets in the clip were polished. Nevertheless, Andy took the clip out and made sure the gun was empty with no round in the chamber. Then he took all the bullets out of the clip and polished each one carefully. Next, he took the clip apart and polished and oiled it. Admiring the beauty of polished ammunition and smoothly functioning clip, he reloaded the gleaming bullets into the clip.

Then he turned to the pistol. Brows furrowed with concentration, Andy stripped the gun down until it was a collection of pieces and springs on the desktop.

Using oil and swabs from the cleaning kit, Andy meticulously cleaned and oiled the already-clean and oiled pistol parts. He leaned back in his chair, thinking that whoever designed and built the gun had to be a genius. The policeman walked in on his hourly visit to make sure everything was okay. Andy gave him a smile and thumbs-up. Then he started to reassemble the gun as the policeman returned to his kiosk.

The gun was all put back together. Andy polished it and the clip. Then he worked the slide several times, cocking and uncocking the gun. He put the clip in and took it out several times. Everything worked smoothly. He worked the slide a few more times, moved the clip in and out a few more times, and admired his work. His wristwatch said it was 0500. Only an hour more of guarding the Le Qui Don lobby to go. Then he could go back to his room for a hot shower and shave, pack his bag, and be off to the airport.

He picked up the phone for his next-to-last report that all was well. Feeling happy and content that he was almost out of Vietnam, he chatted with the watch stander on the other end of the line, a soldier from Milwaukee who had just come back from R&R in Bangkok. As they discussed the finer points of Thai pulchritude,

Andy idly polished the gun. Andy was looking at the lone gecko on the wall in front of him. Its buddy was gone.

Andy hung up the phone and, without giving much thought to it, worked the slide for what must have been the thirteenth time since he had cleaned the gun. To make sure the sights had no dust on them, Andy pointed the gun at the gecko and aimed it, lining up the front blade and rear notch sights on the little lizard's head. Certain that he was aiming an unloaded weapon, Andy pulled the trigger to uncock the gun.

The .45 is iconic among hand weapons. It is not very accurate, it packs a big wallop, and it is extremely loud. The .45 in Andy's right hand demonstrated all three of these traits. It was also loaded.

When he pulled the trigger, the gun fired a thunderous roar, momentarily deafening Andy and his instantly awake desk partner, who jolted back in his desk chair and somersaulted backward onto the floor. The heavy bullet knocked a foot-wide crater out of the plaster and cement wall. And it missed the gecko by a good four feet, high and to the right.

The policeman rushed in, his M16 at the ready, and found a horrified Andy trying to help the night manager to his feet. Andy tried to smile and explain with gestures, but then realized that waving a smoking gun around at a guy with an automatic weapon in his hands was not a good idea. He pointed the gun at the floor, took out the clip, worked the slide to eject the round in the chamber, and put on the safety as he placed the gun gingerly on the desk.

With both hands waving in the air with thumbs extended, Andy babbled and gestured to the policeman. "Okay, okay, everything okay. Numbah one. No sweat, okay."

The policeman went out to his kiosk and picked up his phone. About a minute later, the duty officer's phone rang.

It was the soldier from Milwaukee. He said that the Vietnamese police just called the MPs in the watch center and reported that a shot went off in the Le Qui Don's lobby. Andy, his voice and hands still shaking, confirmed the report and nervously giggled that it was an accidental discharge. Nobody hurt. Everything okay.

Andy spent the remaining hour of his watch cleaning the .45 and sweeping up the plaster and cement pieces.

The gecko was still in its spot on the wall. Andy wondered if it was dead and somehow still held on, or if geckos were too stupid or too brave to get scared and leave.

After 0600 that morning, Andy never touched a handgun again in his life. That is quite a remarkable feat for someone who made a thirty-year career out of the military.

GRAVE ROBBERS

Le Dinh Truoc was born in 1947 in Cao Bang, a village on the banks of the Bang Giang River, close to Vietnam's northern border with China. His father owned half a dozen cargo-carrying sampans, moving goods up and down the river. In 1954, after the French left and the country was partitioned, his family stayed in Cao Bang rather than emigrate to the South. While being a successful trader was not exactly a classical socialist profession, Truoc's family preferred the government of the North to what they considered the crooks of the South.

Truoc attended the military academy and graduated at the age of twenty-one. The Tet Offensive had just ended. Many People's Army and National Liberation Front units had suffered devastating casualties. In several provinces in the south, the NLF was completely annihilated. Whole cadres of southerners loyal to unification had been wiped out, with no reserves to take their places.

Because of his familiarity with the riverine environment, Truoc and a platoon of People's Army soldiers were sent down the Ho Chi Minh trail to the Saigon River. Truoc and his men were to replace a now-dead unit of NLF fighters who had operated along the river's banks. Out of the twenty-eight men who started the journey,

149

twenty reached the Saigon River. Eight succumbed to malaria, dysentery, bombs, and napalm.

Three months later, Truoc's platoon was down to fourteen. Dysentery, American soldiers, and helicopter gunships had taken their toll. But his platoon was making the Americans and their puppets pay dearly.

With careful use of ambushes and booby-trapped landing areas, his men strangled the amphibious landings of the South Vietnamese Navy's river assault boats. Underwater mines, rockets, machine guns, and mortars killed the South Vietnamese and American soldiers as the boats tried to drop their bow ramps and send the troops ashore. Those soldiers that did reach the riverbanks found themselves in fields of claymore minds and Bouncing Betties, or a crossfire of AK-47s.

Truoc ordered his men to retreat into the underground bunkers and tunnels as soon as the artillery, air strikes, or gunships appeared. He was a brave man, always making sure his men were safely into the tunnels before he followed them.

The South Vietnamese boats moved upriver early one spring morning. Villagers from the little hamlet near the big bridge at Phu Cuong had watched them leave. One of the farmers reported to Comrade Truoc that the boats had been empty except for their crewmen. No soldiers. Seven boats had motored upriver: the two little ones that trailed the minesweeping gear, the big monitor bristling with guns, the command boat with more guns and radios, and three big troop carriers.

After thanking the villager, Truoc shared the information with the provincial cadre leader. They knew that a platoon of American soldiers and two platoons of their puppets were on a sweep near the Michelin rubber plantation. About one hundred men. The boats were obviously going upriver to extract the three platoons and bring them back to Phu Cuong.

An ambush was planned. Just north of the village of Phu Hiep, the river curved back on itself, forcing the column of boats to slow down and telescope, clumping the seven boats into one easy target. That would be the killing zone.

Slow and cumbersome, the assault boats could not race out of harm's way. Instead, they relied on their steel armor for protection, and always narrowed their exposure by turning into the heart of the incoming fire while they returned fire with heavy machineguns, cannons, and mortars. Often helicopter gunships or air strikes joined in. Sometimes artillery. Then the assault boats would land their troops on the riverbank and the soldiers would sweep through the area, looking for the ambushers and counting the dead.

Before Tet, the Americans and southerners found very little during their sweeps. But now they often found themselves the hunted instead of the hunters as they walked, then crawled on their bellies, through minefields and booby traps, pinned down by a murderous crossfire.

Truoc was a shrewd battlefield tactician. He had an intuitive feel for battle. His men's ammunition, casualties, enemy's capabilities, and an uncanny sense of timing dictated his commands.

In the late afternoon, the platoon sat in wait, hiding along the sharp bend in the river just north of Phu Hiep. They were waiting for the column of boats with its cargo of troops. The plan was simple and proven: detonate an underwater mine and open fire with rockets and AK-47s until the boats turned toward them and returned fire; wait until the bow ramps dropped and the soldiers were exposed, and recommence firing; watch the advisors on the command boat, and if the American advisor picked up his radio, withdraw to the tunnels. A radio call meant that soon artillery, helicopter gunships, or an air strike would rain death on the platoon.

Truoc could hear the low diesel rumble from the boat engines upriver. Within a few minutes, he could see the two little minesweepers and then the big monitor, troop carriers, and command boat. When the monitor was past and the first of the three troop carriers directly in front of him, Truoc gave a silent hand signal.

A column of water a meter in diameter shot up from the river, lifting the front of the leading troop carrier out of the water. The boat stopped and drifted. Three rocket trails snaked out from the riverbank, two passing between boats and striking the tree line across the river. The third rocket exploded on the monitor's deckhouse. The monitor wheeled out of control across the river current. The other boats turned toward Truoc and his men, shooting blindly with their machineguns, raking the riverbank. With buzzing bumblebee noises, the bullets flew over his men's heads.

The two troop carriers that remained operational dropped their bow ramps, and the soldiers spilled out onto the hard laterite soil. Truoc's men reopened fire, trying to kill the soldiers. Through his binoculars, Truoc watched the American advisor on the command boat, radio handset to his ear, a finger in his other ear trying to block out the cacophony of gunfire. Another American stood beside him, a map in his hand. It was time to retreat.

Truoc signaled his men to move back to the tunnels. He heard the sharp crack of booby traps as the soldiers tried to move inland. Running in a crouched position through the tree line, Truoc made sure that every one of his men was on his way to the sanctuary of the tunnels. Satisfied that no weapons had been discarded and happy that he saw no blood trails, he turned to follow his men. One of the squad leaders was waiting for him, holding the camouflaged tunnel entrance open. With a wave and a smile, Truoc shouldered his AK-47 and stooped to enter the tunnel.

An American 155 mm howitzer shell exploded about five meters above the tunnel entrance. The squad leader and Truoc died instantly, killed by the concussion. The rest of the platoon, although temporarily deafened and dazed, was saved by the thick tunnel walls.

That night the twelve surviving members of the platoon wrote Truoc's name, rank, and the date of his death on a piece of paper and put it into a little plastic bottle emptied of DEET insect repellent. They capped the bottle and tied it around Truoc's neck with a nylon cord salvaged from an American flare parachute. Then they took his broken body to a nearby sugarcane field and buried him in the hard soil. For Truoc's shroud they used one of the black plastic bags the Americans used for garbage or when they cleaned out their latrines. The platoon wrote down the grave's location in a log they had carried since leaving the North. Truoc was the sixteenth entry.

Truoc's body lay in the ground of the land for which he had fought and died. But it was not the soil of his family, of his ancestors. That soil was far north, near the Bang Giang River, near his mother and father and sister.

Eight years later, after the reunification of the country, a team of People's Army of Vietnam soldiers, guided by the platoon's logbook and its one surviving member, exhumed a skeleton wrapped in black plastic. Around the skeleton's neck was a nylon cord necklace with a DEET bottle attached.

A few months later, the skeleton's mother received a letter from the Ministry of Defense. It said that on the first of March 1977, her son Truoc had been buried as a Hero of the People in the new veterans' cemetery near Cu Chi.

* * *

A dozen years had passed since the letter from the Ministry of Defense. Truoc's father had passed away. His mother was a healthy and active sixty-seven, the grandmother of two boys twelve and ten years old. Their mother, Truoc's sister, was married to a rice merchant. They all lived in the same house that Truoc had grown up in.

All five were in Cu Chi at the veterans' cemetery, standing by Truoc's grave, having traveled the 1,300 kilometers from Cao Bang by bus, train, taxi, and foot. They were there to bring Truoc home.

The day before, they had visited the local government officials and asked to have Truoc's remains transferred to the veterans' cemetery in Cao Bang. While sympathetic to the family's request, the cemetery manager said he could not do that. Official policy said that veterans of the American war were to be buried near where they fell. And he had no funds to either exhume a body or to ship remains to another cemetery. He, like all the other cemetery managers, had funds only to bury veterans.

Truoc's sister looked at her brother's headstone, adorned with the engraving "Hero of the People." She scuffed the soil with her sandal. Unlike most of the hard laterite of the area, the cemetery's dirt was soft and loose. Her husband was staring at her, watching her studying the ground. She raised her head and locked eyes with him. He nodded and she smiled. They took the bus back to the guesthouse. While the grandmother napped, the parents and children shopped.

Just before midnight, a taxi dropped the five of them at the cemetery. As her son-in-law took a burlap bag out of the taxi's trunk, Truoc's mother told the driver to come back in two hours.

For the next two hours, the two boys and their father used the shovel and spade from the burlap bag to dig down to Truoc's remains. Truoc's sister and mother took turns holding the flashlight and giving unsolicited digging advice. A wooden box, a half a meter square by a quarter meter in depth was opened. A cotton bag of bones was lifted out and put into the burlap bag. With considerable effort, the two boys and their father wrestled the small headstone out of the earth, brushed it off, and put it in the bag. Then they shoveled the dirt back into the hole and walked back to the cemetery access road where the taxi was waiting.

Three days later, Truoc's mother asked the government officials in Cao Bang for permission to bury her son in the local veterans' cemetery. The cemetery manager said he would be happy to arrange it but that he needed documentation to obtain a headstone. Her son-in-law walked back to his motorbike. He returned with the headstone and the cotton bag holding Truoc's remains, stenciled with his name, rank, and date of death.

And so, twenty years after his death, Le Dinh Truoc was laid to rest in the soil of his ancestors.

MARK-MARK

The dogs of Vietnam, except for the few that led the pampered lives as pets of the rich in Saigon, were a scruffy lot. Medium size, low foreheads, short coats, nondescript colors, slit eyes. Shifty, wary. Always on the lookout for something to sniff and eat. Slinking around the edges of villages and bases. They were the product of centuries of mixed breeding. No pedigrees there. No inbreeding with genetic weaknesses. The beasts were hardy and tough. Survivors. Ugly. Even the puppies were ugly, not cute nor cuddly. That description fit all the dogs of Phu Cuong, except for one.

Phu Cuong was a small town on the Saigon River, well north of the urban sprawl of the South Vietnamese capital. It was the provincial capital of the area that bordered Cambodia. Small, smelly, Phu Cuong was where the river assault group parked its boats when not on an operation. It was the place where the fuel trucks could reach the boats, where the officer's jeep was parked, where the mail was dropped off, where the American and Vietnamese sailors could walk around during the day relatively secure that as long as the sun was up they would probably not get shot. It was the place where the monotony of military rations could be broken with a bowl of *pho*—the ubiquitous Vietnamese noodle soup—or a beer, or a croissant with a bittersweet caffeine-laden cup of *cafe sua*.

At the east end of Phu Cuong was a lacquer factory. Despite the war going on around them, old men artists produced masterpieces on scrap plywood with eggshells and lacquer. After his first full night's sleep in over a week of combat operations on the river, the American treated himself to a breakfast of *pho*, checked his men and boats, left instructions with his senior enlisted sailor, and drove the jeep to the lacquer factory to watch the old men work. He often did this when coming off the river operations. The river and its war seemed far away, although it was just a kilometer to the west.

The owner of the factory acknowledged Lieutenant Richard Berman's presence with a wave and a cigarette-dangling smile. A dog ran up to Berman, stood on its hind legs and put its front paws on the man's knees. The American bent down and scratched the dog's ears and chest. The dog followed Berman around the factory.

Unlike all the other dogs of the villages, the creature must have been the product of an rich man's escaped pet, probably a dachshund, and a village dog. It had a sleek, lustrous red short-haired coat. Although just past puppyhood, a wrinkled forehead with scowl lines gave its handsome face a wizened and worried look. Muscular chest and neck, short stubby legs, long trunk—a dwarf of a dog. It was gregarious, inquisitive, running, and scooting. The dog was bold, full of life. Happy. It was an unusual dog for Vietnam.

After sharing a beer with the factory owner while the dog rested in the sun between them, Berman climbed back into his jeep to return to his men and boats and the river war. The dog jumped into the jeep. Berman gently pushed him out of the jeep and the dog jumped back in. To the amusement of the factory owner and some of the old artists, the American could not keep the dog out of the jeep long enough to drive away. The factory owner told the American to keep the dog. He laughingly refused the piasters the American tried to give him for the animal.

The dog rode regally in the passenger seat of the jeep back to the riverfront. As soon as the jeep was parked, the dog scampered out and greeted the sailors with metronome wags of its tail and yips that only ceased when petted. He moved aboard the command boat, sniffed out his territory, appropriated one of the sailors' ponchos as a bed and settled comfortably beneath the forward .50 caliber machine gun mount.

There was a popular sailors' riddle of the time, typical rough and cruel sailor humor. What has four legs, is covered with fur and goes "mark mark"?: a dog with a harelip.

The dog did not have a harelip. But it was soon named Mark-Mark. Or just plain Mark.

Mark owned the command boat. It was his turf. He went on operations. He ate C-rations and whatever else the sailors would throw at him. He drank bug juice—Kool Aid—beer and river water. He grew sleek and his coat glistened on this diet.

During firefights he would bark furiously, running fore and aft on the boat and directing the fire of the machine guns and mortars. And afterward would sniff the blood on the deck or paw at the body bags.

He followed the American who took him from the factory. If you saw one, you saw the other. But after a few weeks of operations and a night of Mark's barking when everyone was trying to catch some badly needed sleep, Berman decided that Mark and riverborne life might not be a good combination.

Once every month or six weeks, Berman's boss in Saigon tried to take him—and the other young officers he was responsible for—off the river and bring him back to the city to debrief the people in the embassy, talk to the admiral, take a hot shower, eat a steak, and sleep between clean sheets. And, most importantly, he wanted to assess his young officers' state of mind.

Berman, like most American advisors in Vietnam, had lost weight. His skin was taut and tanned. His smiles grew rarer with each visit. Little made him laugh. At most he smiled with his lips together, rarely showing his teeth. He'd sit and stare, unfocused, lost in thoughts of what he had seen and done on the river. The sunken old man's eyes and deep lines set into a young man's face told the senior officer a lot about his young officer. And so, the boss ordered his charge to come down to Saigon for two days.

Berman drove the miserable Highway 1 corridor from Phu Cuong to Saigon, arriving at the South Vietnamese Navy head-quarters compound across the river from the city's downtown. The boss's offices and hooch for him and his staff were in a compound surrounded by concertina wire, sandbags, and a minefield.

In the passenger seat of Berman's jeep sat Mark—tongue out with his handsome head swiveling to take in all the new sights, sounds, and smells. After barking at the South Vietnamese Marine guards that inspected the jeep at the base entrance, Mark rode in royal silence up to the boss's hooch. As the boss came out to greet his young officer, Mark leaped out of the jeep and placed himself between the two men, greeting the boss with his trademark yips and front paws on the senior officer's knees.

During the two days in Saigon, Mark soon learned the lay of the compound, and became an expert gecko hunter. Geckos may be the most efficient insect catcher nature ever created. Mark would stalk the little lizards, pounce on the harmless reptiles and, with a shake of his muzzle, kill them. After rolling on the dead gecko, he would start the hunt for his next victim. The Vietnamese base com-mander expressed concern that Mark would destroy this mosquito protection and everyone would get malaria. Despite scoldings and an occasional boot-toe to the ribs or haunches, Mark resolutely continued to rid the world of geckos.

The boss agreed that Mark's home should not be the com-mand boat on the river. So, at the end of the two days, the boss took custody of Mark, holding him in his arms until his young officer drove away in his jeep.

While on the river Berman, made daily radio reports to the boss back in Saigon. Although officially prohibited, the radio com-munications often drifted from the official to the casual conver-sation of respected friends. Often Mark's yips could be heard in the background as he recognized the sound of Berman's voice. The boss complained that Mark's gecko hunting and nocturnal serenades were causing trouble, but Mark remained the boss of the compound.

At each monthly visit to Saigon, Mark renewed acquaintances with his friend from the river, nobly forgiving the transgression of departing in the jeep without him. During these visits, Mark slept on Berman's bunk, his warm body giving off uncomfortable heat in the muggy Saigon night. But Berman would not push him off. He had tried before and it was futile. Mark just climbed back on as soon as he recognized the even breathing of the young officer's sleep.

As Berman packed his gear to drive back to Phu Cuong, Mark yipped and nosed around the holster, canteen, flak vest, helmet, and web belt of equipment on the floor by the bunk. He knew the signs that his best friend was going to climb back into his jeep and drive away. Mark stayed underfoot through the packing, the walk over to the boss's office, the walk to the jeep, the final handshakes. The boss reached down to pick up Mark, as he had done at every other departure.

And as he had also done at every departure, Mark started his chorus of yipping and barks, imploring the young officer to let him sit in the passenger seat and ride with him to the boats and the river. Berman waved at his boss and the dog, started the jeep and drove to the compound gate, waiting for the marine sentry to open it. Mark's yapping became frenzied and he wriggled free of the boss's arms as the gate opened and the jeep went through. The jeep turned left onto the perimeter road outside the concertina wire and minefield.

Mark ran directly toward the jeep as it moved down the dirt road. Ears sleeked back, tongue out, tail wagging, Mark ran between the sandbags, barking furiously. And tripped a land mine.

The orange-and-dirt bloom of the explosion threw Mark's body thirty feet into the air. Berman turned at the sound of the mine's eruption. At first, he could only see the dust and smoke cloud moving in the breeze. A lustrous red fur coat mottled with darker red blood lay lifeless on the ground.

He stopped the jeep and stared. He could see his boss at the other end of the minefield, hands shading the sun as he looked back at him. The young man thought he should feel like crying or something, but there was no feeling there, nothing. He put the jeep in gear and drove back to Phu Cuong. Back to the river.

Mark's body lay there until it rotted. It was in a minefield. It was too dangerous to try to recover a dead dog's body.

And so the war went on.

The Joke of 1968

There's really nothing funny about the war in Vietnam. One joke, however, did surface after Tet. Sort of funny.

A road ran along the Saigon River. A patrol boat's crew noticed something lying on the road and beached the boat. There was a dead Vietnamese, all smashed and cut up, his AK-47 broken into pieces. And an American soldier, almost as badly cut and busted, but still alive. It was obvious to the patrol boat crew that a vicious hand-to-hand fight had occurred between the two men. The American won. If he survived.

After over a month in the army hospital in Vung Tau, the American had recovered enough to walk around the hospital ward. He looked healthy.

One day a nurse gave him a shave while another gave him a crew cut. Then he put on new blue pajamas and robe. The soldier was going to be interviewed by a *Stars and Stripes* reporter.

With a colonel from public relations and a photographer in tow, the reporter showed up and started directing a camera shoot. Then he sat down next to the bed, a portable tape recorder and note pad at the ready. He waved the microphone like a baton as he interviewed the soldier.

After some preliminary questions about his hometown and his military unit, the reporter asked the wounded soldier, "Corporal, tell me what happened before that patrol boat found you. It must have been pretty rough."

"My squad had a bunch of VC trapped between the road and the river. At night. Hell of a firefight. We were on one side of that road, Charlie on the other. Pretty soon we were low on ammo and our canteens were empty. The VC must have been the same. It was getting light and the sergeant ordered us to pull out. The gooks must have been doing the same because the shooting stopped.

"I was the last of the squad to pull out. It was light now. But as soon as I tried to get up, a bullet would go whizzing by me so I hunkered down. I could see a dink on the other side of the road. So when he stood up, I'd take a shot at him. We were going on like that for I don't know how long. Him shooting at me, me shooting at him.

"I guess we were both nearly out of ammunition. I figured what the fuck and yell out to him. I yell, 'Ho Chi Minh is a dirty cocksucker.' And he yells back, 'LBJ eats shit.' "

"Then what happened?"

"The tank ran us over while we were shaking hands in the middle of the road."

MASSACRE

"What's that, Hung?" The white-haired American pointed at a circular scar in the Citadel's stone wall.

The guide turned to where the tall man pointed and nodded his head. "That's from an artillery shell, Mr. Brody."

"From Tet in 1968?"

Hung smiled and shook his head. "No. From the French. This wall is over 175 years old. It's one of the few original walls left. Most of what you see has been reconstructed."

Brody looked around, squinting behind his sunglasses in the brilliant sunshine. It was late February and the temperature and humidity could be described with the same number: 95. "This weather typical, Hung?"

"Yes, this is typical Hue weather at this time of year. In Hanoi, everyone is in heavy coats. Here we are in shorts and sandals." Hung smiled and looked down at his legs and feet.

"So the 1968 Tet's battles here were fought in this kind of heat? Wearing helmets and flak vests?"

"The Americans could afford helmets and armor, Mr. Brody. We could not."

"Yeah, Hung. I guess."

Hung waved his hand at the reconstructed walls and buildings. "This was all destroyed by the Americans and the southerners' artillery and bombs. After the war we rebuilt it, to preserve the Vietnamese history." He paused and looked at the American. "Were you a soldier here, Mr. Brody?"

"No, Hung. I got here after Tet. Stationed near Quang Ngai. Didn't do any fighting."

"What did you do in Quang Ngai?"

"Doctor. *Bac si.* Worked in the refugee camp hospitals for a year."

"Ah, Bac si." Hung nodded in approval. "I should call you 'Doctor Brody,' yes?"

"Forget the doctor, Hung. Mister or Bruce work fine."

Hung studied Brody's face for a few silent seconds. "Quang Ngai is near My Lai, Doctor. Were you near there when the massacre occurred?"

"No, I got in-country after that. Didn't even know about it until I got back to the states."

The two men walked in silence down the stone stairs and to the outer wall where an elephant carrying two tourists shambled by. Brody took off his baseball hat and ran his hands through his hair. He looked around him and then at Hung who was looking at his smart phone.

"Doctor, we can go to a historical temple near here or, if you are tired, back to the resort and Mrs. Brody."

"Hung, I'm templed out. No more. How about we find a place for something cold to drink and then you take me back to the room? I'm buying."

The two men sat in the shade of a small cafe. A made-in-China fan stirred the air. Two glasses of thick iced *cafe sua* sweetened with condensed milk sat on the tiny table. Hung studied his smart phone, Brody thumbed through the thick book he had carried in his backpack. The book was well worn, its paperback cover taped together. It was Stanley Karnow's *Vietnam, A History.* Hung looked up from his phone.

"Big book, Doctor."

"Yes, Hung. It's a heavy one. And a remarkable history of Vietnam and the war. The fellow who wrote it just died a month ago. Eighty-eight years old."

"You have obviously read it many times, Doctor. It is very used."

"Yes, I guess I have. Probably read it at least half a dozen times. There was even a television documentary based on this book." Brody took a swallow of the iced coffee, made a face at its bitterness and looked at the young man across from him.

"Hung, during that Tet there was a very big massacre at Hue. Much bigger than My Lai. You never mentioned it and there are no signs mentioning it. At least none that I have seen these last two days. But this book, and several others that I have read, describe it in detail."

Hung just stared at Brody, blinking his eyes behind his wire-rimmed glasses, licking his lips.

"Thousands were killed, Hung," Brody continued. "All civilians. Many were buried in a mass grave. But there's nothing to commemorate that. No signs, no memorial, no plaques. It's as if it didn't happen, Hung."

Hung sat silent. Listening. Not responding.

"Don't you people acknowledge what happened?" asked Brody.

"Many die in war. The enemy killed many during our war for liberation, Doctor Brody."

"Yes, Hung, you are right. Sending our troops into Vietnam was a mistake that cannot be redone. My Lai is a tragic lesson. But Tet and the massacre here in Hue, Hung? Your people initiated that, not us or the South Vietnamese."

Hung sat stonefaced, looking at Brody.

Brody smiled and shook his head. "Hung, you weren't even born then, were you? When were you born?"

Hung relaxed and sipped his coffee. "1981. North of Hanoi."

"You have to study a lot to be a certified guide?"

The young man laughed. "Oh, yes. Many examinations to get licensed are required. History, culture, geography, language."

"You studied the war?"

"Of course, Doctor."

"And the Tet in 1968?"

"Yes, Doctor Brody."

The older man leaned forward and lowered his voice. He locked eyes with Hung. "Your people started the Tet uprising. Hue was destroyed. Thousands died. Hell, hundreds of thousands died. Was it worth it, Hung?"

Hung replied in a flat, mechanical tone, as if reading a technical report out loud. "The people of Vietnam rose up against the aggressor forces during that time to turn the American public against the war. To make the American public demand that their leaders take their soldiers out of our country. The people of Vietnam were willing to sacrifice their lives to shorten the war and drive the Americans out."

Brody drummed his fingers on Karnow's book as he listened. Hung sat emotionless, only his mouth moving as it spewed forth words. Then he stopped.

"Did you hope to start an uprising of the population to throw the Americans out and replace the southern government, Hung?"

"The fighting during that Tet was the uprising of the population, Doctor."

"Maybe, Hung. Maybe. But it took a fucking long time for it all too happen, didn't it? It took years before the war was over."

"Doctor, maybe it did. Maybe. But we had time, we had patience, we had the conviction that we would reunite our country. It was our fate. All you had were bullets and bombs and money. You could not win."

"You are right, Hung. And you won. Although I don't think anyone really wins a war. You just lose less than the other guy. And since you won, you get to write the history." Brody finished his coffee, put three US dollars on the table and stood up. "C'mon, let's go back."

Brody's wife was waiting for him in their air-conditioned room. Having just finished a shower after a swim, she was drying her hair. "How'd it go, Bruce?"

"Interesting, Hon'. Hard to believe there was ever a battle. No signs of it anywhere. Just old cannon ball holes from the French days. Hung was spewing the party line bullshit like a fire hydrant. But you have to respect these people. Hell, they won."

LUAU

He had not realized how much the war had changed him. Not in the thing that seemed to matter most to him, his love for his wife. But in other things. Ten months in a combat zone as a Swift boat skipper at the mouth of the Mekong Delta had changed him. He knew his wife hoped these changes were temporary.

Finishing his coffee, Lieutenant Jay Cole put the cup on the little balcony table. Leaning on the railing, he looked out across the Waikiki beach. The sun was just coming up. Waves hitting the sand drowned out the traffic noise of the early rush hour. For the previous four days of his R&R in Honolulu, he and Charlene had had no schedule. They slept in, made love, swam in the pool, swam in the ocean, toured a bit, shopped a bit, went to a Don Ho show and sang *Tiny Bubbles*, visited the Polynesian Cultural Center, and called his parents.

Jay and Charlene had only two mandatory items on their schedule for the seven days. One was to attend the big luau tonight in the hotel's spectacular garden. The other was to impregnate Charlene and start on kid number one. From all the clippings she had sent, Jay learned that conception was a miracle that occurred despite the odds against it. But the odds could be improved by timing and frequency. Charlene said the timing was perfect. And Jay was quite happy to do his part about frequency. In fact, maybe he'd wake her up by climbing into bed and snuggling up behind her. She had slept enough.

* * *

Jay watched Charlene swim a few lengths of the pool and climb up the shallow-end steps. She stood by their lounges and dried herself off as he gave her a critical inspection from behind his dark sunglass. Short, cute, beautiful figure, great legs, and a smile that could melt granite.

"Just what are you looking at, Lieutenant Cole?" she asked in her most stern second-grade school teacher voice.

"Well, teacher, I don't know how well I did on my last assignment. I mean, I think I missed a lot. My teachers before always made me do things over. Okay if I do it again? And I don't suppose you'd show me your panties, Mrs. Cole?" He leered at her.

"I don't know what they do to you over there, but you have become totally corrupted," she said with mock severity as she sat in her lounge chair, drying her hair. "When you come back to San Diego, you are immediately going into a rehabilitation program. In fact, I'm thinking about having you turned into a eunuch."

"Damn, Mrs. Cole. All my other teachers just made me stay after school."

She lay back and reached over and held his hand, squeezing it. "Little Jay, Mrs. Cole is tired now and needs her rest. She has had a very exhausting morning."

"Little! Why don't you just rip open my chest and stomp on my heart? Little? Well, I'm sorry about the inadequacies, Mrs. Cole. Excuse me while I whimper for a couple of hours."

She threw her wet towel on his face.

Smiling, he pillowed her wet towel behind his head and closed his eyes. Two more days and then he'd return to Vietnam and she back to San Diego. But he was a short-timer. Another month and a half skippering his boat and then his relief would arrive.

A week to train him, a week of debriefing, and then back to San Diego. Pack up their household goods, gas up the car, and off to Boston for three years at MIT courtesy of the United States Navy. After that, he would probably specialize in engineering and naval architecture and spend most of his remaining twenty years or so in the navy in shipyards and Washington, DC. Not much sea duty, hopefully no more wars.

In retrospect, Jay was glad that Charlene's ovulation and teaching schedules forced them to take his week's R&R near the end of his time in-country. Most of the other officers took their R&R during the middle of their tours. They all remarked that the time really dragged after R&R. He was sure the days would go by slowly, but there were fewer days to go by for him.

The Hawaiian R&R was really nice. He could truly relax without worrying that the guy walking down the street would try to kill him.

Smiling to himself, he remembered how the first few days went.

"Just what are you smiling at, Jay? You're going to get sunburned gums."

"I'm thinking about all the women in the world who would be much nicer to me and not treat me like an untrained poodle."

"Consider yourself very lucky that I saved you from the SPCA. The reason you're in my domain is that none of those other women would take you."

He chuckled. "And I take that to mean you're referring to my less-than-civilized behavior?"

"Exactly, Fido."

* * *

It had started when they unpacked their bags. He had a few sport shirts, a pair of khaki trousers, a pair of shorts, swimming suit, Keds, shower shoes, some socks, and toiletries. But no underwear. When she said he had forgotten his underwear, he said he hadn't. The army and navy doctors had recommended loose fitting clothing and not wearing underwear to avoid crotch rot in-country. He followed their recommendations and found that not only did he not have crotch rot or diaper rash or any other skin ailments, the prescribed wardrobe was also very comfortable. That scene inspired their first Hawaiian shopping experience—to Sears for a package of Jockey shorts.

Then there were his trips to the bathroom. He never shut the door and visually inspected the products of his efforts before flushing. While she accepted his plea that the medicos advised that color and consistency of bowel movements could tell a lot, she did not accept that he had grown used to using the stern of his boat as a bathroom and the stern had no doors.

After that, Jay knew he had no excuse for the random farting and belching. Telling her to pull his finger, he quickly learned, was one big mistake.

The night before, at a Japanese restaurant, he had held the rim of his rice bowl against his lower lip and shoveled the rice into his wide-open mouth with his chopsticks. When he put the bowl down, she was looking at him with her mouth open.

"Just what are you doing, Jay?"

"Eating rice. What did you think I was doing?"

"What kind of animal have you turned into? You were shoveling food into your mouth like a glutton. Look, you've got rice grains stuck to your nose and chin." She reached over the table and wiped his face with her napkin.

"Char, this is how they eat in Asia. No knives and forks and no dainty picking up one rice grain one at a time with chopsticks. There's a big communal bowl and everyone has a little bowl. You reach in and plop some into your little rice bowl. Then you pick it up and shovel it in. That's how it's done by the Vietnamese." He then demonstrated his eating prowess to her again.

"Really, Jay? How about those two over there?" She discreetly pointed with her chopsticks at two South Vietnamese Army officers in uniform across the room eating dinner. They were picking up small mouthfuls of rice and fish with their chopsticks. Their bowls never came near their faces.

Charlene had more serious concerns than underwear, toilet habits, and table manners, however. The first thing Jay had done when they arrived at their hotel room from the airport was to take a long, hot shower, then shave. He had been in transit for over thirty hours, and had not had a hot-water shower in ten months. She surprised him by joining him in the shower stall. When she soaped his back, she saw the ugly red scar that ran from his left shoulder blade down his back to his left side, stopping at the bottom of his ribcage. There were smaller, circular scars on his left hip and thigh.

"Jay, what are these?"

As they dried themselves off, Jay told her about a firefight and how a rocket had hit his boat's wheelhouse, sending shrapnel into him and the coxswain. He assured her that he was all right and that the wounds looked worse than they actually had been. The coxswain was also okay.

She was horrified, dismayed. When did it happen? Why hadn't he told her?

He wrapped his arms around her and held her close. "Because I didn't want you to worry. I know you worry about me being over there and I didn't want you to worry more than you already do. I'm fine. Really, honey. I'm fine."

He led her to the bed and held onto her for over an hour as she cried tears of anger, concern, and love for him. After they made love, she made him promise to never keep things from her. Never.

He did promise. But there were things he knew that he still would never tell her. He would never share with her the feelings and images and smells that he wished he could erase from his mind and dreams. Watching that baby-faced soldier die, the burning chicken-feather smell of napalm-blackened flesh, killing a fisherman because he was in a free-fire zone trying to feed his family, the sweet-stink of a rotting corpse, tossing a severed foot still in its boot over the side, green tracers, white rocket trails, writing letters home to the next of kin. His promise would not include these.

Then there were the times, especially during dinner, when he would just stare off into space, mechanically eating and drinking. She asked if he was okay or what was he thinking about and he always lied and said, "Nothing, just tired. Maybe still a little jet lagged."

* * *

Arm in arm, Charlene in a muumuu and Jay in an aloha shirt from Sears, walked through the hotel lobby to the gardens. The luau was in the big Oahu Paradise Garden, next to the smaller Kauai Tropical Forest, where a traditional Chinese wedding was being held. As they entered the garden, young women in grass skirts and leis put an orchid lei over Charlene's head and another over Jay's. The scene was pure kitsch. Tiki torches, a Hawaiian trio crooning to ukuleles, a sea of tables covered in banana-leaf table-cloths, and waiters passing around drinks in plastic cups with little paper umbrellas. Two beefy men in sarongs were digging up the pit-roasted pigs.

Like several other of the hotels on Waikiki, their hotel offered big discounts to military families on R&R. That included the hotel's famous luau—an evening of food, drink, entertainment, and danc-ing. After a few incidents of alcohol-fueled debates between civilians and military, the hotel's event manager wisely decided to seat the military families together. The master of ceremonies always made it a point to recognize the young servicemen and their guests.

Most of the guests at the luau were Midwesterners and Southerners on vacation, Japanese honeymooners, Japanese tour-ists, and two or three tables of R&R families. The Nebraskans, Japanese tourists, and shy honeymooners were unknowingly subsi-dizing the R&R tables.

Jay found their table by the big hedge that separated the luau from the Chinese wedding next door. Four couples were already seated. The young wives were trim, tan, and pretty. The men were fit, tan, and had that taut skin and deep-eyed look that identified them as combat veterans. The short haircuts sealed the deal.

Jay recognized two of the men from the flight from Saigon to Honolulu. After a lot of "what unit you with" and "where you from" questions, the five couples settled into a friendly and easy chatter, enjoying the evening and the company. All the men were officers: three army, one marine, and Jay. Charlene found out that two of the other wives were fellow schoolteachers, and the other two were housewives taking care of their little children. For the week, the kids had been farmed out to various sets of grandparents.

Mai tais flowed as they ate their meal with their fingers, trying weird dishes like sashimi and poi.

"Y'know, Charlene has been having a terrible time with my table manners since I got here, and now she takes me to a place where I have to use my fingers," remarked Jay to the table.

"Same thing with me," said the marine, who then pointed at his wife. "She's been telling me what a terrible example I'll make for the kids when I get home. And now look at her." She smiled around her two fingers as she ate a glob of poi.

The entertainment took an intermission and the trio played quiet background music as the five couples ate and talked.

About fifteen yards away from them on the other side of the hedge, the Chinese wedding ceremony was coming to a traditional end with strings of firecrackers.

Crack! Crack! Crachcrackcerackcrackcrackcrack....

By the second explosion, Jay had grabbed Charlene's arm, thrown her on the grass, rolled her under the table, and covered her body with his, holding his hands over the back of his head. She was trying to push him off of her. He looked up and saw the other four men beneath the table, two on top of their wives, who were also trying to wiggle away from their husbands. The men stared at each other for a few seconds then smiled and started to nervously giggle.

Jay was the first man to pop his head over the table. The remaining two seated wives looked at him with dumbfounded expressions. The two tables on either side of them, also R&R families, were devoid of men, with a few women still seated. The tourists and honeymoon couples stared.

"Jay, what is the matter with you?" sputtered Charlene, the first of the women from under their table to surface.

By now they were all up and taking their seats. Laughing, relieved.

"Aw, jeez, I'm sorry. Those firecrackers sounded just like some-one shooting at us. I didn't think, I just acted. You okay, Char?"

"Well, other than having grass stains on my muumuu, I guess so. Are you?"

Jay didn't answer because the two women who had not been dragged under the table were now giving their husbands hell. They wanted to know why their husbands hadn't tried to protect them as the other three gallant men had?

That night as Jay brushed his teeth getting ready for bed, Charlene walked up behind him and wrapped her arms around his waist. She kissed the red scar on his shoulder blade.

"Jay, I love you so much. And I don't want you to change. But I think this war has changed you. Are you okay?"

He smiled at her in the mirror. "You're right, Char. I have changed. I don't know how you go to war and not change. Unless you're a nut or a robot. But, yeah, I'm okay."

THE THREE BOXES

"Hey, Mr. Josephs, after you get the boat tied up, the boss wants to see you, sir."

Lieutenant Alexander Josephs, US Navy, looked out the wheelhouse door of the Swift boat. On the wooden pier stood the boss's administration assistant, Yeoman First Class Gene Scrivener. Josephs waved and shouted over the engine noise, "Got it, Scrivener. A couple of minutes more. Do I have time to shit, shower, and shave?"

"No, sir. Boss is waiting."

"Am I in the shits?"

The yeoman laughed. "I don't think so, sir." He turned and walked back to the Quonset huts that made up the small US Navy base of Cat Lo, South Vietnam.

The young officer turned to the older man standing by the wheel and throttles, holding the boat in place while the rest of the crew tied it to the pier. "Chief, I gotta see the boss. After you get her secured, let's refuel and rearm, resupply with chow, freshwater wash down, and have the snipes look at that starboard engine. It was running rough."

177

"Aye aye, Mr. Josephs. Think I can tell the crew we won't be going out for a day or two? Let 'em sleep and get some pussy?"

"Hope so, Chief. Unless the boss tells me otherwise. But he'd have given us a heads-up on the radio, so let's plan on hanging around here for a while. After a week of snotty weather and two firefights, I think we deserve a rest."

"Roger that, *Dai Uy*. If you need me, I'll be in the chiefs' mess."

Scrivener didn't look up from his typewriter as the headquarters Quonset screen door slammed behind Josephs. "Boss is in the head, sir. Grab some panther piss—freshly brewed about three days ago—and go on in. He'll be here in a few seconds."

After filling a chipped stained cup with the viscous black coffee and dumping in powdered creamer and two spoons of sugar, Josephs sat on the couch in the office of Commander Louis Edington—the "boss." He nursed the bittersweet hot liquid.

"Good morning, Alex. Thanks for coming in so quick." Husky, fortyish, Commander Edington was the senior naval officer in this part of South Vietnam. He was in charge of all the US Navy personnel and equipment and was also the senior advisor to the local South Vietnamese Navy. Edington was a "hot runner," on his way to early promotion and eventually admiral stars. He cared for his people. And they tried to take care of him.

"I read your after-action reports, Alex. Sounds like a rough week out there. Crew okay?"

"Yes, sir. In need of sleep and hot showers but they're fine. I've got a great crew, sir. "

The boss smiled and nodded his head. "How's the boat?"

"Pretty good, sir. No holes, no leaks. One of the engine's running rough, but we'll get that fixed."

"Good." Edington pushed himself back from his desk, ran a meaty palm over his mouth and then stared at his junior officer for several seconds before saying anything.

"Alex," he began in a low, quiet voice, "Rick Traynor died two nights ago."

Josephs felt a sudden chill and his scalp tightened. Rick Traynor—Lieutenant Richard Traynor, was a SEAL. He was also Josephs's roommate and close friend.

"Aw, Jesus, Commander. What happened?"

"Training exercise with the *nguoi nhai* and the Aussie EOD team." *Nguoi nhai* were the South Vietnamese Navy's frogmen, their special forces. The Australian Navy's Explosive Ordnance Demolition Team were also special warfare swimmers.

Evington continued. "They walked right into a real shithole. Someone knew they were coming. Booby traps and mines. Rick stepped on a mine and blew his leg off. He bled out before they could bring in a medevac. Two *nguoi nhai* killed. Everyone else caught some shrapnel, but they'll be okay."

"Oh, fuck, sir. Where's Rick now?"

"Body's with the army at Graves Registration. Closed casket. He's being shipped home today. Wife and two little girls. Mother and father. I think he has a brother and a sister."

Josephs slumped on the couch. He felt numb.

"You okay, Alex?"

"Uh...sure, sir. Just sort of.... No...I'm not okay, sir. I mean Rick..." Josephs took a gulp of his coffee and made a face. Dumbly staring at the edge of Edington's desk, he took a deep breath, shook his head, and looked at his boss.

"Sorry, sir. I'm okay. What do you need me to do?"

"I want you to inventory his goods. Locker, footlocker, duffel, whatever he had here. You know the drill, Alex. Get some chow, take a nap, and then get to it. Scrivener will help. I want everything boxed up and taken care of today."

"Sir, I'd rather get to it right now. I don't think I could eat or sleep just yet. If Scrivener's ready, so am I."

The senior officer studied the young man's face. It had the look that all his officers had—tight, stretched, tanned skin, sunken eyes, dark circles, old men's features in young men's faces. "Fine. The quicker the better."

Edington knew the effect on morale when physical reminders of a fallen comrade haunted the survivors. He yelled for Scrivener, who immediately appeared in the doorway with three empty cardboard cartons, a bolt cutter, a bucket filled with cleaning supplies, and a clipboard. "Ready to go, Commander. Any time you're ready, Mr. Josephs."

The young officer and the enlisted man walked in silence to the Bachelor Officers Quarters Quonset hut. Josephs unlocked the door to the room he had shared with Traynor. One desk. Two bunks neatly made up with poncho liners as bed spreads and mosquito netting bunched to the side. Two steel lockers. A safe. A small footlocker at the end of one bunk with a brown paper bag next to neatly folded laundry on top. A green duffel sat on the floor next to the footlocker. Two unopened letters lay on that bunk's pillow.

Josephs sighed and looked at Scrivener. "I hate this more than anything else I've ever had to do in my life. This is the third time I've done this since I got here. How many have you done?"

"A dozen counting this one, sir. It doesn't get any easier."

Contrary to many things in the navy, the inventory of a deceased's property at Cat Lo followed no written procedure. Somewhere in navy regulations must have been a step-by-step guide on what to inventory and how to do it, including necessary forms and notifications. But at Cat Lo, as well as almost every US military unit in South Vietnam, only one rule was followed: protect the dead man's family. No one had ever told Josephs and Scrivener that rule. But they knew it as well as they knew their own names.

Every object would be looked at closely. If a letter, every word would be read. If a book or a magazine, every page would be scanned. Then the object would be put into one of the three cartons. To be sent home, to be returned to the navy, or to be burned. A detailed inventory would be kept of the contents for the first two cartons. No inventory would be made of the items burned. For all practical purposes, they never existed.

Josephs spilled the contents of the brown paper bag onto the bed. It was from Graves Registration and included a list of personal items found on the body. Scrivener looked at the list and the items, making sure all were there.

Gold wedding band, US Naval Academy ring class of 1960, two dog tags on a metal chain, an Omega diver's watch with a compass attached to its metal link band, two keys on a metal ring, Skilcraft black ballpoint pen, wallet, green pocket memo book, and two quarters, and three pennies. The rings, dog tags, and watch were thick with dried blood. The pen's barrel was cracked, a piece of shrapnel was embedded in the memo book, and the wallet was heavily scuffed.

Silently, the two men cleaned the blood off the rings, dog tags, and watch with rags, soap solution, and alcohol. The gold and steel shined brilliantly when they were done.

"Sir, is this watch navy issued? Don't they issue these to the SEALs?" asked Scrivener.

"I don't know. Let's send it to his wife. If some bean counter in the Pentagon wants the watch back, let them go find it."

"Aye aye, sir." Scrivener put the rings, tags, and watch along with the 53 cents into the carton to be sent home. He made notes on the clipboard, then tossed the broken pen into the burn box. Picking up the memo book, he started going through it page by page.

Josephs opened Traynor's wallet. It contained about twenty dollars' worth of Military Payment Certificates and about five dollars' worth of Vietnamese piasters. He put the money on the desktop. "We'll have to change these into greenbacks," he said more to himself than to Scrivener. There was a California driver's license, military ID card, Geneva Convention card, Shell gasoline credit card, a black-and-white photo of a young Rick Traynor with a pretty brunette, a color photo of Traynor holding a toddler and the dark-haired woman obviously pregnant, and a color photo of Traynor, the woman, a little girl, and another toddler all in bathing suits standing in the surf smiling into the sun and camera.

Scrivener looked over his shoulder. "That's a handsome family. What a fucking shame."

Josephs shook the wallet and a foil-wrapped condom fell out. He tossed it into the burn box. After rubbing the wallet all over with a clean rag, Joseph put it and the photos and identification cards into the home box. Scrivener kept a running inventory.

"Sir, this wheel-book is nothing but call signs, frequencies, and operations notes. All business, nothing else." Scrivener looked at Josephs, who nodded with his head toward the burn box. The memo book was tossed in.

They dumped the duffel onto the floor. Blood-soaked and shredded uniform, socks, underwear, reef shoes, and jungle hat went into the burn box. A 9 mm pistol, holster, belt, ammunition and ammunition clips, first aid kit, web gear, and a Swedish-K machine gun with two full clips, flashlight, and sheath knife, all soaked with blood and mud, were made safe, inventoried, and placed into the box for the navy, along with the empty duffel. The two men made no attempt to clean the equipment.

One of the two keys on the ring opened Traynor's steel locker. On the top shelf was a hairbrush and comb, deodorant, toothbrush, toothpaste, aftershave, and a leather shaving kit. Inside the kit were a razor, blades, four condoms in foil, and a vial of penicillin pills. The brush, comb, razor, and empty leather kit went into the box for home. All the rest went into the burn box.

Hanging in the locker were a set of whites, two sets of khakis, a field jacket, and two sets of jungle fatigues. Pinned on the left breast of the whites were gold jump wings and three rows of ribbons. The top row of ribbons was a silver star, bronze star, and navy commendation medal ribbons, the first ribbon in the middle row was a purple heart with two small gold stars. A combination hat with white cover and two khaki covers hung on hooks at the back of the locker. Underwear and socks were stacked neatly on a shelf below the uniforms, and on the shelf at the bottom of the locker were a pair of white shoes, brown shoes, jungle boots, and gym shoes. After the pockets were searched, the uniforms went into the box for home.

"Scrivener, let's throw in his poncho liner for home. Kids like those. The army can afford it." Josephs pulled the camouflage patterned quilt off Traynor's bed, folded it and put it in the box for home.

At the very bottom of the locker was a shoebox filled with envelopes and photos. Most of the envelopes were of the same stationary as the two letters sitting on Traynor's pillows. Scrivener put the shoebox next to those letters.

The locker was empty except for a bottle of Remy Martel cognac. Josephs picked it up, smiled, and said to Scrivener, "Let's save this for a drink after we finish."

On top of the locker was a helmet sitting on a folded flak vest. "These wouldn't have made a difference," said Josephs as he dumped them in the navy box.

Josephs opened the safe that he shared with Traynor. He took out an envelope and two booklets, leaving his own envelope in the safe. Traynor's envelope held a copy of his will, insurance beneficiary forms, and $250. Josephs sealed the envelope and put it in the box to home.

"What should we do with these manuals?" asked Josephs. "They're classified special warfare stuff. He must have signed for these, huh?"

Scrivener thumbed through the two books. "He didn't get these from here, sir. We don't have a 'need to know' so we can't even keep them here. I'll call the guys at NAVFORV in Saigon and asked them what to do. Until then, I think they should go back in the safe."

"What do you think next, Scrivener? Footlocker or letters? I think we need to go through both of those together."

"Let's tackle those letters first, sir. That's usually the worst part, so let's get it over with."

"You're right. Let's start." Josephs took the box full of letters and gave half to Scrivener. The two men started reading each letter, placing the completed ones on the other man's pile.

As much as they disliked intruding, they knew from bitter experience that sometimes a careless scribble could hurt deeply.

One man had written "stupid fucking bitch" on a letter from his wife when she described how she bumped their new car into the neighbor's. Another had mixed his letters from his wife with letters from his high school girlfriend, who was rekindling old flames. So, they read every sheet and looked at every picture.

They were all letters from Traynor's wife, often including photos or a child's drawings. The letters told of daily happenings and family news, of how lonely a beautiful wife was for her husband, and how their eldest daughter wanted to know when Daddy was coming home. One letter was sexually explicit as she recalled how vigorously they made love during his R&R in Hawaii. A photograph in that envelope showed her naked in a Waikiki hotel bedroom.

Scrivener started to cry. Josephs felt a lump in his throat but did not cry. He didn't trust his voice and just shared silent stares with the enlisted man. After nearly an hour, they put all the letters back into their envelopes and placed them in the box for home.

"What do you think about these two?" asked Josephs, pointing at the two unopened envelopes sitting on the pillow. "Same envelope, return address and handwriting. I don't think we have to worry about anything embarrassing her in those, do you?"

"Hell, sir, I've read too much already," said Scrivener as he put the two unopened letters in the box for home. "We know there's nothing that's going to hurt her in those two."

"Want to take a break for a cup of coffee or something and then get to the footlocker?" suggested Josephs.

"Yes, sir. I need a break. I'll call Saigon about those manuals and hit the head."

"Good idea, Scrivener. Let's lock up and start again in thirty minutes."

After locking the room, Josephs walked into the head. He peed and while he washed his hands, stared at his face in the mirror above the sink. A mask stared back at him. No emotions visible, unblinking, ugly. He walked back to his room, unlocked the door and lay down on his bunk, leaving the door wide open. He shut his eyes.

"Lieutenant? You okay?"

Josephs opened his eyes. He had fallen into a deep dreamless sleep and was disoriented. Scrivener was leaning over him.

"Yeah, thanks, I'm okay, Scrivener. I must have fallen asleep. I feel like a catfish shit in my mouth."

"Well, here's some coffee I brought you, Mr. Josephs. It won't make your mouth taste any better, just different."

Josephs sat on the edge of his bed and drank the coffee while Scrivener checked the inventories in the navy and home boxes.

With the other key from Traynor's ring, the two men opened his footlocker. A compartmented tray rested on top. It contained Traynor's medals, a 35 mm single lens reflex camera with no film in it, aviator sunglasses, and a Buck knife in a leather sheath. These all went into the home box. The tray also contained a box of 9 mm ammunition and another pistol with two empty clips. Those objects went into the navy box.

Under the tray was a pile of neatly folded civilian clothes—sport shirts, khaki trousers, a pair of Levis, belts, windbreaker, sweater, sport coat, tie, white shirt, socks, loafers, shorts, and bathing suit. They piled all the clothes on the bed and went through the pockets, finding another $10.15.

"Funny, I can't picture Lieutenant Traynor wearing any of these," said Scrivener as he added the items to the inventory for the home box.

Under the civilian clothes were the last items they had to go through. A leather-bound bible, half a dozen magazines, and an ammunition can. They fanned the bible's pages, held the book open and shook it. Nothing fell out, there were no scribbles on the pages. It went into the box for home.

The magazines were a collection of well-thumbed *Playboys* and *Penthouses.* Josephs thought that he had never seen Traynor reading these as he tossed them into the burn box.

Scrivener opened the metal ammunition box and made a low whistle. He got up and shut the door to the room, locked it, then dumped the box onto the bed. A hypodermic needle, bent spoon, matches, surgical tubing, and three 35 mm film cans fell onto the bed, along with a cigar wrapped in twine and an envelope stuffed with photos.

Josephs opened the film cans and found coarse white and brown powders. The cigar was a Buddha stick—marijuana wrapped in LSD-soaked cotton string. The two men went into the head and flushed the powders down the toilet, rinsing the film cans and the ammunition box thoroughly. The drug paraphernalia, film canisters, ammunition box, and the Buddha stick went into the burn box.

"Fuck, that was a surprise," said Josephs as he sat on the bed and opened the envelope. After a few quiet seconds, he added, "So is this."

The photos were all of naked women who worked in a bar in Vung Tau, a few kilometers from Cat Lo. Both Scrivener and Josephs recognized them. Traynor was in many of the pictures, usually naked and performing sex acts on the women.

Silently, Joseph handed each photo to Scrivener who looked at it and then put it in the burn box.

They were nearly done. Scrivener added the two classified manuals to the navy box, rechecked the inventories and, together with Josephs, went through the locker and safe one more time.

"I'll get the fire going on the beach, sir. Then I'll burn this stuff."

"That's all right, Scrivener. Let's get these two boxes ready to ship. You start the fire, I'll do the burn. I'm already in a dirty uniform, let me do it."

"Fine with me, Mr. Josephs."

They took the navy box and the home box to the headquarters Quonset hut, leaving the burn box locked in the room. They inventoried the contents of each box one more time, made sure that Traynor's MPCs and piasters were converted into greenbacks, and repacked and sealed the boxes for shipping.

Commander Edington watched them as they finished.

"Good job, you two. That's a terrible thing to do. I appreciate your work. You all done?"

"No, sir, not yet," answered Josephs. "We still have to burn the remaining stuff. And there's a bottle of cognac we want to sample."

Twenty minutes later, Josephs stood on the beach upwind of the cement block and steel incinerator the navy had jury-rigged at

Cat Lo. It was fueled with diesel oil and used a makeshift electric blower, producing a heat that would melt and burn most metals. Scrivener had started the fire, which was now roaring.

Opening the burn box, Joseph fed an item at a time into the incinerator. Paper and photos turned into a white powder ash instantaneously, the hypodermic needle popped like a small firecracker as it hit the heat, and the metal items groaned and snapped. When the burn box was empty, he collapsed the cardboard carton and ripped off a flap at a time and fed it into the fire.

He stood there, staring into the fire. The wind shifted and blew the smoke into his eyes. Josephs blinked several times. He felt tears running down his face, streaking the soot on his cheeks. His nose was running. And so, he just stood there, as tears dripped off his face onto the beach.

Suddenly, he realized that Scrivener was next to him. He didn't know how long the other man had been standing there. With a long metal bar, Scrivener stoked the incinerator and stirred the ashes.

"All gone, sir. The boss says to clean up and then meet him in his office at 1700."

Clean-shaven, showered, wearing clean khakis, and with a bowl of ramen in his stomach, Josephs walked into Edington's office at 1700.

"Sit down, Alex. Scrivener!" shouted Edington.

"Yes, sir," said Scrivener from his desk in the outer office.

"Come on in here, please."

Scrivener walked into the office, nodded at Josephs and said, "You look a whole lot better, Mr. Josephs."

"Soap and hot water can do marvelous things, Scrivener," answered the young officer.

Commander Edington had Traynor's bottle of cognac on his desk and three glasses. He poured two fingers into each glass and gave one to Josephs and the other to Scrivener. Josephs stood up with the other two.

"What you burned out there never existed," said Edington. "To Rick Traynor."

The three men drank the dead man's cognac.

MARLBORO MAN

"That dink looks like he's thirteen years old."

"Who knows, sir? Hard to tell their age. He sure is pale."

"Roger that, Chief. This is probably the first time he's been out of the tunnels in daylight for months. Looks scared."

The two big Americans were looking at the prisoner sitting on his haunches on the hot steel deck of the South Vietnamese Navy's River Assault Group's command boat. Bareheaded and clad in peasant's rough cotton black pajamas and sandals made of truck-tire tread and rubber straps cut from an inner tube, the young VC soldier's hands were tied behind his back. An armed and bored Vietnamese sailor guarded him.

In their ten months as advisors to the river assault group, the two Americans had never seen a captured VC before that wasn't wounded. They had counted plenty of bodies and body parts, and had loaded a few—a very few—badly wounded prisoners on mede-vac helicopters, but this young man was all in one piece. He wasn't looking very happy, but he did look healthy.

A few hours before, one of the assault group's small mine-sweepers had been hit by a rocket and machinegun fire as the group headed back to base. The attack was a surprise since that part of the river was considered "pacified" and supportive of the Saigon government. There had been no enemy activity in the area since Tet eight months earlier.

The boats opened fire and the advisors called in artillery and then attack helicopters. After fifteen minutes, the firing stopped and a squad of sailors went ashore to count bodies. Blood, brains, and yellow-pink tissue was spattered on the riverbank foliage. Brass cartridge casings littered the mud and truck-tire sandal prints marred the wet dirt. But there were no dead bodies, no body parts.

On their way back to the boats, one of the sailors stepped into a hole near the riverbank. It was the shallow mouth of a tunnel that had been camouflaged with palm fronds. They threw a grenade into the tunnel mouth. After the smoke cleared, a sailor was ordered into the tunnel, armed with a flashlight and pistol. A meter inside the tunnel was a supply cache. The sailor reported that several hundred kilograms of rice in bags blocked the tunnel.

Bags of rice were muscled out of the tunnel by the squad. Behind the rice they found boxes of bandages, antiseptic, and French pharmaceuticals. Then tins of Chinese field rations, and then more bags of rice. And behind the last of the rice bags, they found the prisoner, cradling an empty AK-47 and a canteen.

Normally, he would have been shot as soon as he was discovered. But the sailors hauling out the supplies had left their weapons at the tunnel mouth. The VC was dragged out by his ankles, slapped and punched, then marched to the riverbank with hands tied behind his back. The South Vietnamese Navy officer was going to execute him until he noticed that the two Americans and the Vietnamese commanding officer were watching him through binoculars from the command boat. The Americans valued prisoners as good sources of intelligence. With a shrug, he waved the command boat onto the riverbank to take the VC aboard.

The VC stayed in the sun on the hot deck while the sailors loaded one of the other boats with the booty from the tunnel. His hair hung down over his knitted eyebrows and worried face. The senior advisor, a youngish US Navy lieutenant, looked at him from the shade of the canopy on the stern of the boat. He turned to the other American, a chief petty officer.

"You know, Chief, I feel sorry for that fucker. Look at him. Poor kid doesn't know what's going to happen to him."

"Yeah, me too, sir," replied the older man. "I think if we weren't watching they'd have wasted him. Frankly, I'm surprised he even made it to the riverbank."

"How old do you think he is, Chief?"

"Can't tell, sir. Twenty? Maybe."

"Think he'll *chieu hoi*, Chief?" asked the Lieutenant. *Chieu hoi* was a program of surrender or treason, although no one ever used those words. VC and NVA soldiers could *chieu hoi*, which meant forsaking communism and Hanoi and joining the South Vietnamese government's side. According to the propaganda coming out of Saigon, a *chieu hoi* would be welcomed with open arms, interrogated, indoctrinated, repatriated, and integrated into the southern society. Many became scouts for US forces.

"Sir, if I was him I'd sure *chieu hoi*," answered the chief as he lit a cigarette. "Better than being a POW stuck in some tiger cage in Phu Quoc."

The prisoner looked at the two Americans, locking eyes with first the older man and then the younger. He licked his lips and then dropped his head, looking at his dirty feet.

The lieutenant stood up, reached for one of the cracked and chipped teacups sitting by the helmsman's station and poured some water out of his canteen into it. He walked over to the VC, bent over, and held the cup in front of the young man's lips.

The prisoner looked at the cup and then at the American. He shook his head.

"It's water. Water. *Nuoc*. Okay. *Rat tot*."

The prisoner looked at the cup but wouldn't drink. The American looked at the guard who just shrugged his shoulders.

"It's water. *Nuoc*. Okay? Watch me." The Lieutenant put the teacup to his lips and drained it. He refilled the cup from his canteen, took another sip, and then held it to the prisoner's lips.

The VC leaned forward and slurped the water as the American tilted the cup. Water spilled down the prisoner's chin. The chief was standing by them. As the lieutenant refilled the cup, the chief untied the prisoner's hands. The guarding sailor watched with bored eyes.

"This kid's dehydrated," said the lieutenant.

After another cup, the chief handed his own canteen to the VC who drained it. The guard giggled, amused that the Americans would share their own canteens with the enemy.

The VC kept silent but nodded his head at the two Americans. As the chief stubbed out his cigarette the prisoner's eyes looked at the butt. The Americans moved back to the shade of the canopy as the boat's engines coughed back to life. The chief rummaged through some C-rations boxes and took out several of the small packs of cigarettes that accompanied the canned food, coffee powder, and toilet paper. Each pack contained four cigarettes. The chief had two little packs of Winstons and three of Salems. While the lieutenant talked to his Vietnamese counterpart and made his radio reports, the chief walked forward to the prisoner whose hands had been retied and undid the ropes around he VC's wrists.

The American officer was busy as the river assault group made its way back to its base, handling radio communications and navigating the river shoals. He noticed that the chief stayed with the prisoner and his guard, talking, and gesturing. After the boats tied up and the VC was escorted off by two Vietnamese Army intelligence officers, the chief walked aft to the lieutenant, shaking his head with a thin smile.

"Sir," said the chief, "I think we're going to lose this war."

"Why you saying that?" asked the officer.

The older man smiled, looked down at his boots and shook his head. Then he looked at the VC being roughly shoved into the back of a jeep and handcuffed to the seat frame.

"Unless that kid *chieu hois*, I don't think he's going to make it to any POW camp, sir. They're being pretty rough with him," said the chief as he watched the jeep leave the compound.

"I went up to that VC and offered him a cigarette," continued the chief. "He doesn't say anything but takes it. I give him a light. He still doesn't say anything. So I try to get him talking and ask him some questions in Vietnamese." The chief, like all the advisors, spoke Vietnamese. "He just stares at me, doesn't seem to under-stand a word I'm saying. And I know my Vietnamese ain't *that* bad, sir. I'm carrying on a monologue. The guy might as well not been there. So, I'm getting tired of my own voice and offer him another cigarette. He puts it in his shirt pocket. Saving it for later, I guess."

The chief paused and look around the command boat, check-ing to make sure equipment was properly stowed and secured.

"I had these C-ration cigarette packets, some Winstons and Salems, sir," continued the chief. "Life is going to get pretty shitty for him from now on, so I figure these cigarettes would probably be the only good thing to happen to him for a very long time."

"Sure, Chief. Good thing to do," said the lieutenant. "Might make him a little more willing to provide information or *chieu hoi.*"

The chief nodded, paused for a second or two and went on. "So I hand him the packs of cigarettes. He shakes his head. I tell him to take them, they're good American cigarettes. He shakes his head again, won't put his hands out to take them. We go back and forth with me telling him to take them and him shaking his head. Then the guard reties his hands since we're almost at the pier and the kid looks at me." The chief stopped talking and started to chuckle.

"What's so funny, Chief?"

"Well sir, the kid looks at me and makes the first sounds since he's been captured. He says in perfect English, 'I prefer Marlboros.' "

WIA

H e didn't feel much at first. Just a punch in his wrist. But whatever it was made him drop his M16. Surprised, he bent down to pick up his rifle and saw bright red spatter on the black plastic stock. What the fuck was that? And his hand was all covered with red liquid and he couldn't grab his rifle and the firing was deafening but it sounded sort of muffled. He looked around. The coxswain was yelling something he couldn't understand, pointing with one hand while steering the boat with the other. What in the hell was he saying?

Then he felt a sting in his wrist and forearm, which turned into burning pain. Like a hot steel rod was being shoved up the inside of his arm. Damn, he was thirsty and his scalp was tingling beneath his helmet. Itching almost. He could see the guns firing and the tracers and the coxswain trying to reach him. The firing and diesel sounds turned into a noise like air rushing through his ears. Muffling everything.

Someone put a pad or something on his wrist and tried to push him down to the deck. Cold, he felt cold, chilled. His vision turned into a tunnel and lost color. Nausea choked him. He shut his eyes. It was dark, black, but filled with squiggles and blotches of color.

Someone was rolling him and then shoving him. And he was rising and then shaken and then it all just sort of turned into a deep dark nothing.

He could hear voices, mumbling. Something was touching his right wrist. Like a trout coming to the surface to eat mosquito larvae, he opened his eyes. Bright light shot painful lightning into his brain. He shut his eyes, trying to squeeze them together tightly.

"...ope...eyes...doct..." A female voice entered the fog of his brain.

He didn't know how much later—maybe minutes, maybe hours, maybe days—he twisted his head to the side and squinted. A green wall and metal table and some crib bars or something. Then a white thing that moved. It came closer and he heard that voice again. "Lieutenant? Can you hear me?"

"Yeah," he tried to say, but his throat was too dry. He tried to nod his head. Again time passed. He felt restless, agitated, tired, sore, confused, uncomfortable, and angry.

"Good. Good morning, Lieutenant. You just lie there, don't try to move." The voice was a man's. A gentle hand kept firm pressure on his chest. He opened this eyes fully. The room lights had been dimmed. A man's face wearing a surgical mask beneath his chin was looking into his eyes. He tried to raise his head but he didn't have the strength.

"Don't try to move, Lieutenant, we'll crank the bed up for you." A pretty face above a nurse's uniform entered his vision. He shut his eyes.

Someone put a straw between his lips and told him to take a sip. An elixir of cold water filled his mouth and dribbled down his throat and chin. He tried to talk but his mind was too befuddled and all he could do was grunt.

"Drink some more water, Lieutenant."

His girlfriend stood next to the bed and held his hand. He looked at her for a bit and tried to smile, but then went back to the darkness.

One time he saw, or thought he saw, his boat's chief boatswain standing at the foot of the bed. But hadn't the chief been killed? Or was that the gunner?

Mom and Dad had visited. He remembered seeing them. And the doctors and the nurses were starting to look familiar. He even recognized the sounds of their footsteps.

Blackness was replaced with increasingly longer moments of looking around and sipping water and even eating soup. One time he was fed a waffle by a nurse. His right arm was in a cast from his fingers to his shoulder; traction held it in a bizarre Heil Hitler position.

The doctors and nurses told him he was in Oaknoll Naval Hospital in Oakland, California. They thought they had saved his arm after picking out the shrapnel and reassembling the shattered bones like a jigsaw puzzle. He had sensation in his fingers, which was a good thing. Whether or not he would ever be able to use his arm normally was a question that could not be answered for a long time to come.

"Think I'll be able to stay in the navy, doc? Or am I done with this man's outfit?"

"I don't know, Bert. It will be a while before we have to consider that. Right now we have to get you healed. Tomorrow we're taking off the cast and I'm pretty sure you'll start physical therapy soon."

Months of pain, frustration, anger, and boredom followed. He never saw his girlfriend again. The chief came by to visit and Mom or Dad or both were usually around on the weekends. Then, one day over a year after he was wounded, he left Oaknoll Naval Hospital and the navy.

With his GI Bill and VA benefits, Bert studied for his doctorate in mathematics. At a math department party for the teaching assistants, he met Lois. They dated and after he was awarded his PhD, they married. A teaching stint at UCLA turned into a tenured professorship. Around campus he was known as that math professor with the stiff arm and terrible handwriting.

THE CONTEST

They appeared as different as two men could be. One tall, rangy, raw-boned, and sinewy; the other short, baby-faced, heavily muscled, and husky. A floppy jungle hat, sleeveless uniform shirt, khaki shorts, and buckskin chukka boots without socks on the big man; olive drab T-shirt, tan swim trunks, and reef shoes on the shorter. Neither man wore any rank or unit insignia, but everyone in Vung Tau knew who they were. These two men were the senior and junior members of the four-man Royal Australian Navy's Explosive Ordnance Disposal team. Lieutenant Clem Small and Petty Officer Burt Williams.

The American navy officer looked up from his paperwork as the two men walked into his hooch. "Hey, you two. Good morning."

"G'day, *Dai Uy*." Lieutenant Small smiled. His persona was anything but small. The wide grin in his handsome, craggy face revealed several gaps in his teeth. "You and your mates left early last night."

"Yep," said the American as he stood up, opened the refrigerator and handed each man a can of Swan Lager. "There was no way we could keep up with you and the SEALs. Figured we'd retreat while we could still drive the jeep down the hill without running it into a ditch."

He looked at Petty Officer Williams. "You feeling okay, Burt? You look sort of...I don't know...sort of a cross between blue and green and maybe a little red if I include your eyes."

Clem laughed as Burt smiled and opened his lager.

"Fit as a fiddle, sir," replied Burt as he raised his can. "Cheers." He took a sip, leaned back in his chair, smiled again, and belched loudly. "You going to join us, sir?"

"I can't keep up with you guys. If I had a beer now, I'd fall asleep writing these reports. I'll stick with coffee," answered the American. "You guys want some?"

"Nah, mate, takes up too much room in the bladder." Clem took a gulp of his beer. "Burt's okay. At least he is now. We dived on six ships this morning and he's still here, so he must be okay."

Every morning, two of the Australian EOD team took their skimmer out to the merchant ships swinging at anchor off of Vung Tau. The ships were waiting for pilots to take them from the South China Sea up the Long Tau shipping channel to the port of Nha Be near Saigon. The EOD team swam down the hulls and anchor chains looking for explosives and booby traps. And every morning, schedule permitting, they stopped by the South Vietnamese Navy's Coastal Group's junk base and dropped in to the US Navy's advisors' hooch for a chat, maybe some coffee, and often a beer.

The invitation to visit was always open; they were welcome guests. Full of life, ever cheerful, and using richly onomatopoeic Australian slang, their arrival was a delightful diversion from the Americans' futile tedium of advising the Vietnamese sailors in how to run a navy. And about once a month, the Aussies pitched in a case or two of Australian beer to replenish the hooch's refrigerator.

The EOD team did far more than check ships for hidden explosives and drink beer in the hooch. Stationed in a hilltop cave near the communications center and the old French lighthouse, the Australians disarmed and disposed of unexploded ordnance and booby traps, and supported the nearby Royal Australian Army units, US Air Force detachments, and the American and

Vietnamese navies. Once, they even found themselves in the operating room of the American army's medical center assisting a surgeon in the removal of a live projectile from a soldier's chest cavity. Trained in both diving and land tactics, they often found themselves in the shallows of the mangrove swamps of the Rung Sat zone looking for enemy bodies and equipment.

Like the American SEAL teams, the team was considered a special warfare unit. For the last month, they had been working with a SEAL detachment, training the South Vietnamese Navy's *Nguoi Nhai*—frogmen. Two nights earlier the training had come to a successful completion with a covert operation that was described by Clem as a "fuckin' good show, mate."

The night before, the Australians had hosted a farewell barbeque for the SEALs. The coastal group advisors were invited to the festivities at the hillside cave.

"So how was the party after we left?" asked the American.

Burt's cherubic face broke out into a wide smile. But he said nothing. Then he chuckled to himself, blushed, and shook his head. Despite what he did for a living and his apparent self-confidence, Burt was quiet, nearly shy. In that regard, he was very un-Aussie like.

"What's he smiling about, Clem?" asked the American.

Clem drank the final gulp of his beer and pointed at his sailor with the empty can. "Well, *Dai Uy*, Petty Officer Williams of this Royal Australian Navy Explosive Ordnance Disposal team should receive a knighthood. Or at least a full front-page article in the Sydney *Herald*. He has upheld Australia's honor."

"No shit? What did he do?"

Burt sat silent, his wide grin and bright white teeth contrasting attractively with his tanned skin, which had finally lost its greenish tinge.

"Young Burt there set a standard for valorous achievement that will not be matched for many years to come, I reckon. Maybe never." Clem spoke with a mock but deep gravity.

"Really? When we left, you guys were all sitting around that table littered with chicken and spare rib bones and beer cans. And I think I saw a bottle or two of scotch."

"You saw right, *Dai Uy*," confirmed Clem. "It seems that we started a contest of manly virtues just about that time."

The American got up, went to the refrigerator and grabbed three more Swan lagers, giving two to the Aussies and keeping one for himself.

"I think I need a beer to hear this tale," he said as he opened the beer tab and sat down next to Burt. "What, exactly, were these manly virtues? Arm wrestling? Drinking?"

"Only in the preliminaries. It started when one of my fine men demonstrated his repertoire of fart noises, including playing *Waltzing Matilda* with his hand in his arm pit." Clem looked up at the hooch's roof rafters, collecting his thoughts. "I get a little hazy about the right sequence but we and the SEALs started outdoing each other. Lighting farts, booger flinging, gorging on ribs and potato salad, harmonious belching. You know, *Dai Uy*, typical Olympic events. After each event, we took a voice vote, drank some beer or whiskey, and went on to the next."

"Sounds like you guys were a little drunk," observed the American of the obvious.

Burt finally spoke up. "Right, sir. After one of your guys tried to eat a rib bone and chundered, I figured we won."

"Chundered?"

"Right sir, chundered, y'know, vomited, threw up," explained Burt in all earnestness, as if teaching a child. "We were all pretty pissed, smashed off our faces, but the contest wasn't over. One of the SEALs started complaining that we still had two cans of Cheez Whiz, but no more crackers."

"Running out of crackers with surplus Cheez Whiz is forbidden by the US Navy. That's a various serious offense, Burt," said the American.

"Right, sir. Same in our military. So I couldn't allow that to happen. I had been quiet, but couldn't stay quiet any longer, sir. So I went into the cave, found our poker chips, put them on the table and squirted Cheez Whiz on a blue one and red one and ate both."

The American sat in stunned silence, eyes wide.

"Burt did indeed do that, *Dai Uy*. Chewed for quite a while, but got it all down." said Clem. "I'm expecting a colorful turd from this young hero later this morning."

"My gosh, Burt, you do deserve a knighthood for that. As an American, I concede."

Clem said, "You'd think that would be enough. Who could top that one? But one of your SEAL blokes did just that." Clem leaned forward and put his arm on the American's shoulder. "That wanker took the Cheez Whiz and made a bulls-eye of cheese right on my jeep's bonnet. Then he got up there, dropped his trousers and launched a shit right in the center of it."

The American blanched, afraid to swallow his mouthful of beer.

Burt straightened up in his chair, his chest puffed out. "Well, sir, I couldn't let that happen without doing him one better. Which I am proud to say won the contest."

Amazed and in a daze, the American swallowed his mouthful of now warm beer and said, "I can't imagine. What?"

"I quaffed a glass of piss."

Petty Officer Burt Williams left Vietnam as one of the most decorated men in the Australian Navy. He was awarded medals for bravery and merit and was mentioned in a dozen dispatches. A chest full of ribbons on his uniform is a record of these feats. But his single and most valorous and officially unrecognized feat—at least in the minds of his teammates and adversaries—occurred on a Vung Tau hillside on a night in late December 1968. That night Petty Officer Burt Williams became a legend of two great allied navies.

SMOKING'S BAD FOR YOU

The green tracers were so close to his face that he could feel their heat. First Lieutenant Jake Keller was lying on his back in a shallow muddy ditch—a truck track really—pinned down by NVA machine gun fire. The attack on the ARVN compound had started shortly after midnight with a barrage of mortars and B-40 rockets.

The whistles and explosions of the incoming had woken Jake up from a deep, dreamless sleep. He rolled off his cot and became entangled in his mosquito netting like a fly in a spider's web. A rocket passed through the thin walls of the advisors' hooch and out a convenient window on the other side. Jake untangled himself and grabbed his helmet and flak vest. He considered putting on his boots, but thought better of it and scrambled on his belly to the door.

Less than fifty meters away sat the heavily sandbagged headquarters and communication tent. Jake had to get there as fast as he could. The compound looked like a Fourth of July celebration. Ragged arcing lines of green and red tracers crisscrossed and the dark Vietnam night was painted in a ghostly pale light of illumination flares. From the sound of it, ammunition was being wasted at a prodigious rate. The wet air smelled of an odd combination of cordite, shit, and fish sauce.

Jake sensed a lull in the shooting and took a few hunched over steps toward the HQ tent. Bullets that sounded like flies buzzed past his ears; others made odd *pock* sounds as they hit the muddy dirt around him. Realizing that he was about to be shot, Jake had taken a flying leap onto his belly and wormed his way to the ditch and rolled over into it, landing on his back.

Breathing deeply, heart pounding, and sweating profusely, Jake took stock of his situation. He was safe in the ditch for the time being. The HQ tent was still about twenty meters away. At the next lull in the firing, he'd make another try. But for now he was staying put—laying in the mud on his back watching the tracers, flak vest spread over him like a short thick blanket protecting his heart, lungs, and the family jewels.

Man oh man, he wanted a cigarette. Real bad. But there were two problems.

One, Jake had promised his wife the last day of his R&R in Honolulu that he was quitting smoking that very moment. She said that that was the best gift he could ever give her. If he lit up, he'd be breaking his promise and disappointing her.

Two, and more importantly, Jake had only his helmet, flak vest, dog tags, shower shoes, and underpants. He had no cigarettes.

The green tracers stopped zooming over him. Jake took in a deep breath and slowly blew it out. Then he tried to roll onto his side so he could get moving again. As soon as he twisted his shoulders, the tracers came back and the ground made that sound of bullets hitting mud. *Pock. Pock. Pock. Pock.* Jake frantically shifted onto his back. Charlie had him zeroed in. They were waiting for him to move.

"Lieutenant, you okay?" boomed a gravelly whisky tenor over the cacophony of gunfire. It was the voice of one of the other advisors, First Sergeant Molina.

"Yeah, First Sergeant. I'm as good as it gets. Given the situation, I'm fucking outstanding."

"Charlie has you locked in. Better stay where you are, sir."

"Roger that, First Sergeant. Where are you? I don't want to look around given my friends out there with the AKs" asked Jake.

"I'm under the water tank trailer, about three, four meters from your head."

Three mortar rounds whistled in and exploded near the HQ tent, throwing mud and shrapnel in the air.

"You okay, Lieutenant?"

"Got rained on by mud and shit, but no holes that I can find. Other than scared shitless, I really need a cigarette," answered Jake.

"I thought you quit smoking, sir," said First Sergeant Molina.

A spray of machine gun fire swept the water tank, ricocheting off the thick steel. Molina buried his face in the mud, hands holding onto his helmet. Jake tried to turn his head but as soon as his helmet showed above the trench bullets *pocked* into the near mud.

"First Sergeant! You need help? You okay?" shouted Jake as he pressed his head back into the trench bottom.

"Okay, sir. They got us pinned down. We're not going anywhere until this shit stops. They're ahead and on the left flank. How much ammo you got?" replied Molina.

"I don't even have a weapon. I bailed out of the hooch as soon as that rocket went through it."

"Jesus, sir. You left your weapon?"

"Yeah, tell me about it, First Sergeant. The only thing I've got to hold onto is my dick," grumbled Jake.

"Better not, sir," chuckled Molina. "That'll give you a hard-on and as soon as you start showing wood, Charlie's gonna blow it to pieces."

"You gotta promise me, First Sergeant. I get hit in the dick, you shoot me," whined Jake. "Christ I want a cigarette."

"I'm not promising anything, Lieutenant. You can shoot yourself. Oh, yeah, I forgot, you left your fucking weapon in the hooch."

"Rub it in. Go ahead, make me feel dumber than I am. Just get me a cigarette."

Two more mortar rounds dropped out of the sky but fell across the compound near the garbage dump.

"Didn't you quit smoking on R&R, Lieutenant?" asked Molina. "Something about a promise to your wife or something?"

Green tracers sprayed the water tank again. The heavy thud of a .50-caliber machine gun answered the distinctive barks of the AK-47s.

"First Sergeant, right now my chances of dying are much greater than my chances of seeing my wife again. I'll break that promise since I probably won't have to hear about it from her." Jake could hear Molina's low laughter.

He tried to shut his eyes but the glow of tracers and flares were still on his retina. He opened them again and, much to his surprise, calmly calculated that the intensity of gunfire was increasing. One hell of an attack. Charlie was one tough motherfucker.

Something bounced off his helmet onto his chin and then into the mud by his neck. He reached across his throat and grabbed a plastic object from the mud. It was a lighter, a BiC lighter with an orange plastic reservoir. Then a small package landed on the flak vest covering his stomach, and another landed alongside his waist. As soon as he touched the first package, he knew First Sergeant Molina was answering his prayers.

Jake had a lighter and two small packs of cigarettes. The little packs contained four cigarettes each. Every box of C-rations held one of these small packs, along with food, matches, and toilet paper. Jake now had four Winstons and four Salems. Before he quit smoking, he was a Marlboro man. Now he was not particular.

The attack ended twelve minutes after Molina tossed Jake the cigarettes and lighter. Artillery and attack helicopters pounded Charlie into silence. Jake smoked eight cigarettes in those twelve minutes. Inhaling deeply, he watched the green tracers diminish and stop.

Molina walked up to Jake, extended a hand, and pulled the lieutenant out of the mud. Jake was light headed from the nicotine and adrenaline.

"First Sergeant Molina," said Jake. "You have saved my life, but possibly destroyed my marriage. I'm putting you in for a medal. The Phillip and Morris Gallantry Cross."

Four months and three days later, Jake's wife was waiting for him as he got off the plane at Travis Air Force Base outside San Francisco. She ran up to him, put her arms around his neck, and kissed him long and hard. They walked arm-in-arm to the baggage claim to get his duffel.

She put her head on his shoulder as they waited at the baggage carousel. He turned his face to her and breathed in the wonderful smell of her shampoo. Without moving his head he said into her thick brunette hair, "You smell so good. Mary, I missed you so much. When Charlie had me pinned down in the mud, all I could think about was how much I love you. And now here you are." He squeezed her tight.

Mary turned in his arms and buried her face in his chest. Then she put her face up to his and kissed him. Abruptly, she pushed away to arm's length. Looking deep into her husband's eyes, she wrinkled her nose, frowned and said, "You smell like cigarettes. Oh, Jake, you promised. You've been smoking!"

IV AND JIM

O fficially, the *USS Stone Island* was an oceanographic research ship, a designation that conjures up a ship filled with marine biologists, geographers, and oceanographers. In fact, the ship was a spy ship, an electronic spy ship. The ship bristled with antennae of all shapes and sizes. Its crew was a mixture of sailors and officers to operate the ship, and more sailors, marines, and civilians to collect electronic emissions, analyze the signals, decode the messages stolen from the atmosphere, and send all the gathered intelligence back to places like DC, Langley, Pearl Harbor, and Yokosuka. The ship had no weapons to defend itself. Instead, the aircraft carrier task force commanders kept an eye on the *Stone Island* and hoped that, if need be, they could come to its aid in time.

The captain of the *Stone Island* kept his ship in international waters as he steamed up and down hostile coasts, its antennae absorbing valuable signals throughout the electronic spectrum. He tried to avoid confrontations and even steered away from harmless-looking fishing boats or merchant ships. The North Vietnamese, North Koreans, and Chinese knew the *Stone Island* was out there. And they kept an eye on her. An intrusion into their territorial waters would be reason to attack the ship.

Knowing that a mistake could escalate a war or destroy whatever diplomacy was in the works, the captain of the *Stone Island* found his job to be a stressful one. With no defensive armament, and not much speed to run away, he spent little time sleeping and a lot of time on the bridge. His crew was good. And that helped.

One of the junior officers of his crew was Ensign Malcolm C. Satterfield IV, known to his family and friends as IV. Pronounced "eye vee." Malcolm was a New Yorker. Spoiled by his socialite mother and ignored by his prominent attorney father, Malcolm may have also suffered from a bit too much inbreeding. He had an amazing sense of entitlement, was lazy, and had an ego as tough as an eggshell.

He had barely made it through a very expensive string of prep schools, and could not get into any of the colleges befitting someone with his pedigree. He took five years to get his degree from a small college in upstate New York, and then went to work as a junior copywriter with a Madison Avenue advertising firm owned by one of his father's clients.

IV's father and his friends, including the advertising firm's owner, were influential people. Because several of the firm's clients were federal government agencies, a few calls to a senator or deputy secretary earned the advertising firm a designation as a vital government supplier of services. That meant that the young men working at the firm were, for all practical purposes, draft-exempt.

IV was quite content and happy as a junior copywriter...for about six weeks. Then his father's friend called him into his office and said that IV should start looking for someplace that could better utilize his talents. The man gave him two weeks' notice and told him he didn't have to come to work during those two weeks. He'd be paid for another month.

Upset and humiliated, IV sat in an expensive Manhattan hotel bar, sipping fine whiskey on the rocks while he figured out what to do. Two naval officers in their blues were sitting in a booth in the bar with two very fine-looking women. IV stared at them. Twenty minutes later, he sat in the midtown Manhattan recruiting office, talking to a navy chief petty officer. The navy needed junior officers badly, especially surface line officers—ship drivers. To be accepted for Officer Candidate School, he needed a bachelor's degree from an accredited university and an officer aptitude test score above a certain number. He needed to pass a physical, have three reference forms filled out, and pass an interview.

IV had his college send the recruiting office his college transcripts and certification of a bachelor's degree. The chief scheduled him for the aptitude test and a physical, both of which IV passed without a problem. IV wasn't stupid, and squash and tennis kept him fit. His father and mother found him three references among their friends, all of them naval officers during World War II. The interview went well, especially after IV told the two interviewers that he crewed a sailing yacht on Long Island Sound.

After sixteen weeks of training at OCS in Newport, Rhode Island, IV received his commission as an ensign in the naval reserve. Several weeks of additional training at ship handling and damage control schools followed. Finally, in Yokosuka, Japan, he crossed the quarterdeck of the *USS Stone Island*. His orders said he was to relieve the damage control assistant in the engineering department, but the captain had a different job in mind for IV.

Stone Island's previous damage control assistant was long gone, having moved on to a destroyer in Pearl Harbor a month before IV came aboard. The captain could have delayed the old DCA's departure until IV arrived. He could also have accelerated IV's arrival. But making the DCA stay aboard for another month meant that the DCA would have had to cut short his well-deserved leave time between ships. And forcing IV to report to the ship a month early would mean cutting the new officer's post-OCS schooling and leave time. The captain didn't want to shortchange either of the two young men. And he didn't need to because he had Jim Archer.

Chief Warrant Officer Jim Archer was *Stone Island*'s assistant DCA. Jim was a robust career navy man who had left Great Lakes Naval Training Center as a seaman recruit nineteen years ago. He had worked his way up through the enlisted ranks and then entered the warrant officer program as a specialist in damage control and engineering. There was little that Jim did not know about those two areas. And there was absolutely nothing that Jim did not know about the *Stone Island*'s damage control and engineering plant. The captain had no doubt that with Jim around the *Stone Island* was in capable hands. His plan was to let Jim be the DCA. Jim had the experience and proven expertise. A new ensign, untested and fresh out of school with a few months in the navy, still had a steep and difficult learning curve to climb. The captain would make this new Ensign Satterfield Jim Archer's assistant.

Putting an ensign under a warrant officer was unusual and could cause a problem—especially if the ensign was chickenshit, and more concerned about rank and privilege than about the efficiency of the ship.

There are three levels of rank and privilege in the navy. One is the enlisted, the sailors from seaman recruit through master chief petty officer. Next is the warrant officer community, the men like Jim. At the top are the commissioned officers, from ensign through admiral. Jim was at the top of the middle group, IV was at the very bottom of the top group. Theoretically, Jim should salute IV and call him "sir."

While the captain certainly respected and appreciated the rank structure of the military, he had no problem putting someone junior in charge of someone senior. The navy and his country had entrusted him with a very valuable and expensive ship, 352 men, and missions vital to his country. He would do whatever it took to maintain that trust. As commanding officer, violating a protocol of rank and privilege didn't mean much when the operation and safety of his ship were concerned.

Traditionally, the DCA was also the damage control division head, responsible for the division's twenty-five enlisted men. There was no doubt in the captain's mind that Jim could run a division. But he also knew that one of the best training opportunities for a new officer was handling a division of sailors. No one could teach that in the Naval Academy, ROTC, or OCS. The only way to learn was to do. Some officers just could not lead a group of sailors and get results. It wasn't that they were stupid or inept. They simply didn't have a trait that the captain considered inborn. Leadership. He was convinced you either had it or you didn't. It was a human trait just like a sense of rhythm or a quick wit.

His plan was to split the damage control assignment. For the actual operations, Jim would be the DCA, and the new ensign would be his assistant. For the administration of the DC division, the new ensign would be the division officer, and Jim would act as the assistant division officer. It was a bit of a hybrid, but the captain could see no reason why it wouldn't work. After all, he had to assume that both men would be mature about it. They were United States naval officers.

* * *

The scheme did work. Well, sort of.

Stone Island's damage control division ran smoothly and responded well to all casualties and damage, both real and simulated. The division had no disciplinary problems and morale was solid. IV seemed to have quickly grasped the intricacies of running a division of diverse men at sea. And he was progressing well through the various qualifications he needed to become officer of the deck when the ship was under way.

But IV, by his nature, was bit of a complainer. And he had not learned a basic tenet of navy wardrooms: if you complained about something, you would likely be assigned the task of correcting the problem you were complaining about.

IV constantly criticized the food served in the wardroom. When compared to most institutional food services like college dormitories, hospitals, and penitentiaries, *Stone Island's* officers ate pretty well. The food was nutritious and the menus well balanced. There were problems—blandness, monotonous menus, running out of fresh milk and vegetables—but given that the ship was operating at sea near a hostile coast and thousands of miles away from the nearest A&P or Safeway supermarket, those problems were minor. And there wasn't really much that could be done about them.

Those facts were lost on IV, whose grumblings became a ward-room joke. Within a few weeks after reporting aboard, by a vote of fourteen to one, the wardroom elected IV to take over the position of wardroom mess treasurer—the worst officer-collateral duty on any ship. IV was now in charge of the wardroom mess accounts and the menus. He had to deal with all wardroom complaints and suggestions from any one of the other officers on the ship. Of course, IV complained about being the mess treasurer, too, but he couldn't muster any votes other than his own to elect someone else.

The other big gripe IV had was that he worked for a warrant officer. After all, he was an ensign and senior to a warrant officer. He acknowledged that Jim Archer really knew his stuff, but so did he. As a recent graduate of DCA school, IV thought he should be the DCA, not the DCA's assistant.

Jim found this amusing. He had another ten months aboard the *Stone Island* before he received orders and moved on to his next duty station. When that happened, he was sure the captain would make IV the DCA. But until then, he was the DCA, and IV's whining provided a tempting target for some harmless fun. With the help of the rest of the wardroom, Jim sent IV into a rant at least once a day.

One day the communications officer put on an innocent face and asked IV how it was that he was working for a warrant? Wasn't he senior to Jim? Another time the main propulsion assistant asked IV if he could do something about the selection of jelly at breakfast because he and Jim really liked English orange marmalade.

Even the XO got into the act when he looked around the ward-room table at lunch and said, "Who's our junior officer aboard now?" He focused on IV and said, "It's you, isn't it IV?"

"No sir, XO. It's Jim. He's junior to me." IV pointed at the warrant officer sitting next to him.

"Oh, that's right. The DCA is junior to you, isn't he?"

IV was smart enough to limit his answer to the XO. "Yes, sir, he is." But as soon as lunch was over and the XO returned to his office, he started whining to anyone who would listen.

Jim did his part in tormenting IV. During damage control drills and exercises, especially when the captain or XO was in damage control central, Jim would look up from his status board and say, "Hey, IV. How about getting the XO and me a cup of coffee? Black for me, please. XO you want cream and sugar, sir?" IV knew that Jim, as DCA, could not leave his station. And the phone talkers could not be sent on errands since they were restrained by headsets plugged into bulkhead phone jacks. So IV would just turn red, purse his lips tightly together, and fetch Jim and the XO their coffee. But when the drill was over, Jim took every opportunity to complain about the injustice of it all.

Then there was the time in the Philippines. *Stone Island* had pulled into Subic Bay for some new equipment installation, and repairs. Jim and IV were sitting in the officers' club, enjoying steaks, when the captain walked in and joined them. The captain was relaxed and chatty. He told them how happy he was with their division's performance. Both Jim and IV thanked him for the comment, then Jim said the division was a bunch of real good men. The captain agreed but he also said they were well led and smiled at the warrant officer and the ensign.

A tall, gray-haired man wearing two stars on his collar walked up to the table and greeted the captain by his first name. He was the rear admiral in charge of the aircraft carrier task force that had arrived the evening before. Jim and IV stood up as the captain introduced them.

"Admiral Benson, this is Jim Archer, my DCA, and Malcolm Satterfield, his assistant."

The admiral shook hands and looked at the two men closely. If he noticed anything unusual about a warrant officer being in charge of an ensign, he didn't show it. IV whined to Jim as they walked back to his ship. His rant about even a flag officer ignoring navy protocol and tradition went down in wardroom history as his best.

* * *

The captain was tired but happy about the orders the ship had received the night before. After two stressful weeks of tiptoeing along the North Korean coast collecting intelligence, *Stone Island* had been ordered to the South China Sea to listen in on the North Vietnamese and China. Certainly, that stretch of water could be just as harrowing as the North Korean coast, but he had a luxurious four days to get there. He ordered the navigator to lay out a course that would keep them in international waters and clear of shipping lanes.

As the ship steamed south, the weather warmed and the seas calmed. The whole ship relaxed. The sailors took advantage of the sunshine and aired their bedding. Holiday routine was called and an all-hands barbeque of hot dogs and burgers was held on the fantail. The captain was proud of his crew and the ship. They did their job well. And he needed some sleep. They still had a day and a half before they'd be on station and he was going to take advantage of it.

Clad in just his swim trunks and shower shoes, the captain surprised the bridge watch. Acknowledging the bosun's call of "captain on deck," the captain told the officer of the deck that he was going to go up to the flying bridge and try to get some sun and maybe try to nap. If anything came up, he'd be just a deck above them.

The navigator was standing by the windscreen on the flying bridge, enjoying the hot sun and chatting with one of the signalmen. He greeted the captain, who smiled at the two men and said he was going to take a sun bath and to just ignore him. The captain took a stretcher off its bulkhead bracket, opened it up, and put it down on the hot steel deck. Within a few seconds after laying down on the stretcher, the tired man was sound asleep on his stomach.

Ten minutes later, carrying a clipboard full of papers, IV came up the ladder to the flying bridge. He looked around and saw the navigator, the signalman, and a husky man on a stretcher, obviously sound asleep. IV was looking for Jim Archer. The man on the stretcher had his feet nearest IV, his head farthest from him.

Before IV could say anything, the navigator put his finger to his lips and pantomimed someone asleep by putting his head against his two clasped hands. IV nodded, stared at the man on the stretcher, and decided that he was the right size and build to be Jim Archer.

IV held his finger to his lips, turned, and then tiptoed to the foot end of the stretcher. The navigator, realizing what was happening, took a quick step and tried to grab IV's arm. But he was too late.

IV reached down, grabbed both stretcher handles, and with a quick movement, lifted them off the deck and flipped the stretcher over. The captain shouted "what the fuck" as he rolled out of the stretcher and bounced onto the hot steel deck of the flying bridge. He rolled several times, coming to a bewildered halt at the base of an antenna platform.

Directly below in the wheelhouse, the watch standers heard a series of heavy thumps from above and saw Ensign Satterfield scurry down the ladder from the flying bridge. A few minutes later, the captain and the navigator walked down the ladder into the wheelhouse, laughing heartily.

"I'll be in my cabin. Give me a few minutes to shower and then pass the word for Mr. Satterfield to come to my cabin, please," said the captain to the OOD.

* * *

No one knows what happened when IV met with the captain in his cabin that sunny afternoon. No one but the captain and IV, and neither one was talking.

For whatever reason, from then on IV quit complaining and whining. Half a year later, when Jim Archer left the ship to teach at the Damage Control School in San Francisco, IV became the DCA and a brand new ensign became his assistant.

After two years aboard the *Stone Island*, IV was due for orders. The navy's Bureau of Personnel had asked him what he was planning to do. Stay in and make a career of the navy? Leave active duty, but stay in the naval reserves as a "weekend warrior"? Or leave the navy behind and become a full-time civilian?

He had already been mulling over his future when he realized he had only a few months left on the ship. He liked what he was doing. But he was also giving some thought to law school. One night as OOD on a flat Gulf of Siam, IV made up his mind. When he finished his watch, he wrote a letter to the bureau.

IV laid out his plan. He wanted to go to law school and pass the bar. But he also wanted to keep his ties to the navy. So, when his active duty obligations were up, he'd stay in the reserves and go to law school using the GI bill. Mother and father were not going to finance that education. IV wouldn't allow it. Then, when he passed the bar, he'd go practice the law and transfer from the surface officer to the JAG Corps in the naval reserve.

The bureau sent IV to the Damage Control school in San Francisco to be one of the school's department heads for his last nine months in the navy. Jim Archer was one of the instructors in his department. Jim worked for IV this time. After applying to several law schools, IV picked his first choice, Stanford, just down the peninsula from the DC school.

After law school and the bar exam, IV became a Los Angeles County public defender. His father told him that that was an excellent training opportunity, and that IV would make a valuable criminal defense attorney in his firm when he came back to Manhattan.

IV told his father, "Dad, I'm probably going to stay out here. I don't think I'll be returning to New York nor joining your firm."

That evening, IV's parents wondered what had they possibly done wrong? Or was something wrong with their son? Had the navy brainwashed him?

Two years later, Jim Archer was IV's best man. The new Mrs. Satterfield never liked the nickname IV and called him Malcolm from the moment they first met.

One of the guests at the wedding was Jim and IV's captain from the *Stone Island*. Now a vice admiral, he gave a wonderful toast.

PCOD

War evokes many emotions in the so-called normal people who fight in them. These souls are not the super-dedicated and ambitious generals and admirals, nor the psychopaths that if it were not for a war to license their killing would be sitting in some prison back home. These guys are the slugs fighting the war.

Five emotions—maybe "feelings" is a better choice of word— marked the war in Vietnam. Bored, scared, excited, lonely, and horny.

While not as vital as food nor important as ammunition, pussy became the number one topic of conversation, thoughts, and daydreams of US warriors in Vietnam. Young men in their foxholes, hammocks in the field, or bunks at sea weren't thinking about mom's apple pie.

This should not surprise anyone. Virile and healthy men, most well under the age of thirty with adolescent blood and hormones still coursing through their veins, think about pussy whether in war or sitting in a college classroom or taking orders at McDonalds. But in Vietnam there was no girlfriend nearby, no wife between clean white sheets, no nice unstained issue of the latest *Playboy*, *Penthouse* or *Hustler* to spirit into the bathroom or bedroom for nude-photo-enhanced masturbation. Hell, there weren't even any bedrooms, bathrooms were rare, and privacy was even rarer.

Thinking of warm skin and nipples and vaginas and the touch of a female diverted the men's minds from the heat and rain and muck and stink that surrounded them. Of course, there was nothing new or unique about soldiers, marines, and sailors thinking of pussy. As long as there have been men fighting wars, there have been camp followers and whores and hookers and shantytowns.

Wherever there were bases or ports, there were the girls to service the men. Before the United States sent the first troops to Vietnam, the rim of the western Pacific had thriving pussy markets. Subic City, Olangapo, Singapore, Hong Kong, Angel City, and the honchos of Japan had been servicing the US fighting men for years. Vietnam simply switched from French to English.

The big in-country R&R spots of Saigon and Vung Tau had a rotating transient population of Americans with money in their pockets and booze in their bellies. The supply of pussy perfectly matched the demand. Some of the women were beautiful. Some even dyed their hair blond and sported D-cup breasts from a plastic surgeon in Hong Kong.

Others, especially in the boonies, were pocked-marked and hard. Skanky. But they met the demand. A shantytown near the Swift boat base north of Vung Tau sported a bar with cots and partitions in the back. On the road between Saigon and Cu Chi, GI drivers could pull their supply trucks over to the side of the road and get laid behind a berm, then jump back into the cab without ever having had to turn the engine off. That was cheaper, much cheaper, than getting your ashes hauled in Saigon or Vung Tau.

Ugly young soldiers, sailors, marines, and air force men with terrible personalities and lousy hygiene could do something that they never could do back home: they could have sex with a woman who might even say "I love you no shit." All they needed was the price of admission.

There was another price to be paid, which was levied quite arbitrarily. The price of catching the clap. Or syphilis. Or nonspecific urethritis. Or crabs. Venereal disease was a price to pay.

The military preached protection during sex. Wear a condom. Wash afterward. Abstain. Some of the commands even sent their medical personnel into the whorehouses and bars to treat the hookers, issuing them a card certifying that for the time being they were clean. That worked well at the Swift boat base until a new corpsman arrived who thought that treating whores was immoral and stopped the practice. The number of sick sailors increased shortly after that.

There was a rumor that started with the French soldiers in the early 1950s and persisted for another twenty years. The story went that Ho Chi Minh had recruited companies of young comely women willing to contract venereal disease and spread it around. The fact that at one time the occupying French forces had nearly half their men incapacitated by VD lends credence. It also raises questions of what the women did with their earnings? After all, North Vietnam was not overflowing with cash and they were fighting a war.

Another myth grew. Everyone knew someone who knew someone who swore that he had caught the Godzilla of clap. This strain of gonorrhea was so virulent and resistant to cure that the Department of Defense had secretly decided that anyone who had it could not leave Vietnam until a cure was found. Supposedly, somewhere in Saigon or Danang, was a whole barracks full of guys with this disease, long past their rotation dates, all of them waiting for their dicks to fall off. Special forces were recruiting these men for suicide missions, since they'd probably never leave Vietnam and had nothing to live for. The army and navy doctors just shook their heads at this mythical super-disease. Although they said they could cure any of the venereal diseases they encountered in Vietnam, the myth of the monster clap continued.

Most tours in-country were twelve months long. The marines did thirteen months. When their tours were up, the men flew back to the states to new assignments if they stayed in the military, or to civilian life if they didn't. For most, the flight home ended in a reunion with family and friends. And for many of those, sex with their spouse or girlfriend.

Protecting their partners at home from the venereal diseases of Vietnam was paramount for many reasons. Probably the most important reason was not having to answer the question from a wife of how she could have possibly caught the clap from a faithful husband? To avoid this embarrassment, wise men kept track of their PCOD, or Pussy Cut-Off Date.

The PCOD was the last date to have sex before returning home. It was calculated by taking the sum of the amount of time it takes for the symptoms of a venereal disease to appear, the time to diagnose, and the time to treat the disease to the point where the victim was no longer contagious and was also symptom-free. This was subtracted from the last day in-country to determine the PCOD. Prudent calculators used 60 days. Most of the men used six weeks. For example, if a sailor's last day in-country was scheduled to be July 1, six weeks before that would be May 20. From that day until he rotated out of country, the sailor would try to abstain from Vietnamese pussy.

First Lieutenant George Green, US Army Reserve, was due to leave Vietnam and the army the next day, August 16, 1969. Lieutenant Green was a good officer. In his three years in the army, he had served well his country and the men entrusted to his care. His last three months had been spent in Saigon, working for the brass at MACV, the Military Assistance Command, Vietnam. Before that he led an infantry platoon in the boonies.

When Lieutenant Green had arrived in Vietnam a year before, he had left behind his fiancée, Sharon. The week before he reported to his new job at MACV, Sharon and Lieutenant Green married on the beach at Waikiki the first evening of his Hawaiian R&R. Lieutenant Green was faithful to his fiancée, now his wife, the whole twelve months. While a full-blooded and virile twenty-five-year-old man, he just wasn't interested in any woman other than Sharon.

Such fidelity was not rare in Vietnam. It may have even represented the majority.

Maybe not.

Lieutenant Green had become good friends with his officemates at MACV, Captains Charlie Smithers and Bob Sanchez. Both career army officers had another two months left before they rotated to their next duty stations. They had joked that they were going to take Lieutenant Green out on his last night, get him drunk, and then dump him at one of the bars on Tu Do Street to get him laid.

Captain Smithers walked up to Lieutenant Green's desk. "Hey, GG. Let's go shit, shave, and shower and then Bob and I are taking you out to the Rex for a fine steak dinner and drinks. You up for that or are you going to pussy out on us and eat mystery meat at the officers' mess?"

"If you two senior officers are buying the steak and beer, I'm going with you guys. But it's up early in the morning to take the freedom bird home to wife and civilian life."

Captain Sanchez said, "Yeah, yeah, don't rub it in. We know, we know. In fact, we're driving you to Tan Son Nhut in the morning and throwing your ass on the plane."

The three officers sat on the rooftop patio of the Rex, drinking cold beer, eating steaks, and watching red tracers rain down from the sky on the delta many miles to the southeast—killing vegetation, animals, and people, some of whom were probably VC, some not. Lieutenant Green felt relaxed, completely at ease, for the first time in twelve months. Tomorrow he was going home. He hadn't seen or talked to his wife in three months.

A few more officers from MACV came by to chat, wish Lieutenant Green good luck, and have a final drink with him. And then a couple more stopped by. Lieutenant Green was slowly getting as drunk as he had ever been in his life.

At about midnight, the three friends went down the block to one of the more tame nightclubs for a final drink, which turned into a final three drinks for Lieutenant Green.

"GG, get up. Time to get yourself cleaned up and on the freedom bird," said Captain Sanchez as he shook him awake.

Someone had pumped Lieutenant Green's stomach full of sewer gas and had shit in his mouth, then washed it out with Saigon

River mud. The light in the room was about the intensity of half a dozen suns and seemed to melt his retinas and boil his brain. He had never felt so bad in his life. Rolling over he felt his stomach do a somersault.

Stumbling to the bathroom, Lieutenant Green puked up his lungs and guts, turning his internals inside out. He looked over the porcelain thunder throne and saw his two friends standing there, watching him. "Will one of you please shoot me?"

"Normally I'd say 'sure, GG' but we promised the colonel we'd get your ass on that plane. So you'd better empty yourself, and plan to recover from your hangover at 35,000 feet heading east," said Captain Smithers.

"Oh, crap. I feel like shit. What happened? The last thing I remember was sitting at the Rex. How'd I get here?"

"Well, let's see. We went down to Tu Do Street and had a night-cap at the Red Door, then piled your ass into the back of the jeep and dumped you on your bed about six hours ago," said Captain Sanchez.

The words slowly wormed their way into Lieutenant Green's poorly functioning brain. "Tu Do…Red Door? You're shitting me. I was there? You guys didn't get me laid, did you?"

Captain Smithers waited for Green's dry heaves to stop before answering. "Now, would we do a thing like that to our good buddy GG, the short-timer who's leaving us here to fight and die for our country while he goes home to become some insurance salesman or potato farmer? Would we do that to our good buddy, Bob?"

"No way, Charlie. And have GG infect his bride with monster clap? No way," answered Captain Sanchez.

"Come on you guys, be straight with me. Did I get fucked last night? Blow job?"

"I didn't see anything, GG. Of course, I wasn't watching all the time," said Captain Sanchez.

"Me neither, man," said Captain Smithers. "But I don't know what you did when you disappeared for a while. I just thought you were in the bathroom."

"Oh, fuck. You didn't get me laid, tell me you didn't," pleaded Lieutenant Green.

"Let's put it this way, GG. Those women are working ladies. If you got laid, we didn't pay for it, and I don't think they do charity work," said Captain Sanchez.

Several hours later, Lieutenant Green was halfway across the Pacific in a chartered DC-8. He had downed about a gallon of Coca-Cola and was slowly losing his headache and the nausea was almost gone. But he could not remember anything between the Rex and waking up in his bed.

He was pretty sure that his two buddies hadn't gotten him laid. And his wallet didn't seem to be any lighter, which meant he hadn't paid for any pussy. But he still had some doubt. Maybe they did pop for a roll in the hay. Maybe one of the girls did give him a freebie. Probably not, but he wasn't certain.

"Feeling better, Lieutenant?" asked the flight attendant as she put another Coke in front of him. "We still have your sandwich if you want to eat something."

His stomach fluttered and he tried to smile and said, "No, thanks. Just keep these Cokes coming, please."

The cold, sweet soda felt good going down his throat. He would survive. Maybe he'd eat something before the next refueling stop. But what should he tell Sharon? Should he tell her that he wasn't sure if he got laid last night, and they shouldn't have sex for a week or two to see if anything started dripping? Tell her he had some rare combat-related thing that wouldn't let him have sex with his wife for two weeks? Hope nothing happened and just make love to his wife? He was driving himself nuts.

A day and a half after leaving Saigon, Lieutenant Green met his wife at the gate in Seattle's airport. They hugged and kissed, picked up his bags, and she drove to the Olympic Hotel. She had already put out her nightgown and chilled a bottle of champagne. In a travel-lagged and sleep-deprived stupor, he followed her lead and made love to his wife. The thoughts of PCOD and Tu Do Street were buried. He fell into a deep, dreamless sleep.

A month later, George Green, the new project engineer at Boeing, suddenly found himself smiling. He remembered the night at the Rex, the walk to the Red Door on Tu Do Street, and then being tossed into the back of the jeep. Shaking his head, he started to giggle.

WOMAN ALONE

At 0900, the army chaplain, a major, walked into the room of four dozen women and seven children. The women were chatting and drinking coffee or pineapple juice; the children were running around the room, grabbing another cookie or two from the tray next to the paper cups.

Every morning a chartered jet from Saigon and another from Danang arrived at the airport in Honolulu carrying a load of men and an occasional woman or two for a week's R&R—rest and recreation—on Oahu. Usually, two-thirds of them would be met at the airport by a spouse, maybe their kids, or a girl or boyfriend. In the afternoon, the two jets would fly back to Vietnam to return those who had finished their week. Each plane was greeted on Oahu by the major or one of the two other chaplains working for him.

"Ladies, please take a seat. Your husbands and friends are going through customs, and you'll be able to see them in a few minutes. Don't worry about your kids; they can run around as long as the cookies hold out." He checked his clipboard. This group was all wives and children, no girlfriends, no husbands, no parents. Pretty standard.

Grabbing a lei out of a big box on the table in front of the room, he put it around his neck. "*Aloha.* Welcome to Hawaii!"

A ragged *aloha* answered his greeting. He laughed.

"C'mon, you guys can do better than that. *Aloha!*" He cupped his hand to his ear and leaned forward.

The group laughed and shouted back *aloha!* A delayed *aloha* in a three-year-old voice made the chaplain chuckle.

"I'm Major Tripp. Please bear with me for a few minutes. I will be talking to your husbands right after this, but we'll move this along as fast as we can. Each of you has been given this card, right? Please hold it up." He saw that all the adults had a card identical to the one he was holding. "It has my office number and address on it. We're in Fort DeRussy on Waikiki. Someone will pick up that phone no matter when you call. If you need help—and I don't care what kind of help you need—you call this number. I don't care if you ran out of diapers or deodorant or it's a medical or family emergency, you call. We'll be there." The women were looking at him intently. As he had been many times before, he was struck by how attractive these women were.

In the two years he had been stationed here, he had been called at least once a week. Usually the calls were for minor problems like a bad sunburn or the hotel screw-up with the reservations. But sometimes they had been more serious problems, like the marine who woke up screaming and hitting his wife when she tried to calm him, or the air force forward air controller who said he wanted a divorce, or the wife who feared her soldier husband was now a dope addict. Hopefully, these beautiful women would only call because they ran out of sunscreen.

"A few hours ago, these fine men were in a combat zone, so be prepared for some odd behavior. You may have to remind your husband to wear underwear, sleep on the bed instead of under it, to quit swearing, and use a knife and fork." The woman laughed. "If you need help getting him to shower and use the toilet instead of the palms in the hotel lobby, you'd better call." The chaplain raised the card again.

"Okay, I've talked long enough. So here's what I want you to do. First off, in these boxes up here are leis. Take one for each of you and the kids, and also take one for your husband. The custom is to put it on him and then kiss him, but I think you can reverse the order if you want." Again the women laughed. "But if you want to do more than kissing, please wait until you get to your hotel." More laughter.

"There's also a booklet on the table, one for each family." He held up the colorful paperback book. "It's full of great discounts available only to military families on R&R. We've checked all these places and I assure you, you won't get ripped off, the food will be good, and you'll save a wad of money."

A soldier walked in and stood next to the major. "Ladies, this is Sergeant Cermak. After you pick up your leis and your discount book, he'll take you to the reception area. When your husband comes through those doors, greet him with everything you got. You enjoy yourselves and have a wonderful time in Hawaii."

Spontaneously, the women applauded the chaplain as he walked to the back of the room and out into the customs area. He never got accustomed to being applauded. It happened every single time.

He stood at the front of the customs area, watching as the last men cleared customs and grabbed a seat. He introduced himself, made sure each man had a card with his number on it, and gave a more formal welcome than he gave the women.

"Okay, gentlemen. Here's what we're going to do. I want those of you who are not being met by your wives or friends to use that door in the back of the room. It will take you to the baggage claim area. Pick up your gear and have a great R&R. You men without someone waiting here to greet you, you're dismissed."

Twenty-eight men got up, waved goodbye to their buddies, and quickly filed out of the room.

Surveying the room, the major smiled. "There's a whole lot of beautiful women and some adorable kids waiting to see you. Follow me."

The room came alive as chairs scraped back and the men followed the chaplain out of the room, down a short corridor to double doors. "You guys all ready?" shouted the major without turning around. From the other side, Sergeant Cermak opened the doors and the soldiers, marines, sailors, and airmen rushed through to the waiting women. Major Tripp and Sergeant Cermak stood in the corner, watching.

The scene was a happy mob of hugging, kissing, and tossing kids in the air.

"Oh, shit, sir," said the sergeant in a low voice.

"Yeah, I see her," answered the chaplain, his eyes fixed on a tall, pretty brunette with a lei in her hand. He moved toward the young woman as Cermak rushed back into the customs office and to look into the bathrooms. She was searching the thinning crowd, her face a mask that was about to break. Major Tripp stood by her side, saying nothing, watching the crowd and waiting for Cermak.

The pretty woman turned to Major Tripp. "My husband? Where is he? Where is he?"

Cermak walked up to the major and gave him a small shake of his head.

"Misses...?" asked the chaplain.

"Where's Robert? Where is he?"

"Your name please?"

"Oh, yes...Julie, Julie Kedvale. My husband's Robert Kedvale. He's a captain. Army. Where is he?"

Cermak found Captain Robert Kedvale on the manifest. It showed that he had been scheduled for the flight but had not checked in at Tan Son Nhut. He was not on the flight. It also showed that Captain Kedvale belonged to a special operations group in Tam Ky. With a nod from the chaplain, the sergeant ran back into the customs area.

"Mrs. Kedvale, I don't know where your husband is. Sergeant Cermak is checking now. Please come with me so we can sit down." He wrapped his arm around the woman's shoulder and guided her to an office down the corridor. The room was sparsely furnished with a gray steel desk on which sat a phone and a box of tissues. A dark green sofa and an armchair were across from the desk. She sat down heavily on the couch and looked up at the major with pleading eyes. The phone rang before either could say anything.

"Excuse me, Mrs. Kedvale, that's probably Sergeant Cermak." He picked up the phone. It was Cermak.

"Sir, Captain Kedvale never checked into Tan Son Nhut. I talked to I Corps and they're checking, said they'll get back to me in a few minutes. I told them to call the office at DeRussy. Should I bring the car around, and we go back to the office with Mrs. Kedvale?"

"Yes, do that. We'll be outside the baggage pick-up."

"Do they know where Bob is? Is he okay?" she asked as soon as he put the receiver down.

"I still don't know, Mrs. Kedvale. We're waiting for a call back from your husband's headquarters. Let's go to my office. Do you have any luggage or anything?" Seeing her eyes tear up and her nose turn red, he pushed the tissue box across the desk. Her face crumbled as she broke into sobs. Grabbing a handful of tissue, he sat down next to her, put his arm around her shoulder, and held her. She took a wad of tissue from his hand and buried her face, her shoulders shaking as she cried.

With a violent blowing of her nose into the tissue, she sat up, composed herself as best she could, and said, "Uh, no... My suitcase and things are at the hotel. Thank you, major, for...uh..." She wiped her eyes and blew her nose again. "How long until we find out?"

"I don't know, Mrs. Kedvale. It may take a few hours, maybe more. Let's go to my office."

She nodded and together they walked through the terminal and to the olive drab Ford sedan at the curb. Sergeant Cermak held the rear door open for them. The short ride to Fort DeRussy was a silent one.

The outer office was a busy one. Sergeant Cermak immediately went to a cluttered desk and started dialing the phone. Major Tripp led the young woman into the inner office, a mahogany-paneled sanctuary with three large wooden desks and a comfortable seating area. A captain sitting at one of the desks stood up as they entered the office.

"Mrs. Kedvale," said Major Tripp, "I want you to meet Captain Alan Spinoza. He's a rabbi." Spinoza smiled and nodded his head. "Al, this is Mrs. Kedvale."

"Mrs. Kedvale, Sergeant Cermak has already filled me in," said the Jewish chaplain. "I'll be helping him and the major until we get this resolved."

She started to cry and both men handed her boxes of tissues. "Thank you," she sniffed. "What's happened to Robert?"

Major Tripp sat her down on a padded armchair and put his hand on her forearm. "We don't know yet. But we'll find out." Captain Spinoza quietly walked out of the room and shut the door behind him.

Sitting down in a chair next to the crying young woman, the chaplain leaned forward. "Mrs. Kedvale, you need to know that you are not going through this by yourself. We're all here to find out what happened, and then figure out what to do. But it may take some time."

"Is Robert dead? Did he get killed while I was traveling?" She was dry eyed and her voice was steady but muted.

"I can't answer that question now, because I don't know. I know this is a torturous time for you and I won't pretend that it can be anything else." She looked at her knees and nodded her head. Then she seemed to deflate with a long sigh.

"Can I get you anything? Coffee or a cold soda? Can you eat?"

She smiled and shook her head. "I think I'd vomit if I ate anything. But a cold soda would be nice. Thank you, Major."

The rabbi was looking over the sergeant's shoulder, reading his notes, while the sergeant waited for someone on the other end to pick up the phone. Spinoza gave a quick look and raised his eyebrows as the senior chaplain walked to the coffeemaker and refrigerator. On his return trip with two Cokes, Major Tripp patted the two men on their backs and walked back into the inner office. On his desk was a handwritten note. He looked at it then handed one of the cold Cokes to her.

"It says here, home is Fort Bragg?" he asked as he opened his soda. "You from there?"

"No, we're living there now. I'm from Scarsdale, New York. We met when Robert was at West Point."

"Children?"

"No, not yet." She gave a shy smile and then giggled. "We were hoping for one in about nine months from now." Then she broke into tears again. Another violent blowing of the nose and she stopped crying, sighed, and looked up.

"Where are you staying in Hawaii?" he asked.

"The Outrigger on Waikiki."

"Okay, Mrs. Kedvale. Here's what I suggest we do. But it's up to you. Two options. First, I can drive you to the Outrigger and drop you off. You'll be more comfortable there than sitting here, but I imagine you'll be by yourself. Second, you can stay here in the office with us. The library's the building next to us, and there's the PX and base theater just a block over. No matter what you want to do, as soon as we have something definitive to tell you, we will."

After a little discussion, Mrs. Kedvale decided that she'd like to go back to the hotel and maybe try to nap, or just walk around for a while. She hadn't slept for over thirty hours since waking up to catch the flight from Fayetteville to Chicago, the first leg of the long trip to Oahu. Major Tripp drove her to the Outrigger, and walked her to the elevator. Then he stopped at the front desk and asked for the manager.

As soon as he got back to the office, the chaplain called his wife and told her it looked like the day was going to be a long one for him and not to expect him home for dinner, nor breakfast.

"Another missed flight?" she asked.

"Yeah, hon', I'm afraid so."

Half an hour later Spinoza ran into the inner office. "We found him, Major!"

"He alive?"

The rabbi gave him a thumbs-up but his words were drowned out by Sergeant Cermak screaming into the phone. "I don't give a shit you supercilious bitch, give me your fucking commanding officer, now!"

"Major, I think I'd better get on the phone," said Spinoza, and ran back to Cermak's desk. He told Cermak, "Go brief Major Tripp, I got the phone."

Sergeant Cermak stood at the major's desk, his face red and flushed, his eyes on fire. "Sorry about the language, Major, but I was getting more than a little pissed." The sergeant had come to the chaplains' offices from two tours in Vietnam, the last via a month's stay in the hospital. A Combat Infantryman's Badge above two rows of ribbons, which included a Bronze Star and Purple Heart, adorned his starched khaki uniform. He had little tolerance for the chickenshit rules of the military when something important needed to get done.

"I did notice some choice vocabulary, there, Sergeant. 'Supercilious'? I'll make sure to use that in my next sermon. What's the status of Mrs. Kedvale's husband?"

"Sir, he's alive. I don't know what condition he's in. They medevaced him from the field to the navy hospital in Danang. That's where the trail ended and I got pissed. Some lieutenant commander nurse would only acknowledge that he was there and wouldn't give me the time of the day more. Said regulations prevented her from telling me anything without further authorization. I told her about Mrs. Kedvale, and all she said was that wasn't her problem and if Mrs. Kedvale wanted to know something she had to submit a formal request in writing to some commander or admiral or something. That's when I asked for her boss and she told me in some fancy navy talk to follow directions. I think that was about the time Rabbi Spinoza took the phone away from me."

"Just in time, I'd say. But good job, Sergeant. I don't want to go back to Mrs. Kedvale with any information that is incomplete. I certainly don't want to tell her that he's alive and then find out he died while I was talking to her. If Captain Spinoza's off the phone, have him come in here. You stay, too."

The major, captain, and sergeant sat on the armchairs in a circle. Their first job was to determine Captain Kedvale's status and prognosis, then what was going to happen to him. Would he be patched up thrown on the next R&R flight? Were they waiting for him to die? And there were all the possibilities in between. At each new finding, they'd get together and discuss what to do next. No one was to call Mrs. Kedvale until they had something definitive to tell her. And only Major Tripp would make that call. If she called first, he'd talk to her.

For the next twelve hours, the three men worked a bank of phones, napped on the couch in the inner office, and drank cups of dark and sour coffee. At 0500, they were ready to call Mrs. Kedvale. All three were mentally exhausted, bone tired, and needed shaves and clean, unwrinkled uniforms. They had talked to doctors, a division commanding general, an air force colonel, the commander of American forces in the Pacific's chief of staff, the Outrigger Hotel's general manager, and another dozen or so people.

The hotel room phone rang only once and then Major Tripp heard Mrs. Kedvale's anxious "Hello?"

"Good morning, Mrs. Kedvale. It's Major Tripp. I wanted to let you know as soon as possible about your husband. My apologies if I woke you."

"I wasn't asleep. Just lying here in the dark. Where's Robert?"

"Captain Kedvale is in the navy hospital in Danang. He's going to be okay."

"Oh, oh, that's so...so wonderful news. Thank you thank you thank you, Major."

"Your husband was in a helicopter that went down. He has a fractured arm and leg, plus a lot of bruises and cuts. The doctors are more worried about infections from the cuts than anything else. But he's in fine mettle and good hands. He'll be using a sling and crutches for a few months, though. But he'll be okay." He could hear her sniffing as her nose ran while she cried.

"Oh, my, I was so worried. You know. I...I couldn't even think. Oh, this is such good news. I don't even know what to do now."

"Well, I think we can help you with that dilemma. Your husband won't be fit for duty before he has to rotate back to the states and his next duty station. So, he's going to be shipped out in the next space available on one of the medical evacuation flights. He's not what you call 'high priority' for that but we seem to have found him a space. The army was going to send him back to Fort Bragg, but we made a few phone calls and in light of you being here, they're going to send him to Tripler, the hospital just down the block, for a week or two, and then to Fort Bragg. He should be there by midmorning tomorrow. And the Outrigger Hotel says you are welcome to stay another two weeks as their guest."

"Major, that's...I don't know what to say!"

"Mrs. Kedvale, you don't have to say anything. Once we get ourselves cleaned up, Sergeant Cermak will come by your hotel, probably about 0830. He'll drop off a packet of information for you so you don't have to remember everything I just told you. And you still have my card, so you call if you need anything. Okay?" There was silence on the phone. "Okay?" he repeated. Then he heard a loud nose blowing.

"Okay, Major Tripp. I'll see Sergeant Cermak in the lobby at 8:30."

The chaplain drove home and kissed his wife. He showered, shaved, put on a fresh uniform, ate a toasted bagel with cream cheese while his two children ate Eggo waffles and scrambled eggs, kissed his wife goodbye, and then drove to the airport.

It was just before 0900. He looked at the fifty-three women drinking coffee and chatting.

"Ladies, please take a seat. The men are going through customs and you'll be able to see them in a few minutes." He put a lei around his neck. "*Aloha.* Welcome to Hawaii!"

AGENT ORANGE

"I'm sure everyone will benefit from this operation—except Charlie, of course," grinned the Navy veteran. —*Tropic Lightning News*, March 24, 1969

Bethesda Naval Hospital, Bethesda Maryland, March 1982
"Commander?"

Startled out of a deep sleep in a lounge chair in the waiting room, Rick Jeffers opened his eyes. Ben Blumequist, the navy obstetrician stood before him. The doctor wore scrubs, a surgical mask hanging beneath his chin, a scrub cap on his head. It had been seven hours since Jeffers had escorted his wife into the delivery room, and two hours since Doctor Blumequist made the decision that a Caesarean section delivery was necessary and asked Jeffers to sit in the waiting room.

"Doc, how's Sandi? Baby?"

"Your wife's fine. She's fine. You'll be able to see her in an hour or so." The doctor looked around the waiting room. It was empty except for him and Jeffers. He sat down on the edge of the chair next to Jeffers, pulled off his scrub hat, rubbed his eyes, and looked at the other man's worried face. "The baby died. I'm sorry."

"Aw, shit. Aw, fucking shit. Doc...aw, shit..." Jeffers felt his throat constrict and tears started to run down his cheeks. "What...what happened? What...?"

"The fetus was malformed, severely malformed. It died soon after delivery. There was nothing anybody could do."

"What do you mean malformed? Can I see him...her?"

"It was a female. It suffered a rare fetal anomaly. It's called cyclopsia. A severe disfigurement to the point of grotesqueness. I'm sorry for the language, Commander, but I do not want to sugarcoat a serious condition."

"Aw, shit, Doc. Aw..." Jeffers buried his face in his hands. Without lifting his head, he mumbled as much to himself as to the doctor. "We had two miscarriages before. And now this. This will kill Sandi. We bought a crib and a stroller and a playpen..."

"I'm sorry, Commander. There was nothing that we could do."

Jeffers looked up, not bothering to dry the tears on his cheeks. "Thanks, Doc. I know you guys did your best. Can I see my baby?"

"If you want to, yes. But I strongly advise you not do so. And even more, there's nothing to be gained by your wife viewing the fetus. Please follow my advice."

Jeffers nodded his head, leaned back in the chair and shut his eyes, thinking about what to say to his wife.

Thirteen years earlier: 25th Infantry Division Headquarters, Cu Chi, South Vietnam, February 1969

The banks of the Saigon River were verdant and lush. Mangrove trees, sugarcane, robust grasses, and thick scrub flourished, their roots fed by the riverine mother's milk of rich nutrients as the river wound its way to the Mekong Delta and the South China Sea. The flora held the soil in place, stopped the winds, and offered shade. Birds, rodents, crabs, and snakes lived in burrows and branches. Catfish spawned and turtles hatched in the shallows between the mangrove roots. The thick vegetation also provided hiding places for caches of weapons and supplies that were carried on the Ho Chi Minh trail through Laos and Cambodia and then floated downstream. Small base camps, ambush sites, and tunnel entrances were hidden on the riverbanks in the thick vegetation. Helicopters, reconnaissance airplanes, river craft, and even foot patrols could not find the Viet Cong hiding places.

The major general commanding the 25th Infantry Division was not going to let any more of his men get wounded or die in ambushes around the riverbanks. He was pissed that the VC seemed to have more and better weapons and ammunition even with the bullshit coming out of headquarters in Saigon about fucking lights at the end of the fucking tunnel. The 25th's nickname was Tropic Lightning, and he was going to shoot some lightning bolts up Charlie's ass.

The problem wound up in Captain Wayne Lawrence's lap to solve. Captain Lawrence wore the collar insignia of the US Army Chemical Corps. Defoliation was his specialty. Captain Wayne Lawrence, US Army, was going to deprive the enemy of his hiding places. He was going to defoliate ten miles of the northeastern Saigon River banks. He was the man for the job. But, as in most things military, he couldn't do it by himself.

He had the perfect tool for the job. Dioxin, better known as Agent Orange for the color of the 55-gallon drums that contained it. Dioxin would kill the hardiest of plants, but was harmless to humans and animals. Safe to handle, cheap. Easy to apply. Just spray it on. Voila, all the hiding places would be gone. No enemy could hide, at least not on the banks of the Saigon River he was going to denude.

In other parts of Vietnam, Agent Orange was sprayed from the air. C-123 aircraft, like giant crop dusters, flew over their targets of crop fields and paddies to deprive the enemy of their food. In some places, the spray gear was put on the big helicopters. For this location, Lawrence was looking for a more pinpoint application. He wanted something unique that might get him some positive attention from the brass, and maybe even an Army Commendation Medal. The brainstorm hit him while watching the crash trucks spray water and foam on a Huey medevac helicopter that flipped over on landing when its wounded pilot passed out.

He'd connect the Agent Orange pump to a firefighting water cannon. Hook all that up to a large-capacity tank and simply spray the riverbank from the river. He had to find something that floated to carry it all. And he knew just where to go.

Down the Saigon River, just the other side of the Phu Cuong bridge, was a South Vietnamese Navy's River Assault Group. The RAG had several large troop carriers that could easily accommodate the Agent Orange equipment. More importantly, the RAG had two US Navy advisors assigned to it who were always looking for missions for the RAG and its sailors.

Lawrence met with the two American advisors—Lieutenant Junior Grade Rick Jeffers and Chief Petty Officer Frank Sweeney—and the RAG's commanding officer—Lieutenant Kanh Van Thanh—in Phu Cuong. The naval officers and chief embraced the idea enthusiastically. For one thing, their boats were often getting shot at when they were anywhere near the area. And more importantly, both the US Navy and South Vietnamese Navy were on a big push for Vietnamization of naval forces and closer working relations with the other, non-naval, forces. The US Navy, in particular, was pushing to turn over as many US Navy assets and missions in-country to the South Vietnamese as soon as possible. This was a good opportunity to show that the South Vietnamese Navy's RAG was a professional organization.

Early in the morning a week later, two of the RAG's big troop carriers took aboard pumps, tanks, and 55-gallon drums of Agent Orange, a platoon of Tropic Lightning infantry troops, Captain Lawrence, and two of his enlisted helpers. Then they moved upriver. Army helicopters and two US Navy patrol boats escorted them.

For the next three days, the RAG boats sprayed Agent Orange from the river's edge to twenty-five meters inland. The US infantry troops were put ashore to provide land security for the dioxin-spewing boats.

Captain Lawrence and his two assistants handled the spray nozzles for the first few hours. To the US Navy advisors and most of the Vietnamese sailors, it looked like fun, and soon all of them had taken a turn at wielding the nozzles. For the three days, the sky was clear, the sun was hot, and a gentle caressing breeze from the northeast blew a mist of spray right back on the bare-chested sailors and soldiers. Frequent helicopters ferried in teams of AP, UPI, Reuters, CBS, and Armed Forces Radio correspondents, along with uniformed public relations officers from Saigon, to watch, interview, and record the marvelous teamwork that was defoliating the banks of the Saigon River.

By the middle of February, ten miles of Saigon River's northeastern banks had turned from rich green to brown. For twenty-five meters inland from the bank, the land looked like the pictures of the Somme in World War I. Ambushes dropped precipitously. There was no place in that ten-mile verge where the Viet Cong could hide supplies or themselves. Captain Lawrence was awarded an Army Commendation Medal, pinned on by the Tropic Lightning's commanding general.

* * *

Despite the effectiveness of Agent Orange as a defoliant, the South Vietnamese and their American allies lost the war. And because of Agent Orange, much more was lost.

Nearly five million Vietnamese—civilian and military—and forty thousand US military sailors, soldiers, marines, and airmen were directly exposed to the dioxin in Agent Orange. High levels of dioxin were found in the soil, crops, river bottoms, and fish of Vietnam, as well as in the breast milk of Vietnamese mothers and the blood of veterans and Vietnamese civilians. Miscarriages and stillbirths increased; both Vietnamese and American women gave birth to children with cleft palates, physical deformations, severe fetal physical developmental problems, mental disabilities, hernias, and extra fingers and toes. Those people exposed directly to Agent Orange suffered skin lesions; neurological, digestive, and respiratory disorders; throat cancer; acute and chronic leukemia; Hodgkin's lymphoma and non-Hodgkin's lymphoma; prostate cancer; lung cancer; soft tissue sarcoma; and liver cancer. Needless to say, the affected died early.

The use of Agent Orange may have planted a genetic time bomb in the offspring of the veterans and the Vietnamese civilians.

Captain Lawrence of the Army's Chemical Corps rose to the rank of colonel. A lifelong health nut, nonsmoker, and marathon runner, he died at the age of fifty-nine of lung cancer.

Chief Sweeney retired from the navy two years after he returned from his tour in Vietnam. He moved to Alaska and worked in a fishing boat repair yard outside Anchorage. At the age of fifty-four, he was diagnosed with liver cancer and died a few months later.

The RAG's commanding officer, Lieutenant Kanh Van Thanh, broke out in severe skin lesions a week after the spraying. Refusing evacuation to a hospital in Saigon, he stayed with his RAG and the ministrations of his hospital corpsman. During the next patrol, the RAG was ambushed from the southwest bank of the Saigon River in an area that had not been defoliated. Lieutenant Kanh was killed in the firefight.

The steering stations on the two Vietnamese RAG boats that carried the defoliation gear were located just aft of the spray nozzles. Both of the Vietnamese sailors who steered the boats survived the war. One sailor's child was born with an open spine and died a week after birth. His wife miscarried several times after that. The other boat's helmsman emigrated to Oakland, California, with his family in 1981. Thanks to early detection, he is a prostate cancer survivor.

Rick Jeffers and his wife Sandi suffered another miscarriage in 1984. Worried about the effects of pregnancy on Sandi's health, Jeffers had a vasectomy. A year later, they adopted a baby girl. Shortly after seeing his daughter off to college in 2003, Jeffers died of Hodgkin's disease. He was just short of sixty-one years old.

LIVER FIESTA

A steer provides dozens of steaks and roasts, pounds of ground beef, and yards of sausage casings, but only one liver. Liver is packed full of nutrients. It's versatile: it can be fried, broiled, sautéed, even made into sausage. As rare as liver is, with only one per cow, one would think it would be a premium cut sold at premium prices, but that's not the case. Liver is pretty cheap. Even liver from a tiny animal like a chicken is cheap. The reason is that not everyone likes liver. In fact, a whole lot of people do *not* like liver, no matter how it's served. And for even those who do like liver, liver's a meat that needs to be cooked right. It's easy to screw it up. Liver demands a good cook.

US Navy Chief Petty Officer Charles "Cookie" Howell was an outstanding cook. He was the best in the entire Atlantic Fleet. From raw products to finished meals, Cookie knew food. He had kitchen sense. If you liked liver, you'd love Cookie's Liver Fiesta.

The navy cherished men like Cookie. From the days of wooden ships with canvas sails to modern-day ships of steel, sailing has been dangerous, tedious, and boring, requiring teamwork and efficiency. Besides the enemy, the biggest danger to a naval vessel is from within: bad morale. Vietnam-era navy ships offered liberty calls in exotic ports, closed circuit TV, movies, a library, gym, heating, and air conditioning. But despite all this, nothing could make morale plummet quicker than bad food. Not bad as in something that would make the sailor sick, but bad as in boring and tasteless and monotonous. Good food was more than a comfort item to the crew; it was vital. Men like Chief Howell knew how to produce good food for the ships' crews.

Faced with the long deployments and arduous schedules of the precious few ships of a navy operating in two oceans, the admirals wisely kept their focus on food. In the mid-1960s they introduced an award to recognize the best food in the navy. Every year teams went out to ships and naval stations and inspected galleys and tasted food. Besides taste, eye appeal, and aroma, they looked at recipes for both nutrition and cost. And then they made their awards.

In 1967, the *USS Adams Point* won the award, beating out the hundreds of other ships in the Atlantic Fleet. Cookie's ground beef and macaroni casserole received special mention. In a ceremony on the mess deck, he and the ship's captain mounted the award plaque right next to the menu board at the start of the food line.

USS Adams Point was a veteran of World War II in the Pacific and Korea. The ship's keel was laid before most of her 1967 crew had been born. Although the ship was sound and well run, it was scheduled to be decommissioned and scrapped before the next year was out. The modern navy and marines no longer had a mission for the *gator freighter* to land marines on a hostile shore under enemy fire. Most of her remaining time was to be spent as a test platform for new equipment in various stages of research and development, and exercising formation steaming with other ships. It was also turning into a training platform for its crew who, one by one, would be receiving orders to ships in the western Pacific and to boats and stations in-country Vietnam.

Until then, the ship did a quarterly shuttle of a company or two of marines and their equipment to and from Guantánamo Bay in Cuba. Gitmo. The southbound marines and their jeeps and armored personnel carriers came aboard in Morehead City,

North Carolina. The troops meant a couple of hundred more mouths for Cookie and his sailors to feed. Scuttlebutt was that most of these marines had just left boot camp and would be headed to Vietnam after the ship returned them to Morehead City in three months. As far as Cookie was concerned, the *Adams Point* owed the grunts some real fine chow. And he and his men were going to provide it.

And a bit more. After all, these were jarhead marines. Fair game for Chief Howell. Nothing too bad, just enough for a good laugh, and something for them to remember from their trip to Gitmo.

Every week Cookie prepared a detailed menu of the upcoming week's meals for the supply officer and commanding officer's approval. It covered breakfast, lunch, dinner, and midnight rations—midrats—for each of the seven days. The menu had to meet the caloric requirements of hard-working young men, sound good, look good, taste good, be nutritious, and be on budget. A lot of work went into the menu planning, even more work went into preparing the food. The menus always came back from the captain with his initial of approval, a question or two about a recipe he didn't recognize, and an occasional comment like, "Chief, you're making me hungry—and fat."

Every three months the same entrée appeared for crew and the just-embarked troops' dinner the evening after they left Morehead City. That entrée was never served except for that one evening each quarter. It was the first meal the marines would eat aboard the *Adams Point* at sea.

The first evening with the Gitmo-bound marines aboard always found the *Adams Point* in the Atlantic off Cape Hatteras. That meant wind, waves, whitecaps, and green water over the bow. The sea was always rough off Cape Hatteras. The ship was built to withstand much worse. But she rolled, yawed, and heaved in the heavy seas. Sometimes violently. A skilled helmsman at the wheel could mitigate some of this motion with the judicious use of the rudder. A heavy hand would make it much worse.

It was nearly time to call the marines to dinner on the mess deck.

The deck department's senior enlisted man, Master Chief Boatswain "Chief Boats" Martinson, was Cookie's best buddy. They had just finished dinner together in the chiefs' mess. Martinson walked onto the bridge and greeted the officer of the deck with a smile. Four young seamen waited silently behind the master chief.

"Came up to see how it looks, sir. I'd like to get some of the new guys time on the wheel in this heavy weather. Skipper said it was okay if it's okay with you."

The lieutenant in charge of the watch smiled back. "Sure, Chief Boats. You'll be watching them? We'll be waddling around in this muck for a couple of hours."

"Yes, sir. I'll be standing right behind them. This is a good opportunity for training for these lads."

After a few minutes of instruction, one of the young seamen took the wheel, the master chief's hands at the ready to correct him. As the young man steered, the *Adams Point* rolled and yawed even more. The silence of the bridge was interrupted by the loudspeaker's call for the marines to go to dinner. For the next hour, the four trainees took their turns steering the ship.

On the heaving and rolling mess deck, the marines lined up to get their trays and cutlery and their evening meal. For nearly all, this was their first time at sea. For all, this was their first time at sea in Cape Hatteras weather. They read the menu board next to the food award. Tossed green salad with blue cheese dressing. Cream of tomato soup with crackers. Liver Fiesta with rice.

Most of the marines stopped reading after "rice"—they never got to the salsa, broccoli, bread, butter, blueberry pie, vanilla ice cream, coffee, or milk.

Liver Fiesta is a mélange of sautéed beef liver, onions, red and green pepper, garlic, and tomato sauce. Under normal conditions, it has wonderful eye appeal: the brown of the liver, golden yellow of the onions, the colorful peppers and red sauce on a mound of white rice. Its aroma is just as delightful, redolent with onion and garlic. The spicy and piquant salsa is the perfect match to its hearty flavor. If you like liver. And if your stomach isn't doing somersaults. And if your dining room isn't rotating twenty degrees in all dimensions.

Very few of the marines ate dinner that night. Even fewer tried the liver dish.

Just before lights out, the ship was riding easily. Chief Boats put down his reading and announced to Cookie, who was sitting across from him in a lounge chair, that he was going to tour the troops' berthing area, to make sure everything was shipshape. He invited Cookie to join him.

They walked through the hatch into the cavernous berthing compartment, both smoking cigars. The space was clean and un-cluttered except for several buckets and swabs that were at the ready. Pale young men in T-shirts and white boxers lay in their bunks, a few asleep but most just laying there with their mess kit cups handy to catch whatever their stomachs produced.

Cookie and Chief Boats walked into the troops' head. At each of the dozen commodes, a marine was on his knees, head above the porcelain.

Chief Boats nodded at the sight. Cookie took his cigar out of his mouth and yelled in his whiskey baritone, "I wouldn't drink too much of that water, boys. It'll make you sick. Huevos rancheros for breakfast in the morning, lads."

The two navy men walked out of the marines' head to the sound of retching.

WANNA PAHTY?

Most married couples spent the week of rest and recreation together in Hawaii. It was tropical, comfortable, safe, and everybody except the Japanese tourists spoke English. You could drink the water and eat food that was not cremated without getting sick. But some couples, seeking a bit of adventure, picked other spots for their husbands' week out of Vietnam.

Lieutenant Commander Keith Pitken and his wife Sheri decided that they'd spend the seven days in Bangkok. Both of them had a bit of wanderlust and wanted to see someplace different, someplace they had never been before. During the twelve years of her husband's service, Sheri had flown to Singapore, Naples, Tokyo, and Hong Kong to meet her husband's ships.

When Keith received his orders to go in-country Vietnam, they were living on Oahu while Keith served as the executive officer of a Pearl Harbor–based destroyer and then on the fleet commander's staff. For Keith's year in-country, Sheri decided to stay in Hawaii with their two boys. A week's R&R in Hawaii with Keith would be nice, but Sheri needed a break. An R&R at home with the kids was no break. Staying in a hotel with home just a short drive away seemed extravagant and silly. As selfish as she knew it might seem, she didn't want to share her husband with the kids. A week in Bangkok for just the two of them was what their marriage needed.

Keith's mother and father were glad to come out to Hawaii to sit with the two boys. The boys were delighted at the prospects of a week of being spoiled and fed much too much sugar by Grandma and Grandpa. With what she knew to be futile instructions, warnings, and threats to both grandparents and the five- and four-year-old boys, Sheri kissed them all, grabbed her bag from the back of the Chrysler station wagon, and walked into the airport terminal to start her journey to Bangkok.

From the moment they met in the Sheraton's lobby, the Pitkens' R&R was wonderful, everything they hoped for. With three days left, Keith asked the concierge for a good seafood restaurant recommendation. Without hesitation, the man he told Keith about a place that made the best crab in Bangkok, possibly in the whole of Southeast Asia. The concierge drew a route on the hotel's walking map and gave simple instructions. Turn right out of the hotel, walk two blocks, then turn left, then walk two more blocks, then turn left again and walk a block. The restaurant was at the corner. A romantic corner table, the best in the house, was reserved for seven o'clock.

Back in the room, Sheri looked at the walking map while Keith showered. It didn't make sense to her. The map had them walking five blocks to get to the restaurant. But it looked like all they had to do was walk straight out the front door of the hotel, down two short blocks and then turn right a block. Why take this roundabout path the concierge mapped out?

She walked into the bathroom as Keith dried himself off.

"Keith, look at this." She held out the map. "The hotel has us walking way out of the way. The restaurant is just a couple of blocks straight out the front door."

"I hadn't noticed that," said her husband as he studied the map. "Probably he's sending us around the block so we go past all the shops. I don't see any stores marked on the street that starts at the front entrance. He must get a kickback for each tourist that goes into the stores."

He walked into the bedroom and was about to get dressed when he stopped and looked at the bed. The covers were drawn back. She was at the closet deciding what to wear.

"Uh...hon." He walked up behind his wife and put his hands on her hips and then around her waist. "I think that shortcut you found will probably save us a good fifteen, maybe twenty minutes."

She leaned against him. "Yes, so?"

"So I was figuring that rather than waste our precious R&R time walking past stores, we take your shortcut and you donate that saved time to charity."

"Charity? Keith, what are you talking about?"

"Well," he moved his hands up to her breasts. "Like give it to the truly needy. Like me. I truly need some pity sex. Or any other kind you happen to have."

Turning to him, she unwrapped the towel from his waist. "Okay, Mr. Pitken. But this is going to cost you. Big time. We're taking the long way home past all those stores and you're taking me shopping."

At 6:45, Keith and Sheri walked out of the Sheraton into the heavy foot traffic crowd of tourists and shoppers. Everyone leaving the hotel turned left or right out the front door. All of the people arriving came from the left or right. No one walked to or from the street that ended at the front door—the street directly across from the Pitkens.

Keith looked to the right and left at the crowd of pedestrians. He chuckled. "What a bunch of sheep."

Sheri wrapped her arm in his and together they walked past the doorman and crossed onto the quiet street before them. In a little over two short blocks, they'd be at the restaurant with a couple of minutes to spare.

There were no sidewalks and no vehicles on this narrow street. They strolled right down the middle. The first half block seemed to be mainly residences with no signs of life. Just quiet, dark houses.

Down the blocks, they could see lights and what might be tables and chairs, perhaps small and charming outdoor cafés.

"This is so nice. No hawkers, no shops full of tourists. Charming." Sheri squeezed her husband's arm. "What a beautiful evening."

As they neared the end of the block, they could see the lit store-fronts. Garish neon and Christmas tree strings of lights spelled out their wares:

PUSSY-A-GO-GO
LUCKY SUCKY
BIG BOOBY BAR
KNOBBLERS
MOM'S PLACE
PAULINE'S HOUSE OF SENSUAL PLEASURE
SCHOOL GIRL MASSAGE AND BATH
PLAYBOY KLUB

Music, heavy on the bass, spilled out of speakers. The Stones, Beatles, Elvis, Roger Miller, Hendrix. The air smelled of sweet marijuana, cigarettes, spilled beer, body odor, hairspray, curry, mildew, and *pad thai* noodles.

There were three kinds of people on this part of the street. A few crewcut American men, probably GIs, were obviously shopping. Three dozen or so young Thai women in miniskirts or tight pants, high heels, low-cut blouses, and various hair colors and bra cup sizes were obviously selling. And one couple was taking a shortcut to the crab restaurant.

With a two-handed grip that was now turning her knuckles white and cutting off all circulation to her husband's right arm, Sheri tried to get closer to him. "I've never seen anything like this."

"Yeah, pretty gross. Reminds me of Subic City and Olangapo," said Keith trying to keep his eyes straight ahead and ignoring the python grip on his arm.

"Reminds you? What do you mean this reminds you? You've been to places like this?" Sheri was trying to talk as loud as she could through clenched teeth and tight lips. She dug her nails into his arm.

"Jeez, hon. You're hurting me."

"I'll do worse than that. What do you mean this reminds you of Subilongapo?"

"Olangapo, Sheri. Oh-long-ah-poh. It's the town outside the navy base in Subic Bay in the Philippines. Nothing more than a string of bars. Y'know, for the single enlisted guys. I told you about it."

"That place? I had no idea..."

The couple had not noticed the Thai woman with long blond hair, deep purple leather miniskirt, stiletto heels, and bright red knit top stretched to the breaking point over what had to be at least D-sized boobs. She had peeled away from the pack and had taken up her station on Keith's port side.

"Hey, mistah. You wanna pahty?"

Though startled, Keith ignored her, and kept his eyes dead ahead.. Sheri looked across her husband's chest but could only see the warheads of the woman's breasts. The couple said nothing, but both lengthened their strides. They had only a block to go.

"Mistah, c'mon. We go pahty. I got Buddha stick. You big man. You got big dick. I sucky sucky you. C'mon."

Keith looked down at her, scowled, and said forcefully, "Go away!" He quickened his steps. Sheri held on tightly as they accelerated.

"Aw c'mon, mistah. I show you good time. You like. C'mon, we pahty. You play with my titties. They hard. C'mon mistah." The staccato clicks of her heels increased with his pace. She grabbed his left arm to keep up.

Violently shaking his arm free from her grip, Keith whirled toward the hooker, swinging Sheri in an arc. "Go the fuck away! I don't want a party. I don't want to play with you. Go away!"

The whore pouted and looked up at him. "You wanna pahty. You know I sucky you best. We go pahty."

"Goddamnit, leave! Can't you see I'm with my wife?"

The young Thai woman looked up at Sheri, who stood half a foot taller. She looked her up and down, evaluating with a critical eye.

Sheri stared back at the whore as if looking at a rare and dangerous animal in the zoo.

"That okay," said the little woman to Keith. "She come pahty with us."

Leaving the hooker in midstreet, Keith and Sheri turned and ran to the end of the block. Once around the corner they walked up the busy sidewalk to the restaurant, catching their breath. Still wet with sweat, they gave the hostess their name and were seated at a corner table. Keith told her to bring two cold Thai beers, real quick.

They ordered dinner, then drank their beers in exhausted silence. Sheri looked at her husband. He looked at her. The corners of his mouth twitched. As did hers. Within a few seconds, they were laughing so hard that tears rolled down their cheeks and their bellies hurt.

After they finally caught their breaths and controlled their giggles, Keith said, "I think we're taking the long way back." That started the laughter all over again.

The crab was wonderful. The warm night breeze blew through the restaurant's open walls. They walked back the long way and stopped in one of the shops, where Keith bought Sheri a gold baht chain.

Four months later, Sheri and the two boys were waiting outside Honolulu airport customs for Keith. He was done with his tour in Vietnam, had been promoted to Commander, and they were on their way to the commanding officer course at Newport, Rhode Island. Keith was going to be the CO of a Newport-based destroyer. She saw the tall figure in khaki uniform come through the double doors. He looked around and spotted her.

"There's Daddy," she said as she grabbed their hands and waded into the crowd of arriving travelers.

They met him halfway. Dropping his duffel bag, Keith scooped up the boys and hugged and kissed his sons. They wrapped their arms around him, knocking off his hat. He put his sons down; they clung to his legs and je looked up to his wife.

Sheri picked up his hat, and put it on his head. Then she wrapped her arms around his neck and gave him a long welcoming kiss. She leaned back and looked up into his face.

"Hey, mistah, you wanna pahty?"

MACHINE GUNNER

Uncle Basilio stirred his little cup of espresso with the tiny teaspoon, tapped the spoon on the rim of the delicate porcelain cup, and set it on the saucer. With chubby thumb and forefinger squeezing the little handle and pinky finger extended, he lifted the cup to his lips and sipped the hot, bitter, black coffee. His eyes were locked on his nephew Joseph's. The two men were sitting at the corner table in the Piedmont Social Club, a little corner coffee shop. On this Thursday afternoon, like all afternoons, mornings, and evenings, the Pied was sparsely populated, with a seat or two occupied at a few of the five tables. A flow of men trickled through the shop to a back room and out. The music of Verdi mixed with the smells of tobacco smoke and coffee.

The uncle and nephew were in sharp contrast.

Uncle Basilio was short, husky, and had a belly that was proof of eating well for a lifetime. His gabardine suit jacket was unbuttoned, revealing a silk tie on a wide expanse of white shirt. Gold cufflinks, gold wristwatch, gold chain bracelet, gold wedding ring, and gold-and-diamond pinky ring reflected the slats of winter sun coming through the Venetian blinds. Silk black socks and oxblood kid loafers were on his feet. He was seventy-two years old and had no gray in his oiled and styled hair. Whether his hair was dyed or not was a subject never discussed in the Pied. Or anywhere else that Uncle Basilio frequented.

Nephew Joe was tall and well built. He was neatly dressed in the same suit and tie he had worn to high school graduation four years earlier. An olive drab military-type watch on his left wrist was his only visible jewelry, but under his shirt hung dog tags and a silver crucifix. His black hair was in a tight crew cut with high sidewalls. Navy issue shoes, shined to a patent leather black, were on his feet.

Joe was there to pay his respects to his uncle. And more importantly, because his mother had insisted he do so. In front of him sat a half-eaten biscotti and a cup of American-style coffee.

"Joey, your mother wanted me to talk you. Your time in the navy is up in what, three months?"

"Right, Uncle Bas. If I don't reenlist."

"Your mother, she's worried that you won't leave the navy. You know that, right?"

"How could I not, Uncle Bas? She's been crying for a week now."

"You like making my sister cry, Joseph? Haven't you done enough in the navy? They send you to that place near Chicago..."

"Great Lakes, Uncle Bas. Boot camp."

"Yeah, sure, boot camp. Then they put you on that ship in California for over two years, and then they send you to Vietnam for a year. I don't like them pushing you around like that. Your mother and father had a very bad time when you were in Vietnam, Joey." He put his meaty hand on his nephew's and patted it. "Now, where are you located?"

"I'm in Newport, Uncle Bas. Rhode Island. Just a few hours from here."

"So, they'll keep you there until you get out, Joey?"

"If I don't reenlist, they'll keep me there until my enlistment is up, end of March. If I reenlist, they'll send me to an advanced school, and then I'll get assigned to another ship."

"Joey, why would you want to do that? Wasn't it bad enough they send you to Vietnam, but now they want you to go to sea again?"

Joe smiled at his uncle and shook his head. "Uncle Bas, I volunteered to go to Vietnam. I wanted to go."

His uncle's eyebrows went up and he cocked his head to one side in a questioning gesture.

"Really, Uncle Bas. I like the navy. I like what I do. I'm comfortable in the navy. I've got a good start on a career that I can retire from before I'm even forty if I want to. I know Mom and Dad don't like the separation and want me nearby. But I also know they want me happy and fulfilled doing something I like to do."

"I don't understand, Joey. What do you do in the navy? Tell me?" He reached into his coat and took out two cigars, offering one to his nephew. A man at another table walked up to them and held his Zippo lighter at the ready.

"No thanks, Uncle Bas. I don't smoke." His uncle shrugged and gave one of the cigars to the man standing by the table. Uncle Basilio cut off the end of the remaining cigar with a little silver-and-gold penknife, licked the end, and then the silent man lit it with his Zippo. With a nod and a puff of smoke from Basilio, the man went back to his table and coffee cup. Uncle Basilio returned his gaze to his nephew.

"I'm a gunner's mate, Uncle Bas. I just made first class gunners mate. That's pretty fast promotion."

"Sure they promoted you fast, Joey. You're a smart boy. They can see that. So what does a gunner's mate do?"

"We maintain and operate the weapons on the ships. And everything else that supports the weapons systems, like magazines and launchers."

"But Joey, there are lots of jobs for you here. Near your mother and father and family. I can get you a good job. You're smart and a good kid. I'm sure I can use you."

"Uncle Bas, I appreciate that and thank you. But I really like the navy. I've decided that I'm going to reenlist. I'll get a bonus and advanced schooling. Besides, I don't see the expertise I've developed since boot camp having any real applications around here."

"Don't be so sure, Joey. Tell me, what did you do on that boat in Vietnam? I never knew what you were doing over there." He leaned forward and tapped the cigar ash into his empty espresso cup. "It was called a...a PBJ?"

Joe laughed. "PBR, Uncle Bas. River patrol boat."

"Okay, PBR. But what were you doing on it?"

"I was one of the boat crewmen. Four of us. We all did each other's job, but we each had a primary area of responsibility. We patrolled the rivers and canals. Put in troops and took them out. Supported land operations. Interdiction. Ambushes. Medical evacuations." He smiled at his uncle. "Nothing that has any civilian job applications around here, Uncle Bas."

Putting the cigar in the middle of his lips, Uncle Basilio leaned back in his chair and folded his arms across his chest, resting them on the deep shelf of his belly. He studied his nephew, then took the cigar out of his mouth.

"But what did you do on those boats, Joey? Your job on these ambushes and stuff?"

"Me? I was the machine gunner."

Joe's uncle put the cigar back into his mouth and took a deep puff. Then he leaned across the table and again patted his nephew's hand. Through a thick cloud of cigar smoke he smiled and said, "Machine gunner? Joey, I could use a machine gunner."

* * *

Despite the offer of high pay in Uncle Basilio's employment, and the tear-lubricated guilt trips of his mother and father, Joe stood his ground and reenlisted in the navy. His mother's mantle became a photographic shrine to Joe's career. Until the old man died, every time Joe was in town, Uncle Basilio made it a point to take him around town and show him off, introducing his chief petty officer nephew to the deputy mayor, police commissioner, several judges, and every restaurant owner as "my sister's son, Joey, the admiral."

THE RELUCTANT HERO

The bar in the Singapore Holiday Inn on Orchid Street contained a couple of the engineering officers and half the air wing pilots from the aircraft carrier at anchor in the harbor, and a pair of ex-pat Americans—oil rig workers from the looks of them—and their girlfriends. The room was cool, light, comfortable. White jacketed waiters in crisp shirts and bow ties hustled about taking orders and delivering drinks and bowls of peanuts. Lieutenant Commander Ed Steiner and Lieutenant George Baylis sat comfortably in a corner booth on overstuffed leather cushions.

Mutt and Jeff. Ed was tall, big-boned, lanky, and fair. George was short, slight but muscular, dark. The two were friends and shared a stateroom on the carrier. They were principal assistants in the big ship's engineering department, responsible for everything mechanical that made the big ship move and function as a small floating city with a busy airport on its roof.

The ship had been operating at a high tempo since leaving Alameda five months earler. Nearly continuous steaming and flying were taking their toll on the air wing and ship's crew. Several planes and air crewmen had been lost on flights over Vietnam. Two planes had been lost in flight deck accidents. Stress and fatigue were evident in both men and equipment. The ship was pulled off the line and sent to Singapore for a week and a half of repairs and maintenance. And for the crew to get some badly needed recreation and rest.

The port call in Singapore had been planned before the ship left Alameda. Many of the wives had made plans to visit their husbands there. Both Ed and George were single and had no wives or girlfriends waiting for them. But Judy Brown, the wife of Lieutenant Commander Craig Brown—one of the other engineering officers—was flying to Singapore to spend a week with her husband.

Since neither had the engineering department duty watch for the first few days, Ed and George decided to get a room at the Singapore Hyatt as soon as they could get off the ship. They needed the break. Judy and Craig would also be staying at the Hyatt. The night before the ship arrived in the harbor, Craig, Ed, and George decided to meet for drinks and dinner the first night in. They'd meet in the lobby at 1800.

Once the engineering plant was secured, Ed and George changed into civilian clothes, threw their toilet kits and a couple changes of clothing into their gym bags, and ran up to the hangar deck to grab the first liberty boat ashore. They checked into the Hyatt, took deliciously long hot showers not restrained by the water limitations of the ship, changed into swim trunks and T-shirts and went down to the pool. After poolside club sandwiches and beer and a few laps, both fell asleep in the deck chairs. When they awoke an hour later, the pool was crowded with wives, aviators, and other members of the ship's crew, as well as a handful of tourists. This was the life.

Another dip in the pool, another beer, and a bit of a nap, and then the two friends went back to the room for more hot showers. They lounged around in the hotel's terry cloth robes. Diminutive George puffed his pipe, lanky Ed smoked a Cuban cigar he had picked up in the hotel's lobby store. They had an hour and a half before they'd meet Judy and Craig, and decided to go across the street and check out the Holiday Inn's bar.

Happily sucking on pipe and cigar, the two sat in the corner booth, surveying the busy bar. Along one side sat a lively and noisy gaggle of pilots and flight officers from the squadrons on the carrier. Across from then sat the two oil rig workers and their two attractive companions. Judging from their accents, Ed guessed the women were Australians, maybe Kiwis. A pride of large, well-built young men wearing rugby uniform shirts that identified them as members of a Melbourne team came in, loudly seated themselves at a bunch of tables near the oil rig workers, and ordered beer, plenty of beer, mate. Ed and George had switched to Coke to rehydrate and get ready for a pleasant evening with Judy and Craig.

The bar was loud with laughter and chatter. An attractive Asian woman with long, thick hair down to her shoulders weaved through the crowd and stopped at the oil rig quartet. She spoke to one of the men, a burly, thick-necked, bullet-headed man in slacks and a white shirt, his sleeves rolled up to expose thick and hairy forearms. Ed thought his hands looked like catchers' mitts. The Asian woman was short. Standing, she was as tall as the burly man was seated. She was pointing a finger at him, obviously upset, her voice rising above the din of the bar.

"This where I find you? This where you tell me you have business?" she yelled in accented English. "This is where you meet your English whores?"

The big man tried to calm her as the room got very quiet. In a West Texas gravel-voiced drawl, he told her to calm down, to be quiet.

"Quiet? You want me to be quiet? While you fuck these whores?" Her voice was surprisingly loud for such a small woman. "I won't be quiet, you bastard! I tell everyone what you do!" She raised her arm and hit him on the top of his head with her little manicured hand.

He stood up and grabbed her around the waist with his big hands. "You want to tell everyone? Okay, you bitch, you tell them." Her hands pummeled his arms as he picked her up and put her on the bandstand in the center of the room. Without letting go, he yelled at her again. "Bitch, you fucking bitch, you tell them! C'mon, you're on stage, bitch!"

She yelled at him to let go of her and tried to kick him. The two women and the other oil rigger hurried out of the bar. No one noticed; everyone was looking at the big brute and the little woman.

One of her kicks landed in his crotch. Infuriated, he grabbed her by the shoulders and squeezed, lifting her off the stage. Then he shook her back and forth, her long hair whipping with her head.

"You snotty Chinese bitch!" the big man yelled as he tossed her violently back and forth like a rag doll.

Ed watched with fascination, then realized George was talking to him. "We gotta stop this, Ed."

We? Ed looked around the room. He and George were the two wimpiest guys in the place. The gorilla must weigh 275 pounds or more and he was mean. Let the Aussie rugby team or the hot-shot jet jocks take care of that monster.

The rugby players just sat and watched, as did the aviators. The only person to move was the shortest man in the room. George stood up his full five feet and six inches. Ed stood up next to him, reaching his hand to George's shoulder to try to get him to sit down.

"Hey, you! Stop that!" yelled George before Ed could get him to sit down. "Leave her alone!"

The madman turned and saw two men standing at the corner booth—one about the size of a dwarf, the other a tall, rangy fellow. He roughly threw the woman onto the bandstand floor and started walking toward them.

"You going to stop me, you tall skinny cocksucker?" The man's porcine eyes were locked onto Ed. His right hand was balled into a fist about the size and hardness of a bowling ball. When he was two steps away from Ed, he cocked his arm.

Ed thought *Holy shit. I'm about to get my ass whipped by some Neanderthal. I just hope he doesn't kill me.* The man started to throw his punch at Ed's face. Ed closed his eyes, hunched his shoulders, and tried to duck. He felt air move past his face but nothing else. Could he be dead? Was that what it felt like?

Ed opened his eyes and at his feet was the man, out stone cold. The aviators and Aussies started cheering. Then two waiters and the bar manager jumped on the comatose oil rigger, and the little Asian woman started beating on them, trying to save her man.

Shaking, his knees weak, Ed stepped over the waiters, bar manager, screaming Asian woman, and the big man and looked around for George.

"I got him under the jaw with an uppercut just as he started to swing at you. Then hit him with a cross," said George, his little face flushed with excitement. Tiny George had boxed at the Naval Academy for four years. He was the bantamweight champ of Annapolis.

"Shit, George, I thought I was gonna die. You saved my ass. I owe you, big time."

"Bullshit. You'd have done the same for me, Ed. We'd better go across the street and meet Judy and Craig."

"Listen, I'm buying you dinner tonight." They left the Holiday Inn as four policemen rushed in.

Twenty minutes later, Ed had resumed his normal color and had quit shaking. Judy and Craig walked out of the elevator. She hugged George and then Ed in the crowded lobby.

By anyone's standards, Judy was beautiful. From top to bottom, no matter the angle. She was just naturally beautiful. And she was a really nice person to boot.

After a few minutes, they decided to go to the Raffles Hotel for a Singapore Sling, then to the Troika restaurant for dinner. They crammed into a small taxi. Craig, being the biggest, sat in front; Judy sat between Ed and George in the back. At Raffles, which was also busy with members of the carrier's crew, Ed held the door open for Judy, who took his arm and walked with the three men into the bar.

Over their sticky cough-syrup sweet Singapore Slings in disposable plastic tumblers, Ed told the story of the monster man and the Asian damsel and the gallant Wee Georgie. Everyone had a good laugh and then climbed into another taxi for a delicious, lengthy and alcohol-lubricated Russian meal.

Back at the Hyatt, they sat in the lobby talking, Ed and Judy on a love seat, George and Craig in easy chairs across from them. They made plans to meet again at the pool, do some shopping together, and try the local cuisines. Before she and her husband got out of the crowded elevator, beautiful Judy gave Ed and George hugs.

* * *

The ship was steaming back to the war, its crew refreshed.

At first Ed thought it was his imagination. For whatever reason, the sailors all seemed to be smiling at him. Several times he had overheard the sailors referring to him as "the man" and "slugger." Occasionally a sailor would wink at him after saying hello or do a quick shadow box then smile. This was all unusual behavior. Not bad behavior, just unusual. At least morale was high. Still, Ed was puzzled.

Ed settled into the Engineering Officer of the Watch seat in the big ship's central control room. He sipped his coffee as he reviewed the logs and the readings—the vital signs of the complex propulsion plant. It looked like it would be a quiet watch—steaming through the night with no drills or exercises planned. Seated at the desk next to his was Petty Officer Perez, the leading machinist on the watch.

"Looks like it's going to be pretty quiet, sir," said Perez.

"Yep. You get any good liberty in Singapore, Perez?" inquired Ed.

"If running out of money is any sign, I had a great time in Singapore. But nothing like you had, Mr. Steiner." Perez smiled and shadow boxed a right and left cross with his fists. The other watch standers in central control laughed.

Ed didn't get what they were laughing at. And now here was Perez shadow boxing.

"Perez, tell me what the hell's going on. Every one of you guys seems to be smiling, winking, and throwing boxing punches at me."

"Sir, you know. We heard about how you cleaned out the bar and saved that woman some guy was trying to kill. And that hot babe you were with." Perez winked at Ed.

Eyes wide, mouth open, Ed was speechless.

"The guys in the squadron were talking about that fight, and everyone at the Hyatt and Raffles saw you with that Playmate of the Month, Mr. Steiner. You're our idol, sir."

"Perez, it never happened," said Ed, regaining his speech. "Mr. Baylis punched out some guy who was about to hit me. I was just standing there trying not to get killed. I didn't do anything."

Perez looked at the other watch standers in central control, all who were listening intently and smiling. Then he turned back to Ed.

"Mr. Steiner, c'mon now. You're being too modest, sir. Mr. Baylis is a good guy and all, but he's pretty tiny. We know this guy you clobbered was like an NFL lineman, only meaner. You really nailed him. I heard it from two of the pilots who were there, sitting right by you. Besides, what about that blonde? You going to tell us that she was Mr. Baylis?"

"Aw, jeez, Perez. That blonde had to be Judy Brown, Mr. Brown's wife. They were staying at the Hyatt, and so was I. And Mr. Baylis. We had drinks and dinner and met again at the pool a couple of times."

One of the other watch standers broke in. "Maybe so, Mr. Steiner, but I was in the elevator and I saw you two wrassling each other in front of everyone. She's one fine-looking lady, sir."

"We weren't wrestling anyone. We're good friends. She just gave me a hug."

"If you say so, sir," said Perez with a smirk and gave the rest of the control room watch a wink. "Whatever you say."

To Ed's frustration, conversations like the one he had with Perez occurred with other sailors and some of the junior officers throughout the rest of the ship's deployment. The more he protested his lack of heroics and lady killer skills, the more the story grew. By the time the ship turned east to return to Alameda, Ed was a legend on the mess decks. He had single-handedly wiped out a bar filled with deranged rapists. And had a girlfriend who was going to be the Playmate of the Month in the upcoming November, or maybe the February, issue.

George and Craig thought Ed's predicament great fun and did everything they could to keep the legend growing. They toyed with hiring some actress to meet Ed when the ship pulled into Alameda and pretend to have the ever-loving hots for him. But they nixed that idea for budgetary reasons.

The crew of that aircraft carrier garnered many medals and commendations during that deployment. Two Navy Crosses, a dozen Distinguished Flying Crosses, a Silver Star, several Air Medals, and many Navy Commendation and Achievement medals. But the biggest hero on the ship, at least to the crew, was the modest and unassuming Lieutenant Commander Edward Steiner, who single-handedly wiped out a bar of hooligans and had a Playmate of the Month for a girlfriend.

Rumor had it that while Ed drove a VW bug around the naval air station, he had a gull-wing Mercedes coupe in his garage at home.

THE AMBUSH

Ambushes were frequent and bloody in Vietnam. Both sides used them. The Viet Cong and North Vietnamese were better at it than the South Vietnamese and the Americans—if more effective killing can be ever termed "better."

An ambush is a clandestine, sneaky thing. It can easily backfire. But it can be an effective leveler, letting the small and ill-equipped inflict severe damage on the large and powerful. The trick to an effective ambush is to get the ambushing force into place without alerting the target. The target—men, husbands, sons, and fathers—then unknowingly move into the killing zone and the trap is sprung.

Once in place, the ambushers must remain stealthy and quiet. Any motion, noise, light, or even smell, and the cover is blown. The ambush will be a failure.

A lone American officer was in a ragtag group of South Vietnamese sailors and CIA-sponsored Cambodian mercenaries called PRUs. PRU stood for Provincial Reconnaissance Unit, a euphemism for a terrorist organization equipped and paid for by the US government. Its purpose was to use the Viet Cong's own terror tactics against them—assassinations, sabotage, kidnapping, ambushes. The official CIA title was the Phoenix Program, after the mythical Phoenix bird that rises from the ashes of its own destruction.

Intelligence analysts had said that an NVA battalion commander and his staff were going to be moving down a canal in the delta. The plan was to ambush them and kill them. Deep in Charlie country.

Early on a moonless night, using rubber boats with muffled outboard motors and then paddles, the ambushers were inserted several kilometers downstream of the killing zone. Led by one of the Cambodians with the American right behind him, they slogged their way up river along the banks and rice paddy dikes. Dressed in camouflage with olive drab greasepaint on their hands and faces, the twelve men moved without talking, treading quietly in the riverbank mud to avoid detection. After an hour, they reached the ambush site, a bend in the canal. They checked their weapons and the American's radio and hid themselves along the bank. The American sat with his back against a rice paddy dike, facing the canal. It was his job to initiate the ambush by firing a flare when the NVA sampans rounded the bend.

Ambushes end in one of four ways. Usually, nothing happened: the ambushers sat in the mud all night fighting to stay awake until the sun came up, then they pulled out. The enemy target never shows. Next second-most common was that the cover was blown— too much noise, or an early fisherman or farmer stumbled across the ambushers. When that happened, the team would just pack up and pull out before the target arrived. Next was the ambush of the ambushers themselves, a disastrous backfire. And lastly, and the most rare ending, was that the ambush occurred exactly as planned.

Dogs were common in Vietnam. Every village had a pack of medium-size dogs of nondescript color, with low foreheads. Usually skittish and mangy. They were never vicious or biters. Nor cute or affectionate. They just were.

In the village of Phu Thanh Lo, one of these dogs, for whatever canine reason, could not sleep. It sensed some activity worth investigating down by the canal that bordered the village. Strange smells and noises in the muggy air were picked up by its naturally sensitive, cold, wet nose and upright ears. The dog moved along a paddy dike perpendicular to the canal, and then turned upriver along the dike that bordered the canal. The strange smells grew stronger. The dog padded past the smell of men mixed with the smell of greasepaint and the smell of the oil that protected the men's weapons. Just as the dike started its curve along the bend in the canal, the dog smelled a man-smell that was different than the other man-smells.

Through lupine eyes it could make out the shape of a man that seemed to be the origin of the strange man-smells. There was the shape of a man-head and man-shoulders above the dike. A hat covered the man-head. A mottled uniform covered the man-shoulders. Above the man-shoulders and beneath the man-head was sweaty greasepaint-covered skin. The strange man-smell seemed to be strongest there. The dog slunk forward, snout outstretched, following the scent. It put its cold wet nose by the back of the man's bare neck, silently sniffing.

The night was very hot and muggy. The greasepaint prevented the normal evaporation of sweat. The American was overheated and uncomfortable. Having been crouching in one position for over an hour, his muscles were cramped. He was hungry. He was tired. He was cranky. It was one of those times, one of many times when he asked himself, as did many others, "What the fuck am I doing here?" The canal stank, the mosquitoes were sucking his blood and making him itch. This would probably be another night of unbelievable boredom, fighting to stay awake and alert until the sun came up when they could all pull out and trudge downriver back to their waiting boats and crews.

The American was jittery. They were deep in very dangerous and unfriendly territory. His mind kept on shifting from nervous watchfulness to daydreaming, mixing fear with escape. Two more months and he could go on R&R in Hawaii. Four more months and men were going to walk on the moon for the first time. Five more months and he would be going home to either life as a civilian or the navy's graduate school. He could study...

The dog's cold and wet nose pressed against the back of the American's hot and sweaty neck as its warm tongue licked the human sweat.

In his chest, the American's heart *lub-dubbed* two tremendous beats and he jumped to his feet and screamed. With a terrified whine and bark, the dog ran away. The man's heart started an adrenaline dance.

The ambush was blown. They moved back downriver and found their boats. When the American made it back to his base and his hooch, he tried to write an after-action report for his boss, but his hands were still shaking too much to hold a pencil. He sat down, and as the sun came up drank half a glass of Early Times, wondering if the VC were now using dogs to fight their war.

THE PSYOP

P SYOPS—or psychological operations—were military operations, just like going out and finding and killing the enemy.
But PSYOPS used psychological techniques ranging from terror to
"winning the hearts and minds of the Vietnamese people." That
phrase usually brought a derisive grimace or a snort to the faces of
the grunts in Vietnam. In the late 1960s and early 1970s, winning
the hearts and minds of the American people was more important
to the Pentagon and White House.

Following the 1968 Tet fighting, the Viet Cong hunkered down,
licking their wounds, reorganizing, and replenishing. After about
a year, their activity started to increase again. Early one morning
they even had the temerity to launch half a dozen rockets at the
LSTs sitting at the cargo terminal in Vung Tau. One of the ships
was hit and two sailors died.

Rockets and death were not unusual in Vietnam. But they were
rare in Vung Tau. There was an informal, unwritten, and unspoken
agreement that Vung Tau was off-limits to war. It was the anchorage for ships going up the vital shipping channel to Saigon, carrying cargo that was coveted by all sides in the war. Vung Tau was also
the in-country rest and recreation site for the US, Australian, and

Korean troops, and probably a place for the VC to get away from it all, too. Rockets falling on Vung Tau got the brass's attention.

Analysis of the rockets' trajectories and tips from informers pinpointed the launch site of the rockets to the little village of Ben Da on the back side of an island across the shipping channel from Vung Tau. The hamlet was over ten kilometers from the cargo terminal and behind a hill 120 meters high. If the VC had been trying to impress with their rocketry skill and marksmanship, they succeeded.

A sweep of Ben Da by US and South Vietnamese Army troops found only sullen villagers unwilling to say anything other than they were not VC, had not seen any VC, and knew nothing about rockets. That night, two more rockets plowed into Vung Tau, hitting the garbage dump. A second sweep of the entire island found no more than the first, but the rocketing stopped. The local military intelligence officers said it was only a respite. The VC were entrenched in Ben Da.

Two weeks later, a psychological operation was launched. A South Vietnamese Navy medical team of a doctor and two corpsmen, a US Army nurse, and a US Navy chief hospital corpsman went to Ben Da and set up a one-day clinic. The South Vietnamese coastal group transported them on their Yabuta junks and provided security during the clinic.

Captain Sharon Byrne, Nurse Corps, US Army, was glad to be out of the operating room. She had spent eleven months working in the medical evacuation hospital in Vung Tau and was leaving Vietnam in thirty-five days for Texas, civilian life, and marriage. The day trip to some little village was a change that she needed. She had traded her comfortable pajama-like scrubs for jungle fatigues, boots, flak vest, and helmet.

After the junk got under way, she asked the South Vietnamese Army PSYOPS officer to take pictures of her with her camera. Smiling and squinting into the sun as she stood at the bow, holding onto the .50-caliber machine gun splinter shield, her medical bag slung over her shoulder, she knew these would be pictures that she'd look at in later years and cherish.

The sailors set up a perimeter and the medical team walked into the center of the little village. Besides a few dogs and several ducks, nothing greeted them. While the doctor, nurse, and corpsmen set up their tables and chairs, the PSYOPS officer directed the placement of a small generator, two large cone-shaped speakers, and a tape deck. As soon as the generator came to life, the speakers blared out the South Vietnamese national anthem and then a nasal twang song. Some children came out of the huts and cautiously watched, hands behind their backs.

The PSYOPS officer picked up a microphone and interrupted the music. He announced that a free medical clinic was being conducted, and everyone was invited. Candy and soap would be given to the children. The music continued as a few more children appeared.

The US Navy chief hospital corpsman, a big man, waved the children over but none of them moved. He opened a carton, scooped out candy with his big hands, and walked over to the nearest child, a girl of about four or five. She backed away from him, but had her eyes glued on the candy. He stopped. And so did she, still staring at the candy.

After a two-minute stalemate, she looked at the other kids, stared back at the chief, who smiled broadly at her, glanced quickly to her playmates then boldly walked up and took a piece of candy out of his big cupped hands. Within seconds, two dozen children were around the big man, politely waiting for their candy handout.

Like a pied piper, he led the children back to the tables the sailors had set up, replenished his candy stock, and handed out small bars of soap with little cartoons layered in the surface. Sharon took the stethoscope from around her neck, put it on one of the little boys, and placed the bell on his chest. His eyes widened as he listened to his heart.

Slowly, women emerged from the village, the younger ones carrying an infant or leading a toddler by the hand. The PSYOPS officer guided one of the women to the tables and introduced her to the doctor and the Vietnamese corpsman. He then picked up the microphone and again announced that the free clinic was open to all. The other women got in line. More women and children appeared. But no men.

For the next six hours, the doctor, nurse, and corpsman looked down throats and up noses, took temperatures, measured blood pressure, listened to heartbeats, poked, and prodded. They gave vaccinations, cleaned infected insect bites, extracted three teeth, removed splinters, and handed out antiseptics and analgesics. Sharon found a suspicious lump on one women's breast, and together with the doctor tried to convince her to come to Vung Tau for a biopsy and X-rays. With a skeptical frown, the woman said she'd have to talk to her husband, who was out fishing.

The infants and toddlers were, for the most part, healthy. In fact, due to being fed sweetened, condensed milk once weaned, they were chubby. And cute.

One mother stood aside, holding her baby wrapped in a blanket. She smiled at Sharon but didn't approach the tables. Stretching her legs and taking a break, Sharon walked over to her and gently pushed the blanket away from the baby's face. The young mother just held her child quietly.

The baby's big, dark brown eyes smiled at Sharon, its chubby cheeks dimpled. Its mouth smiled gruesomely. A bilateral cleft palate disfigured the little girl's face. Sharon reached for the baby and held her, looking closely at the upper lip and into the child's mouth. The navy chief walked up and looked over her shoulder.

The big man gently rubbed his thumb against the baby's face. He spread her cheek aside and put a finger against the gap in her upper gum.

"Captain, I think we can fix this, don't you?" asked the chief.

"We've got a great oral surgeon back at the hospital," replied Sharon as the Vietnamese doctor and PSYOPS officer walked over.

After a few minutes of discussion, the PSYOPS officer and doctor tried to persuade the young mother to take her baby to the American hospital in Vung Tau. They could leave with the medical team on the junks and start the cleft palate and lip repairs the next morning. The mother and baby would stay in the hospital.

Despite their pleas, the mother refused, nervously looking at the other women who had gathered around. The medical team and the sailors left without her and her baby girl. Sharon was frustrated and upset with the woman.

The Vietnamese doctor sat next to Sharon on the gunwale of the junk as they motored back to the coastal group's base. He sensed Sharon's frustration. They talked quietly. He explained that the baby girl and her parents were probably already being treated as outcasts in the village because of the child's disfigurement; if they turned to the South Vietnamese government or the US forces for help, they'd probably be treated even worse.

"I understand that, Doctor," said Sharon. She looked around at the junk's bow wake and cleared her throat. "But to condemn a little baby to a life of being the village freak when it doesn't have to be...." Her voice trailed off as she shook her head.

A week later, a sampan sculled up to the junk base. The young mother tied the sampan to the float and carried her baby girl up the wooden plank to the shore. She asked the first sailor how she could get to the American hospital. Half an hour later, the US Navy chief drove them in his jeep from the junk base to the hospital where Sharon, in her scrubs, and an army medic greeted them.

The next day, the baby's left cleft palate and lip were repaired by a team of an oral surgeon, dentist, and plastic surgeon. The mother and baby stayed at the hospital for another three days, and then were told to return home and come back in four weeks for the repair of the right cleft palate and lip. The mother was ecstatic and chirping like a bird over the results so far. Despite the swelling, she could see that her baby daughter would soon be a beautiful little girl.

The coastal group sailors took the mother and daughter back to Ben Da, towing the sampan behind one of their junks. When they put them ashore, they told her they'd be back in twenty-five days to pick her up and take her back to the hospital. With a broad smile, the woman thanked the sailors and ran up the path to show a miracle to the villagers.

Twenty-five days later two of the coastal group junks tied up to the rickety pier at Ben Da. The South Vietnamese Navy lieutenant—the coastal group's executive officer—led two of his corpsmen and half a dozen armed sailors into the center of the village. A few women and an older man watched them from their huts.

The officer asked the man where the woman and her baby lived. The man shook his head and said he didn't know any such woman. When asked, the other villagers either remained sullenly silent or said the woman, her husband, and her baby were gone. They didn't know where.

Frustrated, the officer ordered his sailors to search the village, hut by hut. There was no sign of the woman or her child. One of the corpsmen went up to a little girl he remembered having seen at the PSYOPS medical clinic table the month before. He handed her a small bar of cartoon soap. Then he asked the child if she knew what happened to the baby with the broken face?

The little girl shrugged her shoulders and shook her head. "They are all gone."

"Where?" asked the corpsman.

"Gone. I don't know where."

"Do you know when they left?"

The girl looked at her feet and shrugged her shoulders again. Then she ran from the corpsman and into one of the huts.

The two junks returned to their base without the woman and the baby. Waiting for them at the float was the US Navy chief hospital corpsman.

When he saw the coastal group's officer's face, the chief kicked at a sandbag. "Aw, fuck it. Fucking miserable war."

Sharon was at Ton San Nhut, waiting to board her flight to Travis Air Force Base in California. She asked an MP where she could get a landline and he directed her to an office.

The oral surgeon in Vung Tau answered the phone.

"Hi, this is Sharon Byrne. I've got some time before my flight and wanted to check. When are you going to operate on that cleft palate baby?"

In a hoarse quiet voice, he answered. "Hi, Sharon. No operation. The baby and her mother have disappeared. The Vietnamese Navy officer thinks the VC had them killed. I'm sorry." His voice started to choke.

A sudden chill came over Sharon and her scalp started prickling; a painful lump restricted her throat. She hung up the phone, sat down on the nearest chair, and buried her face in her hands. She sat like that for nearly ten minutes, on the brink of crying but not.

"You okay, Captain?" asked one of the MPs.

"Uh...not really Sergeant. Just give me a few minutes. My flight's going to be boarding at 1300."

After a few minutes, she walked out of the MP office and back to the terminal waiting room. The MP looked over at another MP and shrugged his shoulders. "Must be PMS," he said.

The young mother and her baby girl were never found.

PROSPERITY

He was just under four years old. His parents had named him
Hung, which meant "prosperity." By any standards, Hung
was cute. Cute looking, cute acting. Always smiling. Always happy.
Everyone's favorite.

Hung's father and mother made charcoal in the three clay and
brick beehive-shaped kilns in the field where the road from Vung
Tau teed into the highway that led to Saigon and Nha Be. With the
arrival of his little sister a year ago, his grandmother encouraged
Hung to play outside their small house but to not go too far away.
It was okay to go to the side of the road and watch the trucks, but
no farther.

It was the start of the rainy season and Hung was playing in
the puddles behind his house with one of the neighbor kids. They
herded the ducks around the yard and built little dams to collect
the rain runoff. His grandmother called him in and gave him a
bundle of warm rice, a bit of fish, and some vegetables to take to
his parents, who were tending the kilns.

At the kiln, Hung's mother gave him a hug and a kiss and took
the bundle of food. She had been stacking wood. Hung's father
crawled out of the oven of the kiln. What had once been white rags

but were now nearly black were wrapped over his nose and mouth and around the top of his head. Gloves covered his hands. He took off his gloves and his wrappings, revealing pale hands and smiling handsome features beneath a mop of thick, black hair, and a raccoon mask of charcoal dust.

While his parents ate and rested, Hung walked over to the road. A cement tetrahedron left over from the French stood at the road junction, pointing the direction to Cape St. Jacques and Saigon with the distances in kilometers. Hung stood there and watched a column of big, green trucks led by a jeep drive by. The helmeted driver of the jeep smiled at Hung and waved. Next to the driver sat another soldier wearing a helmet, but he was as dark as Hung's father when he was covered with charcoal dust. Two soldiers in helmets sat in the cab of each of the eight trucks that rumbled behind the jeep.

The first truck tooted its horn as it went past Hung, startling him. Then each truck did the same, but something flew out of their cabs, landing near the tetrahedron. Hung ran over and picked up the little packages. They were American candy bars and tiny packs of four cigarettes. He ran back to the kiln and showed his parents his treasures. His father laughed, took the cigarettes, and told him to take the candies to Grandma. Grandma spat out dark red betel nut juice and giggled at the largesse and said Hung could have one piece of candy each day after his nap.

The next day Hung stood at the flat-topped tetrahedron marker and watched another convoy of green vehicles go by in the other direction. He tentatively waved at the lead driver, who waved back, yelled "fuck you, kid!" and tossed a can out of the cab. Continuing to wave and smile, Hung soon found himself in a pile of C-ration candy, cigarettes, canned fruit, instant coffee, powdered hot chocolate, and even little packets of toilet paper. He wrapped it all in his shirt and rushed back to the house. Grandma was amazed.

Within a week, Hung pretty well knew the truck convoy schedules to and from the Australian and American bases around Vung Tau. And he had mastered the magic phrase.

Standing on top of the tetrahedron, wearing an Australian Army fatigue hat, waving and smiling, Hung yelled at each truck as it passed, "*Fokyewkeed! Fokyewkeed! Fokyewkeed!*" He had to bring an empty rice sack to carry home all the goodies.

Hung's mother and father were amazed. They supplemented their income by selling cigarettes and the foodstuffs they didn't use to their neighbors and in the market at Ba Ria. Grandma had joined Hung in his afternoon candy treat, and even puffed a cigarette or two. One day in late November, an American trucker threw out of the truck cab what looked like a giant chicken dressed and wrapped in plastic. Grandma spent a whole day cutting up the big bird and made packages for Hung to take to their neighbors. The general consensus was that the giant chicken was sort of dry, certainly not as good as their ducks.

By the time Hung was seven years old, the convoys of Americans and Australians had been replaced by convoys of green trucks driven by Vietnamese soldiers. Every once in a while an American could be seen riding in a jeep, but that was getting more and more infrequent. The Vietnamese soldiers sometimes waved, but they never threw anything out of their trucks.

Then one day, when he was nine, there were no more convoys of green trucks and jeeps. The road was empty of army vehicles. Civilians carrying bundles on bicycles or in old Citroëns headed toward Saigon. Families carrying children and the very elderly on their backs walked down the side of the road. Nobody went the other way.

When Hung asked if they should follow the people, his father smiled and told his son there was no reason for them to leave their house and the kilns. They would stay.

And then there was no one on the road. No cars, no trucks, no people. Hung could have taken a nap in the middle of the road, although his grandmother would have been very upset with him if he tried.

Hung was standing by one of the kilns helping his parents stack firewood one day when he saw men walking down the road. He ran to the tetrahedron and watched them approach. They were marching in loose files, wearing pith helmets with red stars centered on the crowns and green uniforms. An odd-looking jeep passed the soldiers and drove toward Hung. His mother, father, and grandmother had come up behind him. The aroma of warm tapioca root came out of the big sack that Grandma was carrying.

Hung's father waved the jeep to a stop and shook hands with the three men in it. His mother was smiling and Grandma was pushing the sack of food into the jeep. Then she hugged the driver.

A man got out of the jeep, smiled broadly at Hung and ordered the third man in their jeep to take their picture. Hung laughed, waved his hand at the camera, and yelled, "*Fokyewkeed!*"

HOMECOMING

N avy Lieutenant Sam Beecher sat in the window seat of United
Flight 818, the red-eye from San Francisco to Boston. He
looked out the window of the DC-8. Black. No moon. The only
light was the airliner's green navigation light on the wingtip. He
hadn't slept for nearly two days. Anxiety, excitement, and caffeine
kept him awake.

Less than thirty-six hours before, he had shaken hands with his
relief and the South Vietnamese commanding officer of the river
squadron, climbed into the front passenger seat of the jeep, and
headed to Tan Son Nhut to board the freedom bird. When the
plane took off, a spontaneous cheer and clapping erupted from
the soldiers, sailors, airmen, and marines. Twenty-one hours later
they had done the same when the plane touched down at Travis
Air Force Base outside of San Francisco. A quick thirty minutes
to clear customs and pee, and then Sam was on the chartered
Greyhound for the late-night hour-long ride to SFO.

Before he checked his bag, Sam went to the men's room and
took off his wrinkled khaki uniform, T-shirt, socks, and shoes,
and washed up at the sink. He shaved. Then he stowed his dirty
uniform and brown shoes in his duffel and took out his starched

whites, ribbons, clean underwear, white socks, white shoes, and white cover for his hat. He stuffed his dirty skivvies in his bag and put on the fresh white underwear, uniform, socks, and shoes. He combed his hair and put on his hat. Probably no one would have said anything, but officers were not supposed to fly in working khakis. The regulations required a service dress uniform. Since it was August, service dress whites.

He checked in, found his gate, and slumped down into a seat with almost an hour before the boarding time. The airport was quiet and the waiting areas nearly empty. The only flights were the red-eyes. For the first time in months, Sam relaxed, truly relaxed. He was comfortable in the air conditioning. No one was going to shoot at him or try to mine his boats or set a booby trap. The airport was clean and didn't stink of river water or the decay of rotting vegetation and bodies. His eyes felt like someone had rubbed sand in them, and his stomach was sour. But he felt good, relaxed. He was out of Nam.

Flight 818 boarded on time. Sam had the whole row to himself. He tried to read the airline's magazine but found all he could do was thumb through it and look at the pictures. Exhausted, he looked out the window then put his head back on the seat's headrest.

"Sir, we're making our approach to Logan. Please check your seatbelt and make sure your seat back is upright." The stewardess had shaken his shoulder, waking Sam with a start. It was light outside the window. He must have slept five hours. His mouth felt like it was full of dirty socks.

Waiting for Sam as he walked off the Jetway was his sister Josie. She ran up and hugged her brother, kissing him on his cheek and knocking his hat off. In two weeks, she would be leaving for Italy to spend her junior year abroad. She wrapped her arm around his as they walked to the baggage claim area.

"Sammy, I was so afraid you'd come back after I had gone. I haven't seen you for a year and then it would have been another nine months on top of that. No way was I going to miss my big brother. Mom and Dad are at home waiting for you."

"Dad's still home? He take a day off?"

"It's Sunday, Sammy."

Sam looked at his watch. It was still on Saigon time. "I lost a few days, Josie. What time is it here?"

She giggled and squeezed his arm. Then she pointed at one of the arriving flight information screens. "It's exactly 7:12. Morning time. Breakfast time."

In the parking lot, she opened the trunk of his Dodge convertible and he tossed his bags in. Josie shut the trunk and gave him the car keys.

"I don't think I should drive, Josie. I'm sort of groggy, and I haven't driven a car in civilized traffic for a year. You'd better drive."

"Put the top down?"

"Uh...no. That's too much like a Jeep." He saw a slight pout on her face. "Oh, what the hell, yeah, sure, put the top down."

The Boston traffic and top-down wind noise made conversation difficult, which was fine with Sam. He felt numb, in a sleep-deprived stupor.

At one stop light, a young woman walked in front of the car. She wore a T-shirt. Buxom, she jiggled with each step. Josie was looking at Sam looking at the woman.

"What's wrong, Sam?"

"Is she wearing a bra?"

"No. Going braless is very popular. Female liberation. Especially with the coeds and hippies."

"That's a change," said Sam, more to himself than to his sister.

"I guess. Dad's not big on it. He gave me 'that look' of his when I came home for Thanksgiving wearing bib overalls and a tee shirt with nothing underneath. Then Mom had a little talk with me about not offending Dad and that home wasn't a dorm. Y'know."

"I don't know, Josie." Sam voice was hoarse and soft from fatigue and the dry air of the airplanes.

"The two of them really shit when I brought up moving in with my boyfriend at school." She looked at her brother. "You haven't met him. You'd like him."

"What do you mean moving in?"

"Y'know, living together. Sharing an apartment. Mom and Dad really shit at that one. They were relieved when I told them I wanted to do my junior year abroad. Hoping the boyfriend fades away."

Sam said nothing for the rest of the drive to Newton. Josie pulled the Dodge up the long driveway. She opened the trunk and Sam took out his bag. The back screen door of the house opened and out came Sam's mother and father.

Like her daughter in the airport, Sam's mother hugged and kissed him, knocking off his hat. While Sam was wrapped in his mother's arms, his father yanked the duffel out of his hands, picked up the cap, put it on his own head, and led the way up the back stairs. Leaving his family in the kitchen, the father carried the duffel up to Sam's old room. Still wearing Sam's hat, he walked back into the kitchen and hugged his son.

"Sammy, you look good. A little skinny, but hard. Tough."

Sam's mother looked closely at her son. Handsome, tan, skin taut. But his eyes were different. They seemed deeper set. Old man eyes.

The smells of his mother's kitchen washed over Sam. It was comforting, nostalgic, familiar. His father poured a cup of coffee and handed it to him.

"I forget, Sammy. You still drink it with sugar and cream or has the navy broken that habit? Sit down, Mom's made waffles and sausages for you. Orange juice?"

Sam felt flat, drained, tired, and emotionless. He sat in his chair at the kitchen table, the same chair and table he had sat at since they moved into the house twenty years ago.

"No, Dad, I still gunk it up with sugar and cream." His mother put a plate of waffles and sausages in front of him. Then she poured him a glass of orange juice from the pitcher on the table.

"Thanks, Mom. This looks good. I haven't had this stuff in a whole year."

"Beats C-rats for breakfast, Sammy?" said his father.

"We didn't eat much C-rations. I ate pretty much what my counterpart ate. Breakfast might be *jook*; that's rice soup. And tea. Maybe some fish. Or sometimes just thick *cafe sua* and French bread. Sometimes, if we were near a decent town, *pho*."

"*Pho*? What's that? It sure has an ugly name."

For the first time in what must have been a week, Sam smiled. "No, Mom. *Pho* is sort of a beef soup with a lot of these noodles, bean sprouts, I don't know what else in it. It was pretty good, filling. A real favorite."

"Noodle soup for breakfast?" remarked Josie as she took her seat across from her brother.

Sam ate a bit of the waffle and half a sausage. He drank all of the orange juice and poured a second glass but let the coffee go cold, untouched. His parents and sister were chatting but it took too much concentration for him to listen and take part in the conversation.

"You okay?" asked his mother. "You're not eating much."

"Mom, I'm beat. I just want to get out of this uniform, take a shower, and hit the sack for a few hours."

His mother reached a hand over and brushed it against his cheek. "Sure, we'll let you sleep. Or do you want us to get you up for lunch?"

"Just let me sleep." Sam was starting to feel irritated, short. But he held it in and stood up. "I'm going upstairs. See you later."

The house had not changed during his year in Vietnam. It looked and smelled the same. In fact, it had looked and smelled the same as it had when he had come home from college and Officer Candidate School and on leave.

His father had put his shaving kit in the bathroom. Sam took off his clothes and tossed them in the hamper. The wire rack by the thunder throne still held *Newsweek* and the Sunday paper's *Parade*. The Dial soap and shampoo were the same. Josie's same pink terry cloth robe hung on one of the hooks by the door. His old faded blue robe from high school hung on the other.

The bathroom was clean. No roaches, no mildew, no spiders, no rats. It didn't smell of rot or shit. The shower stall was dry, its tile dark and the grout white. The chrome fixtures shined.

Sam turned on the shower. Hot water. Lots of hot water. He adjusted the temperature and let the water hit him on the top of his head, running down his back as he leaned his forehead onto the cold tiles.

He brushed his teeth in the shower. He shaved in the shower. He shampooed his hair. He soaped up and rinsed his body. Then he soaped up again, very slowly, rubbing the bar of Dial over his chest and legs and between his buttocks and around his crotch. He rinsed off and then soaped and rinsed again. His tan skin was red from the hot water, the scars on his left shoulder and chest a puckered white. The scars didn't hurt anymore.

Sam let the shower stream hit him squarely in his upturned face. A lump in his throat almost hurt. Then he started to cry. Tears were washed off by the shower spray. But they didn't stop. The sound of the bathroom exhaust fan and the shower spray drumming on the stall's glass door muffled his deep sobbing.

Sam cried but he felt nothing. No sadness, no joy, no relief, nothing. He felt hollow and empty and could not stop crying.

Finally, he stopped crying and shut off the shower. He dried himself with probably the same towel he had last used in this shower over a year before, put on his old bathrobe and walked across the hall to his old bedroom. He dropped the robe on the floor and climbed naked between the cool, clean, white sheets. Sam fell into a deep, dreamless sleep.

"Sammy. Wake up, Sammy." A firm but gentle pressure on his bare shoulder nudged Sam awake. His father was sitting on the edge of the bed. "You've been asleep for nearly 24 hours. We decided to let you sleep through lunch and dinner. Better get up and get some food into you, buddy."

Sam rolled onto his back, blinking his eyes clear. He was disoriented, confused. He focused on the elder man's face. His father looked at Sam's shoulder with a frown.

Gently touching his son's shoulder, the father ran his fingers the length of the scar. "That's something new," he said softly.

"Uh...yeah, Dad. All healed. I'm okay. Fine."

"What happened, Sammy?"

"B-40."

"What's that?"

"Chicom rocket. Sort of a bazooka kind of thing. Costs them about two bucks to make. Inaccurate, short range. But it works."

"I didn't know you got hit, Sammy."

"Shit, Dad. I didn't want you and Mom to worry. I'm fine."

His father smiled and shook his head. "You didn't want us to worry? Sammy, you left to go to war. Cronkite broadcast casualty numbers every evening. We got the newspaper every morning. We were worried. Every single day you were away we worried."

"Well, I'm back and I'm fine."

"Yeah, Sammy. You're back. Get washed up and go downstairs and get some breakfast. I've got to go to work. See you in the evening at dinner." He patted his son's shoulder, leaned over and kissed his forehead, stood up and went to work.

In an old college T-shirt and faded Bermuda madras shorts, Sam padded barefoot into the kitchen. Josie looked up from the newspaper and her cup of coffee.

"Mom, look who's up? Rumpelstiltskin."

Sam sat down heavily in his chair and vigorously scratched his head with both hands. "It's Rip Van Winkle, you dummy."

His mother came over to him with a cup of coffee, put it in front of him and kissed his cheek. "Eggs okay? Bacon, toast?"

"Don't give him anything, Mom. He brushed his hair cooties all over the table. Yuck."

Sam ignored Josie. "Fine, Mom."

"You must be pretty hungry, Sammy. Want some potatoes with that or some cereal?"

Sam wanted a cold beer. A real cold beer. He wasn't hungry. He wanted a beer.

"No, Mom. Eggs and bacon are fine. Got any cold juice?"

As Sam half-heartedly pushed the eggs and bacon around his plate, Josie studied him. He looked different, acted different. She looked up and met her mother's eyes. The older woman tilted her head to one side and smiled a little sadly at her daughter. Josie looked back at Sam, who had finally finished his breakfast and was pouring another glass of juice.

"When are you going to see Linda?" she asked.

He looked at her with flat, expressionless eyes. "I'm not going to see Linda. That's all over. *Het roi.*"

"Who's Hat Roy?" asked his mother.

For the first time since he was home, Sam smiled and chuckled. "*Het roi* is no one. *Het roi* means all over, kaput, finished."

Josie leaned forward toward her brother. "Linda and you are over? Really? I thought she was going to be my sister-in-law one of these days. We really liked Linda."

"Well, Linda is going to be someone else's sister-in-law. About six months ago, she got engaged to some guy in her office. Sent me a 'Dear Sam' letter after the fact. Last I heard from her. Last she heard from me was a letter wishing her well." His mother had walked over to his chair and stood behind him and rubbed his shoulders and neck. She bent over and kissed the top of his head.

The kitchen screen door opened and without knocking Mrs. Kellerman, the next-door neighbor, walked in.

"Sammy! I knew you were home. I couldn't wait and just had to come over and see you!" She bustled over to the kitchen table and bear-hugged Sam as he tried to stand to meet her. She leaned back at looked at him. "We'll need to fatten you up. How long are you going to be here? What are your plans now? Going to leave the navy and settle down and get married and have babies?" She prattled on, not stopping for him to answer, holding him close to her. Sam's mother saved him.

"Sandy, sit down and have a cup of coffee. I just brewed a fresh pot." Sam's mother grabbed her neighbor by the arm and firmly guided her onto a seat. "I want you to try this coffee cake."

"Excuse me, Mrs. Kellerman. I have to hit the head. Be right back."

" 'Head' is navy for bathroom, Sandy," explained Sam's mother.

Sam was irritable, anxious, on edge.

Mrs. Kellerman and her husband had been his second family since they had moved next door. She had always been there to slip him a cookie or a slice of cake, to serve her famous potato salad when Sam's father lit off the charcoal grill, to boost him through the window when he locked himself out. She had attended his high school graduation, his college graduation, and even his commissioning as an ensign seven years ago. Her kids and Sam were best of friends.

But now, she irritated him. He wanted to get away from her noise and energy. For that matter, Josie was irritating and even Dad. Mom seemed to be walking on eggshells around him. He just needed some rest, some more sleep, some quiet. A cold beer would be good. Real good.

Sam flushed the toilet and opened the faucet so he could wash his hands. The distinct, acrid firecracker smell of cordite and chemical smell of brains and blood filled his nostrils. He looked around the bathroom but saw only the clean tub and shower stall and commode and the sink with its running water. The smell stopped. Where in the fuck had it come from? He leaned over and smelled the water in the sink. Nothing. The smell was gone but a few seconds ago had been so intense, so pervasive.

Rather than go back into the kitchen and Mrs. Kellerman, Sam went back to his room and unpacked his duffel. Then he took off his T-shirt and shorts and climbed back into his bed, naked. He lay on his back and looked at the ceiling. The smells came back for a second and then went away. He shut his eyes tight, then let out his breath and opened them. A memory of Linda sitting at the kitchen table came to his mind, but he pushed her out of his thoughts. He fell into a restless sleep.

He could hear the ambush starting to his left. All he could see through the foliage was the fishing sampan and the man and woman sitting in it. As soon as the shooting started, they dropped the nets they were hauling in and crouched in their shallow boat. The ambush target was out of Sam's sight, behind the thick foliage. All he could see were the man and wife in their boat, bent over, conical straw hats pointed at him. He wanted to shoot. Everyone else was shooting.

Sam rested his M16 on the black rubber boat's gunwale. The shooting to his left continued and he heard the bee buzz of bullets coming from the target. They were shooting back. It was a firefight and all Sam could see was that fucking sampan and those two fucking gooks wearing their fucking conical hats.

He lined up his sights on one of the hats and squeezed off a short burst. His rounds hit in the water just before the sampan. Sam sighted just over one of the conical hats and squeezed off another burst. The woman's hat and head exploded in a hot pink mist. The impact of the first rounds pushed her erect and back and the following rounds tore her chest into bloody chunks. He could see her husband's face, but could not hear the wailing from the man's fear-ugly terror-filled lips. Sam heard his own heart thumping like a drum on his boat's inflated hull.

Sam woke with a start, his heart racing, his sheets soaked with sweat. The noise was gone, and all he could hear was the hum of the central air conditioning and his heavy, gasping breathing. The river stink was gone, replaced by the filtered air of his bedroom. He sat on the edge of the bed and rubbed his hands on his sweaty face and wet hair. The clock said he had been asleep about an hour.

After a shit, shave, and shower, Sam put on his old Levis, and a golf shirt. No underwear, no socks. He went downstairs. Mrs. Kellerman was gone. His mother and sister were gone. He looked in the kitchen refrigerator then shut it. In the refrigerator in the laundry room, Sam found the cold beer. He opened a bottle then sat on the back steps in the sunshine. He drained the bottle without taking it from his lips. Then he got another and took a bit more time to finish it. The cold beer made his throat feel better, its bitter taste eliminating the sour and acid in his mouth. He calmed down and sat in the sun, trying to think about anything but the river and the gore.

* * *

For the first time in over a year, the whole family was at the dinner table. Sam had had two more beers in the afternoon and was drinking the red wine his father had opened to celebrate the family meal. Sam picked at the grilled steak, baked potato, and asparagus.

"Sammy," said the father, "you've been pretty quiet since you got back. You okay?"

"Yeah, Dad, I'm fine. Just jet lagged and sort of getting use to civilization and creature comforts."

His father looked at him for a few long silent seconds. "So what's next? Where you going with your life, Sammy?"

Sam took a drink of the wine to wash down a bit of steak.

"What's next, Dad, is I report to Newport, Rhode Island, in five weeks. Detailer sent me to be a navigation instructor at Officer Candidate School."

For the first time since the dinner started, his mother smiled. "Newport? Well that's nice and close for a change."

"My pick. Detailer said I've got all the good tickets for a good career in the navy. He wanted to send me to graduate school at MIT or Monterey, but if I did that, I'd be committing to a career, a navy lifer."

"Not interested in that?"

"Dunno, Dad. Navy's been fine. And it's all swell and interesting while I'm single and unattached. But it's a life of a lot of time away from home, wherever home winds up being. So, I told him I wanted time to think about it. Get out of Nam, get civilized again, decide if I want to stay in or get out. So, I asked for something near Boston for a year. After that, if I decide to stay in they send me to grad school. If not, I'm a civilian."

The table got quiet again. His father broke the silence. "Mom says you and Linda broke up."

Josie said, "She dumped him for someone she works with."

"You going to see her while you're home?" asked Sam's mother.

"I doubt it. She's engaged. Hell, she might even be married by now. History."

"Too bad," said his father. "You doing okay with that?"

"Yep. Fine." Sam poured some wine into his mother's glass and then his.

"Uncle Mike has invited us over. He wants to see you. Or we could invite his family over here." His mother looked at him with the look he remembered from childhood, the look when she knew something was bothering him.

"Mom, can we hold off awhile? I don't want to be an asshole, but when Sandy Kellerman came in babbling and hugging, I just had to leave the room. Let me slide back into normal life gradually, okay?"

"Sure, honey." She only called him honey when he was sick or hurt.

"How about this, Mom? Maybe have a barbeque next weekend and invite whoever you want."

"Can I invite one of my girlfriends?" asked Josie. "She would really like to meet you, Sam."

"One of your friends? What zoo did she come from? Lemme guess, she's really nice and makes her own clothes and don't be put off by her mustache."

Sam's parents laughed as Josie responded. "No, Booger Eater, she's pretty and nice. She's smart, so I have no idea why she'd want to meet you. Probably part of some term paper on sub-humans."

The mother shook her head at her children's antics. "Well, this is like old times, isn't it? Fine, we'll do a cookout Sunday." She looked at her son. "What are you doing tonight?"

"Nothing. Staying home."

His father nodded in agreement. "Good, I don't want you out there driving with a belly full of wine." He paused for a while. "Have you even driven your car since you've been home?"

"No. I was thinking about getting out of the house tomorrow. Maybe go into Cambridge. Look around. I need some new clothes, too." He looked around the table. "Oh, I almost forgot. Everyone stay here."

Sam went upstairs and came back down carrying three small boxes. "These are for you guys." The boxes contained a princess ring of opals for his mother, a jade bracelet for Josie, and a Seiko watch for his father.

Later that night, Sam sat in the den with his parents watching the Democratic Convention from Chicago. The old Sylvania black and white television had been replaced with a Zenith color model. They watched the scenes of the riots in Grant Park.

"Jeezus," muttered Sam. "What the hell is happening? I came home to this shit?"

* * *

Two men in kayaks were racing between the bridges on the Charles River. It was hot and sticky. Sitting on the bench on the Cambridge side, Sam ate his pizza slice and drank his Pepsi. Squinting into the sun's reflection off the river, he watched the two kayakers.

The sulfur swamp stink of the delta mixed with the WD-40 smell of his hot shotgun barrel. The gook in the sampan before him was writhing, but not saying anything. Pointing the red lens of his flashlight, Sam could look inside the man's chest since his right side was missing. Green tracers went by, but there was no gun noise. The man looked up at him, his mouth in an open grimace. Nice teeth, thought Sam. Probably doesn't get much candy or sweets to fuck them up.

Sam looked away from the dying man and at the two kayaks that were now under the downstream bridge. The smells were going away. Just the garlic smell of the pizza remained. He looked back at the water in front of him. No sampan, no man. The only noise was the traffic on the bridges and behind him on the street.

He had left the convertible top down and now the black vinyl seats were burning hot. Shit. He took a pair of khaki trousers out of the shopping bag and laid them on the driver's seat. It kept his ass from burning, but the steering wheel was almost too hot to touch. He took two dirty paper napkins our of the brown bag that had held his pizza slice and soda and used them as hot pads to grab the black plastic steering wheel of the Dodge.

"Hey, get your head out of your ass, you dick! It's a red light, you blind fucker!" yelled some young guy who had to dance around the front of Sam's car. Sam stopped in the middle of the intersection. Horns honked and a braless coed gave him the finger. He let his breath out and tried to back up but there was no space. When the light turned green, he cleared the intersection. That was the third time since he had left the driveway that morning that he had screwed up while driving. Sam forced himself to concentrate.

He drove to Somerville and stopped at the old saloon. The bar's dark interior was cool. It smelled of beer. A few men sat at the bar, a couple at one of the tables. Sam sat at the bar and ordered a shot and a beer. He ordered another beer and nursed it, looking at the television mounted high in the corner.

"Fuckin' Red Sox," said the bartender with a shake of his head.

Just to have something to say, Sam smiled and said, "Yeah, fuckin' Red Sox. Give me another glass of beer, please."

A woman walked in, nodded at the bartender, and sat down at the bar. An empty stool separated her and Sam. She ordered a gin and tonic and, while waiting for her drink, looked at Sam.

"Hot outside," she said as she lifted her blond hair off the back of her neck.

"Yes, it's hot."

The little Vietnamese whore was pressing her thigh against Sam's. She smiled up at him and unsnapped the top of her *ao dai*, revealing her small breasts pushed up by a black bra. Her skin was flawless, a milky golden color. Little beads of sweat dotted her neck and chest. It was so hot and humid. She left her tunic flap open and leaned against Sam.

In a breath that smelled of garlic, fish sauce, and Ipana, she whispered, "You buy me Saigon tea, *Dai Uy*? I love you no shit." Sam wanted to touch her skin, wipe the sweat away. He looked up at the television. The whore was gone. He could smell the beer and the woman's perfume. The bar air was cool, nearly chilly. Pushing his empty glass away, Sam walked out into the hot sun and drove his car to his parents' house. He sat in the driveway for a few minutes and watched the whore come out of the shanty, hike up her miniskirt, squat in the beach gravel and pee.

* * *

Watching his father flip Italian sausages and thick burgers over the charcoal, Sam was startled by a heavy, forceful pat on his back, and then a bear-hug squeeze around his shoulders. Uncle Mike had walked up behind him.

"Sammy, Sammy. Welcome home, kid. You an admiral yet? Where you been? I haven't seen you for what? A couple of months at least."

"Hey, Uncle Mike. You haven't seen me for over a year."

"You're shitting me. It's been a year? Where were you?"

"Vietnam."

"Sent you there, huh? But you weren't in the fighting or anything, right?"

"Sam was in the thick of it," said Sam's father to his brother.

"Yeah, I remember. That's right. I saw that piece in the *Boston Globe* a few months back. Had a big picture of you and some Vietnamese on some boat. Nice paragraph about you." Mike shook hands with his younger brother, but kept his left arm around Sam's shoulders. "Where's the beer, bro? You want one, Sammy?"

Uncle and nephew walked over to the cooler and fished two beers out of the ice. They sat down beneath the big umbrella and away from the crowd around the picnic table and grill. The older man studied the young man's face.

"You look like you lost some weight, Sammy. Look good, but a lot more than a year older."

"You seem to be living well, Uncle Mike," said Sam as he poked a forefinger into his uncle's spare tire.

The older man laughed. "Yes, tell me about it. Your aunt is too good a cook and walking around a golf course is not a whole lot of exercise. Believe it or not, I was once your size, kid."

"I believe it, Uncle Mike. I was looking at your wedding pictures and the ones from when you came home from the war." Sam's uncle nodded and stared at his beer bottle. "What was it like coming home after that, Uncle Mike."

"Hell of an adjustment, Sammy. For better or worse, they shipped us home on slow-moving troop transports. And they had a scheme as to who went home first. So by the time I finally made it home, I had been out of flying missions for nearly half a year. Man, I was glad to see your aunt and your cousins."

"Take a long time to get adjusted?"

"Uh...not really. I was so damned busy and had the GI Bill paying for medical school and taking care of everything, I don't think I really thought about adjusting to life at home. Just did it." Uncle Mike looked at Sam for several long hard seconds. "You're having problems." It wasn't a question.

"I dunno, Uncle Mike. I mean I've only been here a week. Shit, ten days ago I was on some stinking river in a flak vest and helmet." He looked around. "And now I'm here."

"Want to talk about anything, Sam?" His uncle had not used the family nickname "Sammy."

"I wouldn't know what to talk about. And even if I did, I don't think anybody here would understand what I was saying, Uncle Mike."

The older man looked around the back yard, surveying the smiling faces. "You're probably right," he said with a sigh. "You still seeing Linda?"

"Nope, she's moved on. Getting married soon. Or she may already be married."

"Really? I liked her. Too bad."

"The relationship couldn't handle the separation, and she couldn't understand what the hell I was doing over there. Why were we even there kinda stuff."

"Sammy, her loss. She has missed out on a genuine Beecher, the best-bred, highest pedigree of male available. Our shit definitely does not stink." The two men laughed.

Uncle Mike pointed his empty beer bottle at a young woman who just entered the backyard with Josie. "She's cute. Who is that?"

"I think that's Josie's college buddy. She threatened to bring her to this."

"Hmmm. Samuel Beecher, as a trained medical professional, I strongly recommend you conduct a reconnaissance of that young lady and map out your plan of attack."

"I just may, Uncle Mike. But having just come out of the jungle, I'm not fully civilized yet. I'd probably go up to her, introduce myself, and then grab her ass."

The following Friday, Sam was sitting with Josie's friend having dinner at Durgin Park. The food was good, simple, and cheap. The waitresses were notoriously surly. For the first time since he left Vietnam, Sam was relaxed, enjoying himself with a good-looking woman.

"I'm afraid of our waitress," he confided to her. "She scares me. She could easily beat the crap out of me."

Bonnie laughed. "She is imposing, isn't she? But you're a decorated war hero. She can't scare you, can she?"

Sam was uncomfortable with "war hero," even in jest. "So while she's beating me with that tray she's carrying, I'll tell her she can't do that to me. You think she'll listen?"

"You have a point there, Sam. I'll tell you what, if she does beat you up, I promise to call for an ambulance. Or a hearse."

"Thank you, Bonnie, I feel much better about that now." He looked around the dining room then leaned over to Bonnie. "I want to get the check so we can get out of here, but she has disappeared. Maybe I can just sneak out and you follow me a few minutes later?"

"And leave me to deal with Brunhilde? No way, buster. I'm sneaking out and you follow me." They both laughed as the big waitress walked up to the table and slammed the check on the tablecloth. Seeing nothing funny about delivering a check, she shrugged and waddled her ample bosom and ass over to her other victims.

Outside the restaurant, Bonnie put her arm in Sam's. "Want me to drive?"

"Whaddya mean?"

"You okay to drive, Sam? You had a couple of beers along with that wine."

"No, I'm fine, Bonnie."

She looked at him for a few seconds. "Let's walk around awhile, Sam. I need to work off the lobster and that Indian pudding. Let my mind clear a bit, okay?"

They walked through the shuttered produce market to the waterfront piers. The night was warm and clear. A lot of people were about. Bonnie and Sam stood looking out over Boston Harbor, the brackish water smell mixed with Bonnie's perfume.

The dead Vietnamese sailor was on the pavement at his feet. His face was swollen on one side, shutting his right eye in a grotesque wink. His other eye was open wide, staring unblinkingly at Sam. So wide open that Sam could see the white around the dead man's dull brown iris. The man's skin was that white-blue that all dead men seem to get, even the dark skinned. At a glance from the Buddhist priest, the widow screamed and cried, her face twisted in grief, spit drooling off her open lips.

"Sam? Sam! Are you okay?" Bonnie was standing in front of him, her back to the harbor. She was holding his shoulders, looking into his eyes. "You seemed to blank out on me for a few seconds. Are you okay, Sam?"

He took a deep breath and realized he was in a cold sweat. In a quiet voice he answered her. "Yeah, sure, Bonnie. I'm fine. Just thinking of something and sort of got lost in thought."

"What were you thinking about, Sam?"

"Nothing of importance, Bonnie. No big deal. Just sort of popped into my mind." He laughed a mirthless laugh. "Occupational hazard."

She put on a serious, no nonsense face. "Sam, are you drunk?"

"Do I seem drunk?"

"No. You don't. But you weren't with me a few minutes ago. What happened?"

Sam was starting to get irritated, short-tempered. But he didn't want to be mad at Bonnie.

"Just thinking about some shit from Nam. You're better off not knowing that crap. Especially on a night like this. C'mon, let's find the car." He put his arm around her and held her close as they walked back to the Dodge.

The next morning, Sam got out of bed early, put on shorts, T-shirt and running shoes, and ran three miles through the streets of Newton. After his shower and breakfast, he called Bonnie and asked her out for that evening. For the next two weeks, Sam ran increasingly longer distances each morning and saw Bonnie nearly every day. He stopped drinking.

With the Dodge filled with her books, clothes, sheets, towels, ironing board, radio, typewriter, and his single suitcase, Sam and Bonnie drove to Providence. He helped her move into the dorm for her final year of college, took her to lunch, and kissed her goodbye with a "See ya this weekend." An hour later, he checked into the naval station BOQ in Newport. The next morning he reported for duty.

A week after Bonnie's graduation and a month before Sam left the navy for an MBA, Sam and Bonnie were married in the chapel at Harvard Square. The single glass of champagne that lasted Sam through half a dozen toasts was his first alcohol in nine months.

Cornering Sam at the reception, Uncle Mike shook his hand and gave him one of his signature bear hugs. He stuffed an envelope in Sam's hand. "Sammy, congratulations! We love Bonnie. We love you. We love both of you. I'm so fucking happy for you, Sammy."

"Thanks, Uncle Mike. I'm pretty happy myself."

"I can see that. Your mom and dad and I were pretty concerned about you when you came back. It's good to see you like this." Uncle Mike looked around. "Where's that gorgeous wife of yours? She and I are going to dance!"

* * *

Claire Schiller, MD, PsyD, studied her notes. She looked out the window at a gloomy December 2012 Boston afternoon. Good weather to be depressed. "Doubtful pt. will continue tx." was the last entry in her summary of her next patient's previous meeting with her. She smiled to herself and shook her head. Despite her doubts, he was sitting the waiting room. She closed the file, took a deep breath, got up from her desk and let Sam Beecher into her office.

Dr. Schiller studied his appearance as he said hello and walked into her office, seating himself in the overstuffed leather chair. He looked different to her. Not sure what, but different.

She sat down in her chair opposite him, a notebook on her lap. Sam spoke before she could say anything.

"Doctor Schiller, I've been giving this a lot of thought since last week." Then he paused, and looked at her. "Uh...I'm sorry, did you have something planned...uh...an agenda or something for today?"

She shook her head and smiled. "Nope. What kind of thoughts were you having, Sam?"

He leaned forward, his elbows on his knees, looking at her intently. "Okay, I realize you're not judging me and you're to be trusted and you're here...I'm here...to help me. Help me... uh...feel better if that's the right term?" He looked at her. She nodded.

"So, shit, Doctor. Since I'm paying for this and Medicare is paying for this and my insurance is paying for this, I'm going to get my money's worth and throw it all on you." He smiled at her and raised his eyebrows in questions. Despite herself, she burst out laughing.

"Throw it at me, Sam. Let's see how good I can catch."

"We may be seeing how much sticks, not how much you can catch." Again, she laughed and nodded for him to continue.

"Okay. Here's what I've been thinking about so much. I'm just going to start talking." Again, she nodded.

"Bonnie died two years ago. Forty-two years of marriage, a son, a daughter, three grandkids. And fucking cancer takes her away. Ovarian. Diagnosis to the end in less than a year." Although his voice was strong and unwavering, his eyes were tearing and his nose was running. He grabbed a tissue from the box near his chair, stemmed the tears, and kept on talking.

"That left a hole in my life that's so big, so deep..." He paused for nearly half a minute, staring out the window.

"I wonder if I should have left the navy? Hadn't questioned that decision ever but that's what came to my mind. Y'know, stayed with the people who understood what I did, what I went through in-country. That sort of stuff." He looked at her then down at his shoes.

"I hadn't had a drink since my wedding day. I could put the booze away back then, especially when I first came back from Vietnam. I think I went on a two-week bender and didn't even know I was doing it. Sort of stopped. Hell, I did stop, when I realized that drinking could fuck up my relationship with Bonnie." He leaned on his elbows again, looking at Doctor Schiller.

"But after Bonnie died...I dunno...I sort of wanted a drink. Especially when I came home from work. Then maybe a drink at lunch, especially if someone else was drinking. At a social function. Y'know. A beer or two after golf." He stopped talking and just stared at the tissue box.

After nearly two minutes, Doctor Schiller asked, "Sam, how many drinks a week?"

He ignored her question, but started talking again. "Work was a pain in the ass. I made nice money, business was worth something even with this shitty recession. But I was getting irritated, restless, short-tempered at work. Couldn't sleep. So I finally said, 'fuck, it, Beecher' and accepted a bid from the other partners to buy my share, and I packed up and left."

"When was this, Sam?"

"A year ago. Then I sold the house and bought the condo here, in the city." He laughed a mirthless laugh.

"Slept in for a few days, bumbled around, then took a few days to visit friends in Chicago and San Diego. Totaled a rental car outside La Jolla. Cop gave me a break and ignored the booze."

"Were you drunk, Sam?"

"Probably. I guess. I dunno." He shifted in his chair. Stood up and stretched then sat down. "Got back to Boston. Money in the bank, nice condo, nothing to do. Absolutely nothing to do. Went to the gym. Thought about dating but just didn't want to. Couldn't sleep. Weird dreams so I was sort of afraid to go to sleep. Felt miserable. Started haunting bookstores and buying books to read but maybe finished one or two. Grew a beard, shaved it off. Watched fucking daytime television. You ever watched that, Doctor?"

"I have not. I'm working during day time television."

"I was lonely, but whenever I was with people, they all irritated me, made me mad, grumpy. Didn't show it, but I was a real bastard. Started avoiding people."

Sam quit talking and stared at the floor for a long time. Then he blew his breath out and leaned back, his head against the top of the chair back. He looked at the ceiling light fixture.

"That light always been there? I hadn't noticed it before."

"It's been there, Sam."

"Huh. I hadn't noticed it. My kids won't let me see my grandkids anymore."

After another minute of silence, the therapist asked, "Why won't they let you see your grandkids?"

"They think I'm depressed and drinking too much and acting erratic. Jumpy. Get startled when the dishwasher changes cycles. Said they won't let me drive a car with the kids in it. Said they're worried about me and wanted me to see a shrink. Think I'm nuts or something."

"Is that why you came to me?"

"No." Sam was very quiet, barely audible. "Four weeks ago, I think I tried to kill myself. Woke up on the bathroom floor with Bonnie's pills and some prescription painkillers spilled all over the sink and floor. There was an empty Absolut bottle and I had vomit all over me."

"Do you remember what happened, Sam?"

"No. Not a fucking thing. Just woke up on the fucking floor smelling like puke. Pissed in my pants. I don't even know how long I was lying there. Got up, feeling like crap. Showered and tried to clean the mess up. Scared the crap out of myself."

"Did you want to kill yourself, Sam?"

"No. I don't think so, Doctor. Like I said, the thought scared me."

"And then you decided to see me?"

"No, Doctor Schiller. Sitting here today, I know I should have come to you long before that. But I didn't do that even then. It wasn't until the smells and sights came back."

She sat there, waiting for him to interrupt his silence.

"See, Doc, ever since Nam I would see these things that happened over there. Not just see them, but smell things like cordite and rot and that dead sweet sick stench. And I would feel the fear and the excitement and the flatness. Like I was back there. The real world around me goes away, and I'm back there."

He told her about shooting the fisherman's wife, and the dead sailor and his widow, and another sailor puking after trying to siphon diesel fuel, and a body bloated to look like fat gray inner tube that deflated with a putrid hissing stink.

"Sam, did you actually smell these things or did you just remember what they smelled like?"

He quit talking and was staring straight ahead, not moving, catatonic. She let him sit like that for a minute, then five.

"Sam? Sam!"

He jolted, blinked his eyes, and focused on her. "Uh...sorry. I must have...I dunno. I was seeing some soldier trying to get up while the medic held him down."

"What was that like, Sam?"

"He was grunting, sort of gurgling. I could hear him. I could smell the diesel exhaust of the boats and the fish sauce."

"What were you thinking, Sam? Feeling?"

"Die, you miserable fucker. You got yourself shot and now you want me to watch you? Die quick, you fucker."

Sam was exhausted, tired, sweaty, even though the room was not warm. He slumped in his chair, wasted.

"Sam, I'm going to write you a prescription that I want you to start immediately. I also want you to come back here this time tomorrow." He nodded his head.

"Do you feel you're okay to go home and take care of yourself until then? If not, I can admit you to the hospital."

"You mean am I going to blow my brains out before I see you next, Doc? I'm okay. Hell, I don't even own a gun."

"Okay, Sam. I also want you to see Doctor Allen. He's a neurologist, and I want him to evaluate you regarding the smells. That can be an indication of a tumor or lesion. Have you ever suffered a head injury?"

"Not to my head. But I did get knocked around over there. Hit in the body but got knocked into the gun mount."

"Be sure to tell Doctor Allen about that. I want you to go to the lobby drug store and fill these prescriptions. Then go to Doctor Allen's office. It's the floor above this, room 604. I'm going to call him as soon as you leave here, Sam. I'll see you tomorrow." She handed him the scripts.

"You know what's real weird, Doc?"

"What's that, Sam?"

"I really want a cigarette or a cigar. I don't even smoke, never have. But now I want a fucking cigar."

"You going to buy a cigar, Sam? They sell them at the drug store in the lobby."

"No, those Nam smells are bad enough without me adding cigar smoke to 'em." He smiled, then sat up in his chair and fixed her with his eyes. "Doctor Schiller, am I going to be all right? Y'know, where I can play with my grandkids again and feel like I'm worth a shit with something to do in the morning?"

"That's going to depend more on you than anybody else, Sam. You came here for help. That's a big step that took strength. You and I are going to work on this together. But it is going to take work and time, Sam."

He stood and turned to leave the office. Then he turned around and shook her hand. "Thanks, Doctor Schiller. See you tomorrow at three."

She watched him walk out of the office and shut the door behind himself. Then she picked up the phone and called Doctor Allen.

At 3:15 the next morning, a Cambridge police patrol found a Lexus smashed into a lamppost on the Seventh Street Bridge. The lamppost was knocked flat against the sidewalk railing. The car's engine was still running, lights on, gear in drive, front air bags inflated. There was no one in the car or near it, no blood. Just a crumpled cigar, which the air bags must have crushed. A check of the registration revealed that the Lexus was leased to Mr. Samuel M. Beecher of Boston.

A week later Boston police found a body in the Charles River at the foot of the Western Avenue bridge. The dead man's driver's license identified him as Samuel M. Beecher, born February 2, 1942, white hair, brown eyes, 70 inches tall and 155 pounds. On his blazer lapel was an enameled red, white, and blue Bronze Star pin. The body was wedged between a piling and the concrete base of the bridge, a dead spot where debris and garbage collected and rotted.

"MY SWEET DADDY..."

This is true. At the request of the family, the names have been changed to protect their privacy. —KL

Sergeant Le Van Hien was with his men at the Cambodian border in Tay Ninh when the news came over the platoon's radio. Saigon had fallen, and the People's Army was in control of the city and all of Vietnam. Ho Chi Minh's goal of reunification finally occurred.

Hien was speechless. He grabbed the hand of his radio operator and shook it. Then he did the same to each of his comrades. No one said a word. They were stunned. Happy. Smiling.

The terrible fighting was over. The soldiers hugged each other, some crying. Hien's dark penetrating eyes looked at his men. For the first time in years, his brilliant smile had returned to his handsome face. They were alive. The impossible had happened. Many brave fighters had died, but not these men. He brought them through the war alive.

Wanting to savor the moment, Hien sat on his haunches, his strong farmer forearms resting on his knees. It was 1975. He had been fighting for over six years. Fighting the Americans and their puppets. Fighting the mites, fungus, and illnesses. Fighting the sadness and sorrows of losing comrades—men who were his responsibility to lead and protect. Fighting the loneliness and the boredom and the fear. And fighting the certainty that he would never again see his parents nor his half-brother or sister, never see the rice paddies and vegetable garden of his home in Dai Duc.

They had won. Hien and his platoon and the Vietnamese people had won. He was so happy. For the first time since 1969, he let himself think about a reunion with his family, and about the land nearly nine hundred kilometers to the north of the little clearing in which he sat on the Cambodian border in Tay Ninh province. Hien lay on his back in the shade of a mud wall and shut his eyes. He just lay there on the hard dirt, happy, thinking of home. The tender scar on his back from an artillery shell rubbed against a pebble and reminded him of what he, his country, and his men had endured.

Hien thought about the day he had joined the People's Army. It was 1969, and he was seventeen years old. The minimum age to become a soldier was eighteen. He could not wait another year. His country was in danger; his land and family needed to be protected. Sitting in a classroom while his country bled made him feel selfish, useless. He was a young man, naive about battle, with a fervent patriot's passion. A year before he had joined Uncle Ho's Youth Union, but he wanted more than a youth brigade. So, Hien affirmed to the People's Army recruiter that he was eighteen. The recruiter didn't question Hien's age. Here was a strong young man volunteering to serve his country. He certainly looked older than eighteen. Let him serve.

During basic training and indoctrination at Kinh Mon, Hien learned to shoot, throw grenades, tunnel, and drill. He learned to kill. His comrades became his brothers, his family. They marched south nearly a thousand unforgiving kilometers through Laos and Cambodia to the revolutionary guerrilla base near Long An and the Mekong Delta. He marched to battle.

Then they moved to the Cambodian border in Tay Ninh. Hien fought and served his country, willing to sacrifice his life for his nation. He fought on, not expecting to live to see his family's land again or the end of the fighting. Hien the farmer and schoolboy became Hien the soldier and leader, rising through the ranks to sergeant and a leader of his platoon.

Besides the dangerous Americans and southerners, the soldiers had to fight the forest diseases. Malaria, scabies, ringworm, dengue fever, malnutrition. Despite medicines from China, the men were slow to heal. They had no time to rest, moving constantly from camp to camp, bleeding from their noses and mouths. As many died from viruses, parasites, and bacteria as died from bullets and napalm.

The worst for Hien had been his capture in November of 1972. He spent several months shackled and tortured in the infamous tiger cages on the island of Phu Quoc. Only an agreement signed by diplomats eleven thousand kilometers away in Paris on January 27, 1973, had saved Hien from more pain, hopelessness, despair, and certain death.

The prisoners of war held by both sides were to be released. Within days, the American POWs left Hanoi in large jet aircraft to be reunited with families in Hawaii. Their war was over. Freed from prison March of 1973, Hien was in the last group of prisoners to be released. The prison camp was closed after he walked through the gates. Hien returned to his men and his country's battle. His war went on.

Despite the horrors of war, Hien and his men were treated to glimpses of humanity. As poor as the Cambodian peasants were, they shared their shelter and food with the soldiers, providing the fighters a rare opportunity for respite and comfort.

Now, in 1975, the fighting had stopped, the men could heal. But the end of fighting did not mean the platoon's mission was over. Their nation needed them to stay in Tay Ninh on the border to guard against uprisings, to maintain the new peace. Although Hien wanted desperately to go home, he and his men knew they must do their duty.

Nearly nine months after the fall of Saigon, Sergeant Hien was given a ninety-day furlough and allowed to visit his home. A bus took him to Vinh in the middle of the reunited country. Then a train carried him the remaining four hundred kilometers to the Kim Thanh district of Hai Dugong province. His feet took him the rest of the way home.

From the moment he unexpectedly appeared in their kitchen, the reunion of Hien's parents with their son was happy beyond description. The three stood silent, hugging, smiling, not letting go. Tears of joy flooded his family's eyes every time they looked at him. They had never given up hope, although they knew the chances of his surviving until reunification were slim. Hien could not believe he was really home, standing on his land, and hugging his family. The village was untouched by the war, but not the villagers. Many young men and women had not come back.

For several days, neighbors and friends came by to welcome back Sergeant Hien. His mother made his favorite meal of fiddler crab soup. The aroma and flavors flooded him with memories. After years of eating what he could forage, captured rations, weevil-filled rice, river rats, and starchy tapioca root, his mother's simple soup was an unimaginable feast. Half the soup stayed in the bowl; his shrunken stomach could not hold anymore. Uncomfortably full, he couldn't stop smiling.

Hien's father's closest friend had a daughter, Pham Thi Tham, who by any standard was already a beauty at the age of eighteen. Statuesque and graceful, she was the embodiment of femininity. Together the two farmers arranged a meeting of their children with hopes for a wedding and grandchildren in the future.

Hien's father had given Tham's father an old photograph of the handsome young Hien to share with his daughter. She had liked what she saw in the picture—a handsome, muscular young man with soulful penetrating eyes, a thick head of hair, and a heart-melting smile. She agreed to meet him. The two fathers happily predicted that a marriage was in the making.

However, the meeting was stiffly formal and very brief. Neither Hien nor Tham said a word. After Hien and his parents left, Tham announced that there was no way she would marry that young soldier who looked absolutely nothing like his image in the old photograph. He was ugly, skinny, dark, and sickly. She'd rather stay a spinster than marry Hien.

Tham's mother sat down with her daughter and talked. She pointed out that Hien came from a wonderful family. His parents were good people. And so was Hien. He was industrious, smart, and kind. And maybe after he fattened up a bit and the effects of the forest disease and other ravages of the war waned, he might not be so ugly. After a long pause, Tham admitted that he did have a wonderful smile. Not said was the fact that there were few eligible men for any woman, no matter how beautiful, to pick from.

For his part, Hien thought Tham was beautiful, but he sensed that she, on the other hand, did not like what she saw. He certainly did not want to marry any woman who did not want to marry him. But he hoped he was wrong.

The two farmers' hopes came to fruition when their children put their faith in their fathers' wisdom and agreed to marry. A marriage was immediately planned. Neither Hien nor Tham had yet spoken to each other.

The local church had no vicar, so the small wedding party bicycled nearly forty kilometers on a dusty dirt road through rice fields and fruit orchards to the church in Hai Duong city. The mothers held onto the pedaling fathers. The bride and groom rode their own bicycles. And then they bicycled back. After ten days of a modest wedding celebration, Tham moved into Hien's family's house and their life as husband and wife began in earnest.

Tham's mother was right. Hien was a good man. Eating nutritious food, sleeping well, and sharing his life with Pham transformed him. His gaunt frame filled out and muscle returned. The dark shadows around his eyes faded. His skin cleared. The natural luster of his hair returned. And his warm smile rarely left his face. He had grown less ugly. In fact, he grew even more handsome than the young man in the photograph. But war had turned his eyes into the eyes of a much older man, a man who had seen much and remembered it all. The scar on his back grew less tender but it did not go away.

The young couple felt emotions they had never felt before. Intense, passionate, pleasurable. They were feeling the deep, indescribable love between a man and a woman. Together they were much more than the mere sum of a man and woman.

Sergeant Hien had to return to his comrades in Tay Ninh. His furlough was over. He had his duty to do as a soldier and platoon leader. So, he took the train and bus back to Tay Ninh. Saying goodbye to his beautiful wife was the most difficult thing he had ever done in a life full of difficult things. Tham felt as if her heart was leaving her.

Loneliness and misery plagued Hien from the moment he boarded the train. He had never felt like that in all his years fighting the war. He missed his wife with all his heart and wanted so much to be back with her in the North. But his country needed its patriot and soldier in Tay Ninh at the Cambodian border.

Tham missed Hien just as much. She kept busy helping her mother-in-law manage the house and her father-in-law work the rice paddies and vegetable plot. But she missed her husband's passionate warmth, strength, and smile and longed for the day she would again see him walking down the dirt road to their land. The waiting was harder than anything she had ever experienced before.

In late 1976, Hien's war finally ended. His country gave him a choice. The People's Army liked Sergeant Hien and wanted him to stay in the military. He would undoubtedly be promoted to higher ranks and be offered all the considerable privileges and the benefits a military career provided. Or he could leave the army and start life anew as a civilian. The choice was his.

For Hien, there was no choice. He left the military and returned to the love of his life and the land of his family. After seven years of fighting, illness, horror, pain, misery, and separation, Hien went home for good.

It took Hien nearly another year before he really felt as though he was not on the front lines. Often he dreamt or imagined he was still with his comrades, marching, shooting his rifle, ducking explosions and bullets.

Hien threw himself into his life as a husband and farmer. Now a member of the Communist Party, he was appointed to lead the farming cooperative. He worked hard on commune matters: agricultural projects, farming, land division, taxes, and administration. For his hard work and long hours, he was paid in rice, not money. Tham was not happy that his duties often took him away from home. Even when he was around, his enthusiasm for hard work bothered her. She respected his dedication, but he had a wife and family to take care of in addition to trying to feed the entire province.

That family soon grew from two to six as a two sons and two daughters arrived. Life was not easy, but love softened all the calluses of hard work. The war became a thing of the past. Their youngest child, a pretty little girl, often massaged her father's aching back after a day's hard work. She never noticed the scar.

In 2012, their youngest daughter, then a strikingly beautiful woman with her father's eyes and smile and her mother's elegant stature and grace, wrote the following:

"When I was young, in the evening time, the electricity cut off. In the dark, my father often told us how hard it was and I cried because I felt how much I love him, my great Daddy. I don't think my generation could do what he and his comrades did. It was much harder than could be imagined..."

WRITING ON A BARRACKS WALL

This is a true story The poem is punctuated as it was found.. —KL

After the fall of Saigon and reunification of Vietnam in the spring of 1975, hundreds of thousands of Vietnamese left what had been South Vietnam. Although not all fled by sea, these refugees were known as "boat people." Many died during their journeys. Refugee and resettlement camps were set up in countries around the world to receive the survivors.

Several of these camps were in the United Sates. Most were located in remote military installations. The resettlement centers were run by Civil Affairs Army Reservists who volunteered, leaving their jobs and graduate schools for this humanitarian service.

One of these resettlement camps was set up in Fort Indiantown Gap, about a hundred miles northwest of Philadelphia. Over two thousand Vietnamese and Cambodian refugees were housed in old World War II barracks while they were processed for sponsorship and then relocation throughout America.

For those people, Pennsylvania was as foreign as the moon. The hot and humid southern Vietnam and Cambodia had two seasons, the dry and the wet. Pennsylvania had four, ranging from

321

freezing to summer heat to rain to blizzard. The Americans who processed them were big. Even the American women outweighed the Vietnamese men. And the food was heavy, starchy, constipating, and tasteless. Vietnamese fish sauce had not yet made it to the American supermarket. Coffee was weak.

The barracks were plain but well heated and solid. No mildew, no roaches. Sewage disappeared from porcelain urinals and commodes into underground pipes. Rain ran down gutters and through grates into sewers. Cold and hot water flowed out of stainless steel and chrome-plated faucets. There were mattresses, pillows, and blankets. Tree leaves turned colors and then fell, leaving branches bare. And one day it snowed, something they had never seen. Central Pennsylvania was nothing like the land they had left behind.

Pennsylvania was not their ancestral home. Their relatives were not a walk or even a *xyclo* ride away. If they were still alive, those lost relatives were thousands of kilometers away, back in Vietnam or Laos or Cambodia or in other resettlement centers in places like Thailand or Australia. Jobs and professions were gone—as were most, if not all, of their worldly possessions. They had to start their lives all over again. Or wither and die.

The week before Thanksgiving, a young Civil Affairs captain walked by a barracks that housed several families. He had put his law school studies on hold to work in the refugee processing and resettlement center. The late afternoon temperature was in the low forties and dropping, the wind was gusty and mist laden, the sky overcast. Everything seemed to be a shade of gray. Something on the barracks caught the young officer's eye. He walked over to look.

Three sentences in delicate handwriting had been painted on the old barracks' front siding. Taking out his note pad and one of the ubiquitous Skilcraft ballpoint pens that the US military bought by the millions, the captain copied the writing.

A few hours later, he shared the writing with two other officers over dinner at the O Club. One of them, a rigid-minded martinet who lived according to military decorum and regulations instead of his brains, was incensed. How could someone deface US Government property like that? The miscreant had to be found, punished, and made to whitewash over the graffiti. But that did not happen. He drank another whiskey and soda, and then another. And forgot about it in an alcoholic haze.

Today Fort Indiantown Gap is a training center for the National Guard. It is modern. Clean. Sharp. That old WW II barracks and the black painted handwriting are gone.

But words of the poem are not gone. For thirty-seven years, they passed from hand to hand until one day, in a San Francisco burger joint, they were given to a guy who likes to write.

Here they are as found on the barracks wall on November 21, 1975:

> *To separate and scatter across the land is not a thing to mourn;*
> *seeds leave the pod just so and spread new life where none has been*
> *before and add new beauty to the old that may exist.*
> *so let it be with you...be glad to leave the pod and seek a place to root*
> *and grow and let others see what you have become because of what*
> *you have been.*
> *It is the seed, you will not lose what has been given to you in the past—*
> *it will always be a part of you, do not wither or weaken because you*
> *must leave, get stronger so that on the day your seed is sown, it too*
> *will be better than what has been before.*

The poet remains unknown.

Acknowledgements

This book would not have been written if not for a young woman from Hanoi. In 2012, I was in Vietnam trying to find People's Army and National Liberation Front veterans to talk to. These survivors who fought for their country were on the other side, the "bad guys." I needed to talk to them to verify the draft of my first book, *Crazy Razor*—to find out if my research and guesses were anywhere near reality. And I was having little luck in finding anyone who would answer my questions.

This beautiful woman overheard my grousing, came up to me, and told me her father was a veteran. She wanted to know about my writing. I showed her the list of two dozen questions I wanted to ask these men—if I could find one. She took my list, skimmed through it, and then offered to translate it into Vietnamese and ask her father, who was a fruit farmer northeast of Hanoi.

Back in Oakland six weeks later, I received an email from her. It contained an attachment, in perfect English, with not only her father's answers to my questions but much more. Feelings, family, tears, and smiles. I realized that this was a story in and of itself. It could be a book. Or a short story. Or both.

The tale of her father became the seed for this book. I added tales that *Crazy Razor* could not hold, stories from memories and experience, and stories told to me by others. And that is this book. It all started with her.

Despite my cajoling and repeated requests, that beautiful young woman would not let me use her name in this book. I am sure modesty and culture as well as government oversight is involved in her reluctance. But I must acknowledge her, albeit without naming her, foremost.

Fortunately, everyone else I want to acknowledge can be named. Jim Likowski was the first reader of the first draft and, as always, gave me invaluable feedback in his characteristic way that made me feel I was being educated rather than criticized. Jim was followed by Ted Blanckenburg, who took the draft to Hawaii and reviewed it during an all-nighter punctuated by bird chirping, beer, and a sunrise. Ted's critique should be a magazine article. I wish I could write like Ted. Reviews of the draft by Captain Eric Dohm and Mushroom Stamp Productions' Danny Levin provided valuable validation of style and arrangement. Mary Ann Dohm's review added badly needed taste and refinement.

My tireless wife, Eileen Levin, suffered through many reviews of various drafts and then a final proofreading. She must be obeyed.

While Anne Tuffin, a most erudite Kiwi, did not review any drafts of this book, the lessons she taught me from her review of *Crazy Razor* were always in my mind.

Mike Miller told me his experiences as young army officer who took a break from civilian life and put his uniform back on to work at a Pennsylvania refugee relocation camp. The final short story in this book is essentially his.

Two beautiful women, Cherie Pipkin and Lisa Guevara, reviewed stories for me and provided comments that turned the tales into stories worth reading.

Tyler Fahr is a young man who makes me feel very old. Tyler did what for me would have been impossible. He created the maps in the book.

And, finally there is Maddie, who danced with Grandpa.

Acknowledgements

Thank you to the young woman I cannot name, Jim, Ted, Eric, Danny, Mary Ann, Ann, Mike, Cherie, Lisa, Tyler, Maddie, and my wonderful Eileen. This book could not be what it is without you. If there are warts on the pages, it's because I ignored your advice.

GLOSSARY

I, II, III, IV Corps: Military divisions of South Vietnam, each an area of operation for the US Army or US Marine Corps. I Corps's northern border was the DMZ, II Corps covered the center of South Vietnam, and III and IV Corps were the most southern.

AO: Area of operations.

Ao dai: Traditional Vietnamese female garb of full-length, tight-fitting silk tunic split from the hip down and worn over silk trousers.

ARVN: Army of the Republic of Vietnam, the regular army of South Vietnam.

B-40: Rocket-propelled grenade used by VC and NVA.

Ba: Misses, ma'am, title for mature woman. Feminine equivalent of Ong.

BUPERS: US Navy's Bureau of Personnel.

BOQ: Bachelor Officers Quarters, lodging for single and unaccompanied married officers.

Charlie: VC or member of the National Liberation Front.

CHICOM; Chinese communist..

Chief, Chief Petty Officer, CPO: The most senior of US Navy enlisted ranks. The three levels of CPO: Chief Petty Officer, Senior Chief Petty Officer, and Master Chief Petty Officer.

Chieu hoi: South Vietnamese government's program of VC/NVA defection. Also, the term to describe the defectors, who were interrogated, trained, or indoctrinated, and who then often worked for Southern and allied forces as "Kit Carson" scouts, or interpreters.

Civvies: Civilian clothes as opposed to a military uniform.

Commanding Officer, CO, Charley Oscar: The officer in command of a commissioned military unit such as a navy ship or aircraft squadron, and an army or marine corps company. Referred to in the navy as "Captain," "Skipper," or "the Old Man," no matter what rank. Senior to an Officer in Charge.

Cumshaw: Bartered goods and services.

Dai Uy: Vietnamese rank equivalent to US Army, Air Force, and Marine Corps captain or US Navy lieutenant.

Dust-off: Helicopter medical evacuation of wounded and, space permitting, dead.

Executive Officer, Exec, XO: Officer second in rank and seniority to the commanding officer of a unit.

FAC: Forward Air Controller'

Fitrep: Fitness report by a senior officer, usually a commanding officer, evaluating a junior officer in the senior's command. Fitreps are important in determining assignments and selection for promotion;

Gator freighter, gators: US Navy ships and landing craft designed to put amphibious forces, usually US Marine Corps, onto hostile shores.

H&I: Harassment and interdiction.

HE: High explosives.

Ho Chi Minh sandals: Sandals made from truck-tire-tread soles and inner tube rubber straps.

Ho Chi Minh Trail: Logistics routes from North Vietnam through Laos, Cambodia, and South Vietnam, used to supply VC/NLF and NVA forces. The North Vietnamese referred to the trail as the Truong Son Strategic Supply Route.

Hooch: Quarters hut.

Illum: Illumination.

Jaygee, JG: US Navy rank of lieutenant (junior grade), equivalent of US Army, US Air Force and US Marine Corps first lieutenant.

Junior Officer, JO: Junior ranks of US Navy commissioned and warrant officers, usually referring to ensign and lieutenant (junior grade) but sometimes extended to lieutenant.

KIA: Killed in action.

MACV, Military Assistance Command, Vietnam: Senior overriding military command in Vietnam, commanded by a US Army four-star general.

Medevac: Medical evacuation of wounded and ill.

My Lai Massacre: The mass destruction of the village and residents of My Lai by a unit of the US Army on March 16, 1968.

Naval Supply Center, NSC: Major US Navy logistics center.

NAVFORV, Naval Forces Vietnam: All US Naval forces operating in and around Vietnam. Commanded by a vice admiral—three stars—whose title was Commander Naval Forces Vietnam or COMNAVFORV.

NLF, National Liberation Front: Viet Cong.

Non-Commissioned Officer, NCO, noncom: Military enlisted ranks from E4 through E9. In the Navy this corresponds to third class petty officer through master chief petty officer.

North Vietnamese Army, NVA: American term for the People's Army of Vietnam, as opposed to the NLF or Viet Cong.

Number one: Vietnamese term for good, excellent.

Number ten: Vietnamese term for bad, lousy.

Oaknoll: Oaknoll Naval Medical Center, a large navy hospital in Oakland, California.

Officer in Charge, OinC: The senior officer in charge of a unit or detachment. OinC reports to a commanding officer.

Officer of the Deck, OOD: Officer authorized by the commanding officer to control the movement of the vessel or operation of a naval unit.

Officer Candidate School, OCS: School that trains candidates for commissioning as officers. Training usually consists of four months before commissioning, with additional training following. Navy graduates are usually commissioned in the reserves as USNR as opposed to USN.

PACFLT: Pacific fleet, commanded by a four-star admiral.

PCOD, Pussy Cut-Off Date: Last day to have sex to allow time for venereal disease to be diagnosed, treated, and cured before returning home. Six weeks before end of tour.

PBR, River Patrol Boat: Fiberglass-hulled boat used by US Navy for riverine patrols. Made famous in the movie *Apocalypse Now.*

People's Army of Vietnam: NVA.

Pho: Noodle soup.

PRC-25, Prick-25: Portable two-way radio.

Provincial Reconnaissance Unit, PRU: Special counter-insurgency military forces composed of mercenaries and special operations personnel.

PSYOPS: Psychological operations as opposed to armed combat operations.

RAG: River Assault Group.

Rat tot: Vietnamese for very good.

R&R: Rest and recreation, a vacation from the combat zone.

Round eye: Caucasian.

Skivvy: Underwear.

Smoke: Colored smoke grenade used for identification and location.

Spooks: Intelligence personnel, spies, and personnel on classified and covert missions.

Swift Boat, PCF: Aluminum-hulled, high-speed coastal patrol craft.

Tactical Operations Center, TOC: Centralized communication center for tactical combat operations.

Tet Offensive: NLF/VC and NVA major military campaign launched at the start of Tet, the lunar new year holidays, on January 31, 1968. Although a tactical defeat for the communists, the Tet offensive marked the turning point of the war. US and South Vietnamese forces were caught by surprise. US public opinion turned against the war from that point forward.

Trung Uy: Vietnamese rank equivalent to US Army, Air Force, and Marine Corps first lieutenant or US Navy lieutenant (junior grade).

Tsu mot: Vietnamese for number one, excellent.

Viet Cong, VC: Southern Vietnamese members of the National Liberation Front. Titular Vietnamese communist.

WESTPAC: Western Pacific.

WIA: Wounded in action.

MAPS

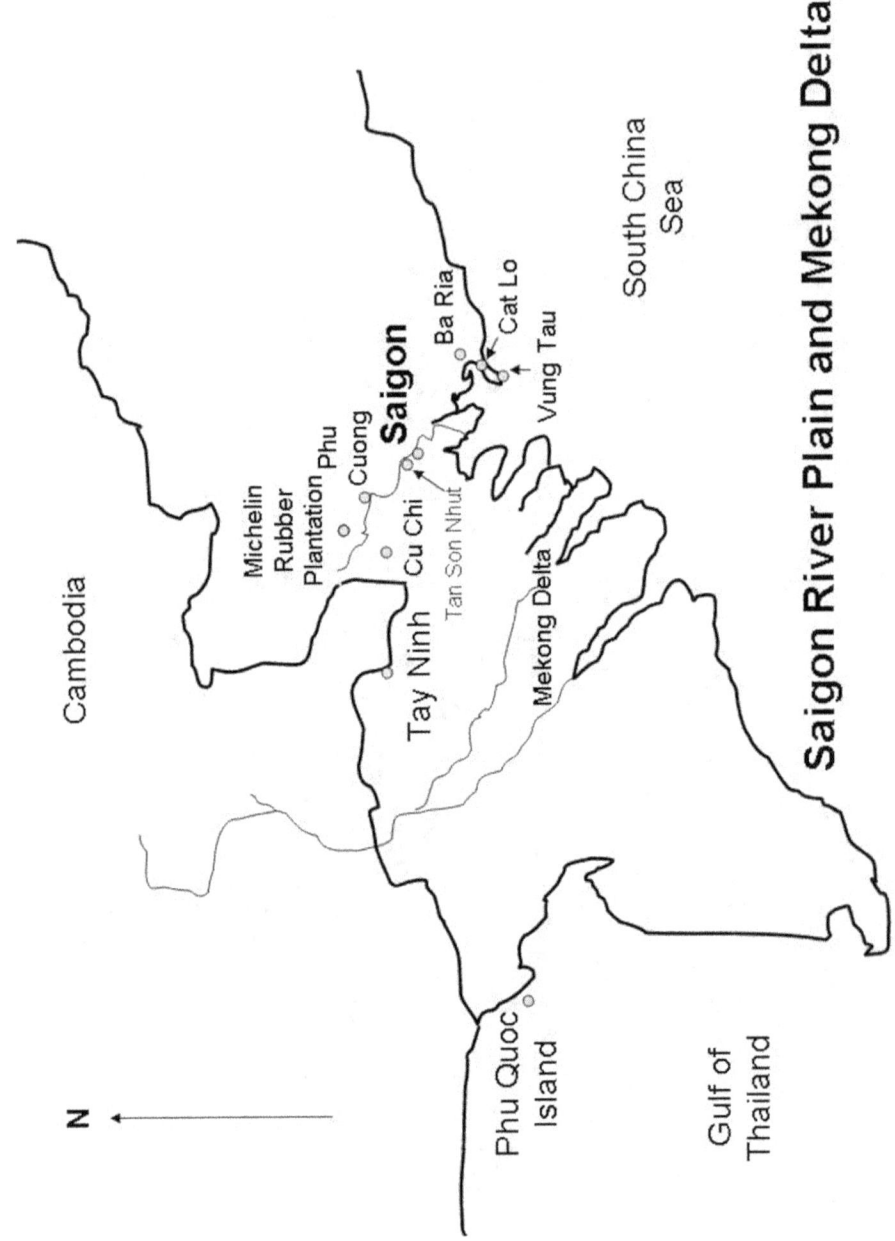

Saigon River Plain and Mekong Delta

www.ingramcontent.com/pod-product-compliance
Lightning Source LLC
Chambersburg PA
CBHW051230260626
47162CB00002B/362